THE BLACK EVOLUTION

TITLES BY PAUL E. COOLEY

The Children of Garaaga
Legends of Garaaga
Daemons of Garaaga

Tony Downs
The Hunt
After Image

The Dark Recesses Collection
Lamashtu
Mimes

Other Titles
Closet Treats
Fiends
Ghere's Inferno
Station 3
Tattoo

Collaborations
The Rider (with Scott Sigler)
Contact This! (anthology)
Dead Ends (anthology)
Luck Is Not A Factor (anthology)
On Deadly Ground (anthology)

The Black Series
The Black
The Black: Arrival
The Black: Outbreak
The Black: Evolution
The Black: Oceania (2024)
The Black: Extinction (2024)

Sol and Beyond
The Derelict Saga
Derelict: Marines
Derelict: Tomb
Derelict: Destruction
Derelict: Trident

Gravity's Bane
Neptune Scars (2024)
Proxima Ghosts (2025)

Suits
Station 3
An Ancient Trap

THE BLACK
EVOLUTION

Paul E. Cooley

SHADOW
PUBLICATIONS

First Edition

Paperback ISBN: 978-1-942137-18-4
eBook ISBN: 978-1-942137-17-7

Visit our website at https://shadowpublications.com

To stalk Paul on social media:
Mastodon: @paul_e_cooley@vyrse.social
YouTube: https://youtube.com/paulecooley
Email: paul@shadowpublications.com
Mailing List: http://mailinglist.shadowpublications.com

Printed in the United States of America

Published by Paul E. Cooley and Shadow Publications
Cover art, cover design, and internal layout by Scott E. Pond
Scott E. Pond Designs: www.scottpond.com

10 9 8 7 6 5 4 3 2 1

THE BLACK

EVOLUTION

CHAPTER ONE

She spent three long days in the lifeboat after *Leaguer* sank. Three days and nights of ocean waves buffeting the mostly empty craft and pushing it further and farther away from where so many had died. Farther away from *It*, but not the memory of *It*.

Catfish, the only other survivor, had been concussed severely. She'd tended to him as best she could, comforting him when he was awake and holding him when he wasn't. Even when he was unconscious, the feel of his body against hers was enough to set her at ease.

She'd been afraid to fall asleep the first night. The moon, a bare sliver in the dark sky, did little to illuminate the ocean beyond the portholes, much less the lifeboat's interior. The darkness seemed to crowd her, envelop her, and worst of all were the shadows.

The storm had moved on, as had its malevolent clouds, but it wasn't long before wisps of white and gray appeared against the day's dark blue sky. Was another storm coming? The shivers that wracked her weren't just for the possibility of more water, thunder, lightning, and the inevitable fear of the small craft capsizing and dropping her and Catfish into ten thousand meters of water.

No. If the light disappeared, there would be nothing to keep *It* from chasing them, finding them, and consuming them. Memories of the impossibly black liquid flowing over the top of the rig, encompassing it like a death shroud, and then spilling onto the deck, which was their only place of safety, kept playing in her mind. She remembered Catfish yelling at the top of his lungs to fire the flare gun at the barrel of fuel oil on the grated deck. She remembered the look on Thomas' face, part wonder and part terror, as he stood tall in the face of death, as well as the screams of the few crew that had survived as they ran for their lives or were taken by the thing, one by one.

Worst of all, she remembered the branches of deep space black rising out of the pool, their ends sprouting orbs that teemed with alien intelligence. Even against the howling wind, she had heard the crackle and crunch of the creature extruding more limbs, tentacles, and eyestalks. And those eyes. They'd all been staring at her. Or had they?

She'd been terrified to fall asleep. As soon as the sun had disappeared below the horizon, her heart thumped hard in a rapid, arrhythmic stumble. The lifeboat sank into impenetrable darkness, and the fun began.

She focused on Catfish at first, cradling his head on her knees while she sat cross-legged on the hard deck. The white of the bandage around his head seemed to be the only remnant of color save for the gray walls.

As she started to slip into sleep, the image of a tentacle slashing through the boat's walls and crushing her like an aluminum can chased away the drowsiness in an instant. Her spine went rigid, and her body shook from the shock. Catfish moaned when her legs dislodged his head from her knees.

Heart racing, eyes still darting around the cabin to make sure the thing wasn't inside with them, she gently pushed until his head returned to the cradle of her knees. He started to snore softly, the sound contrasting with the harsh spray of the water and the waves lapping against the metal hull.

It took a long time before she could close her eyes again and convince herself the monster was gone. Nearly 10,000 meters below *Leaguer*, the thing that had once occupied the M2 trench had been destroyed. She was sure of it. And its progeny that had killed her boss and all the other folks on the rig? They'd burned it up. Correction. She'd burned it up.

But it didn't matter. The boat rocked on the waves, the bare moonlight casting strange shadows through the portholes. Here a tentacle, there a talon and at the back? Was that an eyestalk peering at her?

She didn't stop shivering until she saw the first rays of dawn break through the oppressive darkness. Then, she slept.

When she awoke, Catfish had somehow managed to move himself onto one of the benches. He was once more asleep and snoring loudly. She rolled him over onto his side and slid one of the life preservers beneath his wounded head. She was sure it wasn't comfortable, but it had to be better than laying directly on the hard bench.

She spent the second day dozing when she wasn't checking their supplies, checking them again, and counting every drop of water she consumed. Shawna woke Catfish twice: once to give him water with some anti-inflammatories and once to get some food down his gullet.

He'd been in a daze both times, barely aware of his surroundings, but at least he'd flashed his shit-eating grin. That was enough to make her feel like they might live through this.

Catfish was running a fever, and while he lay dead to the world, she held his hand and sat cross-legged on the floor with her back against the bench. Catfish's arm dangled over the side and touched her shoulder. Things hadn't started that way, but after she was sure he was asleep, she'd moved his arm far enough to drape over her. He didn't seem to mind.

It kept her calm for a while, his clammy skin slowly warming from her body heat. She felt like she could stay awake a little longer without panic, without fear. But then night came again.

High clouds streaked across the night sky, the stars appearing and disappearing like low stuttering strobe lights. The sliver of moonlight, larger than the night before, merely cast more shadows. The clouds scattered the light coming through the portholes, leaving horror in their wake.

Instead of the tentacles and talons from the night before, it was the eyes. The goddamned eyes. They were everywhere in the darkness. Wherever she looked, another eyestalk waved at her from the shadows.

Shawna didn't know how long she sat petrified with fear, too afraid to move. She knew she was squeezing Catfish's hand too hard but didn't stop until he moaned. He was sleeping. He was safe. He might be dying from an infection, but at least the black thing couldn't get him. No, it was going to get her instead.

Sometime before dawn, back screaming with pain and her legs filled with pins and needles from lack of blood flow, her eyelids became too heavy for her to keep open.

She awoke with a start sometime later and found herself looking at the ceiling. A shadow stared down at her. It was here. Her heart thumped loud and fast enough to make her body shiver.

It's here, girl, her late father's voice whispered in her mind. *See you soon.*

The shadow widened and became the entire ceiling. A giant, lifeless eye stared down at her. Another appeared below the space-black maw, which curled into a mirthless smile. Her mouth opened in a silent scream while her head filled with the sound of frying pork fat. The smell of burning hair and the fetid stench of sun-bathed roadkill filled her nostrils.

"Shawna?"

She snapped awake, arms flailing at nothing. For a moment, she was sure the creature would drop down upon her, snatch her up with its teeth, and dissolve her flesh. But it was just a shadow.

"Shawna?" The voice came again. She glanced to the side and saw Catfish's eyes glittering in the moonlight. He swallowed hard and then spoke through a larynx so raw and dry that it might as well have been full of broken glass. "You okay?"

She quickly raised herself, reached for a bottle of water, and returned to him. "I'm fine. How are you feeling?"

He raised a hand, put it on her shoulder, and managed a weak smile, his dingy teeth ghostly gray in the shadows. "Head hurts. And I think I did something to my leg."

She nodded. "I'll get you some medicine. Hang on." She made to move away from him, but his hand tightened on her shoulder. "What?"

"Thomas didn't make it," he said softly. "No one did."

"No one but us," she said. "And I don't even know how we made it."

He coughed and winced. Whatever infection he had seemed to be moving into his lungs. "Very carefully," he said with a grin. "When that, that thing exploded, I think it must have been close to one of the shacks. Either that or the shockwave detonated it. Shrapnel all over the place. You're lucky that falling wooden beam just barely bopped you. Could have been a lot worse."

"I guess so," she said.

"Dragged you into the boat while--" He broke off, his eyes staring past her into the darkness. "While the others died."

She shivered. She didn't know what he'd seen before they escaped *Leaguer* in the lifeboat and wasn't sure she wanted to know either. One day, maybe, but not tonight, while the sun was below the horizon, and her imagination turned every shadow into a creature from a goddamned B-movie.

Shawna brushed a hand against his face. "Thank you. For saving my life."

His grin returned in an instant. "I was glad to do it," he said. "And you're welcome."

A tear tried to escape her eye, but she wiped it away before it had the chance. "Let me get you something." She patted his hand and shuffled to the emergency supply cabinet.

Using the kinetic flashlight, she rummaged until she found the lever that opened the bench against the opposite wall, revealing food and water bottles. Grabbing a bottle of water, she headed back to him. Although his eyes were closed again, she could tell he wasn't asleep.

"Can you sit up?"

He lazily opened his eyes and squinted at her in the darkness. "Maybe with a little help."

Shawna wasn't a large woman, but she easily maneuvered Catfish into a sitting position. Catfish, a little over six feet tall with long hair and a hint of a paunch, somehow seemed smaller, as if the events on *Leaguer* had diminished him.

Or maybe, she thought, *you've just become some sort of badass.*

"What are you smiling at?"

She looked up at him, her cheeks flushing slightly. "Nothing. Here." She handed him the bottle of water. He took it and immediately placed the plastic nipple between his teeth. "Drink slow. I don't need you throwing up all over the place."

"No, ma'am," he said.

The paper packet containing the tablets opened easily between her fingers. She popped the two white ovals into her hand and waited for Catfish to finish sipping at the water. He finally stopped, swallowed noisily, and moaned in satisfaction. "Didn't know I'd ever miss water that much."

"Well, don't miss it too much," Shawna said, "because we're surrounded by it."

He blinked at her and slowly nodded before taking the pills from her, popping them into his mouth, grimacing, and taking a sip of water. "Don't happen to have any cigarettes in that damned supply chest, do you?"

"Um, no," she said, narrowing her eyes. "No vape either, so don't even ask."

"No energy drinks?"

"Cut it out. You need to rest." She placed a hand on his forehead. He still felt too warm. "You have a fever."

"No kidding," he said. "I thought I was just burning up and freezing at the same time."

"You want a blanket?"

He shook his head. "Not yet. Maybe in a while." He tried to turn his neck and look out the porthole but stopped with a grunt of pain. "Any idea where the fuck we are?"

"No. The SOS beacon has been going off for a while now, though. I can't imagine they don't know where we are."

Catfish harrumphed. "Just because they know where we are doesn't mean they're in any kind of hurry to pick us up."

"What do you mean?"

He shrugged. "Think about it. They knew what was happening on the rig and didn't do jack shit to help us. For all they know, this lifeboat has one of those things in it." He rubbed his arms together as if trying to warm them. "I'm surprised they haven't dropped a bomb on us."

What was it Thomas had said? Fuel air bomb? She shivered again. They were lucky to have escaped the thing on the rig. She wondered how close they had come to getting obliterated by a plane from Australia. "I guess you're right," she said, her words tumbling out in a barely audible whisper.

Catfish winced and held his knee, doing his best to keep the leg still. "Yeah, I think I fucked myself up pretty good."

Frowning, Shawna turned the flashlight back on and shined it at Catfish's leg. A long, jagged line ran from his thigh to the shin. It didn't look to have bled much, and a fine crust of scab had already begun to cover the open wound, but his foot looked odd. The purple bruising and swelling told her he'd done a little more than just sprained his ankle. "Yeah," she said, "I think you did. We need to keep you off your feet."

He grunted. "Not like there's anywhere to go. But I do need to piss."

She helped him to the rear of the boat and through the hatch leading to the rail. The moonlight pierced the blanket of high clouds, and for a moment, Shawna couldn't breathe. It was beautiful. As far as she could see, there were only light waves, the occasional foam spray, and the moon's reflection. Whenever a hole in the clouds appeared, more stars than she'd ever seen crowded the night sky.

Using her shoulder to prop himself up, he fumbled for his zipper with one hand, managed to unzip, made sure he wasn't pissing into the breeze, and let go. Shawna tried not to laugh. Of all the firsts she'd experienced over the past week or two, this was the latest.

When Catfish's stream finally turned into a trickle, he bounced his member up and down, slid it back into his underwear, and struggled to rezip. "Shit," he said. "I can't zip it up."

Shawna rolled her eyes. *In for a penny,* she thought. She snaked her free hand around and held the top of his shorts. Her fingers touched bare skin, and even as absurd as the situation was, she felt a tremble of desire.

Stop that shit, she told herself as he zipped up his shorts. *He's like a brother to you.*

"Okay," Catfish said. "Thank you for not making fun of me."

She helped him turn around, and they staggered back into the cabin. "It was difficult," she said.

"I'm sure." They reached the bench, and he managed to sit, legs hanging over the edge, back against the wall. He smiled at her. "Thank you."

"Don't mention it," she said. "Just remember that if you ever have to help me take a piss."

"Deal," Catfish said. "But you're the one in one piece." He shivered and rubbed his hands against his arm. "Hell of a draft coming through those doors."

"That and you need to lie down and let the meds work their way through your system. Kill that fever."

"Yeah," he said. "I guess."

"I'll close the door and get some more blankets, try and make you more comfortable."

"Shit," he said, "how much more comfortable can I get? Ankle's blown, my head feels like it's full of broken glass, my lungs are cheese graters, I'm burning up from the inside, and you're worried about me being comfortable."

"Catfish?"

"Yes?"

"Shut the fuck up."

CHAPTER TWO

She held his hand while he slept and raged with fever. His ankle continued to balloon, and it seemed no matter how much medicine she gave him, the fever returned with a vengeance. She was beginning to worry that in a day or two, it would just be her on the boat.

There was little to do besides doze and listen to the sound of the waves lapping against the hull and Catfish's serrated lungs taking in air. That said, her mind started playing tricks on her. Several times, she thought she heard a helicopter in the distance. Each incident stirred her from her restless sleep and sent her to the deck to look for hope, but there was nothing but the blue sky laced with white puffy clouds and the endless water.

She woke Catfish up every six hours to give him more medicine. Shawna didn't want to tell him they were already running out, that they had enough supply for a few more days if she rationed it, but after that, his body was either going to fight off the illness, or he was going to die. No, that was not something she wanted to think about, let alone speak aloud.

When she was sure Catfish was asleep, she went up on deck and vented all the grief. Thomas. JP. Hell, the entire crew of *Leaguer* was dead. Gone. If the creature hadn't consumed them, they surely perished in the fire they had set to kill it. Or they drowned when the rig finally sank into the abyssal.

Thomas Calhoun, her late boss, had taken her under his wing

and made her something more than a simple petroleum chemist. He trained her to think like an engineer. He treated her like a daughter instead of an employee. And now his body would never be found. There would be no burial. He would simply be marked as "lost at sea."

And JP. The former SEAL and rig diver had been consumed by a creature after being infected. He'd never smile at her again. She'd never have to listen to him and Catfish argue over minute details as they maintained Catfish's infamous AUVs or his other gear. Neither of them would fantasize about spear diving and catching something huge while sharks circled them.

Those conversations, those moments, could only live in memory now. The threads had been snipped once and for all, and there was no going back.

The heartache was worse than being dumped or discovering your boyfriend had decided you were too straight-laced and, therefore, had affair after affair until he finally came clean without so much as a tear. This was much, much worse.

But the absolute final cosmic joke was watching the last of her team, her last good friend, dying in the middle of the ocean while she could do nothing to save his life.

Head in her hands and eyes full of tears, her ears picked up the chop-chop-chop of blades slicing the air. It sounded kilometers away. Had to be another auditory hallucination. She ignored it, focusing instead on the memory of Thomas' lined and kind face, his gruff voice, and the twinkle of mischief in his blue eyes, so much like her father but so different.

The sound picked up in volume. A wave, larger than the rest, crashed into the boat, making it wobble just enough to give her vertigo and knock her off balance. She caught herself before she flipped over the side railing. And then she saw it.

It looked like a brick flying straight at them; its nose tilted slightly toward the water. Her tired eyes and mind finally made sense of what she was seeing. Her heart picked up speed, and she wiped away hopeful tears as it moved closer and closer.

If it was a hallucination, she didn't want to know. If it was a dream, she didn't want to wake up. And when the helicopter reached them, she finally believed it was over.

* * *

She and Catfish spent two days in Port Moresby, the capital of Papua/New Guinea, in a building surrounded by men and women carrying weapons. Although he didn't enter the building, she saw one of the men through a window carrying what looked like a flame thrower.

A pair of Australian doctors wearing HAZMAT suits checked on her every three hours, their faces friendly but stressed behind their helmets. Somewhere in the building, she'd no doubt Catfish was in a closed-off room like hers, IVs hooked up to his body while tests were run on every ounce of blood they could squeeze from his veins.

There were no newspapers. There was no mention of what was happening in the world, no answers to her questions about PPE, *Leaguer*'s owner, and her employer, or HAL, the Houston lab they'd sent the samples to. She hadn't expected the doctors to know anything about either company, but even if they did, she knew it was a long shot they'd tell her. They wanted her calm. They wanted her to read the romance novels they brought her. They wanted her to rest. Finally, they'd put something in her IV to make her do just that.

On the third day of her incarceration, the doctors entered her room without their bulky suits. They told her she had recovered, and while she still had a mild concussion, she was healthy and infection-free. Catfish's ankle would require minor surgery, but his concussion symptoms were fading fast, and the bacteria causing his pneumonia had lost the battle. She'd see him the next day.

They ushered her, against her complaints, to a private jet. Then they were in Japan. Then, they were airborne again and heading for the United States. The plane reached LA and stayed on the tarmac long enough to refuel before returning to the air. Destination? Houston, Texas.

Upon landing at a private airport, Catfish was carried off on a stretcher while she walked on rubbery legs down the airstairs and to the tarmac. The two men who had sat near her the entire flight gestured to a black SUV.

Another group of men rolled Catfish's gurney to a private ambulance.

"Hey! Where are they taking him?" she asked the large man standing before her.

He glanced down at her and said simply, "Same place as you. But he had surgery. Needs to be monitored."

She shook her head. "I want to go where he's going. I mean with him."

The man shook his head. "Those aren't my orders, ma'am. My orders are to get you to your destination. Please get in the backseat."

Exhausted, terrified, and unsure whether or not this was a dream, Shawna opened her mouth to protest but realized there was no point. They had numbers. They had guns. She didn't. She'd have to do what they said.

After climbing into the SUV's spacious backseat, she saw the partition blocking her from the windshield. She had no way to see where they were going.

The SUV drove quickly away from the airport, found the freeway, and rumbled as it accelerated. She tried to look out the windows and figure out where she was, but they were tinted so strongly that she couldn't even make out road signs.

Upon reaching their destination, she heard a conversation through an open window. Someone asked to see ID. Someone said "sir" a lot, and they were moving again for another five minutes.

Through the reinforced glass, she barely heard the buzz of aircraft propellers. The SUV stopped, the doors opened, and she stepped out into bright sunlight beneath a blameless blue sky.

Armed men escorted her into a stark concrete building. She walked through the halls while men and women in uniforms glanced at her with either mild disinterest or unease. The government had her, and she got the feeling they would never let her go.

CHAPTER THREE

She didn't want for food. They brought it at regular intervals when they weren't "debriefing" her and asking the same questions over and over again in a small, windowless room. The single mirror in the room was no doubt one-way glass, and she knew they were recording her every word, every facial expression, everything. And each time she asked a question of her interrogators, they frowned, then told her they'd give her answers. Eventually.

Shawna used her fingernail to scrape a line in the sheetrock each time they brought her a meal. The number was seven now. Assuming they'd brought her three meals a day, that meant she'd been here for more than two days while suffering countless hours of the same questions. Now, she waited for more of the same.

Lost in her thoughts, she barely heard the knock on the door. Shawna warily looked up at the thick, steel door, unsure if she'd heard anything. When the knock came again, she took in a deep breath. "Come in."

The heavy door opened on silent hinges. Through the widening crack in the door, she glimpsed a man dressed in a nondescript military uniform holding an assault rifle pointed at the ceiling. When the door finished opening, a woman dressed in a white lab coat stood in the entryway. She smiled at Shawna, walked inside carrying a stool, and closed the door behind her. A bolt shot home with a loud clank.

The woman stood there for a moment, eyes focused on Shawna's.

"Hello, Ms. Sigler. I'm Dr. Shannon Moore."

Shawna said nothing, and the woman's lips parted in a slight smile.

Moore placed the stool on the floor in front of Shawna's bed and sat down. "I'm sure you have lots of questions. And I'll answer them in a moment."

Shawna said a little more nothing.

The woman sighed and folded her hands in her lap. "Do you know where you are?" When Shawna didn't reply, Moore nodded to herself. "Well, if you don't want to know about me or this place, then surely you want to know about Mr. Standlee."

Shawna stiffened. When Moore's smile widened, Shawna felt like leaping from the bed and beating the shit out of the woman. "Stop wasting my time," Shawna said in a low rasp. "Where is he?"

"He's safe and he's doing well," Moore said. "His ankle required another surgery, but he's had the best care possible. And his concussion has healed up nicely." Moore paused. "As has yours."

"Where is he?" Shawna asked again.

"In this facility," Moore said. "You'll see him later today. Tomorrow if he's not up to it."

"After another round of interrogation?" She spat out the last word with vitriol.

Moore blanched slightly. "There will be no more interrogations," she said. "You have told us everything we needed to know."

Here it comes, Shawna thought. "So now what?"

"That's the question I hoped you would ask," Moore said. Her grin was back and wider than ever. "I have an opportunity for you."

"Opportunity," Shawna echoed. Something in the way the woman held herself sent shivers up and down Shawna's spine. "What kind of opportunity?"

"The organism you encountered on *Leaguer*--"

"Organism? You mean the goddamned monster?"

Moore's lips clamped shut, her smile disappearing into an emotionless line. Shawna wasn't sure, but the woman appeared to be grinding her teeth. Moore sat in silence, eyes boring into Shawna's. "May I continue?" Moore asked a moment later.

Shawna suddenly felt a little afraid of this woman. Moore's emotions seemed to turn on a dime, making Shawna think this was the real person, not the grinning, polite woman who had walked into the room a moment ago. The rest was just a facade. "Yes," Shawna said. "Please."

Moore's grin reappeared as if a switch had been flipped. "Thank you. As I was saying, the organism you discovered on *Leaguer* made it to Houston. But you already know that."

The barrel, Shawna thought. They'd brought up a barrel's worth of oil from the M2 trench. She'd tested it. It had scared her. No, "scare" wasn't the right word. More like "terrified."

"I put a warning in the report. I tried to—"

"Calm down," Moore said.

Shawna stopped in mid-rant, heart thumping in her ears. Until Moore interrupted her, she hadn't realized she'd balled up her fists or noticed the swell of anger making her face flush. She managed to regain control of her emotions and looked down at the bed. "I tried to warn them." The words tumbled out in something like a sob. "I tried."

"I know," Moore said. Shawna looked up at the strange woman, Moore's face a mask of empathy, eyes soft and light. "And it was ignored. I'm sorry."

"Me too," Shawna said.

"You did everything you could, Ms. Sigler. I hope you accept that."

Despite Shawna's suspicion that the woman was anything more than a cipher, the words sounded genuine. "I'll try," Shawna said.

Moore nodded. "Do you need a moment?"

Shawna swiped away the beginnings of a tear. "I'm fine," she said. "Go on."

Moore paused a beat. "The sample from the barrel infected one of the chemists at HAL. The patient was taken to Ben Taub Hospital, where she died. The organism had incubated inside her, consumed her, and most of the CDC team trying to help her. Between the incidents at *Leaguer*, HAL, and Ben Taub, hundreds of people lost their lives. Fortunately, both HAL and Ben Taub were secured."

"Secured," Shawna said. "Secured how?"

"Ingenuity and hard work," Moore said, eyes twinkling. "The entities--"

"Entities?"

Moore's face once again went blank except for a slight twitch at the corners of her lips. "Yes," she said. "That's the preferred term for the organism in question."

Shawna nodded, but the way Moore said it made her feel dumb. "Okay. Entities."

The smile reappeared as though it had never left. "The entities that could not be captured were destroyed."

Captured. Shawna felt like someone had punched her in the stomach. The air seemed too thick to breathe, and her skin bristled with gooseflesh. "You-- You--"

Moore nodded. "We managed to recover two of the entities and have them safely contained."

Shawna was shivering now. "There's no containment," she said in a trembling voice. "There's no way to contain that."

"Ms. Sigler, please calm--"

"You don't get it, do you? One of your so-called 'entities' brought down a fucking oil rig. What do you think that shit's going to do if it gets loose out here where it has all the food it could ever want?"

Shawna's heart thumped so loudly that she wasn't sure she could have heard Moore's reply, not that there was one. That outburst had exhausted every bit of her, and she suddenly struggled to get enough air in her lungs. Even after many days of monitored "rest," she felt like she hadn't slept in a year.

Moore finally raised a hand as though to stop Shawna from speaking again. "Ms. Sigler? Do you need a drink of water? Maybe a sedative?"

Sedative? When her heart slowed slightly and she felt back in control, she said, "No. I don't need a sedative. But a glass of water wouldn't go amiss."

Moore stared at a corner of the ceiling and nodded her head. When she turned back to face Shawna, the grin had returned. "Just a moment," she said, "and we'll take care of that. Now, may I continue?"

Shawna didn't trust herself to speak, so she nodded instead.

Moore laced her fingers together. "During your interviews, you mentioned the entities couldn't escape glass or metal. Correct?"

Shawna said nothing.

"Well, that's consistent from our observations and interviews of the other sites and survivors. But you don't look convinced," Moore said. "Why is that?"

Shawna shrugged. "Catfish said he and JP found metal that had been weakened. Crumbled under strain."

"Iron?"

"No idea," Shawna said. "But that's a good guess."

"Was Mr. Standlee certain it wasn't from rust?"

"Dr. Moore, *Leaguer* was a brand new rig. It hadn't had time to rust through."

Moore raised a hand. "I know it was a new rig, Ms. Sigler. I'm simply asking the obvious question."

Shawna tried not to bristle at that. Moore knew it was a stupid question, so why the hell did she ask it? "It wasn't rust," Shawna said. "The metal, the steel or iron, was brittle. And if I know your entity, it was probably shining like it was brand new."

"That also confirms the other accounts." Moore tented her hands. "What about glass?"

Yes, Shawna, Thomas' voice said in her mind, *what about glass?*

Good question.

"I never had the opportunity to study any glass it touched." Shawna sighed. "I didn't have the chance to run half the tests I wanted."

Moore's fingers played with one another in a silent rhythm. "So you're not certain it can damage glass?"

"No," she said. "I assume its appendages could shatter or break glass, but I don't know if its—" Shawna searched for a word and couldn't find it. "Its—"

"Essence?" Moore suggested.

"No, but that's close." Shawna stared down at her lap. "You have to understand, it moved like liquid. It acted like liquid. Chemically, it tests like a hydrocarbon. But it dissolved nearly every substance it touched." Shawna raised her eyes back to Moore's. "In short, I couldn't hazard a guess as to what it does to glass or other materials that have tightly packed atoms."

"So you don't think the entities can be contained?"

"No," Shawna said. She leaned forward on the bed. "I don't. And I think anyone who does is a fool."

Moore's cheeks tightened for an instant before relaxing back into her easy smile. "Prudent attitude," she said. "Do you consider yourself a scientist, Ms. Sigler?"

"Of sorts," Shawna said. "Thomas used to say the difference between an engineer and a scientist is knowing what to do with the research, how to apply it, and make it into something useful. Scientists want to know. Engineers want to use. Thomas trained me to think more like an engineer."

"You obviously liked him," Moore said. "My condolences."

Shawna didn't realize she was on the verge of crying until she felt a single, hot tear roll down her cheek. She wiped it away absently.

Moore's eyes had softened. "And what would Mr. Calhoun say about this?"

Shawna let out a short bark of laughter and smiled. "He'd have said you're out of your goddamned mind for keeping that shit alive. But—" Shawna's voice trailed off.

"But?" Moore prodded.

"But he would have been interested to know the results of the insanity."

"He sounds like a pragmatist."

"He was," Shawna said. "Also a dreamer. Passionate about his field, more so than having a regular life."

"And you?"

Shawna raised an eyebrow. "What about me?"

"Are you more passionate about your field than a regular life?"

One day, you're gonna have to make a choice, her father had said before he died. *You're gonna have to choose between being a wife and mother or being a scientist because I don't think you're going to be able to do both.*

"I don't think that's relevant," Shawna said. "What's relevant is that you have at least two of these things under lock and key."

"That's right," Moore said. "Under lock and key."

Shawna ground her teeth as she tried to hold back an exasperated scream. "What you don't understand," she said through a clenched jaw, "is that you're not a locksmith. You don't get to put this shit in a box and expect it to stay there." Her voice rose in volume and lowered in pitch. "You're a goddamned child playing with a venomous snake! And when you least expect it, it's going to bite you in the face and leave you dying. Only difference is the rest of us die with you."

The room echoed with her last words before falling into silence. The whoosh of air through the vents and her heartbeat were all she could hear. Moore's face was impassive, but Shawna could see the seething anger beneath the facade. *No, not just anger,* she thought. *I think she's afraid, too.*

Finally, Moore cleared her throat. "Ms. Sigler. I came here to offer you an opportunity. I was hopeful you'd want to take advantage of it, but now I'm not so certain."

"Opportunity," Shawna repeated. "And what opportunity might that be?"

"To help find a way to destroy it once and for all."

Shawna searched Moore's face for a moment. The woman's hard eyes burned with passion mixed with something close to hate. Moore was no doubt capable of deceit, and something seemed wrong with her as if she teetered on the edge of madness. But Shawna saw something behind that hard stare and impassive face. Moore was serious about killing it. Shawna just wasn't sure why.

Putting her hands on her knees, Shawna bent forward slightly. Each whispered word had its own weight. "We. Destroyed. It. We. On *Leaguer.* We got ours."

"Of course you did, Ms. Sigler," Moore said. "And the cost was extremely high."

"Goddamned right it was."

Moore tapped her fingers on the table as though waiting for Shawna to finish.

Finally, Moore said, "When you have committed to the project, you'll get much more information, but I need you to make that decision."

"And what is this project?"

Moore smiled. "We've assembled a team of experts from the encounters at HAL and Ben Taub Hospital. The scientists from HAL will analyze the specimens. Members from the SWAT team that helped clear Ben Taub will provide security and training. Between the two teams, we hope to design weapons to control any future outbreaks."

"Hope," Shawna said. "You hope to contain them. You hope to learn how to destroy them. I think you should abandon that hope and just fry the bastards right now."

Moore's fingers slid across one another in her lap as if she played cat's cradle without any string. "I understand your reservations. And if there were any other way, I'd do that right now."

That, Shawna thought, *is a lie.* Instead, she said, "You have your team. What do you need me for?"

"The same thing we need Mr. Standlee for—your experience."

"Experience?"

"Your observations," Moore said. "*Leaguer* is the only encounter that isn't fully documented. We didn't have access to cameras to watch the entity's progression from its initial state to whatever it became at the end."

"What it became was death. For everyone."

"I understand that," Moore said, a hint of exasperation in her voice. "But your experience was with the 'pure' strain."

Shawna cocked an eyebrow. "What do you mean?"

Moore waved the question away. "So you can either help us study the entities, help fill in the blanks in our shared knowledge, or you can learn to live with nightmares for the rest of your life, wondering when one of the M2 creatures will pop up in your A/C vent or travel up your plumbing while you're sitting on the toilet."

Shawna shivered. Even as Moore spoke, her mind traveled into a terrifying nightmare where no place was safe, no human activity was without danger of the black things appearing and eating everything they could.

Nightmares. They'd no doubt been watching her sleep, heard her muted screams, and seen the sweat-stained sheets. Moore no doubt knew Shawna from dossiers and interviews, but Shawna wagered her time in this place had given the woman more insight than Moore would ever need.

"And if I refuse to join up?" Shawna finally asked.

Moore frowned. "We can't force you or Mr. Standlee to stay or agree to help. The two of you have already filled in several remaining blanks, but there are more questions we need answered, and I think the only way to get them is to have the two of you on the team. While you compare notes with the other team members, I'm certain new information will come to light."

"You didn't answer my question."

The impassive, stony expression returned to Moore's face. "You'll sign non-disclosure agreements. Those agreements will bind you to never speak of the incident, hold interviews, or provide data to anyone else on the planet regarding the incident. Your passport will be frozen for foreign travel until this project is finished, and any work you undertake will no doubt be watched very carefully."

Shawna considered this for a moment. She was dealing with the Feds, probably the NSA or some other alphabet agency that received its funding from those pesky blank check appropriation bills. If she didn't join their monster project, they would monitor her for the rest of her life. Or, more likely, put a bullet in her brain pan. This woman, certainly half-mad, would have no reservations about doing it, either.

"And if I join?"

"Forgive me for bringing this up," Moore said, "but you are currently unemployed. The Federal government is willing to pay you a contract worth three times your former annual salary for a mere six months of your life."

Well, at least there's that, Shawna thought. Six months of her life. Six months of analyzing something that could kill her and the rest of the damned world. *And Judas only got 30 pieces of silver.*

"You think it'll only take six months." It wasn't a question.

Moore shrugged. "It will take as long as it takes. If we think your services should be extended, then we'll present you with a new contract upon the expiration date."

"Have you talked to Catfish about this yet?"

Moore raised an eyebrow in momentary confusion and smiled. "Oh. You mean Mr. Standlee. Rather than interrupt his recovery, we decided to approach you first. If you decide to join the project, we hope you'll have a word with him."

"And if I decide not to join?"

"Then I expect you'll want to give him your reasoning for that as well."

"You're right," Shawna agreed. "I would." She stared down at the floor, her eyes attempting to look through it. "What are your plans for the end of the project?"

"I'm not sure I understand," Moore said after a moment.

Shawna raised her eyes back to the strange woman's face. "What are you going to do with the entities when you're finished studying them?"

Moore's face twitched into something like a grin. "We will burn them until they no longer exist."

Shawna nodded. "And when do you need an answer?"

"Preferably today," Moore said, "but I can wait until the end of the week. Unfortunately, you'll have to stay in this room, unless escorted, until you make your decision. And there are portions of the facility you may not see."

"So I'm a prisoner of paperwork."

Moore flashed a genuine smile. "Good way to put it. Yes. Yes, you are."

An awkward silence settled over the room. Shawna focused on her breathing as she tried to tamp down the well of self-righteous anger threatening to tear through her throat. Every fiber of her being wanted to scream, punch, rip, and find a way to destroy this place once and for all. What they were doing was too goddamned dangerous, and this woman was obviously insane.

But showing that, now, in this room? No. She needed to hide it and keep her feelings to herself until she knew the play. There was time. There was always time.

"Do you have any questions for me?" Moore finally asked.

Shawna figured Moore would ask that. Shawna shook her head and stared into the woman's eyes. "I think you've said everything you will."

Moore cocked an eyebrow, and then her impassive face slowly transformed into a smile once again. "I hope you decide to join the project, Ms. Sigler. I'd really like to work with you."

"Let me know when I can see Catfish."

The woman stood from the stool, lifted it with her left hand, and turned to the door. She rapped twice, and it swung open; the soldier at the door took the stool and handed Moore a bottle of water. She thanked him and turned back to Shawna.

"Your water is here," Moore said. Shawna stood and grasped the bottle. Moore didn't drop her grip. "Was a pleasure meeting you," she said.

Shawna pulled harder on the bottle of water until Moore released it. Moore looked at her expectantly, but Shawna merely turned and sat back on the bed without meeting Moore's eyes. Moore walked out of the room, closed the door, and it locked with a loud clank.

Shawna opened the water bottle and drank half of it in one gulp. After replacing the cap, she dropped the bottle to the floor and sprawled on the bed. All the rage, the grief, everything she hadn't allowed herself to feel came out in a flood. She put her head in her hands and began to cry.

She knew they were watching her, but she didn't care. This was her new world now, and it didn't seem to matter that she wanted to crawl into a corner and die. They were going to force her to face it. Even if it killed her.

CHAPTER FOUR

Catfish opened his eyes and stared into the fluorescent lights for the thousandth time. Before coming to this place, wherever the hell it was, he didn't know a human being could be so goddamned tired.

Between the bouts of heavy antibiotics, the painkillers for his ankle, and the endless questions a group of lab-coated assholes kept asking, he felt like just covering his head with a pillow and never opening his eyes again.

He hadn't seen Shawna since the plane ride from Papua/New Guinea, and even then, he was so stoned on whatever they put into his IV that he was barely aware of the world around him. His only memories of the trip were her pale, concerned face and her hand holding his while he lay restrained on the stretcher, buckled in like a two-year-old, with men carrying assault rifles standing nearby.

Now, he was in a room large enough to contain a hospital bed and all the medical equipment he could imagine, and he was still guarded by a pair of armed men standing just outside the door. He'd asked, no, begged, for a computer, a tablet, anything to keep his brain working. All requests were denied. Instead, they'd brought him a pile of books he had no interest in reading.

This was torture. If he found out the Feds were involved in this, as they surely were, he'd sue for inhuman treatment of a prisoner. Or some shit like that.

It was difficult to think. The painkillers made the world drift in and out, and the antibiotics they'd given him left his stomach on the verge of upchucking the meals they'd brought him.

After living for weeks on a rig with that awesome Chef Nutchtchas filling their bellies with excellent meals every day, the stuff they brought him tasted like slop. Like military food. The more he thought about it, the more it made sense. They were probably on a military base. Where? He had no clue. Could be Guantanamo.

That would be perfectly apt, he thought. *Round up the only two people who survived a goddamned oil monster and hide them away where there are no lawyers, no due process, and no chance of escape.*

The interrogators wore white lab coats, carried cups of coffee instead of batons, and used questions as torture instead of waterboarding. Catfish lost his temper on the second day when they asked the same series of questions they'd asked the day before. The three stooges, as he'd come to think of them, had left in an exasperated huff without saying a word.

When they showed up the next day, they used a different tactic. They started asking new questions about how he'd come up with the idea to turn his deep sea AUV into an explosive to destroy the creature below the rig. They wanted to know how it had worked and if he still had the code.

They wanted to know about the "rust" on the metal grates. They wanted to know how light affected the creature, how it burned, and how JP became infected. And their questions made him smile because he knew, once and for all, that Shawna Sigler was alive and well and probably in the building.

The only question now was when he'd be able to see her or if he'd be allowed to see her. They had purposely put the bed against the far wall in such a position that he couldn't see much through the constantly guarded door, but that didn't mean he hadn't heard the sounds of construction, the click of heavy boots on concrete and tile, and the occasional errant squawk of a radio. Wherever he and Shawna were, they weren't leaving unless someone allowed them to.

He raised himself slightly, repositioned, and lay back down. His ankle itched and ached. He'd had another surgery, and his foot felt like it was full of shrapnel. Recovery time? Four to six weeks in a boot once he was cleared for it. Catfish was betting on a bullet to the head before he finished "recovery."

In a way, he didn't blame them. Thomas had been right. If the world found out goddamned oil monsters were hiding in the ocean, there'd be panic, chaos, and a brief downturn in global civilization. "But at least maybe we'd get green energy," he muttered with a pained smile.

"Green energy?"

The voice startled him into rigidity, which in turn made his ankle scream with pain. Wincing, he turned his head to see the newcomer.

She stood holding a clipboard to her chest. Even dressed like all the other doctors before her, he could tell she was different. The newcomer's eyes shined with both curiosity and confidence, which put his guard up. This was a predator.

"Who are you?" His voice, unused since the previous day, was a gravelly croak.

Her slight smile grew, and she walked fully into the room. She stood at the foot of the bed to keep him from craning his neck or looking sideways. "Hello, Mr. Standlee. I'm Dr. Shannon Moore."

"No," he said while pointing at her. "Who are you?"

Moore cocked an eyebrow. "What do you mean?"

Catfish fought the frustrated sigh burning in his chest. "Those other idiots? They're just drones. Idiots asking me the same idiot questions over and over again. But I can already tell you're different."

"How so?"

He glared at her. "You look like you're in charge. You don't have that academic bullshit air." He nodded to himself. "You're in charge of them."

She pulled a chair from the wall and moved it catty-corner to the foot of the bed. He didn't have to turn his head to keep his eyes on her.

"That's very astute, Mr. Standlee."

"Knew it," he mumbled. "So, I'll ask again. Who. Are. You?"

Moore placed the clipboard in her lap and raised her hands to encompass the room. "All this? All that out there? I'm in charge of it all."

"Good," Catfish said. "That means you can tell me when I'm getting out of this fucking place."

"Indeed, I can," she said. "And I think our discussion today will answer that question."

"Joy," Catfish said. "In a coffin or in chains?"

Her left eyebrow seemed to jump. "Excuse me?"

"Look, lady. You guys brought me and Shawna here all the way from the other side of the goddamned world. You people quarantined us, gave us medical attention, guarded us, and instead of sitting in a hospital, we're here at some black site?"

"Black site," she said and shook her head. "We don't call it that."

"Whatever. I'll bet no one else in the world knows where we are. Sure as shit, not PPE."

"You are correct, Mr. Standlee. Your employer has no idea where you are. To be honest, they probably wouldn't care either. After all, all hands were lost on *Leaguer.*"

He blinked at her. "Shit. We're listed as lost at sea?"

She nodded. "Yes. All hands."

"Nice. So, since we don't really exist anymore, what the hell are you planning on doing with us?"

"As I said, Mr. Standlee, our discussions here in the next few minutes should make that clear."

He let the words sink in. He'd heard that tone before. Cops, lawyers, shit, even his damned girlfriends had said something like that before. Moore was about to offer him a carrot, and then would come the stick.

"Then let's get to it," he finally said.

"I believe you already know why you are here."

Catfish rolled his eyes. "Obviously. Your minions have asked me so many questions about what happened on *Leaguer*, there's no way I couldn't." He raised himself on his elbows. "And how the hell did you guys find out anything about the monster in the first place?"

She waved away the question. "That will become clear in time. For now, let's just say we have audio, video, text, and all sorts of other evidence. We know what ultimately happened, but not all the details. That's why you are here. That is why my minions, as you call them, have asked all those questions."

He touched the controls on the bed and raised it a few inches. He didn't need to change position, but he wanted to see if he could slow her down and make her give away something in her body language. Stalling and seeming not to listen were ways to do that. *Just keep talking*, he thought.

"And?"

"And," she continued, "you have given us most of what we were looking for. Between you and Shawna--"

"Ah, so she is here."

Moore's easy smile disintegrated into a frown just short of a snarl. "May I continue?"

Catfish grinned and gestured for her to do so. Her laser beam glare only served to widen his smile.

"As I said, we have gathered an enormous amount of additional intelligence between the two of you. And since your information was so valuable, I'm here to offer you a job."

Catfish's grin melted into confusion, his eyebrows arching like frightened caterpillars. "A job?"

She clasped her hands together in her lap again. He stared at her fingers, looking for signs of fidgeting. Nothing. She was cold as granite and just as transparent.

"I believe you are currently unemployed."

"Why? We had a contract with PPE and--"

"PPE no longer exists."

"What? What do you mean?"

Her lips twitched into the ghost of a smile. "PPE is currently in Chapter 7. All assets to be liquidated after their stock crashed and all the bills came due. At least that's what the press releases say."

"Holy shit," Catfish said. "Why the hell would you do that?

"It doesn't matter," she said. "As far as the world is concerned, it's the truth."

"NSA?"

She frowned. "Excuse me?"

"Which fucking Federal alphabet agency are you with?"

"Mr. Standlee, you have dropped several f-bombs during this conversation. Are they really necessary?"

"Fuck, yes."

Moore pursed her lips. "Your profile said you'd be stubborn. Childish even."

"Good profile," Catfish said. "Then you know how I react to bullshit."

"Yes, yes, I do."

"So why are you still jerking me off?"

"Fine." She rose from the chair and sidled closer to him like a spider. With her face a mere half meter from his, she spoke in a low, even tone with a cannibal's smile.

"We want to pay you to work here. If you can behave yourself, it'll be thrice what your PPE contract was worth. Regardless of whether you agree, you'll be forced to sign a binding non-disclosure agreement that the US government will vigorously enforce. Your life will be monitored 24 hours a day, and you'll be placed on a no-fly list anytime I fucking feel like it."

The f-bomb exploded from her mouth with a spray of saliva. She moved back from him, her eyes laughing at the expression on his face. "Am I still jerking you off?"

He shook his head. "No, you're not."

"So, that's the deal. You work here, help us develop new equipment, and you'll be paid a ridiculous sum for six months of your time."

"New equipment?"

"Yes. Weapons, if you like. In case one of those things decides to come knocking on our door again."

"Again? Lady, that thing was in ten thousand meters of water. I don't think it's much of a threat here."

"Except for the sample."

Catfish opened his mouth to reply and stopped. The barrel. Shit, he'd forgotten all about the goddamned barrel. "Yeah, except for that."

"And that's the problem," she said. "You know something happened at HAL. You just don't know what or how bad it was."

He nodded. They'd gotten that news on *Leaguer* before the end. Despite the one-way satellite blackout, he'd still brought back communications on the rig, even if they had been limited.

"I know it got loose. Didn't you guys destroy it?"

She smiled. "Yes, and no. You'll hear and see all the gory details once you agree to the contract. But, I can reveal one fact to you now."

"And what's that?"

The smile grew. Those hard eyes held a manic gleam. "We have a specimen for study."

Catfish flinched and then grimaced. His ankle reminded him why he was in bed and that startled movements were not a good idea. "Specimen?"

"Two, actually."

"Fuck," he said softly. "You have to be kidding me."

She shook her head. "No. I'm not."

"Where the hell are they? They're not here?"

"That is a question I won't answer until you sign the contract. Otherwise, I can't give you any more information."

"Those things will get out. They'll kill everyone."

"Oh, I am quite aware of what they're capable of," Moore said.

"Then why the fuck haven't you set them on fire?" Catfish asked. "Burn them up with napalm or magnesium. Why the hell are you keeping them?"

She sighed and stepped back from him. "Because there may be others hiding in the ocean. Or perhaps trapped in some yet-to-be-tapped well in Saudi Arabia or any one of a dozen other countries."

"Goddamn," he said. He broke his stare with her and flicked his eyes to the ceiling. He tried to imagine ARAMCO bringing up a gusher of black, oily death. At best, it'd happen during the day, and the shit would just explode. At worst? It would crawl out of the ground and eat everything. He fought a giggle, trying to imagine the shit feasting on sand. The humorous thought disappeared. "Or Russia."

"Or Russia," she agreed. "Or Texas, or anywhere in North America where we're drilling, fracking, digging sewers, creating roads, or whatever else."

"Christ."

"That's why we want weapons," she said. "And to study them, know how to kill them. And you can help with that. Think of it as your patriotic duty."

He harrumphed. "The Federal government can kiss my ass."

"I didn't mean to them, Mr. Standlee. I meant as a citizen of the world."

He laughed. "That was cheesy. Going to tell me it's my duty as a human, too?"

"If that'll help."

Catfish lowered his head, eyes looking past her. "Weapons. Study. Analysis. You want me to work on how to kill these things?"

She nodded. "That's what I said."

"And have you asked Shawna?"

"Yes."

"And what did she say?"

He watched the woman's eyes and body language, looking for a hint of a coming lie or indecision of what to say. He saw none.

"Ms. Sigler would like to see you before she makes any decision."

Catfish smiled. “I’m not surprised.”

“You’ll require additional physical therapy for your ankle. If you stay with us, you’ll continue getting the best medical care available. Free, of course.”

“Free.” He uttered a short bark of laughter and gestured to the world beyond the walls of his room. “None of this is free, lady. All us taxpayers are already paying for it.”

Moore slowly nodded. “At least it’s going for something productive.”

Catfish said nothing.

She stood from the chair, pushed it back against the wall, and smiled at him. “It was nice talking to you. I’ll need an answer by the end of the week.”

Catfish waved at her but didn’t speak. Moore turned and knocked on the door. He heard a beep followed by the click of a deadbolt retracting. The door opened, Moore stepped through, and it closed behind her on silent hinges.

CHAPTER FIVE

After the doctor checked his dressings and ensured his cast was secure, he handed Catfish a pair of crutches and helped him out of bed to a standing position. For three minutes, the doc waited to see if he'd pass out. Fat chance. Catfish wasn't going to go down again unless hit in the head; there was shit to do.

The doc left, and a few minutes later, the smack of a pair of knuckles on the steel door broke the room's air-conditioned silence. Catfish had waited for the door to open, but it didn't. After a few more seconds, the rap at the door repeated itself.

He tried to speak, but his voice came out in a hoarse whisper. He suddenly realized he hadn't spoken with anyone since that creepy woman, Dr. Moore, entered his room yesterday and made the offer. After clearing his throat, he tried again.

"Come in. You always do," he croaked.

The door beeped, and an LED on the side of the knob turned green. The door swung open slowly, revealing three soldiers dressed in the same nondescript fatigues as the doctor had worn. Two men and a woman. The woman stood between them but was at the threshold while they remained a meter behind her. It didn't take Catfish but a heartbeat to know who was in charge.

"Mr. Standlee?" the woman said.

"That'd be me," Catfish said. "Nobody else in the room."

A brief, tired smile graced her face, and it melted the part of him that wanted to explode in a tantrum. He'd been brewing one for days, and this unfortunate soldier, or whatever the hell she was, was definitely going to be on the wrong end of it. At the same time, though, that smile.

"My name is Sarah. We're going to escort you to the commissary."

"Commissary," Catfish said. "You mean someplace to eat?"

"And drink coffee, or tea, or whatever," Sarah said. That smile was still there, only now it held a glint of amusement.

"So I need an escort."

Sarah looked around the room with a curt nod. "Yes, until I'm told otherwise, you can't leave this room without an escort." The smile faded. "Understood?"

The two men behind her stood expressionless, but the smaller, thinner one on the right curled his fingers into a fist and back out again. Catfish didn't like what he saw in the man's eyes. While his face might not express anything more than indifference, the man's eyes looked, well, dead. Lifeless. As if there was nothing behind them.

"Mr. Standlee?" Sarah said.

He snapped away from the soldier's eyes and returned his focus to Sarah. "Yes?"

"I asked if you were ready."

"Oh," he said. "Right. Guess you want me out of my room so you can have it cleaned?"

"Maybe," she said. "Or maybe Dr. Moore thought you'd like to see your friend."

Now it was Catfish's turn to grin. "Well, hell, why didn't you say so?" With tentative steps, he crutched his way to the door, making sure not to bang his immobile leg on the doorframe.

The soldiers stood aside, affording him enough space to cross into the corridor. Sarah walked around him until she once more stood in front of him. "Follow me," she said. "And please, take your time. We're not in a hurry."

The sound of construction equipment, the smell of burned metal and solder, and the sharp tang of ozone lit his senses. His eyes hurt beneath the merciless glare of the powerful overhead lights. He had expected to see the normal shadowy corners in a hallway, but there were none. Instead of simple overhead fluorescent lights gracing the ceiling panels every few meters, halogen light fixtures hung down, spaced a meter apart. The walls had the same fixtures, resulting in a completely shadowless tunnel of light.

"Someone sure likes their lights," he said as he crutched behind Sarah.

Without slowing down, she said over her shoulder, "They're special. Some kind of alternative to halogens that has the same ultraviolet frequency as sunlight."

"Stand in here long enough and get a sunburn?" Catfish asked.

"Something like that," she said. "Although I thought you'd be happy about it."

Catfish was suddenly struck with the memory of him and the remaining crew of *Leaguer* waiting out a seemingly endless night, huddled together beneath the wash of construction lights. M2, the featureless, shape-shifting pool of absolute black, surrounded them, waiting for a chance to pluck one of them from safety and into its alien maws. They'd made it through the night with only a single casualty and found safety in the dawn.

He shivered despite himself. Yes, the light was welcome. At least these idiots had realized how dangerous their little pets were. If M2 found itself in this hallway, it would be flash-fried just as easily as if exposed to blazing sunlight.

A thought occurred to him. "Hey, how would you know about that?"

"About what?" Sarah asked.

"About why the lights are here."

"That's classified," she said, sounding amused. "But I guess you'll find that out soon enough. Assuming you sign up."

They turned a corner, and the corridor opened into a foyer of sorts. Gleaming metal covered the walls and ceiling. At the far end, he saw what appeared to be the actual entrance to the building. Damned thing looked like an airlock from a sci-fi movie. Two heavily armed soldiers stood to either side, their bored eyes staring off into nothing.

Unlike any office foyer he'd ever seen, no receptionist sat at a curving desk to greet visitors. No works of art or posters graced the walls. Nothing apart from the stainless steel shine. His murky and blurred reflection stared at him from the room's surfaces, shadowing his every step. It reminded him of those mirror mazes at carnivals. God, he hated carnivals.

Sarah continued toward a doorway branching off the main room. A sign above the heavy steel door said "Commissary."

Well, that was kind of hard to miss.

The door opened, Sarah walked through the doorway, and Catfish followed. He didn't know what he'd been expecting, but this was certainly not it. The scent of freshly cooked bacon, eggs, and baked goods smelled like heaven, and his stomach, unwilling to handle much in the way of food the last few days, gurgled and growled with gluttonous desire.

Six tables with benches sat on the floor in two neat rows. Each was large enough to accommodate three people per side, so thirty-six people could eat here at once. Was the team that large? Or was it even larger, and people ate in shifts? Just what the hell was this place anyway?

Sarah moved aside, and he finally saw a small, round table in the corner, large enough to comfortably seat two people. Catfish smiled. Shawna sat in one of the chairs, a paperback clutched in one hand, a coffee cup in the other.

At that moment, he forgot about the soldiers escorting him and the M2 samples festering in some nearby testing facility. He also forgot they could put a bullet into his head if he stepped out of line. Seeing her face made all those other concerns melt away.

He crutched as quickly as he could into the room. His escort might have said something, probably did, but he didn't hear it, didn't care to hear it. The squeaking of the crutches' rubber pegs echoed in the room, and Shawna turned her head to find the source of the sound. Her eyes immediately widened, and a cheerful smile broke across her face.

Before he could reach her, she'd left the table and met him a few meters away. She stepped to the side so as not to disturb the crutches and hugged him awkwardly.

"About goddamned time," she whispered in his ear. Her warm lips met his cheek, and she held him for a moment, neither of them speaking.

For the first time since he'd been plucked from the ocean, who knows how many days or weeks ago, Catfish genuinely smiled. A tear tried to break free, but he fought it back. That, however, didn't help him keep the choked emotion from his voice. "About fucking time, yeah," he said. He turned his head slightly and kissed her cheek.

She pulled back from him at first, joy turning to surprise. They locked eyes, and she leaned closer and kissed him again, this time meeting his lips. A slight blush rose on her light brown skin as she pulled away.

"You hungry?"

"Got food here? I'm shocked," he said.

Shawna giggled and gestured to the table. "Come on." She walked beside him, her arms near him in case he needed help. Normally, that would have pissed him off, but it felt comforting instead. It was as if she wanted to be there to catch him if he fell.

Sitting down was awkward with his cast, but he immediately realized why Shawna had chosen this table. The lack of a bench meant he could stretch out his damaged leg without worrying about bumping it against the heavy lacquered wood.

After putting aside his crutches, but still within his reach, she sat across from him, her eyes sparkling. He met her gaze and shied away. "Been here long?"

She laughed. "Only an hour or two. First time I've been out of my room in days."

"First time I've seen anything but those goddamned white coats and that, well, that woman."

Shawna's grin faded. "Dr. Moore."

"The very one," Catfish said. He tented his hands on the table, his fingers fidgeting with one another. Shawna blinked twice and flicked her eyes to something behind and above him. Instead of following her gaze, he raised his eyes and looked up at the corner of the ceiling. A small orb hung from it like a plastic tumor.

It was a camera. One of those panoramic jobs that could cover the room from all angles. But based on Shawna's gesture, he was certain there was another behind him. Probably two more, one for each corner of the large room. If they were watching, they were no doubt listening too. Catfish blinked twice, and she moved her head in a subtle nod.

"When did you meet her?" Shawna asked.

"Yesterday," he said. "Right after I got done with the white-coated clowns."

Shawna rolled her eyes. "Just how many different times did they ask the same question?"

"Man," Catfish said, "I lost count. Assholes either don't know how to listen or think I'm stupid. Not sure which."

"Both," Shawna said. "And the second is the more likely—"

"Hey!" Catfish said in a mocking, hurt tone. "That's just mean."

Shawna grinned, her eyes darting to another part of the room. "Sorry. Couldn't help myself."

"Uh-huh," he said. "So—"

"Howdy," a deep Texas drawl said from behind him.

Catfish flinched and turned his head. A tall, slightly built, long-haired, goateed man in stained chef's whites had appeared at their table. He held a ceramic carafe in one hand, a serving tray expertly balanced on the other. Steam rose from the vessel's spout.

"Sorry, sir," he said to Catfish. "Didn't mean to creep up on you like that."

The man's physical appearance was more startling than his presence. Every person Catfish had seen in the building had military-style haircuts or, if they were female, their hair was pinned up in a tightly wrapped bun. He thought he saw the ghostly outline of tattoo sleeves beneath the white uniform.

The man poured steaming coffee from the carafe into the cups until they were 3/4 full. The smell of freshly brewed coffee wafted over the table, and Catfish breathed it in greedily. The ever-present stench of antiseptic, a scent he'd been stuck with since waking up in that damned room, faded away.

Finally, the man placed a pitcher of cream and a container of various sweeteners beside it. "I'm Robbie," he said. "I ain't here to ask any questions. Apart from, would you like something to eat?"

CHAPTER SIX

The breakfast was divine. Chef Robbie graced them with the best omelet Catfish had ever eaten, smothered with green chili and melted cheese. The biscuits, definitely made from scratch, crumbled at the touch and tasted like heaven. Catfish wasn't sure what kind of bargain he'd be asked to make in the next few hours, but if the food would be like this every day, he was beginning to wonder if it wouldn't be worth it.

While they ate, Catfish asked Shawna questions to try and fill in the blanks of his memory—how they were rescued, where they had been, and how they'd ended up here. In truth, he remembered very little of their time immediately following *Leaguer*'s destruction.

The meal finished and coffee in his belly, Catfish leaned back in his chair and tried not to belch. He didn't succeed. Shawna shook a finger at him with a prim look of reproach before a burp escaped her lips. They broke into a shared laugh, which didn't last long enough. He wasn't sure what had suddenly drained the devilish gleam in her eyes, but he imagined it was the same thing he'd thought of and would always think of for the rest of his life.

"Want to tell me what's going on?"

She sat up in her chair and rested her hands in her lap. "What did Moore tell you?"

"That she wants us to join 'her team.' That there are two samples of M2 somewhere in this facility and that if I don't join up, they'll shove surveillance equipment so far up my asshole that I'll be filming every time I open my mouth."

"Wow," she said. "Same old Catfish."

"What?"

"It just amazes me how colorful you can be."

"It's a gift," he said.

"I know." She stared at the table as if studying her reflection in the wood. "Money?"

"A lot," he said. "Big offer for six months of work."

"Is it worth it?"

"What do you mean?"

Shawna raised her head and gestured to the room. "Is all this worth it? To study it?"

"No," Catfish said. "It's not. They have no idea what they brought in here. No idea what they're talking about."

"Not so sure about that," Shawna said. "Moore has data from *Leaguer*. They were watching us through the rig's network. I bet they have every email, every text message, and every frame of video the systems captured before the power went out."

"Shit," Catfish said. "Hadn't considered that."

Did they know everything? Looking back on the conversation with Moore, that seemed likely. The pointed questions the white-coats had asked, and their specificity, meant they knew more about M2 than he had supposed. If he hadn't been so pissed off, he'd have realized that earlier.

"Dammit," he said. "Not sure if that's better or worse."

"Pick one," Shawna said. "You won't be wrong."

He rubbed at his unkempt beard and sighed. "The bad news," he said, "is they're going to fuck with these things no matter what we do."

She nodded. "That's a given. The only question is if they can safely handle the, um, 'samples' without us."

"Moore tell you how they got the other samples?"

"Sort of," Shawna said. "That sample we sent to HAL for analysis?"

The sample barrel. Yes, he remembered it well. Part of oil exploration involved procuring sample barrels from a new find to test its production viability. *Leaguer* had sent that barrel to Houston from the other side of the world before anyone aboard the rig knew what they'd found wasn't oil.

"I remember the voice on the radio telling us something had happened there. Something bad."

"Right," she said. "I don't have the details, but it certainly sounded like it got out and killed at least one person. Then it spread."

Spread. The word sent shivers through his bones, his mind filling with the image of a giant wave of M2 flowing over the rig like a tsunami of doom.

"Spread where?"

"Don't know," she said. "Does it matter?"

"Guess not," he said. "They must have handled it, or else there wouldn't be anything left in this city."

"'Handling it' is how they got the two samples."

"Makes sense." He glanced around and saw two soldiers standing at the commissary entrance. Sarah, the one that had rousted him from his room, was nowhere to be seen, and the two men standing guard duty weren't the same pair he'd seen earlier.

"How many people are at this base?" he asked.

"Good question," Shawna said. "Let's count. We've seen the three soldiers that brought you here, two new ones at the door, the chef, the white coats that kept asking us questions, Moore—"

"That woman—" Catfish said but didn't continue.

"—at least another two soldiers guarding the entrance to the room and a few other special guests."

"Special guests?" Catfish asked.

"Yes," Shawna said. "My understanding is several other survivors have chosen to join us."

Catfish brushed a crumb of croissant off his hospital robe. "HAL?"

"Yup," she said. "And Ben Taub."

"That's a hospital," he said. "Any idea what happened there? Or at the other?"

"No." She absently rolled the coffee cup between her fingers. "They haven't given me access to any news stories, much less explained anything."

"Figures," Catfish said. "Our lives pretty much ended on *Leaguer*, didn't they?"

She shrugged and sipped the dregs of her coffee. "Depends." Shawna gestured to the room as if trying to encompass the entire complex. "I think this is our life now."

"Christ, Shawna. You're supposed to cheer me up. Give me hope."

"Sorry," she said. "Not capable of that right now."

Catfish sighed and plucked a sugar pack from the holder. His fingers scrunched the packet, the sound unnervingly like that of M2 dissolving something. The realization made him drop the packet to the table as though it were a bomb. He stared at it for a moment, unsure how to control the sudden rush of his heart rate.

"Catfish?"

He flinched and looked up at her, a blush slowly heating his cheeks. "Yeah?"

"You okay? Looked like you saw a ghost."

He shook his head. "It's nothing. Just—" He broke off and stared past her at the nondescript concrete and metal walls.

Oh, to be locked in here forever, he thought to himself. *It would never get in here.*

Just as the words formed in his mind, he slowly raised his eyes to the ceiling. Several metal vents shushed air into the room. Catfish shivered again, nervous tension crawling through his stomach. "We're not going to be safe here."

Her eyes widened, her mouth set in a question she didn't ask. When she finally spoke, her words were barely audible. "We're not going to be safe anywhere."

The chair creaked slightly as he leaned back, doing his best to ignore his throbbing leg. The pain meds were wearing off. In an hour or two, all those tortured nerves would wake up and begin their shrill, operatic chorus. He wasn't looking forward to it, but at least it would give him an excuse to bail out of this conversation.

No, he told himself. *You can't bail on this. Not now.*

Shawna reached a hand across the table. Catfish leaned forward slightly, just far enough for his hand to clasp hers. "What did Moore say to you?"

"That they need weapons," Catfish said with a sneer. "And for some reason, she thinks my 'expertise' will be helpful."

Shawna stared at him before hiding a giggle behind her free hand. "Weapons?"

"Yeah," he said. "Guess they know about AUV-5."

"Well," she said, "you did manage to blow up an entire trench. It's probably five hundred meters deeper now."

"At least I got the big son of a bitch."

"You did at that," Shawna said. "Only question is, how many more of them are there?"

They fell silent again. Catfish wondered if she saw the same images in her mind—the black tentacles ending in sharp talons, the eyestalks that waved to and fro as the impossibly dark orbs swiveled, searching for movement or an easy meal—or if maybe the memory of the crunching, chewing, smacking, staticky sound of M2 dissolving its prey had begun echoing inside her skull. It certainly was in his.

"We ever going to be free?" he asked.

A timid smile crossed her face. "Doubt it," she said. "But if we don't deal with what's in this building, we never will be."

"You're going to say 'yes,' aren't you?"

She wiped at her eyes, sliding away the tear threatening to crawl down her cheek. "I don't know that we have a choice."

He growled low in his throat. "Bullshit, Shawna. We always have a choice."

Her fingers squeezed his tightly. "My choice is to finish this," she said. "If you'll stay with me."

As much as he knew it was more than likely a death sentence, another guaranteed dance with the deadly, alien things, he knew what his answer would be. The moment he said the word, he felt great relief and the unsettling ice of terror in his gut.

"Yes." The word dropped between them with a nearly audible thud. "I'll stay with you. And we'll finish this together."

CHAPTER SEVEN

Shawna and Catfish had breakfast the next day but enjoyed little privacy at first. Although they managed to procure the same table again, ten men and women dressed in unmarked fatigues, sidearms on their hips, sat at the long tables and ate with languid effort. They looked like children who had donned their fathers' and mothers' clothes for playtime. The eldest of them couldn't possibly be more than twenty-five.

Robbie, the chef, had taken their orders with a smile, made jokes, and served them food to gracious compliments. Everyone in the facility seemed to work for the military, but the chef certainly didn't. Shawna wondered how that was possible. Maybe Moore would explain it at some point. Maybe not.

Regardless of the unexpected company, she and Catfish made small talk through breakfast, staying at their table long after the others had left, but others soon arrived. The annoying white coats entered the room and sat apart from Shawna and Catfish, but she felt their stares while they ate. She couldn't decide if the eggheads were suspicious of them or thought them insane.

Either wouldn't surprise her. Without evidence, she and Catfish's account of what had occurred on *Leaguer* certainly sounded like drug-induced delusions. Hell, if anyone outside this building heard their tale, they'd both be whisked off to a mental hospital. She wouldn't blame anyone for thinking them insane.

The finale for the meal was the appearance of the three soldiers that had escorted Catfish the day before. Sarah, the woman had said her name was, walked confidently to a table, the two men following her.

Catfish gestured to them with a nod. "I think they were either at Ben Taub or HAL."

"My bet," Shawna said, "is Ben Taub."

He raised an eyebrow. "Why do you say that?"

"The way they carry themselves," she said. "Plus, the rest of the grunts look barely old enough to drive. Those three?" She'd paused while doing her best not to look at the trio but failing all the same. "Their eyes. They look like they've seen more than a few things in their time."

"You might be right," he said. "That thin guy? He's got dead eyes like there's nothing human behind them."

"I'll take your word for it," she said. "Haven't had the pleasure of being that close to him."

"When you are, take a look. Take a long look," he said, drawing out each word. "See if I'm wrong."

She shuddered at the thought. Catfish had a penchant for outbursts bordering on childish tantrums, but she'd learned to pay attention whenever he was serious and thoughtful. He was rarely wrong.

They finally departed the commissary and found Moore waiting outside the commissary entrance. The woman stood before them with perfect posture, her coat and trousers neatly pressed and clean. She might as well have just walked out of the dry cleaners after dressing in their bathroom.

"Hello," she said.

Catfish and Shawna traded a glance before Shawna forced herself to smile. "Dr. Moore. To what do we owe the pleasure?"

Moore's smile didn't falter. Instead, her eyes glittered with elvish glee. "I thought after Mr. Standlee gets dressed in some real clothes, we could meet in the conference room for a little chat."

That was how they ended up in the rectangular room that contained a large round table, a podium, several HD TVs and computer monitors, and a serving cart filled with coffee and water pitchers. Dozens of cans of various sodas and bottles of Topo Chico swam in the slowly melting ice.

A sweating bottle of mineral water sat before Shawna on a stone coaster. Catfish clutched a large aluminum can of energy drink in his left hand, the fingers on his right dexterously thrumming one at a time on the hard wooden table top.

Moore sat across from them, a large cup of coffee to her right and a tablet in front of her. She let them stew in silence for a few seconds before looking up from the gadget. "Just a moment," she said and took a sip of coffee.

"What are we waiting for?" Catfish asked.

Moore's smile contained all the warmth of an arctic ice flow. "Someone to help you make your decision."

Shawna traded a glance with Catfish. "I thought we had until Friday."

"You do," Moore agreed. "And today's Thursday. So I thought you might want to meet the head of the project."

"I thought you were the head of the project," Shawna said.

Moore laughed, the sound like stones rubbing together. "Let's say I'm the chief administrator."

"Isn't that another way of saying 'boss?'" Catfish asked.

The smile all but disappeared. "That is a way of saying 'boss,'" she agreed. "Meaning I have ultimate say over anything in the facility. Which also means I have the authority to order whatever I choose." Moore's expression flattened into an emotionless line. "Such as drastic measures to destroy the remaining M2 samples should anything go wrong."

"Might as well keep those plans handy," Catfish said under his breath.

"Don't worry," she said, the smile reappearing as though it had never left. "They are."

The way she said the words wiped the look off Catfish's face. Shawna cleared her throat and did her best to ignore the silence that had descended over the room. "So we'd be working for you?"

"Or me," a voice said from the doorway. Shawna turned her head and saw a smartly dressed woman in her late thirties or early forties with a pristine lab coat covering her jacket. She nodded at Moore and approached the table.

Shawna reflexively stood up, Catfish following her lead a second or two later, his balance shifting slightly as he kept his damaged foot from hitting the floor. The woman offered a hand to Catfish. "Hi," she said, "I'm Kate Cheevers." When she finished shaking hands with him, Kate did the same with Shawna. Her grip was firm, a definite plus in Shawna's book.

"Catfish," he said. "And that's—"

"Shawna Sigler," Kate said. Catfish continued staring at the woman as though studying her. "Something wrong?"

"You just another white coat?"

She crossed her arms and straightened her posture. For a moment, Shawna thought she might hit him. "No, Mr. Catfish."

"Just Catfish," he said.

"No, Catfish, I'm not."

"Then what are you?"

A forced smile crossed her face. "I'll let you answer that question after I brief you." She gestured to the table. "If you don't mind sitting down?"

Shawna patted Catfish's shoulder. "Yes," she said. "Why don't we do that?" She didn't know why Catfish was being such an asshole, but he was beginning to embarrass her. "Before you say something else stupid."

He turned to her, his eyes hard with something akin to anger. "Something else stupid?" He sighed and turned back to face Kate. "Sorry. My mouth runs away from me."

"That's fine," Kate said. "But I'd really like to get this over with."

"Okay," he said and finally took his seat.

Shawna followed suit as Kate made her way to sit at the table. Instead of sitting next to Moore, she had skipped that seat and chosen one more than a meter away. The newcomer took in a deep breath as if composing herself. In a way, Shawna felt sorry for her; Kate hadn't been prepared to joust with Catfish. Either that or there was something else on the woman's mind.

After taking a moment to compose herself, she folded her hands on the table. "You are both here because we want you to help us analyze M2. Your experience on *Leaguer*, in addition to the other accounts, should help us answer some questions about the organism."

"Organism," Catfish said. "It's not an 'organism.' If you'd been chased by it, you'd know that."

Kate's smile hardened, as did her eyes. "Mr. Standlee—"

"Catfish, please."

"Mr. Standlee," she said, emphasizing his name, "I was at HAL. I know exactly how it feels to be chased by one of them."

Catfish said nothing but swung his eyes at Shawna more than once. "How?"

"The sample," Kate said. "That barrel you sent us was filled with it."

"No," Catfish said. "How did you kill it?"

Kate waved the question away. "If you join the project," she said, "you'll have all the answers you want."

Shawna fought to keep from raising her hand—she felt like she were in the principal's office. "How many others here survived an encounter?"

"That information is classified," Moore said. "But you'll know the answer if you decide to take the deal."

Shawna ignored Moore. "Who will we be working with?"

Kate's smile returned, but it was much more confident, not to mention warmer. "Two chemists and a biochemist," she said. "Also, Catfish will be working on weapons development with our security department. I can't give you any more information than that."

"Unless you take the deal," Moore said again.

Shawna gestured to the room's walls. "These are metal."

"Yes," Kate said. "Concrete fronted by metal sheets. All the glass in the building has been replaced with two-centimeter-thick Pyrex, and the lights are a new kind of UV lamp that doesn't burn as hot as a halogen but has the same characteristics."

"Actually," Moore said with a toothy smile, "they produce quite a bit more UV than the standard halogen."

"Safeguards," Shawna said.

Kate nodded. "Safeguards. The labs are filled with them. We have containment rings, and we'll be under guard at all times."

"How does that work?" Catfish asked.

Moore said, "My understanding is that the creatures burn quite well. We have systems that will incinerate any amount of M2 that escapes its confines."

"Great," Catfish said. "Got the place wired for a nuke, too?"

Moore leaned back in her chair and crossed her arms. "That information is classified," she said.

The room went deathly quiet, enough so that Shawna could hear the carbonation in Catfish's drink can. Kate's confidence seemed to have evaporated, her fingers nervously twitching on the tabletop. Shawna knew how she felt.

"So," Shawna said, "you believe your safety measures will be enough to stop it."

"I do," Moore said. "Although once you join the project, all suggestions will be greatly appreciated. I'll do my best to address any concerns you have."

"Until we run out of budget," Catfish said.

Moore smiled. "Mr. Standlee—"

"Catfish, please."

"Our financial constraints are for me to worry about. Your job," she said, "will be to make sure that if we encounter another of these things in the wild, we're more competently able to deal with it."

"And my job?" Shawna asked.

Kate cleared her throat. "You will work with me in the lab," she said. "We need your expertise in geology as well as the petrochemical chemistry. I mean, my team already has that knowledge, but we don't drill for a living. We don't go out into the field. You may have noticed something we wouldn't even dream of."

"Okay," Shawna said. "So it'll be interesting work."

"Yes," Kate said. "Although I can think of better words for it."

"Like suicide," Catfish said.

Moore glared at him but said nothing.

"And if we don't take the deal?" Shawna asked.

Kate and Moore shared a glance. "Then," Kate said, "we'll be without your skills, and the project will be poorer for it. But it will go ahead."

"Do you have any other questions for Dr. Cheevers?" Moore asked.

"Yes," Shawna said. She leaned forward slightly, her expression hardening. "Why are you doing this?"

"She doesn't have to—" Moore started, but Kate cut her off.

"Because I want to make sure these things never threaten people again. That we aren't defenseless next time we encounter them."

"A real humanitarian, huh?" Catfish asked.

Kate swung her gaze and locked eyes with his. At that moment, Shawna thought she looked like a mother bear protecting a cub. "Something like that."

The words hung in the room, the silence again drawing out and becoming uncomfortable. Shawna reached for her drink and took a long sip of the mineral water. She wasn't sure what to say, and every question she had had gone out of her head.

"Anything else?" Moore asked.

Shawna shook her head. It didn't matter if she did have questions to ask. All the important answers were out of reach unless she joined the project. But did she really want to know the answers? Did she?

"Well," Kate said, rising from her chair, "It was a pleasure to meet you both. I hope to see you tomorrow afternoon." With that, she turned and left the room.

Moore waited until Kate disappeared before speaking again. "The contracts are in your rooms," she said. "The facility will provide your room and board since neither of you has a home here in Houston."

"And," Catfish said, "so you can keep an eye on us."

Moore laughed. "Really, Mr. Standlee. Your paranoia, while certainly useful, is unnecessary here and somewhat redundant. We're watching you every minute you're in the facility and not in your room. We'll be watching you every moment you are outside these walls. We'll be listening to your phone calls, monitoring your computer usage, and every form of digital communication you can imagine." Moore paused. "But that will all end once the project is finished."

"Doesn't exactly make me feel any damned better," he said.

"I'm sure it doesn't," Moore said. "But at least you'll be safe while you work here. As Dr. Cheevers said, we already have chemists on staff. We already have engineers on staff. We'll carry on the project with or without you."

"But this will be secret," Shawna said. "Classified until the world burns."

Moore nodded. "Information in the lab is segregated from outside access. There are no VPNs or lines connecting the internal network to the fat internet pipes running off the facility. Terminals connected to the internet are heavily monitored and isolated from project data."

"No secret lasts," Catfish said.

"Usually true," Moore agreed. "But I think we can keep it for a very long time."

"Sure." Catfish took a long slurp from the energy drink.

Shawna expected him to say something else, but he didn't. Unlike her, Moore seemed to relish the tense silence rather than feel uncomfortable in it. Shawna bet the woman was a great poker player.

"So we sign the contracts and start work tomorrow afternoon?" she asked.

Moore nodded. "Or you leave the facility, we pay you for your time, and you're free to do whatever you like so long as you understand you will be monitored for the rest of your days."

Catfish sighed. "The agony of choice," he said.

"Yes," the director said. "That's the best I can do."

Shawna tried to hide the chill that prickled her flesh. If that was the best Moore could do for them, what was the worst?

"If there are no more questions," Moore said, "then I suggest you retire to your rooms to study the contract and make a decision. I'd like to have it before tomorrow morning, but I need an answer by breakfast. Thank you both for your time and attention."

Moore rose in a fluid motion, her arms expertly cradling her tablet, and disappeared through the door without another word.

Catfish whistled. "That lady creeps the shit out of me."

Shawna punched him in the shoulder.

"Ow," Catfish said. "What was that for?"

"For being an asshole," she said. "If we're going to work here, I'd like everyone not to hate us before we walk into the lab. And if we don't? I don't want Moore looking for an excuse to make our lives hell."

He took another sip, his tongue catching the dregs. His fingers tightened around the can and crushed it. "I think we're screwed," he said.

"Probably." Shawna stared at her Topo Chico. "Wonder if they'll bring us some booze."

"Or something stronger," he said. "Always wanted to get high in a government facility. And not get arrested."

"That's the trick," Shawna said with a laugh. "What do you think?"

"I'll know after I take a peek at the contract," he said. "You?"

She shrugged. "Same, I guess."

Catfish rose from his chair and cracked his back. He tossed the empty can into the recycling bin. "Want to help me crutch back to my room?"

"Sure," she said.

As they approached the door, two soldiers appeared. They'd been standing outside the room, rifles slung. "Ma'am," one of them said. "Sir. Back to your rooms?"

Had they been listening to the conversation? Or did Moore have some kind of crystal ball?

"Yes," Catfish said. "Then I need to find a bar."

CHAPTER EIGHT

She and Catfish reviewed their contracts together, doing their best to parse the rather succinct legalese. As much as Shawna distrusted Moore and whoever else was involved in this place, the mysterious woman had provided them with a deal that was easy to understand and had no obvious loopholes for either side.

If the contract had had walls of text and jargon, she would have asked for a lawyer to look at it. That, of course, would cause issues. In addition to missing Moore's deadline, the director would have to agree to let her see a lawyer. Considering the confidential nature of the document, she wasn't sure Moore would dare let that happen. Shawna couldn't blame her either.

They each signed their contracts without saying a word to one another. Moore appeared a few minutes later, leading them to the security station for all the goodies. That took the rest of the afternoon, the seconds ticking off like molasses flowing in winter.

Sarah ran them through the process while one of her minions, a young man who couldn't possibly be older than twenty-three, took their personal information and medical history, had them sign more liability forms than she thought could exist, and other ephemera. The one that gave her chills was the "Deceased Remains Orders." It consisted of a list of questions regarding next of kin, whether you preferred a coffin or cremation, and your religious affiliation, if any

Catfish snorted at the last form. "If we die," he said, staring at the young man with diamond-hard eyes, "there won't be enough to fill an urn. Let alone a coffin."

Shawna had to give the kid some credit; the soldier's eyes hadn't done more than widen for a second before he managed to get his expression under control.

The onboarding process included fingerprints, DNA swabs—although she imagined they already had both hers and Catfish's genetic code on file somewhere—voice recognition training, and finally, pictures for badges. Shawna thought the entire exercise rather redundant, besides being an excuse for teaching her and Catfish how security in "the facility" worked and what was expected of them.

It came down to a small number of rules. She and Catfish were not to leave the base without permission and an escort. They were not allowed to bring contraband into "the facility" and were not to enter restricted areas without permission and an escort. Their room and board were covered, as well as any clothing or other supplies they required.

If you didn't have your badge, you would be arrested and held until your identity was confirmed using voice analysis and fingerprint scans. Sarah said rather sternly, "Don't lose your badge. The paperwork sucks, and it'll make us very grumpy." Shawna got the message. She thought Catfish did too.

They didn't see Moore the rest of the day, which Shawna thought strange. Then again, Dr. Moore was an odd person to begin with. Shawna still wasn't sure about the woman and her motivations. Her suspicions deepened once Shawna realized what "the facility" actually was.

The abandoned spaceport facility had begun construction, ceased, begun again, and ceased again. As a result, several empty buildings abutted the still functional Ellington Field. "The facility," as everyone annoyingly called it, was a series of empty residential buildings and half-finished lab buildings. But that's what was above ground.

Once they were badged up, Sarah took them to the same conference room where they'd first met Kate and Moore. After closing the door, she gestured for them to take a seat and ran them through "the facility's" layout.

The large lab space ran underground, protected by thick layers of concrete and steel. There were no emergency exits from the lab areas and only a single elevator for supplies and personnel. Neither of them brought it up, but it sounded like a goddamned deathtrap if one of those things escaped its prison.

"We're not going to visit the labs yet," Sarah said. "You'll do that tomorrow with the others."

"What others?" Shawna asked.

Sarah shut down the projector without looking at her. "The other scientists."

"You mean they haven't been here before?" Catfish grabbed another energy drink from the huge tub, popped the top, and drank noisily. "I thought we were late to the party."

"No," Sarah said. "It took some time to get the facility ready. In case you didn't notice, they're still working up here and in the labs."

"Shit, it's still under construction?" Catfish said.

"Yes." Sarah sat down at the table. "Nothing major," she said. "Just finishing up a few odds and ends. The construction up here wasn't nearly as important as the modifications made down below."

Shawna looked around the conference room. There were no pictures, photos, no insignias, labels, nothing. The facility could have belonged to anyone. Or no one. "What is this place?"

"That's a little more complicated," Sarah said. "My understanding is it was built to handle potentially hazardous material from space."

Catfish paused, his lips mere centimeters from the top of the can. "Potentially hazardous material?" His eyes brightened. "Like aliens?"

Sarah shrugged. "I assumed for samples from asteroids or something. But, yeah, I guess it could have been designed for that too."

"How long has it been here?" Shawna asked.

"No idea," Sarah said. "I only know what I've told you."

Catfish gestured with the drink can. "What about the modifications? What was modified?"

"Don't know that either," Sarah said. "I know an awful lot of glass and steel was sent below. And I only know that because of the security recordings."

Shawna's eyebrows knitted together, her forehead wrinkling. "Wait. You weren't always in charge here?"

The soldier smiled. "No. Dr. Moore asked if I would handle the security after the Ben Taub outbreak."

The word "outbreak" echoed in her mind as if shouted in a small metal room. She knew Ben Taub was a hospital. She also knew something had happened there, but now, it was becoming a little more clear. JP had been infected by something aboard *Leaguer*, and the "something" was the M2 organism.

"Did someone get infected? At HAL?"

Sarah nodded. "Yes. You'll hear the whole story tomorrow. I'll personally be handling the Ben Taub briefing. Well, me and one other who was there."

"How many survived?" Catfish asked.

Sarah's eyes dimmed slightly. "Not enough," she said.

After that, she answered every question with: "You'll find out at the briefing tomorrow." Every question except the one about their living spaces.

They were offered trailers or rooms in one of the mostly abandoned residential buildings. Shawna immediately opted for a trailer. Catfish too.

Sarah smiled at that. "Good choice," she'd said. "I have a trailer too. As does Givens."

"Givens?" Catfish asked.

She waved the question away. "You've seen him already, but you'll meet him tomorrow."

Sarah walked them out of the building to a row of golf-cart-like vehicles. "Since Mr. Standlee has mobility problems, and your trailers are more than two hundred meters away, we'll take you over in one of these. I'll leave it there and walk back. That way, you can get to dinner tonight and breakfast tomorrow morning. Of course, you could choose to eat in your trailers, but I doubt you'll want to." She grinned. "Chef Robbie is simply amazing."

"That he is," Catfish said. "Best food I've had since *Leaguer*. Of course, that's not saying much."

The three of them entered the vehicle, Catfish sitting in the back with his crutches. Sarah drove them down the wide concrete street, a row of healthy water oaks lining the median. The unoccupied buildings appeared eerie and foreboding. It reminded her of the pictures of the empty cities the Chinese had built. Modern, beautiful, and completely abandoned, slowly settling into decay as the cities waited for occupants who may never come.

The spaceport was still a "going concern," although you'd hardly know it from the lack of cars, people, and working machinery. Shawna could hear the traffic from the interstate, but it somehow seemed to be coming from another universe. She could see houses in the far distance, telephone poles, and water towers. This place was right smack in the middle of a densely populated area. Less than two klicks away, unsuspecting families would sleep their nights away in ignorance. At the same time, the biological equivalent of a nuclear weapon lay below the earth's surface, waiting for its chance to escape and devour them.

Shawna immediately had the vision of M2 bubbling out of the ground and gathering itself in a nighttime tsunami to flow over the land like a hydrocarbon plague, eating everything in its wake. The thought made her nauseous.

A few moments later, the cart turned through an alley to a grassy, undeveloped area. It also had five trailers.

Sarah parked the vehicle next to the first trailer and put on the brake. "We're here," she said. "Home sweet home."

While working for Thomas Calhoun, Shawna had found herself in some primitive places. Whether you were working a find in Nigeria, West Texas, or Papua/New Guinea, you nearly always found yourself far from urbanity and a long way away from a hot shower. During the fracking frenzy in the US, workers paid over a few thousand dollars a month for a cot and a hotplate in tiny trailers lining the main roads. Upon seeing her trailer, her first thought was, "At least it's bigger than that."

Once Catfish had crutched inside his temporary domicile, Sarah led Shawna to her new home. The trailer, cozy but certainly more than large enough for a single person, appeared to be relatively new and in great shape. Sarah handed her a key.

"There are clothes for you inside," Sarah said, "the fridge should be stocked, and you're more than welcome to relax until you decide what to do about dinner."

"Thank you," Shawna said.

"Welcome." Sarah turned to leave.

"I do have a question," Shawna said.

Sarah turned, her eyebrows arched. "Yes?"

"You really think you can contain these things?"

The head of security lifted her eyes to the darkening sky as another gust of wind ripped through the complex. "I don't know," she said. When she finally lowered her eyes to look at Shawna again, the woman looked a little afraid. "I know I'll do my best to kill them if they break containment." Sarah shrugged. "That's the best I can do."

Without another word, Sarah turned and began the walk back to the facility. Shawna watched her for a moment as a distant rumble of thunder drowned the ambient sound of aircraft and traffic.

Now, she was alone in the trailer. She sat cross-legged on the bed's edge, her eyes staring at nothing. Outside, the rain picked up, adding to her sense of unreality.

Shawna unfolded her legs and lay on the bed, luxuriating in the relative comfort. Regardless of the fact she was in a trailer, the presumed stamp of the white trash and indigent, she found herself liking it. It was large enough not to feel cramped and small enough to be personal.

At least the trailer didn't have vents. It didn't have central air. She wasn't trapped inside a concrete or metal prison waiting for a creature to jump out of the shadows, dissolve her into atoms, and absorb her. Or whatever the hell it was that M2 did to its victims.

The tiny bedroom area had a chest of drawers, and she hurriedly unpacked the few clothes they'd brought her and put them away. She imagined Catfish had received the same nondescript clothing that looked too much like what the soldiers wore. Shawna tried them on and hated them immediately, but not because they weren't comfortable. No. She hated them because they felt like prison garb. And, in a sense, they were.

Simple white cotton panties, tube socks, new, stiff, steel-toed work boots, and two pairs of fatigues. Tomorrow, she'd ask Moore if she could get some real clothes.

The simple bathroom down the small hall had a tiny shower stall with a handheld shower head. It wouldn't exactly provide a luxurious bathing experience, but it would still be better than having an armed guard waiting for you when you finished washing your hair.

With a sigh, Shawna pulled herself off the bed, tossed her clothes to the floor, and headed to the shower. If nothing else, she could wash in private and maybe sit under the hot water for a while. Assuming, of course, there was any.

CHAPTER NINE

Sitting in his chair outside the trailer, Catfish took a long breath and wished for a cigarette. After so many days without nicotine, you'd think he'd be able to ignore the urge, put it out of his mind, and never be tempted again. Yeah, right. Even when he was vaping like a madman, he wanted the real thing between his lips, smoke drizzling out of his nose like steam.

He had a feeling that once the project started in earnest, he'd be bumming smokes off anyone who had them. Unless, of course, Il Duce Moore would allow them off base to go shopping.

What a joke. They were south of the fourth largest city in the USA, yet they might as well be on the moon for all their access to civilization. The briefing Sarah had given him and Shawna had made it clear they weren't allowed to leave the complex. So, for now, the mostly abandoned spaceport was little more than a large prison. And this trailer? His new cell.

He leaned back in the lawn chair and relished the squeak and creak of the metal. Unlike the trailer, which was his new home, the chair was cheap and barely functional. He imagined someone found it lying around and thought he could use it.

The military base had to be a drone launching station or training station. He wasn't sure which. The only constant apart from the cold November wind was the growl and whine of propellers slicing the air as the drones took off or landed on the long runways. Thick metal fencing separated the spaceport from the rest of the mostly abandoned air base, but that didn't keep him from being able to see the small, oddly shaped aircraft lifting off or coming down for a landing.

But that fencing could also work another way—keeping the regular military personnel out. Based on the security around "the facility," he thought that was a good bet. Moore didn't want anyone near the building that didn't have official business there. As far as Catfish could tell, that included nearly 100% of the human population.

A gust of wind ripped through the light, long-sleeved shirt they'd given him, and he shivered. After months on *Leaguer*, the cold felt good. He'd enjoy it while he could. He knew from experience that Houston's weather could flip on a dime. Tomorrow could be 26°C instead of in the teens. But if this shit were going to keep up, he'd need some new clothes.

The trailer's fridge had already been prepped with snack food, TV dinners, and a ton of soda and energy drinks. The tiny kitchen also had a coffee maker, one of those pod jobs, but he preferred the carbonated stuff.

Another empty energy drink can. He'd had three since breakfast. They had had him fasting from real food and anything caffeinated for so long that the very hint of something tasty was enough to send him into a sensory orgasm. He'd gain the weight back fast. Catfish grinned. He looked forward to it.

He crumpled the can between his fingers, enjoying the satisfying crunch of aluminum ripping and collapsing. The previously uniform cylinder was now a misshapen squat thing of edges, rents, and bends. He studied it for a moment, analyzing the shape, the metal stresses, and the cracked and warped label.

A sprinkle of rain fell from the bruised and swollen clouds and pattered on the concrete, the trailer's metal roof, and his shirt. He rose from the metal chair, folded it, and dragged it back inside. He didn't mind the rain, but the last thing he needed was to get sick now. They'd just had to kill one massive infection. Did he really want another?

Instead of closing the trailer door, he left it open and inhaled the cool, moist air through his nose. God, he'd missed that smell. It reminded him of home and was so different from the scent of the ocean where he'd nearly died.

He barely remembered the journey from the M2 Trench to here. The drugs they'd used to keep him alive, or maybe keep him quiet, had made it difficult to string the events together. If he tried to remember, he couldn't, but now and then, a random thought led to an image or a sound.

He tossed the can into the kitchen garbage bin and sat on the couch before the small LED monitor. He pulled the table over to use as an ottoman and carefully placed his leg on top of it. The aches and twinges of pain slowly building up in his leg died down. The doctor had said to elevate it regularly. With a sour expression, he hit the remote and brought the TV to life.

The program guide appeared. As he scrolled through the channels, he noticed most of them were marked with a yellow line. Confused, he brought up the menu. "You have to be fucking kidding me."

They'd locked him out like a little kid. He was allowed to watch the weather channels, movies, sports, and certain TV shows. All the news channels had been blocked. Every single one. Even those in other languages.

"Why?" he asked no one.

Because, a voice said in his mind, *they don't want you to know what's happening in the world. No idea of what's being said about the incidents.*

Catfish pursed his lips. That had been Thomas' voice. It was right. Why else keep him from knowing anything apart from football game scores and what the so-called "weather forecast" entailed?

Not knowing what was happening in the world kept them from being polluted. No concerns about politics, world events, or opinion babble clouding their thoughts. But the most important part was to ward off other questions they could ask. For instance, how was the PPE case being handled in the press? What about HAL or Ben Taub?

He chose a sports station and was immediately bombarded by a commercial for deodorant. The show was back with more inane football commentary a few seconds later. Nothing had apparently changed in the world. Same old useless entertainment shit.

You know they're just going to kill you when all of this is over, right?

Catfish uttered a low bark of laughter.

The dead were certainly coming to speak with him tonight. First Thomas and now his dive partner JP. Both had died aboard *Leaguer* because of those "samples" Moore had. *Or their parent,* he corrected himself, since they were all spawned by the thing at the bottom of the M2 trench.

"Bastard," he said to no one, just as the talking heads broke into laughter.

Killing M2 was worth the risk. He wasn't leaving this place without making sure it never had a chance to kill anyone else.

He realized he'd clenched his fists, his nails digging into the skin of his palm deep enough to squeeze out a drop of blood.

As long as they're made extinct, he thought.

If there were a way to end all of this and ensure M2 never left this complex, he'd find it. Find it, execute it, and do his best to keep Shawna safe.

* * *

Four taps on the door froze Catfish. A beat later, someone rapped five times. Smiling, he finished buttoning up the dungarees, and one hand crutched to the door.

It swung open on a purplish black sky with silver dashes of rain against the door light. Shawna stood on the lowest step, her hair damp but bordering on saturated. He crutched backward and braced himself against the trailer wall while she quickly made her way up the stairs and beneath cover, Catfish closing the door behind her.

"Dammit, Shawna. Shouldn't you have a jacket?"

Her mouth twitched as if she was attempting to hide a smile. "Yes, Dad," she said, emphasizing the last word.

Catfish opened his mouth to reply but didn't know what to say. There was something about the way she said the last word. It reminded him of—

"Christ," he said, raising his hands to his face in mock horror. "I sounded just like Thomas, didn't I?" he said, his voice muffled behind his hands.

She giggled. "Yes, you did."

"Oh, man. How the hell did that happen?"

Shawna wrung water from her hair, the droplets dribbling to the floor mat and the trailer's carpet. "I don't want to know," she said. When she finished, she met his eyes. "Do you have a jacket?"

"No."

She frowned. "These clothes suck. Moore has to let us go shopping."

"No shit," Catfish said. "If I don't get some nicotine, someone may die."

Her eyebrows scrunched together, her forehead wrinkling. He realized how much he'd gotten used to that expression and how much he'd missed it.

"You should be clean, Catfish."

"That's what I was told," he said. "Guess my brain doesn't want to admit that. Besides, tomorrow, we may die. And I'm not going out of this world sober. Fuck that."

"Sober," she said. "Don't say it like that. People will think you've been drinking on the job."

"If only," he said. "Sober from nicotine. Whatever. I refuse to go out of this world without a white cylinder of self-destruction perched between my lips."

"Fine," she said.

Her expression lightened a bit. He thought she was about to say something, her lips quivering to make a sound, but she didn't. Instead, she bowed her head slightly for a beat before looking up.

"You ready for dinner?"

The word brought a growl from his stomach, and he realized they'd missed lunch altogether. "Yeah," he said. "But we're going to get drenched."

"No one said we had to go out in that shit," she said. "Didn't you look in your fridge?"

"Oh, right," he said. Catfish crutched past her to the small kitchen and opened the freezer. "What you in the mood for?"

"I didn't really look at what I had. Is there anything edible?"

"TV dinners, pot pies, shit like that."

Shawna yawned loudly. "They have pizza?"

He shuffled the stacked boxes, scanning the labels of each. "Yeah, they do."

"Thank the wonderful universe of processed food," she said. "Get those things cooking. I don't want to die without pizza."

He snorted and pulled out two boxes. "It's not real pizza. Well, not like we'd get at Steel City."

"Don't care," she said. "Pizza is pizza."

He slotted one into the microwave after removing the packaging. "And a cigarette is a cigarette," he said as he crutched back into what served as a living room.

She sat on the couch, staring at the rain falling from the dark sky. "If we were facing the other way," she said, "we'd see the lights of thousands of houses."

He followed her gaze, trying to figure out what she was staring at. The outlines of buildings were difficult to make out, but the Ellington tower, with its blinking lights, was easy to see. "Yeah," he said. "So? That means we're back in civilization."

Her expression had flattened into an emotionless line, and she continued looking through the window at nothing. The sound of the cheap microwave cooking the pizza and the ting of raindrops on the metal roof had become the only things he could hear. Apart from those stimuli, he and Shawna might as well have been frozen in time.

When she finally spoke, she sounded close to crying. "We are," she said. "And so is M2."

The words caused his brain to freeze for a second. The mention of the creatures, so candidly, brazenly, and openly, brought a flood of images and memories shooting through his mind. In stunned silence, he suddenly knew what she meant. It wasn't about the creatures themselves. It was about what they could do if they escaped.

He limped forward, grimacing in pain as he banged his cast against the side of a cabinet. Doing his best not to plop next to her, he used a hand for support as he sat down. It didn't help much with the built-in furniture.

"Well," he said in a low voice. "Guess you've been thinking about that."

She turned to him and nodded. "A lot. Can't get it out of my mind."

He wanted to tell her they might be able to stop this madness. That as soon as he found a chink in the security system, he'd find a way to burn the goddamned things. Destroy them. Reassure her the nightmare was nearly over.

But the eyes. The ears. They were watching and listening. Security, army intelligence, or whatever the fuck they called themselves were probably masturbating while watching the feeds. Or maybe they were waiting for Shawna to change clothes or shower before engaging in that particular activity.

His cheeks burned, and he clenched his fists in reflex. The thought of being spied on, someone following their every move, parsing their every word, their very facial expressions, was enough to send him into a white rage. With a bit of effort, he managed to staunch the inner fire and unfold his fingers.

"Tomorrow," he said, "we'll get some answers." The words sounded moronic to his ears. "I mean," he said, "we'll find out just how good the security is. Maybe we don't have to worry about it."

"Always have to worry about it." She turned to look at him, her legs crossing in the cramped space. "You're the one who always says there's no such thing as digital safety."

"Point," he said. "Same with machines, network lines, phone lines. Anything you can physically access is vulnerable. You just have to have the knowledge or the drive to figure out how to break it or make it do your bidding."

"Right," Shawna said. "So if M2 has access to the lab, it has access to everything."

He placed a hand on her knee. "Look, we'll find out how bad it is tomorrow. We can't do anything about it tonight anyway." He tentatively reached for her.

The microwave dinged, and they both flinched. They continued staring at one another before breaking into uncomfortable laughter. Catfish rose and headed to the kitchen. "Something to drink?"

"Topo," she said. "I know you have some."

He shook his head, grinning. "Don't be stealing my supply."

"Wouldn't dream of it," she said.

He pulled two bottles from the fridge and popped the caps. Had he nearly kissed her? Had she nearly kissed him? The soft look in her eyes, the way she'd moved toward him. "No," he said under his breath. *Just in your imagination,* he told himself.

He brought her the pizza and the drink, the two of them sharing the meal in thoughtful silence. They watched a movie together, barely speaking, barely acknowledging one another's existence. The TV was still running old films while they slept side by side on the couch.

CHAPTER TEN

When Shawna awoke, her back and neck sang a chorus from a thrash metal song. Neither was happy she'd been cramped up on the couch, her legs practically folded beneath her and her head leaning against— Against? She opened her eyes and gingerly turned her head. Catfish. He was on the next cushion, one arm draped around her neck.

Well, she thought, if we're being watched as Moore said, the security guys must be pissed we didn't get it on.

It shouldn't have brought a smile to her face, but it did.

She had known Catfish for several years, and it wasn't the first time they'd shared a room while working together. She'd fallen asleep in his room, or he in hers, more times than she could remember. Engineering and chemical analyses for Thomas usually took all night, and if JP wasn't around, Catfish was her only company.

JP's never going to be around again, a voice said in her mind.

She frowned deeply and pushed herself off Catfish. He mumbled something in his sleep before his mouth half-opened and began snoring. Shawna stood, regretted it, and slowly stretched her cramped muscles.

The TV played Invasion of the Body Snatchers, the original 1950s black-and-white version. Near the end, too. A lone man yelled and waved his hands at trucks leaving town, all filled with the seed pods to take over humanity. She continued stretching while staring at the screen. When the credits began to roll, she was finally able to lean her head to both sides without excruciating lightning bolts of pain striking in response.

She felt as though dawn had broken, but it was nearly impossible to tell. The storm had cleared out, but the sky wore purplish clothing, and the sun seemed to have had little effect on the darkness. Shawna picked up the remote and pressed the guide button. The date and time flashed on the screen. She scrunched her eyebrows in response. 0615.

Her stomach growled as if letting her know breakfast would be welcome. She turned back to the couch and reached to touch Catfish. He'd spread his legs in her absence and collapsed in a more prone position. It reminded her of their time on the lifeboat, where he'd faded in and out of consciousness. When had that been? Nearly two weeks ago? More?

She'd never felt more alone than when he was finally separated from her and taken to a private hospital room while she lay on a cot in a cell. Whenever the creatures appeared in her nightmares, she did her best to remember the lifeboat and the endless swell and fall of the ocean waves. Once the fear had passed, even while worrying about Catfish's illness, she'd found some modicum of peace there. Some.

While they'd been so isolated from the rest of humanity, she hadn't felt alone, not even while he had slept. His presence had been enough. It had been last night, too.

Regretting it even as she did it, she reached out and touched his shoulder. "Catfish?"

He came awake, arms flailing, punching at nothing, his right fist passing by her nose with a whisper of air. Shawna jumped back, crouching. He opened his eyes and grabbed the couch as if afraid of falling. "What the—" He turned his head and saw her. She must have looked terrified because his expression immediately softened. "Something wrong?"

She slowly stood. "Yeah, you asshole. You nearly punched me."

"Oh," he said. He sat up and rubbed a hand through his knotted ponytail. "Christ, I'm sorry."

"You always wake up like that?"

"Only after watching oil monsters eat an oil rig," Catfish said.

"Touché. Didn't Sarah tell us to be at the facility by nine?"

Catfish said, "Something like that. Why? What time is it?"

"A little after six." Shawna rubbed her arms. It was cold in the trailer. "You forget to turn on the heat?"

"Guess so," he said.

"You want to get breakfast before we start work? Or you want to sleep some more?"

"Nah," he said. "We can get breakfast and come back here for a nap if we need to. Besides, I want to see what chef Robbie is cooking." His stomach gurgled loud enough for her to hear it. "And that pizza sucked."

She giggled. "Got that right. Okay, I'm going to my trailer to change. Maybe take a quick shower. Fifteen minutes?"

He yawned loudly while raising his hands above his head. "Sure. Guessing I need one, too."

Shawna wrinkled her nose. "Yes, you do."

"Shut up. Get out of here."

Laughing, she turned and exited beneath a dark sky, shivering in the wind.

* * *

By the time breakfast ended, neither of them felt like returning to the trailers. The wind had picked up, and the rain had returned with biting frigid teeth. But that meant staying in the commissary another hour.

Catfish didn't mind waiting. Sitting with Shawna and talking about nothing while she drank coffee and he had his second energy drink was preferable to being alone in his trailer. He hoped she felt the same way.

Chef Robbie appeared every ten minutes or so, bringing more coffee and asking if they needed anything from the kitchen. Neither of them took him up on the offer for more breakfast, although Catfish somewhat hated himself for not eating more—the chef looked devastated.

Shawna tapped the table, interrupting his slurp from the can. He met her eyes, and she pointed over his shoulder. Turning his head, he saw three people entering the commissary. One of the men, probably in his early fifties, wore a strange-looking glove on his right hand, while the other wore a lab coat over a heavy sweater. The third was Dr. Kate Cheevers.

He turned back to look at Shawna. "Friends of hers?"

"I'm guessing," she said. "Looks like they've known each other for a while."

"I know it's cool out there," Catfish said, "but who the hell wears gloves this time of year? And why only one? Does he think he's Michael Jackson or something?"

Shawna stirred her coffee, although she hadn't put anything in it. "I don't think those are for warmth," she said. "Looks like a burn glove."

"Burn glove?"

"Yeah," she said. "I think they make them for severe second and third-degree burns." She shook her head. "Probably lucky he didn't lose his hand."

"Hmm," Catfish said.

"What?"

"Just wondering how long he's had it. I mean, we know Cheevers was at HAL. You figure he was, too?"

"Oh," Shawna said. "Can't imagine those two would even be on the project unless they were."

"Point," he said. "You think he got injured with M2?"

Shawna heaved a deep sigh and sipped her cooling coffee. "Guess we'll find out soon enough."

"Speaking of," he said, "what are we going to tell them?"

She looked confused. "What do you mean?"

"What are we going to say at the briefing?" He leaned forward and whispered. "Everything? Is there anything we hold back?"

Shawna leaned back and suddenly looked exhausted, as if she hadn't had a wink of sleep since *Leaguer.* She'd looked beautiful last night, almost renewed, but the way the wrinkles and lines appeared on her face now made him a little afraid.

Had she looked like that last night, and he'd been too distracted even to notice? Hell, maybe she'd looked like that since the first time he'd seen her after *Leaguer.*

"We hold nothing back," she said. "No point."

He opened his mouth to say something but thought better of it. What was there really to hold back? If the others had all fought M2, they would know anyway. He didn't see the point of the briefing.

"Okay," he finally said. "So, same song, second verse."

"It could get better, but it's gonna get worse," she said, finishing the schoolyard rhyme. "With any luck, we won't have to say much anyway. I imagine everyone knows what happened on *Leaguer.*"

"Not so sure about that," he said. "Just because we were the origin doesn't mean everyone knows. Hell, I'll bet there are things Moore doesn't know."

"True," Shawna said. "I'll do my best to skip the boring parts."

"Like the drilling?"

"Like the drilling," she agreed. "Although I'm sure the folks from HAL know damned well what we were doing out there. After all, it's why they got the sample to begin with."

"Sample," he said. "We sent them a plague."

Her expression had gone neutral, but he saw how her fingers tightened on the coffee mug. The plague had been her doing. She had warned Thomas about strange results in her tests. They had written up the anomalies but still sent the sample.

"Do you blame yourself?"

Her eyes jumped to his, a look of surprise on her face. It slowly softened, but he still saw it. It was a look somewhere between outright denial and acceptance. He wasn't even sure if she knew she was doing it.

"No," she said.

He watched her and saw the tell-tale shake in her fingers, the lilt of her voice as she'd said it. "No reason you should," he said. "No reason to take that weight."

"But I'm not," she said, the words sounding false and forced.

Catfish took another loud slurp, wiped at his beard, and placed the can noisily on the table. "Yes, you are. You can't take the weight of this, Shawna," he said softly. "No one can."

She dropped her eyes and studied the table. Her trembling hand picked up the spoon and stirred her coffee again. "I'm not," she said.

"Okay. I just want you to remember that."

"I will," she said in a dead tone. "I will."

Catfish heaved a sigh and finished his drink. He turned slightly and looked at the table Kate and her colleagues had taken. The man with the gloved hands didn't pick up a knife or a fork and seemed hesitant while staring into his coffee. Catfish watched him and saw the brief grimace of pain cross the man's face as he finally raised the cup with his left hand.

Hands. Catfish couldn't imagine losing a hand, let alone both. The ability to type code, the technical know-how to solder and modify circuits, and the rest of everything he did depended on his brain's communication with his fingers. Everything.

The trio seemed to be having a good time catching up, although the man with the gloves didn't smile much and looked in pain. Catfish wondered if that was going to be a problem.

"You know what we need?" Shawna said.

Catfish returned his gaze to her. "What?"

"Some kind of connection to the internet. I haven't seen the news in weeks."

Last night's conversation with himself reran in his head. She apparently hadn't noticed the TV channels. Instead of saying anything, he crumpled his can and placed it on the table. "I need to take a walk," he said.

"A walk."

"Yes."

Shawna smiled. "You mean a crutch."

"Something like that," he said. "Meet you in the conference room in a while?"

"Sure," she said and nodded toward Kate's group. "Maybe Dr. Cheevers has some school supplies."

"Like crayons?"

She laughed. "Hopefully, coloring books, too."

"Right," he said and grabbed his crutches. He crutched toward the exit when he saw a small sign. It said, "Chef will return shortly." Catfish crinkled his eyebrows together and crutched toward the kitchen. He didn't hear the sounds of clanging and banging dishes nor the clink of cooking tools against copper pots. Instead, he heard the low sound of Black Sabbath playing over tiny speakers.

Curious, Catfish opened the kitchen door marked with a handwritten sign, "Authorized Chef Only," and stepped inside. The smell of baking bread, a stew brewing beneath the lid of a large copper pot, and the lingering scent of frying bacon all hit him at once, making his mouth water despite his already full belly. Spying a small pan full of bacon, he couldn't help lifting a piece between his fingers and taking a large bite.

"Hey!" a voice called from behind him.

Catfish turned and saw Chef Robbie standing at the rear of the kitchen, an exit door slightly propped open. Then another smell hit him. A cigarette!

"Oh, hi," he said.

"If you want some bacon, I'll bring you some. You're not supposed to be back here," Chef Robbie said and tossed a spent butt into a small bucket. "Ruins the magic."

"You have cigarettes," Catfish said in a monotone.

Robbie scratched at his beard. "Yeah," he said. "You need to bum?"

Catfish found himself nodding as if on autopilot. The chef smiled, pulled a beaten soft pack of M Reds, and offered it. With shaking fingers, Catfish pulled one loose, and the pack disappeared back into Robbie's shirt pocket while he pulled a silver lighter from his pants.

"Can't smoke in here," the chef said, jerking a thumb to the door. "Just open that sucker and step outside. Gonna get a little wet, though."

"No problem," Catfish said. "Thanks."

Robbie wiped his hands on his apron. "Can I ask you something?"

"Sure."

"I don't want to know what y'all are doing down there," he said, his face a mask of suspicion. "But do me a favor and let me know if I need more life insurance."

Catfish froze. He didn't know what to say. The man held the stare with him for a few beats before he started laughing.

"Go have a smoke," he said. "I got dishes to clean and food to prep. I'm sure y'all are gonna be hungry in a few hours."

"Thanks, man," Catfish said.

Robbie tipped an imaginary hat and walked back to the stoves.

Catfish watched him go for a moment, his heart still beating hard. No telling where Moore pulled him from, but the guy seemed to know something dangerous was going on. How much did he know? Shit, how much did any of them know?

Catfish pulled open the door, and the stench of rain drove away the heavenly kitchen smells, the stiff breeze making his skin prickle. He looked at the cigarette, his hand turning the silver lighter repeatedly, flipping its top, and closing it again, enjoying the familiar ting of metal hitting metal.

"You have the smoke now," he mumbled, "you'll get drenched, and the thing will dissolve on you." He flipped the lighter top again and inhaled. Butane, wonderful butane. Catfish fingered the cigarette and gently pinched the paper. Sighing, he closed the lighter with a flick of his fingers.

He walked back into the kitchen and placed the lighter on the counter. Robbie was already at the sink, scraping off dishes before putting them in the Hobart. "Done already?" he said without turning around.

"For the moment. May try again later once it's finished raining."

The chef turned and shrugged. "Supposed to lighten up. But it's supposed to get down below 7°C tonight, too."

Catfish nodded. "Well, maybe at lunch then."

"All right." The chef turned back to his duties without another word.

Catfish scanned the kitchen and finally found a pad next to the whiteboard Robbie used to list items that needed to be cooked or prepped. Without looking at the entries, he flipped to the last sheet and tore it out. He hurriedly wrote a paragraph, folded the sheet, and placed it atop the yellow pad. Robbie might just throw it away, but Catfish was counting on simple curiosity. He doubted Robbie would comply with the request, but what the hell?

He could go straight to Moore, a voice said in his mind. *Show her the note.*

Yes, Robbie could. It would annoy Moore. That in itself was reason enough to try.

Catfish returned to the dining room, but not before putting the cigarette in his shirt pocket.

* * *

After Catfish left the dining room, Shawna picked up her cup of coffee and headed to Kate's table. The woman had been munching on a croissant while listening to her comrades when she looked up and saw Shawna. Kate raised a hand and waved to her.

With a nervous smile on her face, Shawna approached cautiously. Kate tried to swallow, began to cough, and stifled it with a drink of water. Instead of trying to speak, she gestured to the seat next to her.

Shawna suddenly felt as though she were a waitress about to ask a patron if they needed anything.

As Shawna took a seat, Kate finished swallowing. "Sorry," Kate said. She pointed at the two men in turn. "That's Dr. Neil Illing, and the other is Dr. Jay Hollingsworth."

Neil reached across the table and offered a hand. "Neil. Ms. Sigler?"

"Shawna. Pleased to meet you," she said, shaking his hand. She immediately offered her hand to Jay, but the pained expression on the man's face made her slowly pull back her hand. "Sorry, Dr. Hollingsworth. I guess you're not shaking hands."

"Jay, please," he said. He glanced at his gloved hand and forced a smile. "Yeah, I won't be shaking anything for a while with that hand."

"Sorry to hear that," Shawna said, wincing at the hollow idiocy of her words.

He waved the concern away. "Kate tells us you're a chemist."

"Yes," Shawna said. "Mainly petrochemical the last several years, but I interned for a pharmaceutical company, so I'm a little versed in bio-chem."

Neil smiled. "There are worse things to know."

"Got that right," Jay mumbled under his breath.

"Where's your friend?" Kate asked, her eyes scanning the room.

"Out for a crutch," Shawna said.

"Oh," Jay said. "Is he hurt?"

"Could say that," Shawna said. "Injured his leg, getting us off *Leaguer*."

"*Leaguer*," Jay said and shook his head. "I'm not going to pry. I guess we'll find out all the details in an hour or so. But how the hell did you get off the rig?"

"Lifeboat," Shawna said.

Neil picked up a piece of well-buttered, crispy toast. "One of the ones that launch twenty meters from the ocean surface?"

"Yup," Shawna said. "Although I don't remember much about that."

Which was true. She had fragments of the burning deck, explosions, and the look on Thomas' face as he died. She had flashes of Catfish grabbing her, screaming at her, her vision dizzy and unfocused, and her head ringing from the sound of the explosions. Then, there had been the impact of something against her skull, followed by a yawning darkness that had swallowed her whole. She shivered involuntarily.

Jay seemed to pick up on her thoughts. "Sounds harrowing," he said. "You have a nice trip from Papua/New Guinea?"

She tried not to roll her eyes. "Don't remember much of that, either," she said. "Kind of a blur. Sort of found myself here."

Jay nodded before slurping his coffee.

Neil finished his piece of toast in the awkward silence that followed. "You living in the trailers? Or in the complex?"

"Trailers," Shawna said. "Both Catfish and I."

"Ah," Jay said. "Is that what he calls himself?"

Shawna laughed. "He definitely prefers it."

"Must be a story behind that," Jay said.

"There is," Shawna said. "Isn't there always?"

Another awkward silence fell over the table. Kate scratched her plate with her fork and gathered the dregs of her remaining scrambled eggs and bacon. Shawna, usually shy, felt petrified of these older scientists. Plus, looking at Jay's glove made her feel— Feel what? Guilty? Maybe Catfish was right after all.

"I think," Shawna said, "you should ask him about it. Maybe he'll show you."

Jay raised an eyebrow, his grin slowly widening. "Let me guess. Tattoo."

Shawna giggled. "How'd you know?"

"Makes sense to me. I have one of Yosemite Sam."

"Christ," Neil said and pointed at Jay. "I'll warn you ahead of time. Jay has an unhealthy obsession with Looney Toons."

"I say, I say, that's a lie, son!" Jay said in an excellent Foghorn Leghorn impression.

Shawna laughed despite herself. "That was good. Know any others?"

Jay took a breath, and Neil immediately put a hand in front of the man's face. "Don't," he said to Jay while looking at Shawna. "Don't get him started. It'll be bad enough in the lab. Trust me."

"No fun," Jay said. "You'll have to forgive Dr. Illing. His sense of humor died somewhere between birth and preschool."

"No," Neil said. "I just don't find you funny."

"Oh, the pain," Jay said in an excellent Bugs Bunny impression. "Such a petulant child."

Kate turned slightly to face Shawna. "Ignore them. They're like an old married couple. Thankfully, they don't work together often."

"Until now," Jay said as Daffy Duck.

Neil rolled his eyes. "My apologies, Shawna. I'll try to behave myself." He jerked a thumb at Jay. "I can't speak for him, though. Not sure he's capable."

"He's not," Kate said with a grin. "You married, Shawna?"

The question surprised her, making her blush slightly. "No. I'm not. I don't even have a boyfriend."

Kate nodded. "I have an ex and a daughter," she said. "Regret the ex, but not Maeve."

"Maeve," Shawna said. "Nice name."

"I like it," Kate said. "Old family name."

"Yes," Jay said, "she comes from a long line of fae."

Neil looked from Jay to Shawna. "Any idea what the hell he's talking about?"

Shawna tried to hide her smile and failed. "Fairies," she said. "Irish ones at that."

"Oh, my," Jay said in Marvin the Martian's voice, "I like her already."

"I hope," Kate said, "you're not coming on to her, old man."

Jay raised his hands slightly, as if from decades of routine, to make some gesture. He didn't manage it. Another wince crossed his face, and he lowered them once more. "Sorry."

Shawna shook her head. "Nothing to be sorry for. And please remember, before I was plucked up and brought here, I was on an oil rig."

Neil laughed. "Then you'll know how to keep him in line."

She smiled. "Something like that."

"Good," Kate said. "Although these two really are gentlemen." She glared at Jay. "Even when he tries to prove me wrong."

"Hey, look at the time," Jay said, pretending to look at his sleeved wrist. "Don't we have a meeting to get to?"

"Shit," Shawna said. "Go time already?"

"Sadly," Kate said and downed some water. "Down in ten. Relieve that bladder and get ready to talk and listen."

The party broke up, and Shawna immediately felt alone again. Talking to them had been somewhat cathartic. Each of them had spoken like nothing was wrong, that they hadn't had years taken off their lives in a day. And it was a lie.

Kate, who looked to be in her thirties, had gray streaks through her hair, and her puffy eyes bespoke sleepless nights. Jay's distress didn't stop with his hand either. Like Kate, he looked like he hadn't slept or rested for weeks. Considering the drugs that were no doubt coursing through his system, that was quite the feat. Neil looked the most normal of the three, but even he had a few tells. The way he spoke. The way his eyes had stared at his cup of black coffee as though it were dangerous. It would have been comical if she hadn't found herself doing the same.

Lies. Who did they think they were kidding? Surely, Moore saw through this as easily as Shawna had. Didn't she understand that they hadn't even had the briefing yet, and everyone was a basket case?

Shawna found herself at the door, looking through the window at the cold drizzle pattering against the concrete. The morning light seemed to have been swallowed by the storms making their way across the city.

Wouldn't it be easy just to walk out this door, freeze your ass off, hitch a ride to a bar, and get hammered as all hell? Turn your back on this place and never look back.

She turned around with a sigh and found Moore talking to Kate in what passed for the reception area. The two women seemed to be having a semi-private conversation. Kate looked nervous, while Moore was her usual stone-cold self. Shawna didn't envy Kate—working directly for Moore couldn't possibly be easy. Or pleasant.

Sarah was just glad neither of them had noticed her. Perhaps Moore would have guessed she was thinking of skipping out. Why wasn't everyone thinking that?

The team of survivors from HAL had more or less seen everything she and Catfish had. They'd been trapped in their lab with M2, which sounded much like what happened on *Leaguer.* Perhaps the Ben Taub survivors had been trapped, too.

It doesn't matter what they saw or experienced, Shawna thought. *It's what's in their nightmares that matter.*

That was part of the allure. To kill it. To know it was extinct once and for all. Once she destroyed these samples, maybe she could stop looking for vents and grates and once again feel comfortable in the dark.

The door behind her opened.

"Is it time now?" Catfish asked.

Shawna turned. His hair was a soaked mess, as were his dungarees. "What did you do?"

He shrugged. "I took a walk."

"I see that," she said, trying to maintain a straight face. "Didn't you know it was raining?"

"Yeah, I knew," he said. "I just didn't give a damn." Catfish gestured to the hall. "You ready?"

"No," she said. "But I guess it's time to get to work."

CHAPTER ELEVEN

Moore's eyes flicked to him when he crutched through the door, and her normally fake smile became a frown. He smiled at her, fighting the urge to stick his tongue out instead. It was juvenile, which was exactly how he reacted to pompous authority. He had been in the woman's presence just long enough to get the depth of her, and it was all bad. Moore had turned herself into an angry deity that held their lives and futures within her twitchy-fingered fist. All she had to do was squeeze, and one or all of them could disappear without a trace.

It would be easiest to do that with Shawna and Catfish. All too easy. As far as the world was concerned, they were already dead. Snuffing them out would be simple. Nearly abandoned government facility, soldiers running around with automatic weapons, plenty of places to hide bodies—

Or they could just feed you to M2, said a little voice inside his head.

Catfish twitched as he crutched to the conference table to sit next to Shawna. He grinned as he pushed the crutches beneath the chair. A glass of water and a sweating can of energy drink sat on stone coasters before him.

The catering cart was obscene. Robbie had smashed breakfast's leftovers together in simple yet tasty-looking combinations. Catfish, still full from breakfast, felt a tremor of hunger.

Yup. He needed to smoke. Vape. Something. If he didn't, he was going to overeat and burst.

Kate's two former coworkers, the dude with the glove and the geeky-looking guy she had brought in that morning, sat next to one another two places down. The guy with the glove's name was Jay Hollingsworth. The other was Neil Illing. He imagined that Moore had purposely removed any mention of education bona fides. He was pretty sure there wasn't a person from HAL who didn't have at least one Ph. D.

Kate stood by the catering table and filled her traveling mug from one of the large coffee pots. The sound of low conversation made the room seem even larger than it was. Kate, their supposed boss, looked as nervous as a teacher on their first day at school.

Catfish had noticed a twitch in Jay's hands. Could be from his injuries, but Catfish didn't think so—the dude was scared. So was the Neil guy.

Metal clinked against metal as the rest of the room finished making their meeting nests, fortifying them with drinks and yummies, and, finally, coming to rest in wait for the meeting to start. They didn't have long.

Moore appeared and took her station by the projector. "Good morning, everyone," she said.

When no one immediately returned the salutation, Looney Toons' Porky said cheerfully, "G-g-g-good m-morning."

Catfish swung his head to Jay, grinning at the man's expression. Another awkward silence filled the room before Moore cleared her throat. The entire time, she hadn't made eye contact with Jay.

"I assume you've all met," she said. "But just in case, I'll go through the roll." A gentle smile appeared on her face. "I'll skip the titles if you don't mind. From HAL, we have Kate, Jay, and Neil. From Leaguer, we have Shawna and—"

"Catfish," he said in a low growl.

"Yes," she said. "Catfish."

Moore's eyes twitched in the direction of the room's door. Catfish followed her gaze and saw Sarah and the scary guy with the dead eyes walking in. "And our new arrivals," she said. "You've all met Sarah, of course. And this is Mr. Givens."

The lanky man nodded curtly, his expression cold and emotionless. He and Sarah reached the table and took the last two chairs. Givens didn't make eye contact with anyone—it creeped the hell out of Catfish.

Moore waited for them to settle before continuing. "Instead of spending the next ten hours going through a massive slide presentation with graphs, pictures, embedded videos, and scientific gobbledygook, I'd much rather devote today to talking and putting the series of events in order.

"We do have hours of video," she said, "both from HAL and Ben Taub. We even have some from *Leaguer*, but not as much as we'd like." She glanced at Shawna. "I hope the two of you can help us figure out how this thing got loose and share any ideas about where it came from."

Shawna took a shuddering breath, but Catfish knew she wouldn't say anything. Her stage fright was probably kicking in. Always did when she had to lead a meeting of any kind.

"We'll have many breaks, as many as we need, to get through today." Moore paused for a moment as if gathering her thoughts. "I know each of you was traumatized and pushed to your limits by these encounters. If you feel you need a break, please say something. Any questions?"

"I have a question," Jay said. "Where is the CDC team from Ben Taub?"

Moore's smile disappeared. "We could not come to terms," she said. "Not in the end."

Catfish didn't like the sound of that. Surely, she didn't whack an entire group of government employees. Right?

"So we only have Neil for the biology experiments?"

Moore held up a hand with a forced smile. "Jay? Those are questions for after this meeting. We'll go over that as soon as we're done here."

He started to say something else, but Neil had reached out and touched his arm. Jay sighed, his chair creaking as he leaned back in defeat.

"Thank you," Moore said. "Any questions about what we're going to cover today?" No one said a word, although Jay loudly slurped at his coffee. She pretended not to notice. "I said this wasn't going to be a mammoth slide presentation, but there are a few things I want to cover."

She tapped a button on her phone, and the projector came to life. The room dimmed simultaneously, and the sudden bright white screen made him squint. The image of *Leaguer*, the oil rig where it all began, appeared on the screen. The sight of it made him take a sharp, ragged breath.

He'd spent over a month on it, fought constantly with the deck boss, and made enemies out of damned near everyone in that time. He and JP had spent their off-hours spearfishing a dozen meters below the ocean surface but in 10km of unsurveyed water.

Knowing that had given them both an adrenaline rush. Even now, the thought gave him the shivers, and they weren't all unpleasant.

Shawna's arm bumped his, and he looked down. She'd moved her hand to her knee, and it was shaking. Without thinking, he placed a hand over hers. Shawna didn't flinch, didn't look at him, and didn't react at all when he gently entwined his fingers with hers. A beat later, her fingers squeezed and held for a moment before finally relaxing.

"*Leaguer*," Moore said, "drilled an exploratory well in the M2 trench. They brought up enough oil to fill a test barrel and shipped it to HAL. The creature then infected a member of the HAL staff, and she was rushed to Ben Taub. At the hospital, the infection consumed her and proceeded to multiply throughout the facility." Moore took a breath. "That is the short timeline. Does anyone dispute that general sequence of events?" The room remained silent except for the projector's fan and the crackle and slide of thawing ice in drinks.

Moore tried to make eye contact with everyone in the room, but few met her gaze. Catfish did, though. Locking her stare caused a match to catch in his stomach, a sudden flare of rage making him twitch.

"I have a question," he said.

"Yes?"

Catfish leaned forward. "You forgot to mention how many of our friends died. Not to mention the rig workers, the lab staff, or the innocent people in the damned hospital."

Moore said nothing in reply.

He turned and looked at Jay. "I watched over a hundred people die, two of them my friends. How about you?"

"Mr. Standlee," Moore said. "Please allow—"

"Damned near an entire CDC team," Jay said quietly. "Security guards. Our IT director. One had a heart attack, and one," he spat, "has seemingly disappeared without a trace. And a bright young woman got infected and died." He shook his head. "Too much."

"So," Catfish said, turning back to face Moore. "Maybe you could stop being so clinical and remember what we've been through."

The facility director put her hands behind her back, and her eyes hardened. "My apologies," she said. "I didn't mean to be insensitive. However, keep in mind I know exactly to the person how many died, how many are in mental wards, and how many suffered other wounds." The flash of anger he'd felt started to dampen. "I also know how many people we managed to save."

She tapped the phone on the projector stand, and the slide changed. Two buildings appeared in front of a sunny sky, the letters "HAL" with the words "Houston Analytical Laboratory" clearly visible below the acronym.

"Pasadena, Texas," she said. "HAL received the test barrel from *Leaguer.* They immediately fed the barrel into their dispersal system, thus allowing the creature to fill the metal pipes." Another picture showed smashed walls, rusting, crumbling metal, dangling ceiling tiles, and burned carpet. That was one hallway. The picture changed again, affording them a view of a destroyed lab. Debris lay strewn about the large area as though a frat kegger featuring crystal meth had been held.

"Thanks to security footage reclaimed from the damaged server arrays, we have a more or less complete account of the events leading to the creature's escape from the dispersal system and into the facility." She looked over at Kate. "What I don't understand," she said, "is how Marie Krieger was infected."

"Yes, you do," Kate said in a cold voice. "We've told you a thousand times."

Moore smiled, the corners of her mouth straining from the effort. "Perhaps you'll recount it for our new arrivals?"

Catfish heard a click in Kate's throat before she began speaking. "Marie cut herself on the cap removal tool we use on barrels. It wasn't too deep of a cut but deep enough to need bandages. She complained about a burning sensation in her finger, but it seemed to abate." The last words faded to a near whisper, and Kate cleared her throat. "Over the next few hours, Marie developed a very high fever. Mike, our boss, called an ambulance for her, and she was taken to Ben Taub. We didn't receive any real updates after that."

Kate reached forward and took a sip of water with a shaking hand. "The creature escaped the dispersal system after we had begun our petroleum quality tests."

Shawna's head immediately swung in her direction. "How did it react?"

"Let's cover that in a while, Shawna," Moore said.

Shawna squeezed Catfish's fingers hard. "Okay," she said. "But we are going to talk about it."

"Yes," Moore said. "We will." She smiled at Shawna before looking back at Kate. "Anything else?"

Kate frowned before looking at Jay. "You were there too."

Jay nodded. "I saw a black speck in the cut. I mean tiny."

"How tiny?" Moore asked.

"Was kind of hard to tell," Jay said. "I guess no larger than the width of a sewing pin."

Moore grinned. "Thank you, Jay. Okay. Let's table that for now. As I said, I'd like to spend this morning talking about the actual events, not the science."

You mean you enjoy being an emotional voyeur, Catfish thought. The woman looked as though she was getting off watching them relive it all. If he ever had the chance, he'd knock her block off.

"Now," Moore said, "a CDC team was dispatched to Ben Taub to quarantine Ms. Krieger. Ms. Krieger died, and during attempts to resuscitate her, the creature consumed her. Because of a phone call to 911 from the HAL employee that accompanied Ms. Krieger to the hospital, a SWAT team was activated and sent to Ben Taub to contain a security situation and enforce the quarantine."

Catfish flipped his eyes toward Sarah and Givens. He didn't see any signs of distress on the woman's face, but her posture had changed, unlike her stony-faced colleague. He looked bored, as though this was a meeting about corporate finance instead of true-life monster tales.

"Several members of the medical staff," Moore continued, "died while trapped with one of the creatures in the quarantine area. The SWAT team engaged the creatures and managed to destroy nearly all of them."

"Nearly?" Catfish asked.

"The creature ended up in the hospital's waste system. When the systems were shut down, it became trapped in the metal tank."

"Then how did it get out?" Jay asked.

Moore gestured to Kate.

"I have a theory," Kate said, "that it tried to escape the waste tank by filling the pipes running from the quarantine and ER area. When the valves closed during the shutdown, I think whatever, well, tendrils it had extruded were isolated from the first creature."

"Shit," Shawna said. "People opened the taps and let them out?"

"No," Kate said. "The creatures would have had to go through the various drains in the building."

"Christ," Shawna said.

The pictures on the projector changed again. It was clear they were of a hospital's interior, specifically an ER or OR. Like the photos of HAL, the images were filled with fragments of machinery, discolored stainless steel, and shattered glass. Not for the first time, Catfish was glad M2 never left any blood behind. It just erased you from existence. Everything but metal and glass. And sometimes wood.

One of the walls from the hospital had puncture marks as if a giant sword had been thrust through them. Only—

"Shit," Catfish breathed, "those are concrete walls."

"Yes," Sarah said.

Catfish whipped his head around to look at her.

She was smiling, although it looked more and more like a quiet scream. "The last, um, thing we dealt with had grown substantially. We had to blow up the top floors to destroy it."

"Wait," Jay said, pointing at the screen. "You mean one of these things got big enough to do that?"

"That's nothing," Sarah said. "It more or less destroyed an entire floor by itself."

"How large was it?" Neil asked.

"I don't know," Sarah said. She glanced at Givens, but he didn't acknowledge it. "It was very dark. But I'm pretty sure it was at least ten meters wide, and I don't know how long."

"Oh, man," Catfish said. "You are so lucky to be alive."

Givens turned his head slowly as if on rusty hinges, his dead eyes boring into Catfish's. "Luck, blood, and explosives made out of oxygen tanks."

The gentle southern drawl coming out of that hard-lined mouth made Catfish cringe. That was the voice of a gentleman rather than the automaton-like cadence and inflection he'd expected. Who was this guy?

"Oxygen tanks," Kate said. "How--"

Sarah waved the question away. "It's a long story," she said. "We did what we could with what we had." The room went silent, leaving Catfish wishing someone would say something. Anything. Just break the awkward, stifling silence threatening to—

"Sarah?" Moore said. "Regardless of the creature's size, what other traits did it display?"

The head of security looked at the table as if searching for an answer. "I don't know," she said. "It moved like a spider, but at the same time, it didn't. Also," she said, "they're cannibals."

"Wait," Kate said. "What?"

"Yeah," Sarah said. "We watched one of them consume the other. The larger ate, or absorbed, I guess, the smaller creature."

Jay's gravel-filled voice broke over the ensuing silence. "What happened?"

"Huh?" Sarah asked.

"After it ate the smaller one. Was there some reaction?"

She nodded. "Yes. It got bigger. And it got bigger fast."

Jay traded glances with Kate, and Catfish realized Shawna was staring at him.

"What?" Catfish asked Shawna.

"The big one ate the little one," she said.

"So?" Catfish said. "That wave wasn't—"

"Yes," she said. "Think about it. Once M2 got out on the deck, it acted like a single creature. But we saw multiples inside the rig. We didn't see them at the end."

He thought for a moment. Jay, Kate, and Neil were speaking in a heated conversation, although he found himself tuning it out. Multiple creatures, then one.

At the very end, a malevolent tsunami of absolute darkness washed over the rig, consuming anything biological and growing larger. No, there weren't individual creatures; that had been a single contiguous entity, thing, blob, or whatever the hell you wanted to call it.

"You're right," he said to Shawna. "There was only one. So the others either took the night off or—"

"Or," Shawna said, "the bigger one absorbed the others."

"Makes sense," Catfish said. He made eye contact with Sarah. "Hey. You said the bigger one ate the smaller one, right?"

"That's what she said," Givens mumbled.

Catfish remembered a story he had read in high school. Had to do with a hunter that brought other people to his island to hunt them. Why? Because if you're at the top of the food chain, there is nothing else to hunt that presents any challenge. At least, that's the impression he got.

"Did it, I don't know, hunt the other one?" Catfish asked.

Sarah looked at Givens, the pair staring at one another. Finally, Givens twitched into something like a nod. She swung her gaze to Catfish. "If I remember correctly, it did."

"Why?" Jay said. "Why do you say that?"

Sarah and Givens exchanged another long stare before she spoke again. "It ignored us," she said, Givens nodding. "It could have kept attacking us but rushed toward the smaller one instead."

Catfish realized the room had gone silent again. Jay, Kate, and Neil must have given up on their conversation to listen. In a way, he wished the room was still filled with ambient noise. Sarah looked uncomfortable, Givens more stoic than ever. And Shawna? He'd noticed her breathing had picked up. Shit, his had too.

"Spiders are cannibalistic," Neil said. All heads at the table turned to look at him. He shrugged in response. "They weren't spiders, I know that, but they had a lot of similar traits. Multi-legged, a central body, and they could jump as well as run fast."

"Too damned fast," Givens muttered.

Moore waited for a beat before speaking. "Shawna? Catfish? What did you see?"

What did we see? On the deck? In the rig interior?

"Tentacles," Catfish said. "Talons."

Neil scrunched his eyebrows. "Did it remind you of anything?"

"Maybe," Catfish said. "The ones that weren't simply liquid, they—" Tentacles, mandibles, maws that might as well have been holes in reality.

He felt pressure on his fingers and looked down. Shawna had moved her hand atop his, gently squeezing as if to reassure him. "They hunted us," he said. "Tore down walls, dissolved wood and sheetrock, and the way they moved—" He trailed off again as he tried to put the images into words.

"I think," Shawna said, "ours acted differently than yours."

"How so?" Jay asked.

"You described them as arachnids," she said. "Or rather arachnid-like. Ours reminded me of deep-sea life. Like a mix of squid, crab, starfish, and insects. But I'd have to see what yours looked like to know for sure."

"I can arrange that," Moore said. The woman's expression was as remote and serene as ever. Shawna practically flinched. "We have plenty of footage of the creatures from both HAL and Ben Taub."

Shawna opened her mouth to say something but closed it without making a sound. Instead, she looked at the floor and squeezed Catfish's hand again. He knew what was going through her mind. It was the same thing going through his. The idea of seeing that thing again, even on screen, filled him with dread and made him wary of the shadows in the dimly lit room.

Shit, if you can't handle seeing it on screen, how are you going to be able to handle seeing it in person? How is Shawna going to be able to do that?

"Perhaps later," Moore said. She glanced at Kate. "You have enough information?"

The scientist nodded with a barely visible smile. "Confirms a lot of my experiment plan," she said. "Also brings up a few new things. I'll have to sort those out with the team."

"Excellent," Moore said. She killed the projector, and the lights in the room slowly came back to life. Moore left the makeshift podium and took a seat two down from Kate. "Now," she said. "We're going to begin with *Leaguer,* and we're going to end with Ben Taub. I want to know everything."

Catfish and Shawna looked at one another.

"You or me?" Catfish asked, his words barely audible even to himself.

Shawna took a deep breath, tented her hands on the table, and stared at nothing. "PPE discovered a new find in the M2 Trench off of Papua/New Guinea. Thomas Calhoun," she said, nearly choking on the words, "brought JP Harvey, Catfish, and me to the new exploration rig sent to validate the find, which happened to be in over ten kilometers of water." She trailed off for another moment and continued the tale.

As she spoke, Catfish relived every second of it. He and JP testing the new automated underwater vehicles (AUV) Catfish had designed, working out the bugs a full month before *Leaguer* drilled the first test well, spearfishing, enjoying the freedom and adrenaline of swimming with untold depths beneath them, the trips in the speedboat to retrieve the AUVs for inspection and maintenance as well as the hours spent watching recordings, looking for out of the ordinary details exposed by the new lighting systems.

Of all the rigs he'd been to, all the work he'd done with Thomas, Shawna, and JP, *Leaguer* was the best experience he'd ever had, even on the worst days. But that was before they drilled, and it all went to shit.

JP got infected, although no one knew exactly how. Richardson, a roughneck Catfish had liked, had too. All the hours Catfish had spent in the hospital had given him plenty of time to think. The only conclusion he'd come to is that the creature incubated before turning on its host—unless it simply absorbed the host.

Something ten kilometers below the rig had grabbed onto the drill pipe and wrenched *Leaguer* downward. Once the rig was incapacitated, the casualties quickly piled up. Catfish and the other survivors had fought to recover supplies to last the night, but one by one, more and more of the humans aboard *Leaguer* disappeared, becoming one with the creature. Or maybe the creature had become one with them.

Now and then, Shawna looked at him to confirm one of their shared suspicions or to verify her memory. She did well. He only had to add his own theory once.

Shawna finished the tale by recounting their last night aboard *Leaguer* with the storm and the darkness around them, the tidal wave of black liquid covering the rig's superstructure and flowing down to swallow everything. Tentacles, mouths, dozens and dozens of each, had appeared in the liquid, extruding and reaching for them.

That's when she blasted the fuel barrel on the deck. The massive creature quickly caught fire, and the deck's metal surface disappeared beneath thick smoke and flame. She skipped how Thomas had died along with the others. She also chose not to try to recount how she and Catfish ended up together in the boat or how they managed to remain safe in the following days.

There wouldn't have been any point. Who cared how you managed to get rescued after hearing over a hundred people had been consumed by living oil?

When Shawna finished, the room went silent. Catfish raised his can of energy drink and tried to sip as noiselessly as he could. He only realized when the can was to his lips that his hand had developed a tremor.

"Any questions?" Moore said.

No one made eye contact with one another. Catfish stared at the table, his translucent reflection staring back at him.

Shawna's hand found his again and squeezed firmly. "You okay?"

He nodded but said nothing.

"Okay," Moore said. "I suggest we take a break. Let's reconvene in fifteen minutes."

The stillness in the room quickly broke as the scientists rose from their places to find the restroom or get a refill. Catfish quickly downed the rest of his drink. He had never needed a cigarette more in his life.

"Hey," Shawna said quietly.

He swung his head to look at her. Her eyes were dry, but her face appeared haggard and haunted. He crumpled the can. "Yeah?"

She squeezed his hand a little harder. "Are you okay?"

He looked down at her hand, the light brown of her skin contrasting with his sun-deprived flesh. He squeezed her back. "Yeah. You?"

"Sure," she said and squeezed harder. "Want to take a quick walk?"

"Absofuckinglutely," he said. What he really needed was a cigarette. Shit, a whole carton of the damned things. Line 'em up in his mouth like in the cartoons and light them with a blowtorch. One inhale, hold for five seconds, and exhale enough carbon monoxide to kill all the insects nearby. Yeah. Sounded like a damned good idea.

He felt the scientists' eyes on his back, or maybe it was that Givens guy, the one with the dead eyes. Who was he kidding? There were cameras everywhere. Anyone could be watching them. Still, it took some effort to keep from glancing backward.

"I need some air," Shawna said, heading toward the front doors. Catfish followed.

The stink of rain flowed into his nose as he breathed deeply. Compared to the persistent smell of sawdust and the faint scent of freshly ground metal, the rain was a welcome change.

He stood with Shawna beneath the nearly two-meter-long overhang, a lonely butt tree standing in the corner of the sheltered area. Catfish took another deep breath, and the ghostly scent of burned tobacco hit him. He grinned.

"What are you smiling at?" Shawna asked.

"Nothing good for me," he said. "What'd you make of all that bullshit?"

"You know they're listening to us, right?"

"Of course they are," he said. "So say hi and spill it.

She rolled her eyes. "Hello, Orwell," she said, arms spread wide as she turned in a slow circle. When her arms came down, she put her hands on her hips. "Happy?"

"No," he said, barely able to keep from laughing. "Answer the damned question."

Shawna ran a hand through her thick hair. "Moore is leading us."

"You think?"

She nodded. "Either Kate came up with those questions, or Moore did. But either way, this morning was about letting us fill in details without even telling the story."

"Meaning what?" he asked.

"That she and Kate could have written all that crap down and put it in front of us. But they didn't. Instead, they did that little dog and pony to get us to think."

"So, what, they get real reactions from us?"

"Sort of," she said. "More like so the details would pop back in our minds." She smiled, but it had no warmth in it. "Bitch is smart."

"It was like brainstorming a horror movie," he said.

"Yeah. And that was only the first one. There are two more in the trilogy. When Kate and Sarah tell their side, we'll have the whole picture."

"No, we won't," Catfish said. "We'll still only have the pieces. Not sure how we're supposed to put them together."

"That's what the experiments will be for," she said. "And I can already tell they're going to be fun."

He glared at the butt tree, wishing like hell a half-burned, lit cigarette poked out of the hole. No such luck. He'd have to talk to Moore about it before he ended up killing someone.

"What's your problem?" Shawna asked.

"Need to go shopping."

"Don't we all," Shawna said. With another sigh, she stared up at the cold rain falling from the dark clouds. "Time to go back."

"At least the worst part is over," he said. "We don't have to go through remembering all that shit again."

"Worst part," she echoed. "I hope you're right."

CHAPTER TWELVE

Shawna didn't have a watch, a phone, or anything to tell time. The conference room didn't have a clock on the wall. It didn't even have a window.

At least when they'd been trapped on the lifeboat, the sun and moon still rose and set. Time passed, and the lapping waves rocking the boat had been the only things that had kept her sane while Catfish slumbered in his ill exhaustion. She had promised herself she would get a watch. Too late now.

After the scientists, Sarah, and Givens piled into their chairs with fresh provisions, an awkward silence filled the room. Less than a minute later, Moore entered and returned to her seat at the table.

"Hope everyone had a good break," she said. "Find everything okay?" A few nods and whispers responded. Moore's fake smile faltered. "Does anyone have questions for Shawna or Mister—" She stopped herself before glancing at Catfish with a shark's grin. "Or questions for Catfish?"

No one said a word. Moore nodded to herself. "Okay, then. Let's move on. The M2 test barrel ended up at HAL. Kate?"

Kate looked more than a little nervous. She gathered herself for a moment and then began to speak. She told them about the barrel's arrival, Krieger becoming infected, and the first round of tests they'd run on the sample.

HAL's initial tests of the "oil" had confirmed Shawna's analysis.

The substance was the sweetest crude ever recovered despite its color. Additional analyses provided similar information until they got to the tests that included light.

The substance seemed to absorb all spectrums of light except bright white. That had made the sample simply explode with a pop and had scared the hell out of everyone. Kate said it was then that they knew something was very wrong.

"Finally, M2 got loose in the lab. It started as a puddle," Kate said, "but eventually consumed enough material to grow. And it grew damned fast."

Shawna saw motion out of the corner of her eye. Givens and Sarah were nodding to one another. More commonalities. Shawna had seen the same thing in the lab on *Leaguer* when one of the samples nearly consumed her. If not for Thomas' quick thinking, she would have perished inside the sealed lab. The thought made her eyes moist. Thomas had saved them again and again, but in the end, she hadn't been able to save him.

"After that," Kate said, "it ate or destroyed sheetrock, carpet, people, anything biological. Jay, my daughter, and I ended up in the basement of the new building. M2 followed us through the HVAC. Jay created a makeshift battery bomb, and we killed the damned thing."

"Battery bomb?" Catfish asked, his eyes focused on Jay.

The older scientist grinned. "Yeah. Short the leads, and the battery heats the wire to a high temperature. Especially once you cut away the insulation."

"How'd you make that?" Catfish asked.

Jay held up his gloved hand. "Not very well. Had to use some cloth to hold things together. It caught fire."

"Christ," Catfish said. "But it worked."

"It did," Jay said. "Exploded the thing like it was a firecracker."

"Anything left of it?" Shawna asked.

Kate shook her head. "No. Dr. Moore's team combed the facility looking for other signs of the creatures but found nothing."

"At least there's that," Catfish said.

Moore cleared her throat. "Any other details you want to add, Kate?"

The chemist slowly shook her head. Shawna thought for a moment that Kate would say something else, but she didn't. She scribbled a note on her pad. Perhaps Kate would be more forthcoming once they were down in the lab.

Moore looked around the room, purposely making eye contact with everyone. Damn, but she was intimidating. Shawna could feel the tension coming off Catfish in waves and knew he'd like nothing more than to punch Moore in the mouth.

Shawna understood the rage boiling beneath his skin. Catfish wanted answers, and Moore wanted to play games and try to cow them all instead. Shawna nearly chuckled aloud. Moore didn't seem to understand that Catfish was immune to those tactics. When he finally made that clear, Shawna wondered how Moore would respond.

"Any questions for Kate or the other HAL survivors?" Moore asked.

Survivors. The word echoed in Shawna's mind as though shouted at the mountains from a valley floor. They should get T-shirts. "I survived M2, and all I got was this lousy t-shirt!" It would be a perfect addition to this clusterfuck.

No one said a word.

"Thank you, Kate," Moore said. "Let's take a five-minute break and then cover the last third of this meeting." The head of the facility drank from her cup while swiping at the tablet before her.

Catfish sighed. "Might as well get my heart racing again," he said.

"You want another over-caffeinated energy drink that's driving you one step closer to a heart attack?" Shawna asked.

"Yes, please. Extra heart attack on the side."

She rolled her eyes and stepped away from the table. A shadow fell across her as she reached the iced bucket of cans. She quickly turned and nearly ran into Kate. The woman stepped back in surprise.

"I'm sorry, Shawna," Kate said.

Shawna managed to tamp down the brief rush of adrenaline. "No problem," Shawna said. "A little jumpy."

Kate made a sound that might have been a laugh. "Aren't we all?"

Shawna nodded, her shaking hands pulling the energy drink from the bucket. "Have you been down to the labs?"

Kate smiled. "Of course. I helped design two of the retrofits. Well, with Neil's help, of course."

"The biochemist?"

"Right," she said. "We, um, spent some time brainstorming about what we'd need, and Moore gave us the means to put it together."

"Makes sense, I guess," Shawna said.

"Look," Kate said, "I can't promise nothing bad will happen. Shit, who can? But I know we've taken every precaution we know to. If there's any suggestion you want to make, I'll be more than happy to hear it and take you up on it. It's not like I have a budget."

"Seriously?"

Kate's grin widened. "I don't know what kind of paycheck you're getting, but I can't imagine it's small."

"It's not," Shawna said.

"Let's just say then that this is a well-funded project. I don't want to know how or by whom, but if we need something, we get it."

Shawna nodded. It was almost like working for Thomas again. If they had a new idea, something that would require some bootstrapping, he found the money. He always did. *Always had,* she corrected herself. *Had.*

"You okay?" Kate asked.

"Yeah," Shawna said, wiping at one eye. "I'm fine. Just tired. These meetings," she said apologetically, "aren't easy."

"No," Kate agreed. "They're not."

"Ladies? Gentlemen?" Moore called. "Can we get started?"

Sarah's account of the Ben Taub incident took less than ten

minutes. An infected scientist had been brought into the emergency quarantine area at Ben Taub Hospital, the CDC took over, and something had happened. Something bad. Sarah, it turned out, worked for HPD SWAT. Or had. Same with Givens. They hadn't known what they would be fighting and were completely unprepared for what happened.

Dr. Krieger, the scientist from HAL, had been eaten by the creature from the inside out, replacing her body with a large pool of oil, which quickly decimated the CDC team. By the time SWAT arrived, the creature had already taken several lives and destroyed much of the ER wing. Then, it escaped containment.

Sans communication with the outside world, her SWAT team found themselves trapped inside Ben Taub with the creatures. Without Dr. Moore's assistance over the radio, all of Ben Taub would have been destroyed, and everyone lost.

Shawna scribbled on the pad. She reoriented the pen in her fingers and delicately flipped it from one end to the other. The words "M on radio. Did she already know?" stared back at her in black ink.

Sarah spoke about how the creatures changed, their exteriors hardening once they reached a certain size, how their talons clicked on the tiled floors, and how they moved. She and her team had acquired several infant blankets made for jaundice and used the high-intensity UV rays to corral one of the creatures, but before they could destroy it, a larger creature had burst through the walls and devoured its smaller brethren.

Once again, Shawna was struck by that fact. Somehow, it was important, although she couldn't say why. She wrote it down, her scribbles practically indecipherable even to herself.

By the time Sarah finished, Shawna had pretty much stopped listening. The ending to Sarah's story had been more or less the same as HAL's, although the creature the SWAT team had destroyed was monstrous. Not as large as she imagined *Leaguer*'s M2 had been, but still a massive creature. *Leaguer*'s large M2 creature hadn't moved like that. It hadn't taken a well-defined shape. It sprouted tentacles, horrid maws, and eyestalks, but it had never had a distinct body.

Both the HAL and Ben Taub creatures had somehow managed to transform themselves. The carapace, insectile, crustaceous features, working mandibles, all those details had been missing from the M2 hostiles that destroyed *Leaguer.*

But the Ben Taub tale was even more worrisome than the HAL encounter. For one thing, the creatures moved both intelligently and purposefully. They sought out food like hunters, not slime molds. They had also managed to take out light sources and other obstacles.

M2 had evolved, or maybe differentiated was the correct word. Either way, the creature had changed radically between the three encounters. Shawna wrote the word "evolution" in messy block letters. It stared back at her like an accusation. She added a question mark to it. The word caused another shiver, but she couldn't say why.

* * *

By the time Sarah and Givens had finished telling their story, Catfish felt exhausted. They hadn't been in that room for more than a few hours, which included several breaks, but it seemed much longer. Like days. He had a feeling that it was only going to get worse. He was both right and wrong.

After they ate lunch in the conference room, catered by Chef Robbie, of course, Moore put on a slide show of sorts. It mainly included reiterating the facility rules of conduct, security, use of the commissary, and the custodial schedules. Moore made it clear they weren't responsible for cleaning their domiciles or washing their clothes; all that was handled for them.

Catfish wanted to ask Moore if that meant he could throw a kegger in his trailer but decided it wasn't worth it. Getting the "someone just shit in my coffee" look from Moore would have brought him great joy, but it would have made the meeting last longer, and that was the last goddamned thing he wanted.

Besides, Shawna looked as antsy as he felt. She wanted out of there, too. A glance around the table told Catfish everyone felt that way. Well, everyone but Givens; that man didn't seem to react to anything.

When Moore finished repeating all the rules, boring them stupid with cautions about security infractions and the armed sentries walking the perimeter at night, he'd nearly chuckled. All that to impress them? Or scare them? Bullshit.

He'd noticed the mounted cameras on the fences and those on the surrounding buildings. Moore had this place on lockdown. Cameras everywhere, probably infrared capable. Even the idea of armed sentries was a joke. No one was getting in here that hadn't already been cleared.

It was probably even worse in the building where the HAL folks stayed. They wouldn't even have to attempt to hide them there. Every centimeter of those buildings was watched. He was sure of it.

Which begged another question. Were the sentries, cameras, and constant cautions aimed at keeping someone else out or the scientists in?

While Moore would no doubt suffer an embolism if any of her prized eggheads escaped the compound, an interloper gaining access to the facility would make her vaporize it with a nuclear blast. He knew what was beneath that woman's mask.

And who would want to get in here? Good question. Who could possibly know anything about what happened at HAL or Ben Taub, much less *Leaguer*? Catfish smirked as Moore finished up her list of informational drivel.

Moore might be able to cover up the HAL incident completely, but Ben Taub? Between the high number of casualties and the number of patients and staff that survived, keeping a lid on that little train wreck would be much more difficult. Was the NSA going to follow the survivors around for the rest of their lives? Monitor their internet usage? Who they talked to, what they wrote down, what they said, anything indicating treachery or rumor-mongering?

He doubted it. Well, the internet part? All too easy. But the rest? No. No goddamn way.

With the lunch debris cleared and fresh cups of coffee and iced cans of soda distributed, Moore brought up three new slides. Each contained a map of the facility lying beneath them. Four levels. One level for engineering, one for labs, and another for quarantine. She didn't mention the fourth.

When she said the "q" word, Catfish sat up in his chair, the meeting daze and glaze gone from his eyes. "Quarantine?" he asked.

Moore didn't bother meeting his stare. "Quarantine is the most secure of the levels," she said. "It's where any samples are flushed. Also, it's where anyone having had physical contact with M2 will be kept for observation."

Observation, he thought. Great word. You kept a subject for observation to see how the disease manifests and how the creature might consume you from the inside until you are little more than a pool of living black. The image of an eyestalk rising out of the darkness filled his mind. Catfish shook away the mental movie trying to play through his skull.

"We will walk you through each emergency system when we have the tour later," she said.

"Tour?" Shawna asked.

Moore's fake smile returned, thinner and more forced than ever. "Yes, a tour."

"Wait," Catfish said. "You said four levels." He pointed at the slide on the screen. "What's the fourth level?"

Moore's smile completely disappeared. "Maintenance," she said. "Facility emergency power, bilge, etc. Nothing you need to worry about."

"Wait," Catfish said. "Bilge?"

Moore's gaze turned to him with slight disinterest. "You do know how shallow the water table is here."

"I have an idea." Catfish scratched at his beard. "What does that have to—" Catfish gritted his teeth as he realized what she meant. "You mean in case the lower levels flood."

"That is correct," Moore said. "Although we have updated as much as we can, the facility has been here a long time, and the movement of the aquifer has caused some leaks here and there."

"So you can burn us to death, or we could drown," Catfish said. "Are those my only options?"

"Besides getting eaten?" Jay said.

With a hiss of exasperation, Kate said, "People? Focus. Memorize the layout. I want to ensure everyone knows what to do if something happens." She cleared her throat and swallowed hard. "We all need to remember that the facility's security itself is a far second in priorities."

"First priority being?" Jay asked.

Kate pointed vaguely at the conference room wall. "That out there, above us and less than a kilometer or two away, human beings live in their houses, their children play, and attend school." She shifted her finger and tapped it hard on the table. "If we don't do our jobs, if we aren't vigilant, M2 will wipe them out. And then the rest of the city."

The room went cold with a crushing silence. Damn, but Kate looked furious at the idea. Not wistful or nervous. Her eyes burned with something personal. Her daughter, perhaps? Yeah, Catfish thought to himself. Only a mother could look like that, one whose child had been threatened. Or killed.

"Any questions?" Moore asked finally.

CHAPTER THIRTEEN

When Moore had finished the rest of her presentation, she ushered them to the elevator, and they began their descent.

The elevator display changed from "Transit" to "Eng," the car came to a gentle stop, and the door dinged cheerily.

"First stop." Moore glanced at Catfish. "Kate will show you around."

"Wait," Shawna said, "what if I want to see?"

The director said icily, "Then you can do so on your own time."

Catfish once again found himself wanting to hit Moore. He'd never met anyone so capable of condescension without raising their voice or needing sarcasm to do it. The clipped, precise words and perfect diction, accompanied by the ever-present automaton-like grin, combined to form the most asshole of a human being he could have imagined.

He opened his mouth to pelt her with obscenities, but Shawna touched his shoulder. "Let it go," she whispered.

Forcing his fingers to unclench from fists, fingernail marks buried in the flesh of his palm, he smiled at her and stepped across the threshold and into an unmarked, brightly lit, white corridor.

The faint memory of fresh paint underlay the normally antiseptic smell that recycled air usually had. The elevator dinged, and he glanced backward and waved to Shawna. She returned it as the car doors slid shut, and the lift continued downward.

Kate was looking at him.

"What?"

"Nothing," she said with a smile.

Shaking his head, Catfish looked down the hall, which ended in a large metal door. A guard armed with an incinerator stood beside it, his dungarees unmarked by insignias, rank, or hardware. A pair of dark goggles peeked out from beneath a hood, fabric covering nearly every piece of skin, protecting as if from a harsh desert sun. The soldier, guard, or whatever the hell he was, nodded to Kate as they made their way down the hall.

The bright lights and the white-painted floor, walls, and ceiling combined to hurt his eyes. He needed sunglasses.

"Bright enough in here?" Catfish said. His crutches squeaking on the floor was the only sound apart from the soft pad of her athletic shoes on the thick steel floor.

"The halls have the new bulbs installed. They pump out the same UV spectrum as sunlight. However," she said, "we're beginning to find out just how reliable they aren't."

He glanced at her, his face screwed up in a frown. "What the hell does that mean?"

They had reached the large steel door, which might have been torn from a bank vault. Probably had been. Kate waved her bracelet at the sensor, and the door slid aside, revealing an airlock.

"Really?"

Kate laughed. "Did you forget this was designed to hold in ETs?"

"Not on the engineering level."

"No," she agreed. "Security precaution in case pollutants get into the air recycling system."

He nodded toward the corridor behind them. "That's on a different system?"

"They all are," Kate said. "But there are air shafts connecting the levels. Guessing the architects of this monstrosity weren't too worried about anything getting up here. We had to retrofit this area extensively, and we're still having some power problems."

"Great," he said. "So how the hell do you know they're going to work when they need to?"

She took in a shuddering breath as they walked through the airlock. "I don't."

A chill crawled down his spine.

"Well?" Kate said, gesturing to the large space. "What do you think?"

The rectangular floor had a single recessed area marked "Printing" enclosed in what looked like soundproof walls. Tools, sheet metal, shelves and shelves of printer material, and a steel wall with a hatch marked "Testing" filled out the room.

"Looks like someone shit out a high-end Home Despot."

She laughed. "Fairly accurate. The testing area is both explosion and fireproof. Just, um, don't make anything too big."

"Is that a challenge?" Catfish asked with a grin.

"No, it certainly isn't." She led him past the security console, where no one stood, and to the construction area. The curtained-off portion had plenty of space for welding, cutting, and other loud and potentially dirty jobs. "Console is over there," she said, pointing toward a large desk curled in a rough L shape. Multiple monitors hung above it, their screens blank. "You should be able to send blueprints and anything else you need from there. Now, all you need is a bracelet."

He frowned. "Bracelet?"

With a smile, she took him to the security desk. Givens appeared from nowhere, his face set in a stony line, eyes dead and uninterested. Catfish placed his hand on a device, and after it scanned his fingerprints, it spat out a printed bracelet with a chip. He stared at it before slapping it around his wrist.

"That should be that," Kate said, leading him to the consoles. He noticed Givens was following them, the holsters on his hips making him look like a strangely garbed gunslinger.

When they reached the console, she showed him how to log in using the bracelet. Once he did, the console screens came to life, and a black command prompt stared at him from the desktop.

"Um," he said, scratching his head. "This looks like my desktop at home."

"Interesting," Kate said with a knowing smile. "I never would have guessed that."

He listed the files in the directory and stared at the screen. It was his home directory. From the computer at his home. "They fucking mirrored my computer." His voice had become the snarl of a rabid animal brimming with deep fury. It made Kate step away from him. Givens stepped forward.

Catfish glared at the shorter man. "Going to do something?"

"Only if I have to. Just remember," Givens said and gestured to Kate, "she didn't do it."

The words tamped down the fire. A little. He wanted to hit something, smash it, torture it, destroy it. What made it worse was that he knew who did it, and the bitch wasn't here right now. That's who he wanted to threaten, scream at, and punch with as much power as he could muster. Givens was right.

"My apologies," he said to Kate through clenched teeth and forced himself to relax his hands. The hateful glare took more effort. He turned back to the screen and checked the drive assignments. His old drives were there, mounted and ready for him.

Every drive, every directory, every file. Moore had copied everything. Might as well have just lifted the drives out and put them in here. Except for one difference—these mirrored drives had been decrypted.

"How—" Shaking his head, he looked at the drive assignments again and noticed three that didn't belong. One was marked "M2 Surveillance Archives," another marked "M2 Device Research," and the last was marked "M2 Entity Research." He quickly checked the folders to determine how many files were in each.

The archives folder contained over 500 terabytes of data. The other two? Practically empty. Skeleton directories, a few readme files, and not much else. However, the "Device" directory had one interesting subfolder: "AUV5."

He feverishly typed in commands, finding telemetry records and data dumps. "How?"

Kate cleared her throat. "I take it this means you're ready for work?"

He turned to her, his face a mask of confusion. "What are those?"

She followed his finger and leaned forward to look at the file names. "I'm not sure. I think you'll have to ask Moore."

"Tell me," he said to her, "exactly what the hell am I supposed to do here?"

Givens took another step forward until he was practically at Catfish's elbow. "You and I are going to make some weapons," he said coldly. "Something useful."

"Really? And what engineering expertise are you bringing to this endeavor?" The word "engineering" dripped with sarcasm.

Givens' eyes finally came to life. "I fought the things and won. You," he said with a sniff, "ran."

The room went silent as Catfish's mouth opened in surprise. Even Kate seemed taken aback. When Catfish finally managed to find his voice, indignant rage colored every word. "We had no weapons, asshole."

Givens grinned. "We did. We made them."

"Big deal. I blew up the mother of this shit."

"And that's the only reason you don't have a bullet in your brain," Givens said. "So maybe we should get to it instead of me having to listen to your hurt ego."

Catfish swung a fist without even knowing he was going to do it. The blow, awkwardly aimed and difficult to throw with a crutch under his arm, did more than miss. The crutch fell from beneath his arm as his skin flew less than a centimeter from Given's pallid face.

Givens' arm snaked out in a blur, catching Catfish's wrist and turning it while his other hand shot around Catfish's chest.

"Bad mistake," Givens said. He twisted the wrist, and Catfish cried out in pain. "But not a bad throw for a cripple."

Then Catfish realized something. He should have fallen to the ground in a heap. Instead, Givens' arm around his waist held him up and kept him from smashing into the thick steel floor. Catfish said nothing as he limped sideways, leaning on his remaining crutch to stabilize himself while he shrugged away from Givens' embrace. The soldier with the dead eyes let him go but held his hands out as if to catch him if he fell.

Catfish looked into the man's eyes again and saw a hint of amusement. For once, the asshole didn't seem so robotic.

"If you two are done marking your territory," Kate said, "I need to visit the lab level." She nodded to Catfish. "You'll find email addresses in a shared doc on your computer. Send me one if you have questions or need some support, although Givens here should be able to help you with anything you need."

Without breaking his stare with Givens, he smiled and said, "I'm sure we'll get along great. Right?"

Givens smiled. It was somehow more terrifying than his usual expressionless stare. "We sure will."

"Great," Kate said and clapped her hands together. "Then I'll leave you to it."

She turned and walked away without looking back at them. Catfish watched her retreat through the blast door and into the corridor.

"Well," he said at last, "are we done pissing?"

"For now," Givens said. "Just let me know if you want to go again. But," he said, pointing at Catfish's cast, "I think we need to wait until you're healed up."

Catfish chuckled. "Maybe." He turned to look at the computer. "All right, Mr. Givens."

"Just Givens," he said.

"And I'm just Catfish. So. What do you want to make first?"

Givens grinned like a starved shark. "Something that goes boom."

* * *

Catfish sat in his trailer, his fingers clenching and unclenching as he stared at the gray sky. The night was coming fast, and he couldn't wait for it to arrive. Meetings, meetings, meetings. All he wanted was a pack of cigarettes, a cold beer, a bowl of Cindy White, and some chicken wings. Was that too much to ask?

At the end of the day, he and Shawna presented Moore with a list of "necessities." Catfish had included three different models of nicotine vaporizers, a list of brands and flavors, and an order for three cartons of the darkest, foulest, cheapest brand of cigarettes he could think of. That, an economy pack of plastic lighters, and a strong halogen flashlight.

Shawna's list had included a steel flip-top lighter and a request for several halogen flashlights. She hadn't been very specific. Catfish wasn't surprised by the request for lights, but the fact she wanted a Zippo had been confusing until he remembered Jay and his battery bomb.

Moore had looked at the list and nodded at the remarks about needing real clothes, jackets, and footwear. As Moore said it was all doable, she'd seen something on the list that drew her attention. Her voice dropped off in volume and stopped altogether. When she finally looked up from the paper, her cold, fake smile had returned. Her eyes, however, said something else entirely. Catfish thought one of their requests had surprised her or given her an idea. Probably both.

Catfish continued staring into the growing darkness. The sky pissed on the ground again, the droplets spattering against the trailer's roof, ceasing nearly as quickly as they had begun. He opened the trailer's screen door and stepped out. The distant lights of the airfield glowed like halos in the misty air.

He took a sip from the soda and let out a long belch. His stomach responded with a hungry gurgle. Dinner couldn't be far away. Hopefully, Moore would have some "gifts" for him and Shawna. Catfish rubbed at his itchy dungarees. What he wouldn't give for a Skinny Puppy t-shirt and an internet radio thrashing out metal and industrial tunes at top volume loud enough to make the dishes tremble inside the cupboards.

Well, he thought, *that's one way to get around the audio surveillance.* Of course, that would require him and Shawna to hear one another during such a sonic assault. "No, that won't work. Next?"

He'd have to think of something else. Think. That was a joke.

He flinched when he saw motion at the edge of the door, memories of the day evaporating into the present. Shawna stood in the gathering darkness, her fatigue jacket covering the donated sweater. "You ready for dinner?"

He smiled. "Yeah," he said. "Then you can tell me about the rest of your day since I wasn't invited to the lab."

A brief shadow of concern crossed her face but quickly evaporated. Now, he was more than a little curious about how her day had gone. That look didn't exactly reassure him.

She grinned. "I have a feeling something will be waiting for us when we get back to the commissary."

"Like what?" Catfish asked.

"Provisions!"

CHAPTER FOURTEEN

Shawna parked their cart next to three other carts. She imagined one was for Sarah and Givens, whose trailers were just ten or so meters away from hers and Catfish's, and two to cover Moore and the HAL team.

The only question was where Moore slept. If it was in the same building as the HAL folks, then she might have shared one of their carts, but Shawna didn't think Moore was the kind of person who would willingly inhabit the same structure as other people. Let alone the plebeians working for her.

Like Catfish, Shawna didn't like aggressive, arrogant people. However, the difference between her and Catfish was that she knew that not everything was a personal slight. He had plenty of reason to be wary of people in positions of power, but hell, didn't everyone?

If you worked in the oil fields or on the technology side like Catfish, you discovered early on that some people had all the answers, all the power, and all the incompetence imaginable. All too frequently, they ended up managing a mission-critical area of expertise, resulting in accidents and needless casualties.

That's why Thomas' team had worked for him again and again. It wasn't the paycheck, which was great, but the respect he gave his team, that he always listened to their suggestions and often reformulated his plans based on their findings, had more than earned their loyalty.

He'd been adaptive. Confident, yes. Arrogant at times? Sure. But not when it mattered.

The real question with Moore was whether the misanthropic air surrounding her speech and behavior was genuine or manufactured. The idea it was the former terrified the hell out of her.

Moore had the power of M2 sitting beneath this facility. The substance's ability to consume anything biological and reproduce at an astonishing rate made it a threat to the entire planet's ecosystem. Moore held the keys to unleashing or destroying it. That power had been given to her when she rescued the samples from Ben Taub and HAL.

If someone fucked up and a sample escaped? It was because of her power. If the creatures were destroyed? Again, because of her power. And if she wanted to kill everyone who'd ever laid eyes on M2 or knew about it, that was her power, too. Shawna only hoped the woman had been sincere when she said her goal was for everyone to get through this and the samples destroyed. If not, they were all dead.

Shawna stepped out of the cart while Catfish grabbed the crutch from the back and carefully maneuvered himself to stand on the wet concrete.

"Got it?" she asked.

"Got it," Catfish said. "When do you think it's going to stop pissing on us?"

"Didn't you look at the weather report?"

"No. Why would I do that?"

Shawna shook her head. "Because you wanted to know."

"Really miss my phone," he said.

The sentries near the door nodded to them. Catfish smiled at them, although Shawna knew it was fake as hell. It was his way of saying "fuck you" without actually speaking.

The commissary doors were open, and a moody light shone from within. Shawna and Catfish stepped inside and felt like they'd entered the Twilight Zone.

A large round table had been set up in the middle of the dining room, and the unnecessary chairs and tables stood against the far wall. The round table was laden with real plates, real silverware, bottles of red and white wine, and quite a few potholders looking bereft of their payloads.

The HAL team had already been seated. Kate waved to them and pointed at the empty seats around the table.

Jay reached for the bottle of red near him, paused, and gestured to Neil. "You do it."

Nodding at Jay's embarrassed smile, Neil handed the bottle to Catfish and Shawna. "Bottoms up," he said.

Shawna held out her wine glass and allowed him to pour. Catfish sneered at the wine but accepted it. She had to stifle a laugh. He liked all things alcoholic, but wine was probably his least favorite. Now, if Moore had offered him bourbon…

She giggled as Catfish tentatively sniffed at the glass, his face recoiling slightly before trying another sniff. With a sigh, he took a sip. His face wrinkled as he swished the wine around his mouth. At last, he uttered a quiet burp.

"Not bad," he said.

Jay and Neil started laughing. Kate just held her head in her hands.

Shawna clapped him on the shoulder. "Y'all might want to just let it set on your tongue awhile." She leaned closer. "It's the polite way to drink."

"Oh, right," Catfish said, putting the glass down. "That was a very good Texas drawl," he said to her with an imaginary tip of the hat.

"Why, thank you," she said, batting her eyelashes.

Catfish blushed slightly and scratched at the unkempt patch of beard on his left cheek. "Welcome."

"Shawna?" Kate asked.

She turned to look at the lead scientist. Kate had ditched the lab coat for a thin sweater, its cuffs puffed out as though she were constantly pulling the fabric to her elbows. The woman was pretty. It was a shame this was probably the only time Shawna would see her out of a lab coat.

"Yes?" Shawna said.

Kate's smile faltered a little. "I didn't get a chance to catch up with you after the lab tour."

Shawna shivered. "No. You didn't."

"What did you think?"

"Most expensive I've ever worked in," she said.

That was no joke. PPE had had the best people, equipment, and management, but their labs hadn't held anything like what she'd seen in this facility.

Once you entered the airlock using your bracelet, an aerosolized chemical agent streamed through jets hidden in the wall to remove bacteria and virii. You then donned a heavy but flexible, well-air-conditioned pressure suit and a throat-activated mic.

She hadn't believed the procedures they walked her through. Jay and Neil had demonstrated the use of the portable incinerators, the oxygen cutoff system, and a "decontamination" cubicle large enough to fit three people. She'd frowned when she'd realized the cubicle was on a set of tracks.

"Does this thing move?" Shawna had asked.

"Move?" Neil had suddenly looked flustered. "Oh, right. Well, um—"

"For crying out loud, son," Foghorn Leghorn had said, "just get, I say, just get to the point, boy!"

"Shut up," Neil had muttered. "Decontamination might be a bit of a misnomer."

When he hadn't immediately continued, Shawna had said, "And?"

Jay had sighed loudly. "He's trying to tell you that one of two things happen if you go in there. You either get burned to a crisp by those soldiers over there or the lovely sergeant out there. Or, they move you to the quarantine level."

"Move you?" Shawna had asked. "What do you mean move?"

"It has those tracks," Neil had said, "because it's an elevator."

"Oh." Shawna had thought for a moment. "And why is there a

difference?"

"Damn, I wish Moore could have told you this instead," Neil had said.

"Fine, you wimp. I'll do it," Jay had said. "If your suit gets punctured or, um, dissolved in any way, you'll be moved to that chamber. Once you're inside, you'll be observed and asked what happened. While you tell your story and they review the cam footage, they'll assess how bad the damage is. But make no mistake, they'll fry you if there's more than a spot on you."

"Will they fry the lab too?" Shawna had asked, desperately trying to keep the fear from her voice.

Neil had pointed at the stainless steel walls. A large recessed LED monitor showed a split video view with a control panel. A quick look told her you could subdivide the screen into four windows, zoom, and pan.

"The lab room has three levels of security," Jay had said. "The first is a full UV spectrum blast, which your suit will get when you leave here. Any experiments with M2 will include a spotlight of harsh UV. If the sample escapes its box, it'll be instantly fried. The lab is lit so that even if a minuscule dot of M2 gets out, it'll be easy to spot. The placement guarantees there are no dark corners for M2 to hide in. No vents for it to crawl through. No way out.

"The second," he'd continued, "is for the area to be evacuated. The room will be aerosolized and ignited. Will create a fireball similar to a fuel-air bomb."

"Jesus," Shawna had said. "What's the third? A nuke?"

"The third," Neil had said, "is the lab, this corridor, and everyone inside this facility gets immolated, as well as the equipment and anything else. Nothing will escape."

Nothing will escape, she'd thought. *If anything sounded like famous last words, that phrase covered it.*

"Any questions?" Jay had asked.

"None whose answers will make me feel better," she'd said.

"That's how I felt," Neil had said, one hand rubbing absently at his bald spot. "And I helped design this portion of it."

Shawna had raised an eyebrow. "Wait. You, Kate, and Jay designed this?"

"We had a little help," Jay had said. "This facility existed long before we got here. It was made to handle a variety of possible pathogens or, um, biological entities."

"Government thought they would be incarcerating an ET in here. Just not the kind that eats everything," Neil had said.

Jay had said, "Facility underwent an upgrade about fifteen years ago. Guess the prospect of someone being dumb enough to bring down an asteroid sample, Martian soil sample, or something like that, put the fear of Beelzebub in someone. That's when they made the system more modular. We just had to include the stainless steel and a few additional M2-specific safeguards like the UV. The only problem is the goddamned power."

She'd turned from the view screens and frowned at Jay. "Power is a problem?"

"Not power for the facility," Neil had hastily said. "That's pretty well covered. No, it's the UV lights. We didn't exactly have time to reinvent the wheel, so we did the best we could. They can be unreliable."

Goosebumps had covered her skin. "How unreliable?"

Jay and Neil had exchanged a glance. Was this why they hadn't let Catfish down here? So he wouldn't freak out? Or was this particular parcel of information something they'd decided to let her in on rather than counting on Kate to do it?

"We have a lot of them," Jay had said, "to cover any shortfalls. But we can't have them on all the time. The bulbs will burn out too fast." He'd pointed at the lab area behind the glass. "Still, we'll have two soldiers with incinerators standing guard. If something happens inside there, M2 will have to survive the flames and escape the lab before the failsafes kick in. I wouldn't worry about it."

"Impressive," Shawna had said. "So now that I know all the ways I can die, can I see how I'm going to die?"

"That's right, my fellow humans," Jay had said in a radio announcer's voice, "'fatalism' is the word of the day at Miskatonic University!"

"Miska what?" Shawna had asked.

"Miskatonic."

"You mean from Lovecraft?"

"That's right, Shawna," Jay had said, "you win the Kewpie doll!"

Neil had shaken his head in exasperation. "Jay, I know you're nervous, but shut the hell up."

"M2 is such a boring name," Jay had said. "Besides, something with tentacles that we don't understand? Enough to defy the laws of physics, chemistry, and biology? A creature that can eat damned near anything on the planet?" His helmet had slowly shaken to and fro. "I don't know what could be more like an 'Elder God.'"

Shawna had considered that for a moment. "Point taken."

"He's so damned dramatic," Neil had said.

"Oh, my friend," Jay had said and mocked putting an arm around Neil's shoulder. "Let's not give her our old married couple routine until she's gotten to know us."

Shawna had giggled. "You are like an old married couple."

"See what I mean?" Jay had said. "All right. Let's show you the classroom."

* * *

"You okay?" Kate asked.

The lab. Kate was asking her about the lab. She bounced back to the present with a mental lurch. "Fine," Shawna said. "Just trying to remember if I had any questions."

"No worries," Kate said.

"Hey!" Jay said. "No shop talk! This is our inaugural dinner here at Miskatonic University."

Catfish turned to Shawna, a question on his lips. She held up a finger. "I'll explain later."

"Besides," Jay said after he took another sip. "I'm starving."

That didn't last long. A few moments later, Chef Robbie appeared, his hair tastefully tied back and a puffy chef hat poking the air. His chef's whites were immaculate, and she doubted he'd worn this set while cooking.

He placed steaming trays upon the potholders and opened each in turn. Steak. Fried chicken. Herb-crusted salmon. Roasted fingerling potatoes. Steamed mixed vegetables. Salad. Bread. It was like having a buffet at a swanky restaurant.

"I'll bring pitchers of water and iced tea momentarily," Robbie said. He made eyes with Catfish. "You want an energy drink?"

"No, thanks," he said.

Robbie nodded. "All right, tuck in and let me know if anything isn't to your liking," he said, quickly disappearing into the kitchen.

"Who's paying for all this?" Shawna asked.

Jay snorted. "I'm sure we are," he said. "Call it our hazard pay courtesy of the taxpayers. Let's eat."

CHAPTER FIFTEEN

During the meal, Shawna noticed that Robbie had provided Jay with two plates of diced, easily chewable pieces of meat. One look at Jay's burn glove told her he was unlikely to use a knife to cut. Every few bites, he winced as he manipulated the fork.

By the time they'd finished dinner and the dishes had been swept away, Shawna thought she would burst. Her head danced a little from all the wine she'd consumed, and everyone at the table had gone loopy.

Although their plates were set, Givens, Sarah, and Moore never appeared. Shawna thought that odd. They were either too "good" to eat with the geeks, or something else had their attention. She wasn't sure she wanted to know what that "something else" might be.

The lingering taste of peppercorn, heavenly protein, and a healthy serving of greens and beans overpowered her curiosity. Besides, all she wanted now was to waddle to the golf cart and drive to the trailer. Sleep was calling, and she was listening.

Jay, Neil, and Kate shared war stories about working at HAL, while Shawna regaled them with her trips to Nigeria, Saudi, and the UAE. While they discussed chemistry, she spoke more about the dysfunction and danger in the oil patch, some of which they already knew.

Catfish hadn't said much, and she wondered why. He was normally guarded but affable. Something had changed after *Leaguer*, or maybe something else was on his mind. She hadn't had a chance to get the skinny on the engineering area.

Robbie appeared one last time to make sure everyone had everything they needed. Catfish whispered something to him; he smiled and disappeared again into the kitchen. When he returned, he held a small grocery bag, placed it in front of Catfish, tipped his chef hat, and disappeared again.

"What's in there?" Shawna asked.

"Provisions of a sort," he said.

Shawna rolled her eyes.

"Well," Jay said, stifling a mighty belch, "I think it's time to hit the rack, as they say. Have to get up early."

"Early?" Catfish said. "Why early?"

Kate sighed. "Guess no one told you. We're only allowed in the lab between sunup and sunset."

Shawna asked through a yawn, "Another safeguard?"

"Yes," Kate said.

"What? Why only those hours?" Catfish asked.

Shawna touched his shoulder as if to impart a secret. "Because they want to make sure if M2 somehow gets out while we're handling it, it happens when the sun is up."

"Oh," Catfish said. "So it'll fry."

"Exactly," Kate said.

"Got it. Time for sunrise?" Catfish asked.

"0647," Jay said through a yawn. "Sunset at 1726."

Catfish whistled. "Still a long day."

"True," Jay said with a grin. "But we only work from 0730 to 1700, with as many breaks as we need. We can study film and results when we're not testing."

"Gotcha," Catfish said.

Jay looked at Neil. "You ready to go?"

Neil didn't bother stifling his burp, which rang in the dining room. "Yup."

Kate glared at him with exasperation, but it didn't look real to Shawna.

"Disgusting. Both of you." Kate said.

"We are," Neil admitted. "You hanging here?" he asked Kate.

She nodded. "Have work to do and a couple of personal things to handle."

"Ah," Jay said. "Let's go, driver. That cart ain't gonna drive itself."

"Wonder if I can get a DUI while driving a golf cart," Neil said.

"I'm sure you can, but not here," Jay said. "Let's go."

The two men said their goodbyes and disappeared. Shawna and Catfish were out of their chairs nearly as quickly.

Sarah waited for them just beyond the threshold with two large, green duffel bags at her feet. "Hello," she said.

"Hi," Shawna said. "Missed you at dinner."

Sarah smiled. "Don't worry. We ate. Here are the items Dr. Moore managed to get you. I understand there are some choice toiletries and other niceties in there."

"Who went shopping?" Catfish asked.

"I believe it was Dr. Moore," Sarah said.

"Cool." He tried to lean down to grab one but quickly decided that was a bad idea.

"I've got them," Shawna said, reaching down and picking up one of the heavy duffels.

"Shit," Sarah said. "Forgot about that." Sarah lifted the other one and easily placed it on her shoulder. "I'll throw it in the back for you."

The rain had stopped again, but the frigid, humid mist clung to every piece of exposed skin. Shawna knew it wasn't that cold, but dammit, it felt like it.

When they reached the trailers, Catfish couldn't stop himself from yawning. "I need a nap," he said. "It's still too early to sleep."

Shawna said nothing, but he was right. She still didn't know what time it was, but although the sun had been down for a long time, she couldn't believe it wasn't even 2100 yet. If she slept now, she'd be up at

0400. *If you sleep at all,* she thought.

That was the problem. Sleep had been hard to come by, although not for lack of opportunity. And after what she'd seen in the containment area, she wasn't sure she'd ever sleep again.

After unloading the two duffel bags and the small parcel Robbie had given Catfish, Shawna walked him to his trailer, opened the door, and ushered him inside. She left the duffel with her initials at the threshold and carried Catfish's to his bed. He didn't follow her.

When she returned to the living room, he had pulled three items out of the bag. A pint of Jim Beam, a small rectangular box, and an envelope. He stared at the words "Mr. Standlee" signed in neat cursive on the envelope's front.

Shawna wrinkled her nose and sat down next to him. "Who's that from?"

"Don't know," he said, "but I have a pretty damned good idea." With a sigh, he slid his thumb to break the seal and pulled out a single sheet of paper. It had no letterhead, stamp, or marks apart from the handwriting. She read it over his shoulder and grinned. He looked mortified.

"Mr. Standlee," Shawna said aloud, "it has come to my attention you have attempted to acquire cannabis from Chef Robbie. This violates your employment contract as you are to ask the facilities manager, which is myself, for all necessary provisions and not rely upon other employees to gather them for you.

"I also ask you not to imbibe any intoxicating substances two hours before your work hours, during your work hours, or before a scheduled emergency drill.

"Thank you for your understanding."

"Bitch," Catfish said.

"Holy shit," Shawna said. "Open the box."

He did. A small multicolored pipe the shape of a circumcised penis with a bell-shaped head stared back at them. Inside the box was a plastic baggie of plant bulbs, a tiny grinder, and pipe cleaners. Catfish blinked at it.

"She got me weed," he said. "You have to be kidding me."

Shawna laughed. "I can't decide if that woman is the devil or just snowing us all. Either way, she knows how to take care of her employees."

He shook his head. "I don't even know if I can trust smoking this shit. And that asshole Robbie? Ratting on me?"

"How do you know he ratted on you?"

"Because I gave him a damned note!" Catfish said.

"Oh," Shawna said. "And you really believe all those cameras didn't catch you writing the note or giving it to him or him reading it?"

He sighed. "Okay, fine. It was a stupid idea."

She pointed at the box, a wicked grin on her face. "No, seems like it was a perfect idea."

He glanced up at her. "You, um, want to, um—"

"Later," she said. "I need to take a look in my duffel and get it sorted."

"Oh, right," he said, "your OCD is kicking in."

"It is," she said. "Be back in a few minutes. Maybe you can move your lazy ass and unpack your own before you get too relaxed."

"Right," he said. "I'll have everything unpacked by the time you get back."

"You better," she said.

After lugging her duffel into her trailer, she opened it and found more than she'd asked for. Sanitary napkins, tampons, deodorant, toothpaste and toothbrush, dental floss, and condoms. She blinked at the condoms.

When the confusion passed at seeing the last item, she felt a flash of anger. Why the hell had Moore put these in here? And the nerve of her to do it! She just seemed to take it as a given that Shawna would want to fuck someone?

Not someone, a voice said in her mind.

Shawna's expression melted from anger into a sad smile. She picked up the pack of condoms, shook her head, and tossed them aside. The rest of the duffel had the clothes she desperately needed—a hoodie, a jacket, and running shoes. She scanned the sizes, more interested in comfort than style, to ensure they fit. The hoodie would be a little large on her, but so what? She stripped off the old sweater she'd been wearing, removed the tags, and slipped on the brand-new hoodie.

The slight chill in the trailer disappeared at once. Still wearing a smile, she unpacked and stored her supplies in the small chest of drawers while the toiletries ended up in the bathroom. All except, of course, for the cardboard package of condoms.

Sighing, she picked them up and shuffled them beneath one of her pillows. Next time she saw Moore, she'd slug the woman. A sudden blush lit her cheeks. That bitch would probably see the surveillance recordings of her unpacking and lingering over the pack of rubbers. *Hope you enjoyed the show,* she thought.

Shawna left the trailer, returned to Catfish's, and rapped on the metal door, but his voice was already yelling for her to come in.

He sat on the couch, his eyes riveted on the coffee table. Shawna followed his gaze. An unopened carton of cigarettes sat on the table next to an assembled vaporizer and a bottle of nicotine liquid. The unopened pint of Jim Beam and the box of cannabis paraphernalia sat next to it.

"Wow," Shawna said. "All your vices in one place."

He slowly nodded. "Damned near."

She sat beside him on the couch, her hands folded in her lap. "So, what's going on?"

"Ever since we saw that thing on *Leaguer*, I've wanted to smoke an entire carton in one puff."

"Okay," she said. "Apart from that being impossible, why in the hell would you want to do that?"

He shrugged. "Maybe because after seeing an oil slick kill over a hundred people and knowing it killed dozens more back here, I don't know what the hell is what anymore. When I pulled you off *Leaguer*? I thought for sure you were dead." His left eye glistened, but he continued staring at the table. "But I wasn't going to leave you there. Not for that thing to eat you or for you to burn." His lip quivered as though he were trying to hold back a sob. "Not for you to end up like Thomas."

Shawna's eyes moistened with unwelcome tears. She had no idea what to say. What could she say? That she was thankful? That he should have saved himself instead?

The oppressive silence finally broke as he spoke. "And now we're here," he said. "Trapped in this place with no way out but to go through it all over again. Thomas is still dead. JP is still dead. And M2 is alive and well." He shook his head in disgust. "And all I want to do is destroy it."

She tentatively placed a hand on his shoulder. "It will be," she whispered and kissed his cheek.

He flinched, his eyes opening wide in surprise. Catfish slowly turned his head, his gaze finally meeting hers. He wrapped his arms around her and kissed her lips. A few minutes later, she rushed back to the trailer while wishing she'd just brought the damned condoms.

CHAPTER SIXTEEN

Shawna stood near the blast door and peered at the hastily painted sign. The word "CONTAINMENT" had been printed in a clumsy, childish hand, the crimson letters running over a partially scraped away sign reading "Quarantine." Shawna glanced at Jay, a question on her lips.

"Containment is much more precise," he said in Elmer Fudd's voice. His nose grew and shrunk as though he were switching between himself and a human version of Fudd. "Quarantine is what happens when you get infected."

She found herself nodding. "I see what you mean."

Neil snapped his fingers. "Containment isn't more precise. It's more about function than precision."

Jay made a farting noise. "How do you figure that, Doc?"

Ignoring Jay's slip into Bugs Bunny's voice, Neil raised his hands as if it were elementary. "Containment is as precise in function as it is in name."

From behind her, Kate said, "It doesn't matter if it doesn't perform the function. It might as well be called 'security joke.'"

"*A* security joke," Neil corrected her.

"Oh, fuck off already," Kate said.

Shawna turned to look at her boss. Kate had eschewed her lab coat for a black blouse and slacks. Her skin appeared creamy and smooth in the contrast. "You changed."

"Of course I did. It's a party."

"Yeah, a meet-and-greet," Jay said. "An old friend is waiting for you."

"Don't forget the new guy," Neil said. "He's very interested in meeting you."

"More like eating her," Jay snickered.

Kate put her hands on her hips. "Stop that. Be nice to her. They're secure," she said and pointed to the blast door. The heavy steel suddenly turned transparent as if it had been a mirage all along. Beyond where the blast door had been, a large glass and steel enclosure housed a dented and aging oil barrel, the initials "PPE" practically glowing from its side.

"Not that one," Kate said, grabbing the back of Shawna's head and forcing her to gaze at the oversized glass box containing a large oblong tank. The tank's surface looked as though it had been patch-welded repeatedly, uneven seams covering damage that had occurred while it was being moved. Or maybe it was damaged from the inside.

"See?" Kate said, letting go of Shawna's head. "They're safe. But that storage tank? That's our friend Marie in there."

The storage tank marked "Taub" vibrated on its metal stand, the glass surrounding it quivering. A fine mist of dust erupted from the weld seams, and a line of liquid rose through a gap in the weld. The liquid streamed across the tank before breaking into dozens of tendrils.

She could hear the sound of crunching chip bags. Or maybe it was frying bacon. The thick liquid broke the welds, dissolving them as though they were organic instead of metal, and spawned hundreds of more tendrils. Some lightened slightly and rose from the tank's surface, each sprouting sharp talons. They dipped and bent and punched holes in the metal. More and more M2 leaked through, quickly surrounding the tank and obscuring it from view.

Shawna stood stunned, her body feeling like she'd been dropped in icy water.

"It's okay," Kate said from her elbow. Shawna turned to look at her. The scientist's sclera and iris had both turned to the color of dead stars. The orbs spun in their sockets, tiny tentacles squirming from the corners of Kate's eyes. "Marie just wants to thank you." Her voice had become thick as though she were drowning.

A talon extruded from Kate's chest and swung toward Shawna.

* * *

Shawna sat up in bed, her heart thumping in her ears. Catfish let out a snore, and she flinched, her hand immediately rising as if to strike him. She pulled up at the last second, her fear leading to confusion. She could just make out the shape of his body in the darkness before he rolled over on his side, his hand reaching for nothing.

Out of breath, she buried her head in her hands. She'd had nightmares ever since that first night on the lifeboat, but that had been a bad one. The worst.

The nightmares usually included M2 rolling over *Leaguer* like a tidal wave. Only in her dreams, the fire she started didn't destroy the living oil slick. In those, the creature put out the fire by drowning the flames. Its eyestalks then turned as one to look at her. No. Look into her, their dead gaze swallowing her.

But this? This was worse. After seeing the containment area, she shouldn't have been surprised. She sighed and slowly lay back down, doing her best not to bump Catfish. She held her hands together across her belly, fingers tapping in a nearly silent beat, her heart rate eventually slowing to match it.

Catfish grumbled and readjusted his arm, but he was still asleep. At least she hadn't woken him. She traced the edge of his elbow, the lines nearly invisible in the darkness.

I should have told you, she thought. *You asked, and I said I was fine. And now I don't know how to tell you.*

* * *

During her tour, she'd followed Jay and Neil to the elevator, and once it was underway, she'd noticed a tremor in Jay's hands.

"Feeling okay?"

Jay looked at her with a puzzled expression that slowly transformed into an embarrassed grin. "Always. Just have to take a few deep breaths."

The elevator dinged, and Shawna understood exactly what he meant. The facility's bottom level was nothing like the engineering or lab levels. Instead of looking well-maintained and secure, the south wall had developed a slight bow. A trickle of water flowed down the wall from a crack in the steel and concrete foundation.

"Come on," Neil said.

Shawna continued staring at the crack and noticed the constant buzz of the lights. The room wasn't nearly as bright as the lab or engineering levels. The fact it wasn't painted all white had something to do with it, but the concrete floor, aged and water-stained from ancient muck, seemed to dull the light. She knew it was an optical illusion, but it still gave her a shiver.

Unlike the lab and engineering levels, the containment level didn't have an airlock. Slabs of metal, sheets of aluminum, panes of incredibly thick glass, bundles of rebar, and sacks of concrete created a maze leading from the blast door to a large structure near the back wall. The steel on that wall gleamed as though polished, and the glass windows provided viewports into the room.

Shawna pointed with a slightly shaking finger. "Is that—" Her words trailed off into silence.

"Yeah," Jay said. "It's where they are."

Neil glared at Jay before flicking his eyes to hers. "If you don't want to see it, you don't—"

She forced herself to smile. "No, I'm fine. I just needed a second."

"God hates a coward," Jay muttered and walked to the containment enclosure.

Shawna saw that Neil was about to tell her the same thing again and decided to step forward before he could get it out. If she heard him say that again, she might take him up on it. But if she didn't see it for herself and prove the things were safely corralled, she wouldn't be able to sleep again.

Her heart rate hadn't increased, and neither had her breathing. Instead, they were both slowing, her body numbing with every step. She kept her eyes on the floor before her, not daring to look through the approaching windows. After reaching the heavy hatch separating the rest of the room from the containment tank, she stood still for a moment and tried to regain her composure. The fear had been ready to jump in, rule her, and leave her screaming and crying on the floor.

Neil dragged his feet slightly as he walked to join her. She chuckled nervously. The man was smart enough to try and not spook her.

"The hatch," he said, "is something they got from the Space Center. Or so I'm told. Scrap or something. Was the best we could do, although Moore is working on something better."

"What about the glass?"

Neil shrugged. "Same kind of stuff you'd get for a large aquarium. Should be able to handle a lot of stress. Again, Moore is working on something better."

Shawna gestured to the surplus construction supplies. "What happened here?"

"Didn't realize how bad the water damage was. And Moore had to put M2 somewhere. All those supplies?" Neil shook his head. "Those are for the walls. This place is leaking, and they will be plugging holes in it while they can."

"Jesus." Shawna saw a pattern on the wall and blinked. "What is that?"

"Det cord," Neil said. "Part of Moore's final solution protocol." He pointed to the containment enclosure. "Thermite and Semtex. Should create a dual-purpose wave of destruction. Shock wave detonates any

M2, and the thermite burns it to a crisp."

"Nice." Shawna walked around the hatch and to the side while keeping her eyes in front of her. She stood there for a moment with the viewport in her peripheral vision. Something moved. Her heartbeat froze for a beat before she turned her head and peered inside.

The storage tank from Ben Taub sat inside a large glass housing atop a thick sheet of steel. The glass wasn't crystal clear, appearing as though it were slightly fogged. Haphazard blisters riddled the tank's surface. Something inside had been pushing against its prison, and it was making headway.

She swallowed hard. "Neil? How long has it been trying to get out?"

The scientist scratched at his head. "Since the tank was transferred from Ben Taub, which happened a day after the incident. They had a hell of a time getting it down here. The cargo lift had been frozen stiff, and they had to get it fixed first, so the storage tank sat topside rigged with all the incendiaries Moore could find." He shrugged. "I'm guessing it's been trying to get out since it became trapped."

"I feel like I've been lied to," Shawna said. "I thought Moore said this entire facility had been retrofitted."

"It was. Well over a decade ago. And that was mainly to shore up the maintenance level. We had to add all the network lines and new sensors at the last second. Still working out the kinks," Jay said. He'd walked from the other side of the hatch to stand with them. "But even so, this place was never designed for something like M2."

She noticed several instruments connected to the glass enclosure. "Are those sensors?"

Jay nodded and said, "Seismic. Alerts security if M2 gets lively."

"How lively is it?" she asked.

"You don't want to know," Neil said.

Swinging her gaze to the smaller of the two housings, her breath hitched. There it was. The barrel. The stamped initials PPE stared at her in silent accusation. The letters looked odd, as though the ink had been unevenly spread. Then she realized the barrel's surface was warped and covered in blisters similar to those on the Ben Taub tank.

"M2," Shawna said to no one. She had filled and taken samples from that barrel and discovered a life form. Trapped inside the 30-liter barrel was the only known remaining link to the creature *Leaguer* had drilled into and the last sample they had of the original strain.

She pressed her hands against the glass and leaned close enough for her nose to touch. She remembered the oil sample in *Leaguer*'s lab moving off the table and coming after her. Thomas had saved her, but that's how it had all begun.

No, she thought. *JP getting infected was how it began, and you know it.*

That was more true than she wanted to admit. More than a hundred people on *Leaguer* had died because of the liquid organism inside that barrel. The substance had tested as an amazingly pure hydrocarbon, an oil so sweet it would take almost zero refinement. Fate's famous bait and switch had left humanity vulnerable to something otherworldly, something that shouldn't exist.

"How active is the barrel?"

"Active enough," Jay said, "although less so than the storage tank. I'm guessing that may be because it's much lower in volume."

"Do we know how much liquid is inside the tank?"

Jay and Neil exchanged a glance. Shawna suddenly felt as though she'd discovered a deep fear of theirs.

"Attempted measurements have been inaccurate," Neil admitted. "The liquid is moving."

"And changing form," Jay said. "That's not helping us. Best we can guess is between 250 and 300 liters."

Shawna's eyebrows raised in shock, her face paling. "300 liters?"

"Worst case scenario," Neil said. "Absolute worst case."

"Based on what?" Shawna asked.

"How much material was in the storage tank." Jay wiped his sleeve across his chin as if to scratch an itch. "I guess I mean how much we think was in there. Assuming fundamental physics hold."

"Jay," Neil said, "you can't break conservation of matter."

"As we know it. But those things," he said, pointing at the two containment enclosures, "don't seem to have much trouble breaking understood laws."

Neil opened his mouth to reply but dropped his head in grudging agreement.

"Speaking of physical laws, do we know how much damage they're doing to their metal cages?" Shawna asked.

Jay's face lit with an apologetic smile. "We wish."

* * *

Was that why she was awake now? Knowing they couldn't guarantee M2's imprisonment no matter what they did? That without her, the thing never would have made it to land? Was it the fear of the creatures' inevitable escape? Or was it guilt for Marie Krieger's death?

Shawna was an accomplice—unwitting, to be sure, but an accomplice just the same. Nothing would change that. The others who died at HAL and Ben Taub? That was on her for deciding to send the barrel for testing without a more specific warning. But that had been before she knew what it was and what it could do.

M2 was trapped. The barrel and storage tank were still secure. Neil said they were monitored 24/7 with armed guards, and no blind spots in coverage were allowed. Security monitored motion and vibration readings for spikes or signs of metal fatigue, although no one knew the actual readings—Moore wasn't sharing that information.

Catfish said something in his sleep. Suddenly cold, she pulled the blanket up to her neck and rolled over. He twitched slightly as she draped an arm around his shoulder, his body stiffening before relaxing again. Hugging his warm body, she shook off the remnants of the nightmare and fell back asleep.

CHAPTER SEVENTEEN

Catfish's eyes flipped open at the sound of an alarm, and he sat up in confusion, his messy mop of hair falling into his eyes. It took him a moment to determine where the sound was coming from. Something caught his waking eyes, and he swung his head. It was the TV. Instead of the guide channel or a specific program, a notice blinked on the screen.

"Breakfast is at 0630 through 0715. Lab and Engineering work hours begin at 0730. Have a good day." The message remained, but the TV had stopped its alert sound.

'What. The. Hell." Catfish rubbed at his eyes. A hand pressed gently against his back, and he turned like a zombie to peer down at Shawna. A tangled cocoon of sheets wrapped her naked body, leaving her bare from the breasts up. "Hi."

"Hi," she said, her cheeks blushing slightly. "Is it time to be awake?"

"Yeah," he yawned. "I think Orwell's thought-police knew the moment I woke up." He shook his head. "I'm too tired to be creeped out by that." He lay back down next to her, one arm draping over her belly. She nestled into him, and he kissed her cheek. "Is this awkward?"

Shawna blinked at him. "Is it?"

"No," he laughed. "Thought it would be, but it's not."

She smiled. "No," she said, kissing his nose. "It's not."

Even as tired and sore as he was, he felt different somehow.

Yesterday, everything seemed futile. But not today.

Am I really that shallow? I just needed to get laid to find hope? He shook his head.

"What?" she asked.

"Just stupidity," he said. "Fuck breakfast. Let's just stay here and sleep."

"No," Shawna said. "What time did the TV say it was?"

He yawned again. "0600. No one should be awake at this hour."

"Catfish, millions of people in this city are awake right now."

"Exactly," he said. "And imagine how few road rage incidents there would be if they got more sleep."

"I give up," she said, smacking him with the pillow. "I need to get dressed and hit my trailer."

"To what? Change clothes? Or shower?"

"Both," she said.

Catfish pouted. "Was hoping we could shower together."

She laughed while buttoning her jeans. "In there? I doubt you'll fit in that damned thing."

"Shit. You're right. Oh, well."

"Not a bad idea, though." She planted a kiss on his cheek and grinned. "I'll be back soon. Better be ready for breakfast when I am. Because I'm hungry."

"Hungry for—" He let the words trail off and leered at her.

Shawna blushed. "Food," she said and mock punched him in the stomach.

"Hurry. I'm hungry, too."

She left the trailer, and it immediately felt as empty as it had been before last night. With a sigh, he crutched to the shower.

As he stepped into the tiny cubicle, so crowded he could barely move without slamming his elbows into the sides, he turned the tap to "H" and immediately regretted it. Cold water jetted down on his bare shoulders, every pore of his skin turning to gooseflesh.

Shivering and cursing, he held himself as best he could while he waited for the water to warm. He didn't have long to wait. Once the jets reached a temperature high enough to produce steam, he fought to keep all of his body in the water at once. It wasn't possible.

As quickly as he could, he shampooed his hair, soaped himself down, and rinsed. Three-minute shower. That's all he could stand this morning. Maybe he should ask Moore if the project's barracks, the mostly abandoned building where the HAL team slept, had community showers because this was ridiculous.

He wrapped a towel around his head and rapidly rubbed the excess moisture from his skin. As humid as the air was outside, he would probably have a damp shirt for the rest of the day, especially since it would take several hours for his hair to completely dry.

Shivering and wishing he'd turned the heat on, he dressed himself while icy beads of water continued rolling down his back from his wet hair. Damn, it was cold. Errant droplets sprinkled on the trailer's carpet, but he didn't notice.

Once dressed, he crutched back into what passed for the living room, and the table caught his eye. The pot, the alcohol, the vape, and the cigarettes were all still there. Untouched.

Catfish sighed, cracked the seal on the value pack of lighters, and put two in his jeans pockets. He hoped Moore knew he'd be carrying those with him at all times. In truth, the chances of the lighters being helpful were damned near nil, but they were a nice security blanket until he managed to create something better.

"Like she'd ever allow that," he said.

He was sure Moore's people had run all sorts of psychological hoodoo tests on them, profiled them, and had conclusions about what he and the other team members would do in certain situations.

Moore might know he would destroy the entire facility if given half a chance. Maybe one of the reasons he hadn't been invited into the lab area was that she was afraid of what he would do. Then again, she allowed him lighters and did the same for Shawna.

Moore was complicated. Either she was playing a game he had yet to figure out, or she truly wanted them protected from a possible "mishap."

"Or maybe, just maybe, she's insane," Catfish mumbled to himself.

That was a possibility. Only question was whether she was like this before the M2 incidents or after. Maybe the sight of that liquid, alive and dead at the same time, and the horrible things it could do, tore something apart inside, and now she warred with two personalities—one that wanted to do her job and the other that wanted to do the sane thing and nuke the creatures before they threatened anyone.

He shook away the thoughts. None of it mattered right now. Shawna would be back any minute, and he wanted to make sure he was ready. His stomach gurgled and growled as though it were trying to consume him from the inside, but there was something more important than food.

In a little over an hour, he'd be locked inside the engineering floor while she was in the lab. He would be protected by multiple steel walls and UV light. To study M2, a creature that was killed by that very same light, Shawna and her team had only a wall of glass and steel to protect them from the canisters' confines. If the creature got loose from its containment shells or the samples somehow broke through their barriers, Shawna would be facing the things head-on.

In other words, he'd be powerless to help if anything happened.

I'd be stuck on the outside with no way in, he thought.

Not that it would matter if Moore went ahead and just flash-fried everyone to ensure M2 didn't escape the facility.

In light of that, he had to cherish every moment with Shawna. Every meal. Every word. Every touch. Either one of them could die later today. Either one of them could just disappear, never to be seen again. That was the reality now. That was how things would be until the "project" ended.

"Hey!" Shawna called from outside. "You ready?"

Catfish blushed as he fastened his belt. "Be there in a sec." He strode to the table, picked up the vape, smiled at it, and broke open a carton of cigarettes. He placed the liberated pack into his pocket without unzipping the plastic strip. He'd open it later, he was sure of it, but right now, the hard rectangular container of 20 death sticks felt just as reassuring as the touch of Shawna's hand on his.

* * *

After a more subdued breakfast than the day before, Moore waited for them at the commissary door. She was dressed in all black, her pale face appearing to glow in the contrast.

"Mr. Standlee," she said.

"Catfish."

"Yes, Catfish." Her thin smile twitched in annoyance. "It's time for you to see the doctor."

He furrowed his brows. "For what?"

"I believe to get you off those," she said, a long finger pointing at the crutches. "And into a walking boot."

"About time," he said, trying not to show how much the foot already ached. He'd been afraid to take too many of the pain pills, but he'd maxed out on the anti-inflammatories for all the good they were doing him.

After saying goodbye to Shawna in the elevator, Givens appeared from an adjoining hallway, his face set in his typical bored expression.

"You taking me to the doc?"

The man nodded but didn't speak. He pointed to the main door, and Catfish followed him through, the crutches making his pace slower than the soldier's. Givens led him to another golf cart, and Catfish raised an eyebrow.

"Surgeon's here?"

Givens nodded. "You getting in, or you want to crutch?"

With a shrug, he got into the passenger seat after stowing his crutches. "Onward, James."

"Fuck you," Givens muttered and put the cart in drive.

They weaved through several supposedly abandoned buildings until they reached a four-story complex with a caduceus on the side of it. Givens parked in the handicapped space and shuffled out.

"Hey," Catfish said, "we don't have a sticker."

Givens looked amused. "So? You're the only cripple on the spaceport right now."

"Meaning what?"

"Meaning you have a little hospital all to yourself. This puppy," Givens said, pointing to the building, "was never open to the public. Not meant to be either. At least not anymore."

This is insane, Catfish said to himself. The spaceport had been closed and in limbo for years, yet it had a hospital? When he made it inside, he finally understood.

The building's facade may have been complete, but the clinic was barely finished and appeared as though a single surgery room had been brought to completion. He hardly remembered anything about coming off the plane and being whisked straight into a medical facility, but that's what must have happened. When he awoke, he'd been in a guarded room that was not in this building.

Two nurses and a doctor awaited them in the unpainted lobby. They took X-rays. They prodded and poked. They warned him about overdoing it. They told him not to remove the boot unless he was going to sleep, and even then, he had to wear a brace to keep his ankle from moving. Did he understand? Here are some pills. Be a good boy. Now, get the hell out.

The boot's hard plastic crunched on a few kicked-up pieces of gravel, and Givens glanced at him as they returned to the golf cart.

"Ready to work now?" Givens asked.

"Already was." Catfish peered up at the soiled cotton sky. "More rain?"

"Who gives a damn. Hey, about what we talked about yesterday?"

Catfish turned and peered at him. "What about it?"

"How big of a boom?"

In the few hours before work was halted yesterday, he and Givens had written down requirements for a weapon. Fortunately, it appeared they had plenty of material to print nearly as many prototypes as they could imagine.

"I think we're looking for two sticks of dynamite worth. I think that will puncture whatever M2 tries to grow but would probably scatter it all over the goddamned world."

"Doubt it would have done much to what we saw at Ben Taub," Givens said with a shake of his head. "Took a couple of oxygen tanks worth of explosion."

The golf cart squeaked and rattled as Givens drove it down the pockmarked, uneven concrete. Catfish looked out over the fields and listened to the drones constantly landing and taking off before beginning their training sorties.

Boom. He wanted a big boom, and he wanted it portable. Moore had told him she wanted something easy to make, something they could 3D print rather than waiting for large manufacturing facilities. Although he imagined it was mainly to keep the project a secret.

Fewer people involved in the weapon's creation meant fewer possible leaks. Catfish imagined Moore would have a fit if he suggested they bring in outside help. He had some ideas about that, but it would take another conversation with the dragon lady, which was not something he looked forward to.

Big boom. How to create a big boom? He supposed they could print something spherical with the same basic characteristics as a frag grenade. He'd want to test different timing mechanisms for the trigger, but it might work.

"You got any grenades on base we can look at? Hopefully, dud ones?"

Givens laughed. "I'm sure we can find something. What do you need? Frag? Pineapple? Flashbangs?

"Frag. I think it needs to be spherical."

"Shit," the soldier said, "you know your grenades."

"Too many video games."

They left the main road, such as it was, and returned to the facility. After parking in the grass, Givens grabbed the crutches from the back.

"We'll keep 'em here in case you need them," Givens explained.

"Oh, okay," Catfish said. He didn't like the sound of that. In case he needed them? In case of what? If he lost his foot to testing an explosive?

Catfish was learning to walk with the boot now, the rocking motion becoming more and more natural. He'd tried to fight it at first, attempting to force the boot to act like a foot or push it in the right direction, but that's not how it was supposed to function. Instead, you just had to let it do the work and have some trust.

By the time they reached the Engineering level, Catfish's foot was letting him know just how unhappy it was. Fortunately, the pain was below a five. Annoying as hell but workable.

Givens left Catfish alone in the lab while he procured some dummy explosives. At least Catfish hoped like hell they'd be duds; otherwise, his day was about to get a lot more interesting.

After logging in, Catfish looked up information about explosives and metal tensile strengths. It was going to be a long day of researching and designing. Then, he'd have to simulate the explosions and let the computer take out much of the guesswork.

This was going to take a while. He hoped Moore realized that. Otherwise, she would be deeply disappointed.

CHAPTER EIGHTEEN

Shawna stood inside her heavy bio-suit, her hands inserted into the thick gloves protruding through the steel walls and into the room. Darkness bathed the metal piping that delivered the droplets, but the area around the worktable was a UV kill zone. If a sample escaped during distillation, it would be fried instantly by the concentrated slashes of deadly light emanating from the walls, the ceiling, and the floor. If not for the worktable's overhang, the droplets would be vaporized before they left the reservoir.

Still, if M2 managed to get to her gloves, wasn't she dead? Jay had promised that as long as she kept her hands on the tools, M2 couldn't reach her. After she'd worked with the gloves, it was apparent why.

The heavy gloves remained nearly 7 cm away from the shadowy darkness enveloping the stainless steel tools. The room's sensors were calibrated to find temperature deviations. If there was a massive drop in temperature, say from an excess of liquid flowing through the reservoir spouts, the bright white light would erupt into the overhang.

Kate's team seemed to have thought of nearly everything. M2 didn't appear in infrared except as a cool spot before disappearing into the background. The creature either generated its own heat or rapidly absorbed the ambient temperature of its environment. That had been the first official physical test, but it also involved filming the behavior of the droplets from each reservoir in separate workspaces.

Kate had offered Shawna her choice of specimens: M2 from the ocean, which they had named Poppy, or the creature captured at Ben Taub known as Taub. Jay had demanded Cthulhu and Hastur, but Kate nixed both, pointing out how difficult they were to say, much less remember.

Yes, that fight had taken a while. It ended after Kate told Jay he was being childish, and he uttered a Foghorn Leghorn impression that made them all smile. Waggling his eyebrows, he'd finally said, "Boring. But okay. The lady always wins." He glanced at Shawna, holding his hand to the side so only she could see him. "I've also been told she's the boss."

"Jackass," Kate said. "Get to work."

Shawna had picked Poppy. After all, it was the original specimen *Leaguer* had captured from the M2 Trench and drained into a test barrel of oil. That specimen had never seen *Leaguer*'s deck, but it had infected at least three personnel, including JP Harvey, a long-time member of Shawna's team.

The M2 creature from that test barrel had also infected a HAL employee, incubated inside her, and ultimately gave birth to other creatures when it was cut off from escaping the storage tank. The entities remaining in the pipes had then rampaged through the hospital.

Neil took Taub.

"How you doing, Shawna?" Kate asked over the helmet comms.

"Fine," Shawna said as she held the partition no more than a centimeter above the worktable's glass and metal surface. The reservoir dispenser descended until it hung 3cm from the worktable. "Ready," Shawna said.

"Ready here, too," Neil said, his voice crackling slightly through the helmet's comms.

"1 ml of M2, Shawna."

Kate counted down from five, and the dispenser flashed red. A single, measured drop of the creature fell from the nozzle and struck the metal sheet. Holding her breath, heart beating fast, Shawna positioned the partition and quickly lowered it, the thin metal sheet cutting the droplet in half.

Grinning, she activated the worktable's magnetics, and the partition immediately clamped to the worktable. The resulting size of the droplets would hardly be scientifically accurate, but there hadn't been a better, safer way to divide them, not if they wanted to get at least the first round of tests done. Maybe after the first week, they could have engineering print them some new calibration equipment for this task. *If we survive that long*, she thought.

The dispenser rose from her worktable and resumed its position in the bright white light. Shawna pulled her arms out of the lab's glovebox and shivered. She was done with that, at least for the moment.

"Neil?" Kate said and began her countdown. Through the monitor, Shawna watched the bio-chemist perform the same operation. When he was finished, he stepped back and seemed to tremble slightly.

Jay exhaled heavily over the comms. "Well, that went well."

Neil barked something that might have been a laugh or maybe an effort to keep anxious bile from spewing out of his mouth. If it was the latter, she knew how he felt.

"Well done," Kate said. "Security? We are red."

"Copy."

Hopefully, that meant the security desk sergeant no longer had her hand over the big button that would turn the lab into a thousand-degree inferno. That was another reason Shawna had been shivering—it was the first time they had used the equipment, and it was the first time she'd interacted with the substance since *Leaguer*. The memory of her first encounter with the thing while performing the initial analysis of the find haunted her. If not for Thomas, M2 would have consumed her.

The idea that those little droplets could infect her and slowly turn her into a new creature, one large enough to take shape and walk, had terrified her the moment they'd devised this test. But they had to know what they were dealing with; otherwise, if it did get loose, they'd have no data and only guesses. A guess wasn't good enough, not with neighborhoods less than two kilometers away and the fourth largest city in the country just a few kilometers north of the facility.

A ring of glowing yellow lights turned red—a warning indicator someone was playing with the M2 samples, just in case no one else noticed. The color change hardly seemed necessary and did little to relieve her stress. Yellow meant warning, which indicated everything was status quo. Red meant the team was experimenting with M2 and that a sample was contained in one of the labs. Shawna asked what color it changed to when M2 got loose.

Kate swallowed hard. "They'll get bright white, and you'll get a hell of a sunburn," she said. "But at least you'll know."

Shawna shivered again and stepped away from the transparent partition separating them from the inner lab. She followed the other three to the main monitors and sat beside Kate.

Neil activated a control panel, and two metal and glass hemispheres dropped from the ceiling. They each descended to provide another shell around the sample containers. The array of large monitors came to life, each screen displaying a feed from one of the dozen cameras inside the hemisphere.

"Kate?" he said. "You want Poppy or Taub?"

Her face twitched. "Shawna and I will take Poppy."

"Okay, Jay," Neil said. "Let's get to it."

Kate smiled at her. "Now it's time to get geeky. I'll dial in the cameras to study the organism. We can set a few filters for each one so we can observe any physical changes while we run the tests."

"Oh, good," Shawna said. "Can't wait to see down its gullet."

"Not funny," Kate whispered.

Four tiny dots of black lit up beneath the barely visible fluorescent light. Shawna watched as Kate calibrated the cameras, each zooming in like a microscope, making the tiny dots look as large as dinner plates. And there it was. M2 in all its volatile, hazardous, predatory glory. At this size, it was an impossibly smooth pond of darkness rather than an amorphous body sprouting taloned tentacles.

Shawna's heart rate spiked unexpectedly, and her lungs felt as though they couldn't get enough air. Distilling had been terrifying, yes, but that fear had strangely kept her from freezing. Now that she had time to look at it and remember its potential power and ravenous nature, she didn't think she could move.

"You okay?" Kate asked.

Shawna started. "Yeah," she said, the word a shade above a whisper.

"Liar," Kate said. "Don't feel bad. Took me a couple of days to get used to looking at it."

"What? I thought this was the first time?" Shawna said.

Kate kept staring at the droplets on the screen. "Someone had to test the equipment," she said, nodding to the monitor. "We were as safe as we could be, and the sample was only out of the dispenser for less than five seconds before it was obliterated, but yeah." Her voice trailed off for a moment. "Terrifying."

"Okay," Neil said. "We're ready."

"Same here," Kate said. "We're recording."

Shawna and Kate sat in silence while waiting for something to happen. The other two were doing the same with Taub. Why? Because the creatures were there. The cameras had sensors to detect movement, such as ripples in the liquid or if the sample changed shape or position.

But what else was there to do? Have a cup of coffee outside the labs once you went to the trouble of decontaminating your suit and going through it all over again just to get back inside? It wasn't worth it. In a way, she hoped something would happen. The smaller they could keep the samples, the better. If they had to move up to several milliliters, the risk of an escape grew.

After five minutes, Jay began muttering Looney Toons lines. After a minute of that, Neil was telling him to shut up. Then, they were swapping stories. And still, nothing happened.

The temperature sensors didn't trip, the droplets remained motionless, and nothing was out of the ordinary.

Kate sighed. "Is it just begging for trouble to tell you I'm bored?"

Shawna stifled a laugh. "Yes," she said. "But I was thinking it."

"Neil? What do you think?" Kate asked.

"No temperature change," he said. "It matched the tanks' recorded temperatures and immediately rose to the lab's ambient temperature. The same as the worktable."

"Well, that was a letdown," Shawna said. Her brows wrinkled together a moment later. "But it's not. Not really."

"What do you mean?" Kate asked.

Shawna couldn't help but grin. "No data means no data. Okay, so it's not generating heat, and it's not consuming heat. We put the droplets on sterilized metal slabs. There's nothing for them to consume. Nothing. They're in a vacuum."

"Shit," Jay said. "She's right."

"That pushes our timing a bit," Neil said. "We can run the color tests for another ten minutes or so, vary the temperatures of the slabs, and see if there's any significant change."

Shawna waited for Kate to say something, but the silence lingered.

Finally, Kate said, "Won't be scientifically precise."

"Why?" Shawna asked.

"Because the samples are starting at ambient temperature in an ambient environment. Simply cooling the plate isn't the same thing as—"

Jay snorted. "Kate? We can't even put chemical agents on this shit to see what it is. Not until we figure out just how large a sample we need."

"Look," Neil said, "this is going to be guerrilla science no matter what we do. We can't handle the substance, and we can't do something large scale until we determine the small scale." He coughed. "And that's going to take some out-of-the-box thinking."

"Neil?" Jay said. "Say it in non-corporate speak."

Neil shrugged. "We make it up as we go along."

"Right," Kate said. She sounded as if she were smiling. "Do it."

The waiting game continued, but at least they had data now. The substances didn't react until the temperature descended to 0°C.

Their liquid surfaces began to harden as if growing a shell, but there, the similarity ended. The Poppy droplets rippled before hardening. Shawna slid her gaze to the monitors covering the Taub samples and inhaled quickly.

Infinitesimal spikes rose from the Taub droplets' shells. Neil zoomed in on the droplets, the camera resolution decreasing slightly before righting itself. As the lenses refocused, the tiny protrusions became more clear. They weren't spikes. They were hairs.

"Well, I'll be, I say, I'll be dipped in shit!" Foghorn Leghorn said.

"Neil?" Kate pointed at the Taub monitors. "What the hell is that?"

"It's—" He sounded like he was trying not to laugh. "Those are hairs. Like those of a spider."

"A spider," Shawna said.

"Like a tarantula. Plenty of non-mammals have them," he said.

Shawna looked back at Poppy. The twin droplets appeared to have become completely solid, but that didn't mean their surfaces weren't strange, too. No hairs, but the shell seemed more like something you'd find on a lobster or crab.

"Why would they not respond in the same manner?" Shawna asked no one.

Jay laughed. "Different strokes for different homicidal ooze sources?"

"What's the difference," Kate said, ignoring Jay, "between Poppy and Taub?"

"One was in the barrel," Shawna said, "and never came in contact with humans. And the other," she said, voice trailing off.

"The other," Neil said, "ate God only knows what before it was captured in the tank."

Shawna stood from her chair, her eyes flicking between the two. "The creatures that rampaged through Ben Taub," she said. "They looked more, well, spiderish in nature. Maybe crab-like?"

"Yeah?" Neil said. "And?"

Shawna couldn't put the words together to describe the horror movie now running through her thoughts. "Jesus," she said.

"Shawna?" Kate said. "What is it?"

She stepped back from the monitors, struggling to catch her breath. "Crustaceans versus mammals," she said. "Poppy never had a chance to consume anything but what was in the ocean. Or pretty close to it."

"So—" Jay took a deep breath and slowly exhaled. "Taub came out of a human being," he said flatly.

"And I don't know of any non-mammal sea creatures that grow hair for warmth or as sensory organs," Neil said. "I think that's a terra firma thing."

"Okay," Kate said. "So what's the hypothesis?"

"M2 evolves to match its prey?" Shawna whispered.

The comms went silent for a moment. When Jay finally spoke, he sounded as monotonic as she had. "Maybe it evolves to match its environment. The fauna and flora available." He swallowed hard, the clicking sound unmistakable. "Poppy wouldn't know anything about hair or skin. All it would know are crustaceans, cephalopods, some really strange fish, and not much else. Pretty sparse habitat at two kilometers below sea level, let alone ten."

"Harsh habitat, too," Neil said. "Up here, there's no pesky pressure to put up with. Bacteria, viruses, dust from animal hide, pollen, you name it, is flying through the air no matter where you are." He pointed at the wall separating them from the M2 samples. "Unless you keep them in an artificial vacuum."

Taub's surface appeared solid and dully reflected the fluorescent light through what looked like ice crystals. Looked like, but wasn't. When she'd studied a sample of M2 from the test barrel before it was shipped to HAL, she'd found it to be an almost impossibly excellent oil for refining. If it contained any water, she'd have found it then.

She looked back at Poppy. It, too, had produced crystals around itself. "Wow," Shawna said.

Kate turned her helmet to look at her. "What?"

"It's crazy," she said. "But if their evolution has diverged, how much has it diverged?"

"I don't think I want to know where this is going," Jay said.

Neil had stopped watching the monitors and was watching her instead. "What are you suggesting, Shawna?"

"Well," she said. "Once we establish a baseline for heat and cold tolerances, which we're doing now, we start studying stimuli. See if the samples react differently."

"You're insane," Jay said. "Or you need to share your drugs."

"Oh, man," Neil said. "I see what you mean, but I think we're a long way from that."

"I know," Shawna said. "Might take days to get to that step."

"But," Kate said, "we're going to have to feed them at some point if we want to track substantive variations in their growth. We'll just need to see how they respond to different materials. And," she said, "if we have to destroy these, we'll do the same with the next batch. Agreed?"

Jay and Neil agreed. Jay sounded morose, while Neil sounded relieved. After a few seconds, Shawna almost regretted bringing it up. If Catfish were here, he'd be throwing one hell of a tantrum.

"Then let's finish this batch of tests," Neil said.

Shawna looked at the monitor. The temperature inside the sample boxes had dropped to -15°C.

"No other changes," Neil said.

"Well," Kate said, "reverse it slowly, and we'll see how they react."

The team chatted, developing new experiments centered around Shawna's idea. Even Jay seemed to have come around. Kate furiously tapped on her tablet, filling the notepad with their plans while the specimen slabs gradually warmed. Once the ambient temperature reached above freezing, the crystals disappeared. They didn't evaporate or melt. Instead, they seemed to be reabsorbed. At 2°C, the hairs disappeared on the Taub samples, while the Poppy samples lost all solidity. At 5°C, both Taubs returned to their liquid states.

The chatter slowly died down as the team's attention refocused. Scientifically speaking, the 3°C variation between Poppy and Taub reaching their nominal state was significant. The test was hardly as controlled or precise as it needed to be, but the differential suggested, in Neil's words, "Further studies are required."

Shawna smirked. Moore would probably have kittens if she discovered her scientists were being scientists. Then again, there was something to be said for finding M2's limitations. That was the real reason they were here, wasn't it? To discover how to slow it, stop it, and kill it?

"When you were testing M2," she asked Kate, "what's the highest temperature you used?"

Kate thought for a moment. "Jay? Do you remember?"

"Yeah," he said. "350°C."

Shawna pointed at the specimen boxes. "You can't get it that high, can you?"

"No," Jay agreed. "But at that temperature, M2 transformed, or at least attempted to. It ultimately turned to ash and crust, but we don't know at what temp."

350°C was more than high enough to extinguish any complex biological life she could think of save for certain bacteria. "So then the question is, at what temperature does M2 perform a state change?"

"Don't know that either," Kate said. "But we did see water vapor."

Shawna felt the world drop. "That's impossible."

"No," Jay said. "It happened. But we didn't exactly know what we were looking at. Maybe if we'd known it was going to try and eat us later, we'd have been more thorough."

"No doubt," Shawna said, ignoring his sarcasm. "We don't have the means to test that, do we?"

"Not at this second, no," Kate said. "Have to requisition it from Moore."

"Okay," Shawna said. "How hot can we make the sample boxes?"

"About 150°C," Neil said. "Give or take a few degrees."

When Kate spoke, Shawna could hear a grin in her voice. "Security? Going to bring up the temp. We might have a flash."

"Copy," the sergeant said. "Proceed."

Flammability. All the M2 survivors made the same claim—this shit burned hot. A flare gun on *Leaguer*, a battery bomb at HAL, and makeshift oxygen tank bombs at Ben Taub. In each case, M2 caught fire, causing its size to shrink rapidly, its appendages flailing in panic before turning to ash. Or it simply exploded.

But there were some differences. Poppy had never really grown the skin the Taub specimens had. When the Taub creatures had reached a significant size, their shells were different, like a cross between an insect and a mammal. However, no one had seen them form those protective barriers when M2 was this small.

As Shawna watched the green LED numbers for a rise in temperature, she wondered if these specimens were large enough to exhibit the behaviors they were most interested in. She hoped she was wrong.

At 48°C, the changes began to happen. Poppy's surface rippled with bubbles, the droplet seeming to vibrate as the temperature increased. Taub's, on the other hand, jerked spasmodically as though something inside was trying to get out.

Neil and Jay both took a step backward in reflex.

When the temperature reached 100°C, the bubbles on Poppy's surface began to burst. The tiny particles ejected from the mass glittered in the deadly UV light like cinders escaping a campfire.

When the temperature reached 120°C, Poppy detonated as though it had been packed with dynamite and someone had lit an instantaneous fuse. But Taub just kept getting more strange. Whatever jerked and moved inside the droplet finally punched out of the incredibly dark liquid. It froze halfway from the droplet's top to the slab's surface.

A second later, the Taub samples were destroyed in the same fashion as the Poppys. The sample boxes were empty. The stainless steel glowed where the droplets had been and appeared impeccably polished rather than scarred or smudged by the explosions.

Shawna exhaled heavily. "They're destroyed?"

"Good question," Neil said.

While Kate and Neil rolled back the footage of the specimens' destruction, Shawna studied the lab's security feeds. The pristine antiseptic floors and walls shined blemish-free. The UV light concentration was unchanged, and no gases were emitted inside the sample boxes. In essence, the droplets might as well not exist.

"Check this out," Neil said.

He touched the tablet in front of him, and the Taub monitors replayed a time-lapse of the specimens in their frozen state to the moment they exploded. The footage showed Taubs' hairs retract into the droplets, tiny waves of motion rippling across their surfaces. As the temperature indicator rose on the playback, the Taubs seemed to solidify slightly. Shawna hadn't noticed that before, and it wasn't as dramatic a change as it had been as the creature froze, but it was there nonetheless.

Neil had added another filter to the sequence, and the last 200 frames that captured the creatures' destruction dropped in frames per second (FPS) to ten. Those last 20 seconds of footage, the mysterious appendage that popped out and the violent shaking across the droplet before it flashed into nothing, horrified her. It was as though something alive, alive by human standards anyway, had been trapped inside. If given a chance to survive, what would it have done?

The Poppy footage was much less dramatic. There was no movement inside the droplet or radical modifications to its surface apart from the vibrations and waves that had rippled across it. Kate slowed the FPS a few seconds before the specimens disappeared. There was little warning they would explode; their surfaces shook in one galvanic movement before they flash-fried into nothing.

Something tugged at Shawna's mind. "Can you roll that back?"

"Sure," Kate said.

Shawna watched the film loop again, willing her subconscious to point out what she had seen but not understood. "Again." This time, she found the few frames. "Stop."

The feed came to a halt, and Kate looked up at Shawna. "What is it?"

"There," Shawna said, pointing her finger at a speck hovering above the droplet. Dozens of others dotted the top and bottom of the frame. They were ill-defined, but one stood out. It was there for only two frames, but finding the path it had taken wasn't difficult.

The bright yellow particle that had escaped the droplet's surface had left an indentation in the droplet itself. M2 had shed its material. Shed. That was the word her brain had been turning over. She grinned.

"See it now?"

"No," Kate said.

"There. See that pucker mark? I bet every particle that exploded off the droplet's, well, shell left one of those in its wake. It's like M2 was shedding itself. Some form of asexual reproduction, maybe?"

"Reproduction?" Jay sighed. I thought they only reproduced when cut in twain or if another ate them."

"No," Neil said. "I think she's right. Think about it. The organism is about to die. It knows it's going to die on some instinctive level and attempts to spread itself. To live. Survive."

"Christ," Jay said. "So now you're telling me the things send out spores?"

Shawna shivered. She suddenly wished both HAL and Ben Taub had been burned to the ground.

CHAPTER NINETEEN

Exhausted, foot aching with pain, and more than a little tired of looking at figures and simulations, Catfish announced he was done for the day.

Givens, mostly quiet while they dissected the grenades and Catfish studied the mechanisms, blinked at him. "Still another hour until quitting time."

"Not for me," Catfish said. "I'm done."

Givens said nothing and simply left the level, seemingly a little put out that they'd quit early. Well, too goddamn bad. Catfish needed to elevate his leg and get the fuck out of there.

He considered resting his leg on the table while he waited for Shawna but decided lingering was a bad idea. Instead, he took the elevator to the first floor and headed outside, the zip strip still on the cigarette pack in his pocket.

The cool November air's humid chill hit him like a slap in the face, but he was thankful for it just the same. It wasn't cold enough to burn your skin but cold enough to wake you up.

He shivered and pulled his arms around himself when a gust of wind rushed through the gaps between the buildings. Moisture beaded on his cheeks and dampened his beard.

He heard the door open behind him and turned around. No longer wearing a lab coat, Shawna stood with her arms crossed in the freshening breeze. "You trying to get pneumonia?"

"No," he said. "Just needed to get out of there for a while."

Shawna sighed. "I know how that feels."

"Well," he said, "we can stay here for another thirty minutes and get some grub, or we can head back to the trailer and come back for food later."

"We need a damned take-out joint."

"Got that right," he said with a laugh. "Chinese. Indian. Mexican." Catfish smacked his lips, his beard dancing with the movements. "Been a long time since I've had good Tex-Mex."

"That's for damned sure." Shawna held the door open. "Get in here. Get something to drink and relax. I'd rather not have to come back to this—" Her voice trailed off.

"This what?" he asked.

She seemed to shake away a thought. "Doesn't matter. I just want this place in my rearview for the night."

"Fine," Catfish said with a pout. "I'll get out of the cold, Mom."

She punched him on the shoulder as he headed in. "Don't get sassy with me. It'll cost you."

"Like you can spend money here," he said.

Shawna grinned, "Not what I meant at all."

"Wait. What did you mean?"

He tried to get her to share what she meant, but she was having none of it. In a way, it was cute. Maybe that's why she'd done it, offering a game of some kind to keep them occupied.

We're just like little kids, he thought. That brought back the memory of last night, and an embarrassed smile lit his face. *Okay,* he thought, *not like little kids.*

The commissary was open, but the serving area was closed. A few bowls of snack mix, finger sandwiches, and thermoses of hot chocolate graced the few dining tables.

"I love you, Robbie," Shawna said and made a beeline for the hot chocolate.

"What are you, five?"

She stuck her tongue out at Catfish and filled a cup with the steaming frothy drink before dropping three marshmallows inside. "Perfection," she said.

"Perfection?"

Shawna took a small sip and shrugged. "No. It's not perfect. That would require some Irish cream. You know, the alcoholic kind." A dark mustache appeared above her lips, but her smile was as radiant as ever. "You should try it."

Grumbling, he fixed himself a cup. She stood next to the thermos, counting off the steps. He stopped more than once to glare at her but had difficulty fighting a grin. When he finally tasted the concoction, he forced a grimace. "This sucks."

She punched his shoulder again. "Shut up and grab a seat," she said. "You need somewhere to stretch."

He followed her to one of the few remaining tables, one of the small ones, and sat down with an oof.

"Good day?" she asked.

"Not really," Catfish said.

"Aw, little Catfish not up to engineering duties?"

He leaned back and rested his boot on the chair directly across from him. "Givens and I are working on a type of grenade."

"Grenade?" Shawna asked as if the word were something foreign.

He sipped from his hot chocolate. "Grenade. Something that will produce a shockwave big enough to damage M2 when it's solid."

"Good idea," she said. "So long as you don't blow up the facility while testing."

"Too true," he said. "But I think we have that covered. Moore provided us with a shielded container where things can go boom."

"So what's the problem?"

He shrugged. "Lots of calculations. Lots of design based on explosion shape, how best to create the shockwave, possible damage rates, range—"

"Okay, okay, I get it—"

"Plus," he said with a sneer, "I have Lt. Creepy at my elbow. Guy doesn't say jackshit unless I ask him a question or if he wants me to explain something. He practically stared over my shoulder all day, reading whatever I was reading and watching my every goddamned keystroke." He shook his head slowly in exasperation. Shawna giggled, and he glared at her. "I'm unhappy with my coworker."

She coughed twice to get her laughter under control. "Well," she said, trying to hold it together, "could be worse. Moore could be the one looking over your shoulder."

"Gee, thanks for that chilling idea." He flipped off the security camera in the nearest corner of the ceiling. "Hope she heard that, too."

Rolling her eyes, Shawna looked down in her mug.

"Okay," he said.

"What?"

He tapped his fingers on the table. "Something's bothering you."

"No."

Catfish leaned forward. "Talk to me. Tell me about your day. Anything."

She sighed. "Well, you have trouble with your coworker. I think I'm going to have problems with my new ones."

She explained how the dispensers worked and how the lab was set up. He paid close attention to her description of the failsafe systems. Thermite and Semtex. For some reason, he thought that was important. He'd remember it.

"Those two security guards we have inside the lab complex with us? God only knows what the hell they're thinking," Shawna said.

"Really? Why?"

She smirked. "We sectioned two drops of M2, one from each batch, and ran temperature tests on them. That was fun."

A shiver ran down his spine. "Fun?"

"Yeah," she said. "Scared the shit out of me."

"Well, what happened?"

She told him. He wasn't surprised it didn't make him feel better. Four scientists playing with a living bomb, and instead of just dealing with one, why not handle three more of the goddamned things?

He clenched his fingers. "Do I slug Kate or one of the boys?"

"Neither," Shawna said. "It was a group decision."

"So I'd have to smack you, too."

Shawna stirred the dregs of her hot chocolate noisily. "Yes. Yes, you would."

"So what was this supposed to prove?"

"Well," she said, "it was interesting. The M2 from the *Leaguer* test barrel, we call it Poppy, acted differently than the sample from Ben Taub."

He raised an eyebrow. "Called?"

"Taub," she said.

"Man, I thought Jay had more imagination than that," Catfish said.

"Don't ask," she said. "Anyway, we got a strange reaction when they were frozen. Poppy crystallized, but get this: Taub grew hairs."

"What?"

"Taub grew hairs when the temp dipped below freezing."

"Hairs," Catfish said. Of all the things she could have told him, it was the least expected. Based on what he'd seen aboard *Leaguer*, he'd expected crustacean features or at least a passing resemblance. But hairs? "What kind of hairs?"

Shawna's face lit up with excitement. "Neil thinks it's the same kind of hairs a spider grows. But these were—" She broke off, searching for a word. "More like mammal hair. Like it was trying to grow fur."

"Come on. That's bullshit."

"I don't think it is. I don't know how it's possible, but it happened." Shawna looked past him as if replaying the scene in her mind. "The barrel sample never came in contact with non-ocean organisms. If there was any real bacterial growth or dust inside the barrel before we filled it up, it was the only thing M2 had to eat. Therefore, Poppy didn't have a chance to consume any new biological matter."

"Yeah, so?"

She rolled her eyes. "Poppy crystalized. Taub crystallized and grew hair. Taub was, oh, I don't know, 'birthed' from a human being."

He thought for a moment before it clicked. "Shit. Taub ate mammals."

"Right," she said. "I'm sure it also consumed roaches, bugs, mites, any critter that might be hiding in a hospital that large. It also consumed medical waste."

"Jesus," Catfish said. "The films prove that the things at Ben Taub acted differently than ours. The M2 on *Leaguer* didn't want to move around like that. It tried to grab you with a tentacle and pull you in."

"Exactly," she said. "The Taubs moved like some kind of spider-thing out of a horror movie." She noisily slurped one last sip from the cup. "The only explanation is that it, well, learned. Or changed its form based on its food source."

"Food source," he echoed. "You mean it is what it eats."

A bright light gleamed in her eyes. "I think that's exactly what I mean."

"Jesus," he said. "And what does that tell us?"

Shawna shrugged. "It's really just a theory," she said. "It could be a coincidence, but I don't think so. Nothing else really fits." She flicked a finger against the cup. "But if our hunch is right, it means M2 has a completely different lifecycle than anything else in nature. It doesn't just infect like a parasite. It consumes its victim or material and incorporates it into itself." She looked down into her cup. "It's unique."

"God was on too much fucking acid," Catfish said.

"Oh, that's nothing. I'm becoming more and more convinced M2 isn't even from Earth."

His eyes widened. "What?"

She looked around conspiratorially. "I don't think it's from here."

"Why?"

Shawna pushed the cup aside and tented her hands. "We know it survives without the need of sunlight."

"Yeah. So? The damned lanternfish can do that."

"Yes," she agreed. "So can a ton of other creatures. We have plenty of examples of animals that survive without light. Thrive, in fact. But stay with me."

He knew she would eventually get to the point, and it wouldn't help to rush her. He'd known her long enough to realize when she was on a roll. "Continue."

"Okay. It is a life form that is literally liquid. It has no shell, container, or micro-thin barrier to hold in its guts. No solid material at all. I'm sure some things on Earth get close, but I'm willing to bet nothing qualifies, and if it does, it damned sure isn't as intelligent as those things down there," she said, pointing to the floor. "That suggests a lifecycle we've never seen, never encountered, never even dreamed was possible."

He waited a few beats, giving her a chance to roll on, but it seemed she'd finally come to a stop. "Extra-terrestrial," he said dully. While she'd been speaking, the images of thousands of insects and ocean species flashed through his mind. "What if it's not a life form at all?" he said.

Now, it was her turn to look confused. "Explain?"

"Man," he said with a grin, "put on some Floyd, put a bong on the table, and we'll look the parts for this conversation."

"What?"

He waved away the question. "Never mind. You know what the Portuguese man o' war is?"

"That's a jellyfish, right?"

"Not really," he said. "It's actually a group of cells or whatever that— Fuck. Here's the simple version. It's like a colony. They conglomerate with one another and, I don't know, specialize themselves and then get together and make that sail, the long strings of stingers, and everything else. So it's not really one creature, but many, each doing their own thing, but acting in concert."

Shawna reached for the cup, peered into it as though the hot chocolate had somehow replenished itself, and thumbed it away in frustration. "Now I understand what you meant about the bong."

He grinned. "You get what I'm saying?"

"Yeah, okay. I do. So one 'cell' of M2 gets together with another, and they decide to work together."

"Right," he said. "I mean, there's something else going on there. But think about it. Just like you said about your experiment today. In isolation, away from its progenitor? Parent? Shit, I don't know the word. Whatever. It gets cut off from its colony, and the sub-colony that's left decides to work together instead. Create a new M2 entity."

Shawna shivered. "That's terrifying in its plausibility."

He laughed. "Isn't it?"

"I need more hot chocolate."

"You're going to burst or get the 'betes!"

"Whatever," she said and headed back to the thermos, snatching up Catfish's cup on her way.

He smiled while he watched her fill the cup and dunk the marshmallows fully before she finally stirred the concoction. Years ago, when he'd first met her, he thought she was an intelligent idiot. She barely spoke when Thomas wasn't around and seemed terrified of Catfish. She and JP bonded nearly instantly, but he imagined that was more because of JP's personality than anything else—the man was always a big brother to whoever needed one.

But after a few months, she warmed up to Catfish and started spending time around him. More and more. She would sometimes take a break from whatever engineering project Thomas had cooked up to join Catfish and JP in the warehouse. She'd walk in when they were making sexual jokes about the waldos or various other attachments used on AUVs and ROVs.

After that, she even played poker with them. She was good at bluffing and usually took some of everyone's money before the night was through. Drove JP crazy.

But something was different now. He wondered if maybe it had always been different, and he just never noticed.

"Thinking?" she asked as she placed the fresh cup of hot chocolate before him.

He gestured at the cup. "Thanks."

"Welcome."

He said nothing.

"Catfish? Share."

"Maybe that's not a plausible theory after all," he said.

"What? No, it's great."

He shook his head. "It's got a giant gaping hole in it, though."

"What do you mean?"

"Simple," he said. "If one speck of M2 was enough to consume a human body, then where did the rest of the M2 come from? Did it convert all the biomass into more of its own cells? Just magically create them and bend them to its will?"

"Hmm," Shawna said. "I think I see what you're saying. That's more of a question for Neil. He's the bio guy."

"Biochemist, right?" Catfish asked. "I wish we had a xenobiologist."

"You read too much science fiction," she said.

"No," he said through a laugh. "I'm living it."

A grin spread across Shawna's face. "Point taken. If you're right, it's like a virus. It infects the cell, causes it to make more viruses, and destroys it in the process." Her grin faded slightly. "Hmm. That doesn't sound right either."

"But it sounds close," he said.

"Close, but no cigar?"

He snapped his fingers. "Damn."

"What?"

"I should have asked Moore for some cigars."

A moment later, the foyer beyond the door echoed with noise. Catfish turned in time to see the other scientists entering the dining room.

"Well," Shawna said, "there goes the party."

"Nah," Catfish said, "it's just beginning."

CHAPTER TWENTY

By the time they finished dinner and returned to the trailer, Shawna found herself yawning over and over again. It had been a long day, and a huge meal at the end of it hadn't helped. She felt bloated and ready to pop. Dammit, the food here shouldn't be this good.

The rain had decided to stop, but the clouds still obscured the stars and moon. Shit. They couldn't even see airplane lights as they streaked above the low ceiling.

Her teeth chattered as she maneuvered the cart through the breezeway created by the buildings and out the other side. Their trailers sat on the tarmac, the porch lights glowing. Shawna blinked. "You leave your lights on?"

"No," he said. She noticed he had his arms wrapped around himself against the fresh breeze. "I didn't. I always make sure those things are off."

"Well," she said. "That's comforting."

She pulled up to Catfish's trailer and jumped out. "Come on, gimp."

"Whatever," he said.

She waited for him to struggle out of the cart and walk to the door. "I'll go first," she said, climbing the steps and opening the door before he had a chance to speak. She flipped on the interior lights and gazed around the room. A grin slowly lit her face. "I guess the maid has been here." She walked inside, waiting for Catfish to take a look.

The bed was made with fresh linen, the floor had been cleaned, and all the plastic and paper from his new clothes had been swept away as though they had never existed. A neat pile of extra blankets sat on the foot of the bed.

"Wow," Catfish said. "Do they do turndown service as well?"

"That might be asking a bit much," Shawna said dryly.

"How does a maid get security clearance to work here?"

She snickered. "I think this is technically a military facility. They might have some enlisted to handle that."

"Oh. You might be right." He glanced at the door. "Or they're a bunch of mercs."

"I don't think so," Shawna said. "This is too damned government. I mean, we're right next to Ellington Field." Losing the fight to a loud yawn, she covered her mouth and let it loose.

"Jesus, woman," Catfish laughed. "Be a little louder next time."

"Sorry." She stretched her back with a groan of pleasure. "I need a hot shower."

Catfish kicked the floor. "Knew there was something I forgot to do."

"What's that?"

"Was going to ask Moore about using the showers in the dorms." He pointed to the tiny shower cubicle. "I can barely move around in there."

She sighed. "Not a bad idea. Tell you what," she said, nonchalantly undressing, "I've got first. You've got second."

"Um, okay," he said.

She liked the half-embarrassed look on his face. "You'll have to towel me off, of course."

"Of course."

Shawna stepped out of her panties and walked slowly to the shower, enjoying the feel of his hungry gaze sliding over her body. "I'll be quick."

"I hope not," Catfish said.

* * *

Catfish snored lightly. She'd had to pry his arm from around her shoulder and move it next to her. The moment she did, she wished she hadn't. It was comforting to be held, skin on skin, naked, vulnerable, and protected all at the same time, but she was wide awake, and he was dead asleep.

She shuffled out of his grasp to the edge of the bed. He said something in his sleep but didn't wake up. Good. The last thing she wanted to do was awaken him. Someone should be getting some z's.

That was the hell of it. She had been. Until the dream.

She'd been back aboard *Leaguer*, trapped inside the lab. The sample in the beaker had come alive and escaped the lab table. It was somewhere in the shadows, waiting for her, moving toward her. Coming for her.

Thomas banged on the door, his voice still coming through the cell phone in her hands as he forced his way into the sealed lab. "But I have to tell you something," he said as the last bolts gave way and the door swung open, "things are different now."

She swung her head from the threat in the shadows to face the door. Thomas stood there, his face set in that all too familiar grin, but something was wrong. The flesh beneath his pants wriggled as though something crawled up his leg. Then another. And another. Dozens and dozens of them. And then they were beneath his shirt, dark shadows worming their way up his body.

Tendrils of smoke drifted through the fabric, her nose filling with the smell of burned hair. That scent all but disappeared, replaced by the stench of rancid meat. The shadows rose above his waist, impossibly black holes in reality that seemed to bore into him rather than move across him. They reached his chin, and his mouth opened wide. Hundreds of the amorphous, featureless shapes practically leaped inside. He closed his mouth and stood there, still as a statue.

"Thomas?" she wheezed.

His eyes had become distant, as though he were looking at

something far away. She held her breath as she waited for something to happen. In the shadows of the room, something slithered.

She flinched as his gaze swung back to her. His dull eyes became pools of swirling darkness, his mouth opened, and the sound of frying bacon filled her ears. She clamped her hands against her head to stifle the brain-shattering sound. Thomas' lips had turned black, his pale skin rippling in strips of darkness that seemed to erase him a slash at a time.

The crackling sound faded as a pool of black ooze coalesced where he had once been. As she screamed and tried to shuffle further away from the creature, an eyestalk rose from the pool with the crunch of a shattered shell. But instead of a slowly spinning black orb at the stalk's end, the eye wasn't black. It was blue, like the color of Thomas' eyes.

The dream had ended, but not before she heard something that might have been Thomas' dead voice. She had awakened with a start but managed not to scream. That had been what felt like hours ago.

It had taken her a long time to get that image out of her head and quite a while before she could stop shaking. Since then, she'd tried to turn her mind to other matters. Like science.

Evolution. It was a word they'd all used today and the day before. An organism must adapt to changes in its environment, its food supply, and its predators. For instance, if the prey does not adapt to a new predator, they are made extinct. The same goes for massive environmental changes that affect their food supply.

Life needed food. Life needed a way to harness energy to keep its cells humming along. It needed the power provided by its food and environment to satisfy the nearly all-consuming need to reproduce. Life had to have it.

Mutation and other changes happen to more complex creatures over long periods of time, although in some short-lived species, such as fruit flies, several generations can be experimented on in the span of a month. Technically, any generation could spawn a helpful mutation. Its brood would be the ones to bring about the next generation and so on.

But M2 didn't take long to adapt. Not long at all. It had been somewhere in the M2 Trench, hiding beneath the ocean floor and no doubt snacking on the occasional tidbit of food. It shouldn't have been a surprise that it resembled a mixture of oceanic life when it appeared on the rig.

However, it had also made the most of its environment. Inside *Leaguer's* interior, it had used the walls, the corridors, anything it could to stalk its prey. Once on the deck, however, it had alternated between the moving pool of living liquid and slashing the air with manufactured talons.

Another shiver wracked her, and it took her a moment to get it under control.

Face it, or you'll always be hiding from it.

Yes, very true. Also, a bit easier said than done.

Evolve, she said to herself. *Evolve or die.*

That brought up another thought: pressure. The oil they'd brought up had been at a depth of nearly 10km. That meant as the substance rose through the drill string, pressure had fallen away, but the creature that came up in the barrel hadn't seemed to have suffered from the enormous pressure differential.

Maybe we're thinking about this wrong, she thought. *We don't know what M2 actually looked like when it was below the ocean floor. There's no way of knowing that. Did it change to liquid when we brought it up? Or is that its natural, most basic form?*

A good question. She stifled a yawn. Maybe she could sleep now. She rolled over and slid an arm beneath Catfish's. In his sleep, he wrapped his other arm around her. Smiling, Shawna finally slept.

CHAPTER TWENTY-ONE

They had been studying M2 for three days now, and it was officially time to cut bait. They'd learned much but far too little, so they would have to try something else.

Shawna's team sat around a table on the lab level. The makeshift meeting room was large enough to house three or four people comfortably, but with Moore there, it was getting a little crowded.

Neil stood next to the whiteboard, a black marker held before him like a weapon. He'd drawn a grid with the tests and the results.

They had poked and prodded the minuscule samples and run the same tests and same routines, but the specimens hadn't reacted to physical stimulation. They'd even tried feeding the samples with biomass, but Moore had terminated the experiments once the samples grew to a size of five milliliters. She'd been alarmed by the creatures' rapid absorption of nutrients.

They had tested five possible "consumable" materials: chicken, carrots, a chunk of sheetrock, a chicken bone, and a cube of construction-grade plastic. Each specimen had torn through the biological offerings with reckless greed. Jay concluded that the porous nature of flesh and bone allowed M2 to quickly separate the molecules or atoms and absorb the medium. Sounded logical to her.

Plastic was consumed, too, albeit at a slower rate. The same was true for sheetrock and wood. The only things the creatures didn't seem able to eat were metal and glass, but it weakened those materials. They hadn't had time to study how, and that was the next test. First thing tomorrow.

But they were at a standstill on the more important tests. They hadn't been able to recreate the physical characteristics they'd witnessed on *Leaguer* nor at the other two incident sites. Kate had proposed they start with larger samples, say 5ml, and torch them if they grew too large. Moore had nixed it and told them to leave the lab and head to the meeting room. And here they were.

Moore stood at the end of the folding table, her tablet in front of her. She looked over at the whiteboard, seemingly reacquainting herself with their tests and the results, which Shawna knew was bullshit. She didn't believe for a second that Moore hadn't watched every second of every experiment and knew the results down to the decimal point.

"So, no other ideas?" Moore asked.

"No," Kate said. "We're stuck."

"Okay," Moore said and finally sat. She picked up the tablet, tapped it a few times, and put it back down again. Hands folded in front of her, she stared at all and none of them, her eyes finding that perfect balance between the two. "Maybe you're too close to it," she said.

"Like anyone here isn't," Jay muttered.

Moore's fake smile grew. "I'm not," she said. "What do we factually know about the vectors?"

"Vectors?" Neil grinned. "You been spending a lot of time with the CDC?"

Moore ignored him and glanced at Shawna. "You say that at least two workers were infected. Is that correct?"

She nodded. "Best as we figured. I mean, it's possible something else happened, but that's our best guess."

"Kate?" Moore asked.

"One of our samples got loose, and," her voice suddenly sounded choked, "Marie was infected."

"So the facts are: this thing infects," Moore said. "At a certain size, it can move across surfaces, and at another size, it begins to extrude appendages and what looked like feeding organs."

"Looked like," Jay said. "Trust me. Those things had mandibles."

Moore's fake smile dropped away, replaced by a look of reproach. "Be that as it may," she said coldly, "those are what you need to test. How it becomes what it becomes."

"Which means," Kate said, "we need larger specimens."

"No," Shawna said. "She means we need test animals."

"Oh," Kate said. Her skin had turned slightly green. "Like mice?"

Moore nodded. "Mice. Cats Whatever."

"Jesus, lady," Jay said. "I'm not killing a cat."

"I'll call PETA," Moore said. "We'll start with a literal lab rat. I'll get you a few tomorrow. If you need another type of specimen, you'll need to let me know."

The room went quiet. Moore sighed and looked at her watch. "Instead of returning to the lab, I suggest you design your new tests upstairs before dinner. Maybe get something from the commissary."

"Okay," Kate said. "We'll do that."

Moore's shark-like grin reappeared. "Excellent." She stood, her tablet held in the fingers of her left hand. "You've been working hard. You should be proud of yourselves," she said. With that, Moore left the room without looking back or waiting for an acknowledgment.

"She really gives me the creeps," Jay said.

Shawna nodded but said nothing. Moore spooked everyone. Even Kate. Or maybe, especially Kate.

"Well, um, okay," Kate said. "Want to move to the conference room?"

No one spoke as they packed up what they had and headed to the elevator. Shawna yawned twice on her way to the dining room. Damn, she was tired. She had finally managed to get some sleep, but it wasn't nearly enough for a long day in the lab. And although she knew they hadn't even put in a full day, it seemed it had gone on forever.

But they now knew that separate strains of M2 took on different physical properties under extreme temperature variation. They also knew M2 consumed biological matter better than any other substances they'd tried. And, of course, they knew the light frequency that destroyed M2 completely. In short, they knew a lot, but not enough. Not nearly enough.

For instance, how did M2 convert matter into more of itself? Or how about the chemical process of the creatures breaking down matter? Was there a significant life span for the spores if they were to land somewhere? Could they infect other creatures? Start at the bottom of the food chain and work their way up?

She was pretty sure that was the unspoken question on everyone's mind. And now, she guessed, that's what Kate would talk about. Fun. More mental gymnastics.

Shawna smiled the moment they entered the commissary. Chef Robbie had once again placed large thermoses of hot chocolate on the serving table along with all the fixings. At least she could get her sugar shock going early.

* * *

Shawna yawned again and immediately blushed. That one yawn started the entire table going. Jay tried to do an impersonation but couldn't hold it together as his jaws opened wide and gave birth to an ear-splitting howl.

Shaking her head at him, Shawna looked back at the board and sipped lukewarm hot chocolate. They had a fair number of biological tests listed, and she knew Neil had pages and pages of experiments he'd wanted to run on the small samples. Since none of the tiny specimens had reacted to stimuli, those had had to be tossed out the proverbial window. Now they were back in play.

They had to recalibrate everything to deal with larger entities. Maybe something the size of a cat or dog. They had sample cases large enough to house one of the creatures, so that wasn't a problem. The challenge would be keeping themselves safe while performing the tests.

The light arrays had been designed for smaller specimens, preventing M2 from escaping the deadly UV rays while ensuring the samples didn't fry. Kate's team would either have to dump the UV lights or find a way to provide enough shade for the samples to survive. Plus, they needed four specimens again—two each from Poppy and Taub. Four. Four larger creatures that might be able to transform and eat everyone in the facility if they escaped. That was a very sobering thought.

They'd start with lab rats. Infect each with a pin-point worth of M2, observe the gestation period, and measure the resulting creatures' volume and physical size. Weighing the rats as accurately as possible to determine their relevant mass would be important to try and establish the creatures' transformation processes. It couldn't possibly be 100%. Some of the mass had to be lost to conversion. Didn't it?

A rap on the door caused Kate to stop mid-sentence. Shawna turned and saw Sarah standing at the threshold. She looked both apologetic and excited at the same time. "Kate? Can we borrow your team for a few minutes?"

"Sure. Should we bring our drinks?"

"I don't think that's a good idea," Sarah said. "Come on."

She led them to the elevator, and Shawna's heartbeat picked up.

"What's going on?" Kate asked Sarah.

Sarah waved her wristband at the elevator controls and punched the Q button. "There's something down in quarantine I need your collective opinion on." She hissed a sigh. "And probably your prayers."

That stopped everyone in the elevator from talking. It was as if they were holding their breath while they descended deeper into the facility's bowels.

Shawna thumbed the metal top of the lighter in her pocket. The spring's ting was almost inaudible. Almost. But as long as she could hear it, she felt calmer. She was glad she kept adding fuel to the lighter every other day. Today might be the day she needed it.

The elevator door opened, and a blast of bright UV light made her squint. It took a moment for her eyes to adjust to the painful change in illumination. The sight of four men dressed in bio suits, incinerators slung over their shoulders, did nothing to slow her sprinting heart. She continued flipping the top of the lighter, but the sound no longer soothed her. Instead, it sounded like the dripping of black liquid from a frail pipe.

As Sarah led them down the hall, Kate continued asking questions, but Sarah continued saying nothing. When they cleared the airlock entrance to the quarantine interior, Sarah turned left and gestured for them to follow. Finally, they reached the containment tanks. Poppy's barrel sat on its side, suspended on a metal stand, pipes leading out of its lid. The heavy glass and steel composite window offered a view into the room.

"Last night," Sarah said, "we had a monitor trip in Poppy's containment system. There were vibrations."

"Vibrations? That's nothing new," Neil said. "What kind of vibrations?"

She smiled at him, but there was no mirth in it. "The big kind. Taub's tank nearly rocked in its cradle. So did Poppy's barrel."

Silence lingered. Shawna didn't know what to say to that, and even if she did, she wouldn't have tried. Her hands were shaking with fear.

"What do you want from us?" Kate finally asked.

Sarah stared at Taub's enclosure, the incinerator-armed guards standing at the back wall. "A better way to contain them if they burst through their respective metal prisons."

"You burn them," Shawna said. "You fucking burn them."

Sarah sighed again. "I was asked to get your opinion on what we should do. Dr. Moore made it clear that I was to follow your instructions." Shawna opened her mouth to speak, but Sarah continued talking. "So long as it didn't include destroying M2 at this moment."

Neil looked horrified. "No. We can't destroy it. Not yet."

"Well," Jay said, "how else would we contain it?"

"I don't know," Sarah said. "But you might need to come up with a way soon. See that spot?"

It took a few seconds for her eyes to find it, but sure enough, there it was, just beneath one of the barrel's ribs. Several portions of the metal had been pushed out as though from someone hammering at the inside. The dents were much larger than the ones she'd seen the other day.

"Jesus wept," Jay said. "We have no way of knowing how much steel is left, do we?"

"No," Sarah said.

"How thick is that waste tank?" Kate asked. "Thicker than a barrel of oil?"

Sarah shrugged. "I have no idea."

"I'll bet it's thicker," Jay said. "It was designed to hold a lot more mass. A sample barrel's not necessarily made for long-term storage."

Sarah was silent momentarily, her eyes drifting back to the enclosures. "So maybe the tank is thicker. Do you think it will have a more difficult time getting through the steel?"

"I think so," Jay said. "We'll know more after we perform the metal tests tomorrow."

"Metal tests?" Sarah asked.

Neil brightened. "We're going to use larger samples of M2. Should be able to do some bio tests and determine how it affects metal and glass, and rate of deterioration if there is any."

"Oh," Sarah said. A reluctant smile broke across her face. "I guess that's why Moore has me stationed in the lab tomorrow."

"So you'll be with us?" Shawna asked.

"Yup."

"That's something at least," Kate said. "We'll need to batten down the hatches."

"I know," Sarah said. "I'll do my best to make sure this shit doesn't get out of the lab. Like always."

"Good to know," Shawna said.

"Okay, that's all I have. Your answer is to either burn it or think about it?"

Kate and the others glanced at one another. Finally, she said, "That's about the size of it."

"Right," Sarah said, looking more than a little dissatisfied with their answer. "I was hoping for a little bit more. Thought maybe you'd have some ideas."

"We'll discuss it and let you know."

Sarah nodded. "Don't take too long."

* * *

Catfish pulled cans of artesian water from the fridge. Shawna sat on the couch, her eyes moodily fixed on the blank television screen. They hadn't spoken much at dinner. They had shared their meal with the rest of the team, where shop talk was all but forbidden, so they hadn't exactly had a chance to catch up.

As she told him about her day, the abandonment of the small-scale tests, the plans for the larger specimen bio tests, and the containment problem, Catfish began to feel nauseous. It wasn't from the meal or too much caffeine. No, this was fear.

When she finished, he stared at her for a long moment, stifling the urge to touch her face. "So now what?" Catfish asked. "We torch the facility?"

"What? No," Shawna said. "Well, not yet."

"Not yet. My ass. If that thing is close to breaking out of its prison—"

"It's not," Shawna said. "If it bursts from the barrel, it's going to get nuked by all the UV lights. And if that doesn't stop it, then the incinerators will."

He paused for a moment, considering her words. Yes, the creatures were contained in the barrel and storage tank, both encased in that thick glass composite Moore and Kate were so proud of, but it hadn't been tested against M2. Not really. Kate and Moore appeared to accept that the substance would hold up to M2's corrosive nature, but he wasn't convinced. Not at all.

"Can't say I'm happy to think about any of that," he said. "You do realize that the more complicated safety measures are, the more likely they are to fail."

She pulled in a shuddering breath before taking a long sip. "I've read that book too," she said. "And I know that. But if you build enough rings of security, especially making the outer rings pretty formidable, you should be able to keep anything from breaking out."

"Should," Catfish said. "If you're right about these things being from another planet, all bets are off."

"Well, we should know some things tomorrow," Shawna said. "We're going to start with the glass/metal tests and see if we can find a rate of deterioration."

"But you're going to do that after you feed the damned things?"

She stared at the TV's dead screen for a moment as if the answer to his question lay in its unpowered LEDs. Finally, she nodded. "We'll perform the metal and stress tests at the smaller size and then work our way up once we have the samples grown in the rats."

Catfish shivered, the liquid sloshing slightly in the can. "And what happens if those get too big?"

"Incineration," she said. "We have sample boxes large enough. Shouldn't be a problem. Same as the containment area. If the UV doesn't kill it, fire will."

"You hope," he said under his breath. "How long is all that going to take?"

"Depends. We don't know how fast M2 will grow in the rats. For Krieger, it only took a few hours before she—" Shawna broke off. "Before whatever happened happened."

What happened, Catfish thought, *is that the thing absorbed her inside out.* In a way, Marie Krieger had fed it, grown it, and birthed it. All against her will. An unwilling host cut down by the substance's insatiable need to feed and live.

Like JP, like the other rig workers who became infected, they died without warning, and no one had even really noticed they were that sick. Catfish tried to imagine a hospital filled with hundreds of M2-infected humans. Or maybe a mall. Or a school.

He tapped a finger on the can. "You think the infection will be faster in smaller animals?"

"Yup," Shawna said. "I mean, it stands to reason that it would go faster. Not as much mass to rewrite, or consume, or whatever."

"Well, I guess—" He stopped. "Did you say rewrite?"

Shawna paused a moment before finally nodding. "Yeah, I did."

"Explain that."

"Neil put forth the theory that M2 is rewriting the DNA of the biological cells it encounters. Rewriting them to serve itself."

"Then how does it consume sheetrock, plaster, plastic, and anything that's not biological? And it sure as hell doesn't rewrite dead animal DNA."

She slowly smiled. "You're so cute when you think you've found a hole in a theory."

The desperate anger that had welled up from nowhere faded rapidly. He realized he'd been yelling for no reason and sighed. "But it's a hole."

"Yes," Shawna said. Her fingers played with the cuff of his shirt. "That's when Jay suggested it's 'rewriting matter.'"

The thought dangled there for a moment as his mind fought to pluck it and consume it. It was like suggesting that the physical were mere pixels, and all you had to do was rearrange them to create something new and different. "How much had Jay been smoking?"

"You mean the crack or the acid?"

Catfish rolled his eyes. "You don't smoke acid, Shawna."

"Shows you what I know." She brushed his arm. "Jay can really think outside the box. Hate that phrase, but you know what I mean. He just tosses this shit out there during brainstorming. Half the time, it makes sense. Other times?" Her grin brightened. "He just sounds nuts."

"Did he explain how M2 might be rewriting matter?"

"Of course not," she said. "He probably thought it was just a neat idea."

Catfish finished the can of water, crumpled it, and tossed it to the coffee table. "Does sound like a neat idea," he mumbled.

She put her dimpled can on the coffee table and curled her legs beneath her. Catfish shuffled and made room as she lay her head on his chest. She dragged one of his arms across her and the other to match. He brushed her cheek with his fingers.

"You worried about tomorrow?" he asked.

"Yes and no," she said. I know we have the best possible defenses if something goes wrong, but I sure as hell don't want something to go wrong."

"I know that feeling." Catfish stroked her hair. "Think you'll know something definitive tomorrow?"

"I don't think we'll ever find out anything definitive about M2. It just—" She paused. "Whenever we think we've found a consistent rule, it breaks it. Like the freezing thing. All the samples should have acted the same. But Taub reacted differently and used actual hair to defend itself against the cold. What if it can do the same sort of thing for light?"

He felt as though the room had suddenly gotten colder. There were only three things they knew that killed M2—extreme heat, UV light, and fire. And if it somehow managed to grow a defense against UV light, it could venture out during the daylight. There would be no natural defense against it at all.

"That's a terrifying thought," he said.

"Yes, it is. And with the two samples trying to break out of their confines, we need to find out if that's the case."

"Why do you say that?" Catfish asked.

"Because I have a nasty feeling that the larger M2 gets, the more quickly it adapts." She dragged a hand across the inseam of his jeans. "I'm tired of talking."

"Okay," he said dumbly.

She looked up at him as he stroked her hair. "I want to feel safe for a while." Catfish turned out the light.

CHAPTER TWENTY-TWO

When Shawna and the rest of the science team entered the lab, she noticed a stack of containers against the far wall with the words "LIVE ANIMALS" imprinted on their sides. Four of the poor bastards didn't know they would soon be incubators.

Shawna wondered how painful the process would be. It sounded as though Krieger mainly became ill and then unconscious. Maybe she was still out of it when the creature finally killed her. Or perhaps she'd been brain-dead for a long time before it consumed her. Impossible to know.

Neil was the only one comfortable handling the rats. It was difficult to look at an animal, any animal, and admit to yourself you were going to cause harm to it knowingly. Shawna and the others would be complicit, regardless. It was necessary, dammit, but she didn't have to participate physically.

While he plucked two unwilling volunteers from the boxes and transferred them to the sample cases, Shawna, Kate, and Jay headed to the lab to prepare for the test subjects.

The airlock cycled with a hiss she could barely hear. That sound quickly disappeared as vacuum replaced air. The light turned green, and Kate motioned to the door.

"Ready, Shawna?"

Could you ever be ready to walk inside a lab room where two pipes, each a container and distribution system for M2, hung less than

1.5 meters from your head? She knew it was made of metal. She knew it was glass insulated. She didn't care. "Ready."

Shawna entered the room with Kate in front. They unclamped the relatively small sample cases and placed them in the small lab's quarantine area.

After taking care of the cases, Jay ran camera checks on the area where the cases had been. The spot check was meant to ensure that nothing had fallen from the sample containers. In truth, though, it was as much about seeing if the cases had suffered any damage causing flakes or dust. Jay found nothing. Kate and Shawna found nothing. They were good to go.

Why wouldn't that feeling that something bad was about to happen go away? Why couldn't she just focus on what they were doing and make sure she wouldn't be the cause of it?

"Kate?" Neil said. "Are we clear to oxygenate?"

"Shawna?"

"I think we are, Kate."

"Copy, Neil. Let's get some air in here."

"Copy."

A moment later, she heard sounds from outside the suit, meaning the room was no longer in a vacuum. Shawna breathed a happy sigh. Had that been what had made her so antsy? Neil stepped through the airlock doors, a sample case in each hand. Shawna saw the rats through the cases' clear sides. Nope. She was still antsy.

Kate secured the first, marked "Poppy 1," into the slot and locked it down. Neil did the same with the one marked "Taub 1." No cute names for the rats, she noticed. She guessed Neil didn't want to sentimentalize them since they would be dead in a matter of hours. If not sooner.

"Shawna?" Kate said. "Want to get the samples?"

"Samples?"

"Poppy and Taub. The metal syringes."

She froze instantly. "I thought Neil—"

"I will," he said. "I just need them on a tray so I can switch out."

Trembling, Shawna walked to the secured supply cabinet and peered through the translucent surface, her eyes wary for anything that wasn't white or reflective steel. Once she'd convinced herself there was nothing to fear, she reached out and took a syringe from each shelf. She didn't know how much M2 was in each and didn't care. She just wanted this over with.

But you couldn't rush handling M2. One mistake, and it was all over. Stepping as carefully as she could, she walked to Neil and carefully placed the syringes on the tray as if they could explode at the slightest jostle.

Neil's voice, a little less calm than she'd expected, nearly made her cringe. "Nervous?"

"Yes," Shawna admitted. There was no point in hiding it.

"Me, too," he said.

Kate looked through the glass. "Jay? We're ready."

"Okay," he said, "going to red."

The steady yellow light above the cases flickered and flashed between red and yellow, the strobe effect nearly rendering the light green. A second later, it turned a slow, blinking red.

"Shawna? Get about 1.5 meters from me," Neil said. "You too, Kate."

They followed instructions, making sure they were closer to the exit. Ultraviolet light bathed the rat, making its white fur glow. Neil reached through the case's opening, held the rat, and plunged the syringe's needle into its abdomen. The rat squealed but quickly went silent. Shawna's heart pounded.

"Okay," Neil said, placing the one-shot syringe on the tray. He clamped the opening shut again. "Next."

In less than five minutes, he'd infected both rats, and the cases were secure. Shawna led the group into the airlock, probably walking too fast. When she turned at the airlock door, she realized she hadn't been the only one in a hurry to get out of there.

The airlock cycled, they stepped into the corridor, and the metal door slammed shut, effectively putting the room into lockdown.

More like closing the lid on a BBQ grill, she thought.

They snaked around between the labs until they reached Jay in the observation area.

"No reaction, apart from the expected," Jay said.

Shawna looked at the screen. Both rats scratched at the injection sites, the specks of black readily visible amidst the sea of white fur. Both rats eventually settled down and set about exploring their new confines. Neither appeared to be a fan.

"If we were back at HAL," Jay said, "we'd be drinking coffee and having a Danish while we waited for the test results."

"Shit," Neil said, "back at HAL, you didn't have to worry about giving birth to a monster."

"Well, now I don't have to worry about whether or not it's possible. Now I know it's inevitable."

The comms went silent. Jay's voice was without a hint of humor or irony—just the tone of a fatalist stating the obvious. It made Shawna want to run for the exit.

After thirty minutes, things began to happen. The Taub 1 rat lay down but didn't appear to be in pain. Its eyes blinked a few times before closing, its chest rising and falling steadily. A moment later, Poppy 1 did the same, but only after convulsing several times. Its breathing became erratic, the arhythmic thump of its heart visible through its delicate skin.

As Shawna and the others watched, the pink color of Poppy 1's skin darkened as though someone had mixed black onto a painter's pallet. The rat's fur seemed to retract into the dark gray of the animal's belly. Its eyes, a dull red to begin with, turned obsidian before becoming an impenetrable black. Now looking like a naked burned thing, the rat shuddered and flailed its legs once. Twice. The skin parted as though being unzipped. Thick, black liquid erupted over the sides of the animal's exposed ribs. The creature's carcass melted into the black with the crackle of frying bacon.

Shawna stepped away from the glass, her horrified eyes riveted on the bubbling pool of liquid. It was at least a liter in size and seemed to have at least 1 millimeter of thickness. The pool's surface slowly stabilized, becoming smooth as glass.

"Jesus," Jay said. "That happened to Marie."

Kate sounded choked. "Don't remind me."

Shawna switched her gaze to the monitors marked "Taub 1." The rat was still, its heart rising and falling every few seconds.

"Its heart is slowing," Neil said matter-of-factly. He tapped a button and added a marker to the video. "Taub 1 has survived three minutes longer than Poppy 1."

"No," Shawna said, shaking her head. "Taub 1 just still has a body. I don't care if it has a pulse. It's dead."

Neil said nothing, conceding the point. He cleared his throat as if to say something but stopped. Shawna felt her heart slam dance in her chest when she saw what had happened. A talon ruptured the skin of the rat's neck, slicing down from the throat to its midsection. Another popped through the skin. And another. Then liquid broke over the rat's body, consuming it. The taloned appendages, their trunks still embedded in the liquid, clicked and clacked against the sample case's steel bottom.

The taloned branches of darkness slowly retracted into the pool, its size growing slightly. Its surface went still for a moment, but it was short-lived. A large bubble burst from the pool's center, a thin cylindrical appendage rising from the liquid. Upon reaching three centimeters, a black orb extruded from the end. The sensory organ spun as if taking in everything at once.

"Holy fucking shit," Kate said.

"I'll be a be a be a be fucked!" Jay yelled as Porky Pig.

The pool seemed to rise slightly off the sample case's bottom, although that could have been an optical illusion caused by it thickening its edges. The eyestalk bent forward, the orb dead and lifeless as it spun.

"Is it looking at me?" Shawna asked no one.

The pool flowed toward the observation window, the eyestalk bending even further as if trying to assess them as a threat. Neil leaned forward to the glass. The eyestalk waved away from him, getting a few more centimeters of distance between them.

"Neil?" Kate said. "Don't get too close."

"That thing can't get to me," he said. Now, his helmet was practically against the thick partition.

Shawna took another step back. Something was about to happen. She knew it.

"Neil?" she said. "I really don't think—"

The eyestalk descended three or four centimeters until it barely pushed through the pool's surface. At the same time, a stream of amorphous liquid flowed forward toward the window.

"What's it doing?" Jay asked.

Neil made a sound that might have been a laugh but turned into a high-pitched scream. The pool of liquid seemed to fly forward like a wave crashing into a high beach. Shawna noticed the stream of liquid had become hard, and the creature had used the case's floor as a lever.

"Oh, Jesus Christ," she said.

The black liquid covered the sample case's composite wall, leaving the observation window useless, but it couldn't block out the cameras. What Shawna saw made her that much more terrified.

The camera above the translucent sample case showed that the creature had flattened against the glass. Its tail had lengthened slightly, allowing the thing to push its liquid mass further up the side of the glass. The thick ooze rippled up and down as if something tried to burst from it.

When the creature reached the top of the case, it continued clinging to the side, dragging its colloidal-looking tail along with it. Shawna could see how it was doing it even through the observation window glass. The creature's bottom layer appeared corrugated as if it had grown nearly invisible suckers and hairs to crawl like a spider.

The team watched in silence as the ooze continued traveling across the boundaries of its prison, testing each corner again and again. After determining there was no immediate exit, the pool flowed back to the center of the sample case, its edges thickening once again. A short eyestalk extruded from the liquid, the lifeless orb following their movements.

Shawna looked over at Poppy 1. The pool hadn't transformed, but it was now testing its prison, similar to how Taub 1 had done. Poppy 1, however, didn't attempt to crawl up the sides in the same fashion. Instead of growing a tail, it had grown a small tentacle and used it to push itself along. However, once it reached halfway up the glass, it bunched up like a tree, finally bending under its own weight.

"Wow," Shawna said. "Does it know how to climb?"

"Doesn't look like it," Jay said. "Or it's playing one hell of a game of possum."

"No, I think she's right," Kate said. "Poppy 1 is acting very differently from Taub 1. They should be about the same size, so I doubt that enters into it."

Neil reset the motion sensors to prevent alarms from triggering. "Security is going to have to watch these things all night," he said.

"Well," Kate said, "we have another four hours before quitting time. Let's try a couple of things before we start the metal test."

Shawna wasn't sure she wanted any part of this anymore. Every time she tried to focus on something else, the impassive, dead stare of the eyestalk seemed to follow her. She could feel it watching her, waiting for a chance to—

"Shawna?" Kate said. "Help me prep."

"'Right. Prep." She took careful steps to reach Kate, doing her best not to look behind her. But even as she spoke with Kate and began preparing the metal samples, that gnawing feeling of being watched wouldn't go away.

* * *

Jittery. It was the best word to describe the crawling sensation in Catfish's stomach and the tingling in his nerves. It wasn't hurting his focus, but the same thought bounced around his skull every few minutes: "Is Shawna okay?"

The first half hour inside the engineering lab had been excruciating. Every moment that passed, he'd waited for the sirens to start wailing, a booming, robotic voice shouting over the PA, and the sound of napalm going off inside a tin can. Each imagined event triggered more and more consequences, everything from Shawna running out of the lab, her body disappearing as a blob of black washed over her, to a wall of fire rushing toward him, human screams just audible over the roar of superheated air.

Now, those thoughts had become more sporadic. In fact, he could go entire minutes without thinking of disaster.

"Hey!"

Catfish flinched and turned from the computer. "What?"

Givens stood less than half a meter away, glaring at Catfish with an irritated squint. "You've been staring off into space for about two minutes now. What's the problem?"

"Have not," Catfish said. "And there isn't one."

"Then why isn't the next design ready?" Givens asked, a finger gesturing to the computer.

Catfish blinked at him before turning back to face his screen. "Send Job To Printers?" a dialog box said. A mouse click later, and a progress bar appeared. "There. Happy?" He turned to face Givens.

The other man had already left the console and headed for the igniter boxes. Catfish sighed. He couldn't focus, and the last prototypes had failed spectacularly. One hadn't even exploded. He'd somehow managed to get the combinations wrong. Instead of improving the flammability of the explosive, the new chemical combo had only burned the grenade into slag with a pop.

This latest? He'd returned to the drawing board and discarded the idea of adding thermite to the explosive. He couldn't get it to work, and it was unstable as hell. He'd have to find something else a little less likely to blow up if it were accidentally dropped.

He'd considered using phosphorus, like 'ole Willie Pete of the Vietnam era, but stability was once again a serious issue. He couldn't even print using phosphorus. They weren't in a vacuum-sealed clean room, and white phosphorus would be too toxic anyway.

The grenade hadn't been designed to get the creature in one fell swoop. The idea was to pierce any armor it may have formed with an explosion and then ignite the liquid within using a secondary agent. The rest would take care of itself. At least, that was the theory.

But the secondary agent had been a serious issue. Now, he was going back to basics. Givens had suggested using something thermobaric, but that created its own problem. The first and foremost being predictability. If M2 was chasing you, the last thing you wanted to think about was how far you had to throw the thing not to be covered in fuel before the second charge lit you up like a matchstick. Plus, the collateral damage would be significant.

But the magnesium had been a good idea. A great idea, in fact. He grinned at the computer. He and magnesium were old friends now.

The question now was which way worked best. Solid? Powder?

He was leery of the powder. The simulations predicted a sizable cone of fire, but he was concerned about the scatter effect. The mixture couldn't be too thick or thin and would be tricky to get right. Solid? That was the question.

A fragmentation grenade design was optimal so long as untrained personnel were somewhat protected from blowing themselves up or catching themselves on fire. A tight, predictive area of effect is what he needed. Cook, throw, boom. Simple.

With that in mind, his final Hail Mary design included magnesium shards. They should burn for up to a second before disappearing into ash. That was more than long enough to set M2 on fire if you cracked open its shell first. Assuming, of course, it had grown one.

The progress bar had reached 5%. Catfish leaned back and sighed. He should be over with Givens putting together more igniter assemblies. He should be up and fidgeting over the new design. He should be doing so many things except sitting here and waiting for the anxiety monster to reappear.

Get it finished, he told himself. *Then, at least, she'll be armed with something more than good looks.*

If she heard him say that, she would no doubt put her hands on her hips and glare at him. He could almost hear her asking him why he didn't list intelligence, along with the fact she was pretty to look at. He blushed, thinking of how he'd respond to that situation. What would he say to get himself out of trouble? Or maybe he'd just decide to dig a little deeper?

His worried expression faded into a thin smile. Feeling a little better, he got up from the console and carefully walked to join Givens. Test. Retest. Perfect. Yeah. He was on it.

* * *

Shawna's team had clocked out early and headed upstairs to the conference room. They had a lot to talk about, and none of it was good.

In addition to the chorus of yawns constantly repeating around the table, she practically drifted off mid-conversation. The room smelled of sweat and bottled-up fear that had become stale and putrid. They all needed a shower, but the conversation had been too pressing.

The metal and glass tests were quite successful but in the completely wrong way.

After exposing the metal and glass samples to the M2 specimens for thirty minutes, they pulled and bathed them in UV for another five minutes before preparing them both for the microscope.

Jay kept an eye on the monitors while Shawna, Kate, and Neil handled the rest of the tests. The metal's surface, it seemed, had become brittle, the edges no longer uniform as though nearly microscopic bits had flaked off during or after their exposure. The steel also appeared to be the shiniest substance she'd ever seen.

The glass Moore's team had used to isolate the M2 containers was just as susceptible. So were the pipes.

Essentially, M2 slowly ate away at the metal and glass and transformed the two mediums in the process. They just didn't know on what level. Moore flat-out denied their request to send the materials to a lab that could see what was going on at the atomic level.

"Metal and glass are tightly packed," Jay said. "Not much space between the atoms. But this? This looks like metal has been transformed into something else. Maybe something a bit less dense."

Neil and Kate balked at that, but Shawna hadn't. She remembered Catfish mentioning the steel on *Leaguer* that had come in contact with the creature. The metal shouldn't have been clean, and it sure as hell shouldn't have been so brittle.

Before *Leaguer*, she would have said Catfish had exaggerated or hadn't quite known what he was seeing. But now, she was more than willing to believe his account. When you were already beyond the impossible, how could you deny the implausible?

It didn't matter how it was doing it or what it was doing to the materials. The fact that their M2 containment systems were vulnerable to M2's nature meant that they had to fish or cut bait and do it soon. They hadn't even bothered running the biological tests today—the metal and glass tests had been too depressing.

Moore had attended their conference, although briefly. Shawna had been shocked when the head of the facility, the woman so paranoid about containment security, seemed so nonchalant about their findings. "You'll just have to work faster," she said. "Maybe drop some of the more intensive or time-sensitive tests."

"We've been talking about it," Kate said, "and we're not sure how to enhance the containment system other than surrounding it in several more layers."

"I know," Moore said. "We knew that was a possibility from the beginning. We also knew it might be inevitable. Which is why you'll finish what you can in the best time possible. This project will have to end sooner than I thought."

Kate hadn't kept them long after that. Instead of joining Shawna at the commissary, the scientists returned to their dorm to shower and change. Shawna wanted to but just couldn't bring herself to. She felt they'd already lost the fight, and it was just a matter of time before M2 escaped.

The signs were there. The vibrations inside the barrel. The bulging dents on the barrel's surface. Poppy was trying to escape. Although Taub was imprisoned in much thicker confines, it was undoubtedly doing the same. It could take weeks or days, but they would eat through their makeshift prisons and destroy everything in sight.

The hot chocolate tasted sour and left her with heartburn, which didn't improve her mood. All she wanted to do now was crawl into bed. After a shower. Dinner didn't even sound like a good idea, although she knew she should be hungry. It was as if her entire body had simply had enough. Or, maybe it was her mind.

Taub 1 had watched her all day. She knew it. The eyestalk had always seemed to follow her, the orb spinning as if searching for a target, but it had already found one. Taub 1 seemed to have found its intended meal.

That thought had hounded her all day, just as it did now. She didn't want to return to the lab until those things were incinerated, and even after that, she wasn't sure she trusted the containment system to hold much longer.

How long had M2 been imprisoned? Less than a month? The creatures had had weeks to affect their environment, each day gathering more space to push and work on the metal. While Taub was encased in thicker steel, it still faced a layer of glass surrounding the storage tank. Poppy, however, was in a relatively thinly walled barrel within the same kind of glass enclosure as its brethren. Poppy and Taub, upon breaching their prisons, could find any number of ways to escape. Once that happened, the quarantine level would be destroyed in a fireball. She hoped.

"Hey," Catfish said.

She looked up at him with a tired smile. "You're out early."

"No, I'm not. I'm half an hour late. We, um, worked until they kicked us out." He wrinkled his eyebrows at her expression. With a sigh, he sat across from her and leaned forward. "What happened?"

When she finished telling him, he stared down at the table. "I need that bottle of bourbon now," he said. "So that's it? It's just inevitable no matter what we do?"

She nodded. "If we had time, we could experiment and find out how and what it's doing. We might also be able to develop an alloy or polymer that's immune to the effects. But I imagine that would take weeks, if not months."

He leaned back in his chair and looked at the commissary entrance. "Ever get the feeling there's something going on that we don't know about?"

"Yes," Shawna said. "Every day. So, is there anything new going on with you that I should know about?"

The way his smile appeared made her grin. When Catfish had a breakthrough, it was like watching a little kid see their first meteor streaking across the sky. Catfish lived for moments of discovery, just as Thomas had.

"I think we've got the grenades figured out," he said. "Ditched all the other designs and focused on one."

"What makes this one special?"

His grin widened. "Solid magnesium flechettes."

Keeping her face as straight as possible, she said, "You're going to give M2 diarrhea?"

Catfish glared, a dribble of hot chocolate stuck in his beard. "Going to make it shit fire."

He told her about the grenade tests and how he thought they were close.

Shawna tented her hands on the table. "So when does my team get hold of them?"

He blinked. "What?"

"I want one on my belt."

He sighed. "Don't we all. They haven't been fully tested yet. If we have a printing defect, for instance, it could blow up in your hands. We need to run some more stress tests."

"Bullshit," Shawna said.

"Okay," he said, "how about this? As soon as I have one ready, and I'm confident, I'll let you have it."

"Good." Her fingers crawled across the table toward him. "We need to get out of here."

"We do," he said. "Because you need a shower. You're rank."

She laughed. "A shower it is. Let's go to the chariot."

He awkwardly stood with a groan.

"Leg still hurting you?"

"Always," Catfish said. "Getting better, but every once in a while, it lets me know I wrecked it."

"Okay. Shower. Dinner. TLC."

"Dinner? Want to come back here?"

She blushed. "No. We'll eat in your trailer," she said.

"Oh. Okay. I mean—" He stopped for a moment. "Was that a double entendre?"

She grinned at him, and it was his turn to blush. "Guess we'll find out."

CHAPTER TWENTY-THREE

The next day, Shawna again found herself in the lab facing Poppy 1 and Taub 1. However, things were a little different now. Sarah had replaced the sergeant at the security station, and the familiar portable incinerator units had been replaced with the kind you expected to see strapped to a soldier's back.

There were now four suited figures inside the labs instead of two, and a few stainless steel nozzles had descended from the ceiling. Somehow, Shawna didn't think they were there to spray water.

After their chat yesterday, Moore must have gone into security overdrive. Ultra-paranoid level. But could Shawna blame her?

Shit. Hadn't she wanted to burn the things yesterday? Set fire to the facility and walk the hell away? Do something to destroy M2 once and for all?

Moore might be crazy, Jekyll and Hyde crazy, but at least she was taking this part seriously. M2 might destroy the humans inside the labs, but it wasn't getting out of here unless it had been reduced to ash and flushed out the waste vents like the leavings from a million cigarettes.

You're going to die in here too, a voice said in her mind. *Don't you know that?*

Ignoring the voice, she focused on what Neil had put on the monitors. It was the security log from last night. Seven separate instances showed up on the display, and as she read them, she felt both puzzled and more afraid than ever.

The first had happened just after sundown. Taub 1 sprouted more eyestalks and spidery legs before examining its prison. This time, however, it had tested the seams of the sample case by extruding a tail, affixing itself to either side of the intersection like a glob of tar, and pressing with the tail.

The extreme vibration on the glass and steel surfaces triggered the sensors, and security was called to ensure the thing hadn't escaped. Taub 1 hadn't escaped the sample case, but it tested all eight corners of the case in the same manner.

The second security alert summary listed another trigger from Taub 1. More than two hours after it had tested the case and returned to its liquid form, two eyestalks rose from the pool, the black orbs spinning in dizzying revolutions. The alert ended there. No further movements.

Just the summary had been enough to make her skin vibrate. When Neil ran the film loop of the extrusion, her throat burned with bile, and the overwhelming need to run filled her mind. Even though it was only a recording, she felt those dead, lifeless eyes assessing her and its surroundings like an animal desperate to get out. But she felt as though it wanted something more than simply to eat its captors.

Poppy 1 began its nocturnal behaviors around the same time Taub 1 had grown eyestalks. Shortly after the team left the lab, it returned to its liquid state, reabsorbing itself into an obsidian pool. The alert summary listed an unusual 25°C temperature change lasting three seconds, but the chemical sensors had recorded no known toxins or unexpected compositions.

The video, however, showed much more than the alert summary provided. They watched the pool bubble slightly, its surface covered in a heat haze like fresh asphalt drying in the Texas summer sun.

"What the hell?" Jay had said. "Did that thing fart?"

Shawna's mouth opened and closed before she laughed. A few

seconds later, the rest of the team joined her.

"I mean, what was that?"

"Jay?" Kate said. "That was neither helpful nor scientific. But damned funny."

Jay stopped laughing. "I wasn't kidding."

Neil turned back to the monitor. A touch of the trackpad and the loop played again and again. He stepped back from the monitors and tried to cross his arms reflexively. Shawna smiled as he put them back down at his sides. Some movements were damned near impossible in the suits.

"I think you might be right," Neil said.

Kate sighed into the mic. "Okay, so it expels heat. We didn't detect any hydrocarbons, any CO2, nothing."

"Unless it created oxygen," Shawna said. The team went quiet. "Neil? Do we have that?"

He shook his head. "Apart from the actual oxygen levels inside the room, the sensors aren't calibrated or sensitive enough to pick up that small of a deviation. I mean, if it expelled some O2, it would have to be a tremendous amount to tick the meters."

"Shit," Jay said. "You think M2 creates oxygen?"

"No," Neil chuckled. "But I didn't think it farted either."

"Point." Jay walked to the monitor. "Okay. So, do we test that?"

"Don't know, don't care. Yet. Let's see what else it did first," Kate said.

Alert number four occurred when Taub 1 changed color as it reformed itself. Well, transform was a better term. It once again extruded a pseudopod that looked like a misshapen beaver tail, but as it did, the appendage's color lightened from its normal jet black, and its surface dimpled and pitted.

It paused for several seconds before the pool narrowed in diameter and extruded another appendage at an angle. The tail's flat, thick base gave the creature the leverage required to press the new pseudopod against the glass. But this time, Taub 1 had positioned itself no more than a few centimeters from the glass wall, the end of the new appendage hooked and curled to a sharpened point.

A few seconds passed before the tail pumped upward, and the hook swung in a vicious half-circle, Taub 1's normally black surface bubbling as it took on the same texture as its tail. The sharp point glanced off the glass, crumbs of dark debris scattering over that side of the sample case. Taub 1 attacked again, and the case trembled.

Taub 1 tried the same tactic for five minutes. When it finally stopped, the sample case's floor appeared covered in brownie crumbs, and the creature seemed to have grown smaller.

It's losing mass, Shawna thought. *It transformed itself, grew a muscle analog, and something like flesh. Or a carapace.*

After its final attack, Taub 1 collapsed into liquid, spread itself thin to coat the sample case, and coalesced into a pancake. The video loop ended.

"It's learning," Shawna said aloud.

"Learning fast." Jay turned to Neil. "Did it come close to damaging the case?"

Neil shook his head. "I don't think it has enough mass to do that. But no, it didn't. Enough to freak out the sensors, but not enough to affect the glass."

"You don't know that," Shawna said. "Remember what the experiments showed. We can't be sure it's not weakening the entire sample case."

The team fell silent again. Shawna looked over at Taub 1. The creature's lone eyestalk followed her. *Or seems to,* she said to herself. Paranoia was expected, but did she really think the creature cared about who was in the room? Each of them was nothing more than a meal to the lifeform.

"How bad are the rest of the security alerts?" Kate asked.

Neil brought up the additional sensor logs. More of the same. The difference was that Poppy 1 seemed more content in its liquid state than Taub 1. The reason? Good question.

Both samples were bathed in the same frequency of fluorescent light and had been kept at the same ambient temperature, so why did Taub 1 continually probe its confines, often growing limbs and other muscular pseudopods? Poppy 1, on the other hand, seemed to have given it up.

Shawna looked back at Poppy 1. The black liquid sat like a sheen of dirty motor oil on a metal slab. No hint of an eyestalk there, much less any other appendage.

She felt Taub 1's alien stare and kept her eyes focused on Poppy 1's displays. She couldn't bear to look at that spinning, murky eye for another moment.

"So now what?" Jay asked.

Kate pored over the reports and looked back at their tests. "We'll have to destroy them both quite soon," she said. "So what do we want to do? Bisection?"

"I'm in favor of that," Neil said. "We'll slice them down the middle like we did with the small samples. See if the smaller specimens can still manifest physical attributes."

"I swear," Jay said, "when you speak like that, I question if you've ever been laid."

"Only by your mom," Neil said.

"Oh, haha," Jay said. "And yours wears combat boots."

"Bisection," Shawna said, ignoring their repartee. "What do we do if they don't respond?"

Kate sighed heavily. "Then we'll try something else."

Something else. Like what? Feed them radioactive waste? Or maybe insects from the fields? What?

Neil and Kate had already begun prepping for the next round of physical tests. Another bisection would require Neil, Kate, and Shawna to enter the lab and use the partitions built into the sample cases to effectively split the samples, creating 4 of the creatures from the two already in the containers. Four of them.

The plus side? They wouldn't be half as large as they were now. But four of them? She imagined the partitioned sample cases, the things inside all staring at her with those dead, disinterested spinning orbs.

"Shawna?"

The voice made her flinch. Inside the pressurized helmet, she couldn't hear where the sound had come from. She shook away the clenching fear that had grasped her. "Yeah, Kate?"

"You okay?"

"Why wouldn't I be?" The moment she said the words, she realized she had said them between pants.

"You need a break?" Jay asked.

"I'm fine," Shawna said, desperate to keep the tremor from her voice. "We ready?"

Jay sighed through the comms. "Is there such a thing?"

Shawna glanced up at the monitor feeds displaying the inside of the lab. All those angles, all those lights, all those safety precautions. Now, they'd have to put them to the test.

"Ready."

CHAPTER TWENTY-FOUR

It was Shawna's first time in the lab since they'd infected the rats. Her pressure suit muffled the sounds as though they were coming through the walls of a thinly insulated apartment.

More like a dorm room, Shawna thought.

She, Neil, and Kate left the airlock and entered the testing lab. Even with four meters of distance between her and the entities, Shawna felt too close. Way too close. It was one thing to be on the other side of a thick glass and steel partition and quite another to only be protected by the UV lights and the sample case enclosures. Shawna stared through the window and into the diagnostic area beyond. The two soldiers with their incinerators stood still as statues, their eyes scanning the lab for anything out of the ordinary. They made her nervous, too.

If something happened, what would keep them from running inside the lab and torching the scientists as well as the creatures? Hell, why bother with that when you could just use the nuclear option and flood the lab with killing fire?

"Okay," Jay said. "Poppy 1 is pretty chill."

Neil snorted. "How did an old fart like you come up with that one?"

"Nephew," Jay said. "I think you can split Poppy 1 without manually adjusting its position."

The heavy pressure suit was more than a little warm inside, but now it seemed as though her skin had been covered in ice. The last four words Jay had spoken were enough to conjure some pretty damned ugly images.

She slowed her pace, allowing Kate and Neil the first crack at Poppy 1's sample case. When they reached it, Shawna sidestepped for a better view. Jay had been right. Poppy 1 lay more or less in the middle of the sample case. Just as they had cleaved the first samples to create clones, they'd drop a partition and separate the liquid, effectively creating two creatures.

Kate moved to perform the process on Poppy 1, but Neil moved in her way. "I've got it," Neil said.

"Ah," Kate said. "Saving the little old lady?"

"Hardly," he said. "You're neither little nor old. Just thinking of Maeve, that's all."

The comms went dead silent. Neil stood for a moment as though chastising himself for having given voice to the thoughts. Finally, he said, "Here we go," and turned back to the sample case.

Shawna watched as he pulled the safety release and slid the partition down. When the metal and glass came within a few centimeters of the pool, it began bubbling.

"Shit," Jay said. "Neil? Slam it home. Now."

Just as tendrils of black, no thicker than filaments, rose from the pool, their ends reaching for the partition, Neil dropped it and hit the control to fasten it into place. The pool erupted in shudders and bubbles. The Poppy creatures continued exploring the new obstruction with pseudopods for a moment before finally retracting them. The puddle of M2 slowly oozed to the center of its new confines, its twin doing the same.

"What the hell?" Jay asked.

"I saw it too," Kate said. "They both responded in the same fashion."

"So?" Neil gestured at the case. "Probably just an instinctual response if both displayed the same behavior."

Shawna shook her head. "I don't think so," she said, her voice barely above a whisper. "It's a clone. Hell, it's not even a clone. It's just the same creature cut into two pieces. The real question is whether or not the two creatures share the same memories."

"Memories?" Kate said. "Are you suggesting these things are capable of memory?"

"Why not?" Shawna said. "If you can condition a creature, it remembers. Hell, you can even condition a plant to grow more vertically by cutting off the longest limbs. A tree doesn't have memory, but it can be conditioned."

"No," Neil said. "Conditioning is not memory."

Shawna smiled despite herself. "Then a dog remembers, but a plant doesn't?"

"Children?" Kate said. "Can we go ahead and handle Taub 1 so we can get out of here?"

"Oh, right," Neil said.

He stood over the sample case, his eyes examining the locking mechanisms and the status lights. The case was secure, or as secure as possible, with M2 inside.

While Kate stayed near the Poppys, Shawna moved to the side of the Taub 1 sample case. She'd averted her gaze as long as she could, but a twitch of movement caught her attention. A black, spinning orb on the end of a malformed, hooked eyestalk stared at her. For a moment, she forgot there was a wall of glass and steel between her and the creature. Its alien stare froze her thoughts, and time dragged on while she stared into a void.

"Shawna?"

Neil's voice was far away, but he was asking her something. She wanted to care but didn't. The alien appendage and eye came closer. The darkness in the creature's orb beckoned and called to her. Sleep. Silence. Still, the orb and its void came closer until she felt like she was drowning.

"Shawna!"

The voice was so far away that she didn't even know whose it was. Didn't care either. She was listening for something in the dead silence. Something that would speak to her in a language she could understand.

The void before her disappeared, replaced with blinding white light. She stumbled backward and nearly fell before someone caught her.

"Neil? Get her out of here!" Kate was yelling.

Where was she? Where had she been? She blinked rapidly as she tried to clear the terrible afterimage, her retinas practically burning from the light. "Neil?"

"Yes, I've got you. Can you stand?"

Could she? Why was he asking that? She looked down, and her vision cleared. She'd been staring directly into the light array above her. "Where?" The dizziness faded, leaving her breathing rapidly but also feeling more stable. She pushed forward slightly, regained her balance, and stood on her own.

Kate stood near the panic button on the wall, her hand hovering mere centimeters from its glowing red surface.

"Why?" Shawna surveyed the room and saw the Taub 1 sample case. Its stand had moved slightly as though pushed. Instead of being flush with the observation window, it now canted a few centimeters toward the wall. She pointed at the case, the confusion giving way to unease. "What happened?"

"Are you okay?" Neil asked.

Shawna nodded. "I'm here. What happened?"

"You tell me?" Kate said. "Because I don't know what the hell you were doing." The anger in her voice made Shawna turn to face her. The team leader had moved her hand away from the panic button but remained within reach.

Shawna caught motion through the window and looked over. The two soldiers with incinerators were no longer standing in their positions. The pair had moved to the airlock while two new arrivals took position on either side of the experimentation lab.

"What happened?" Shawna said.

"You don't remember?"

She turned to face Neil. "Remember what? I don't understand—"

"It's okay, Shawna," Jay said over the radio. "What's the last thing you remember?"

"I—" She swallowed hard. "I saw Taub 1. It was looking at me. And—" She stopped again. How could she put it into words? It was a delusion, something Lovecraft might have dreamt up. Hell, she didn't want to remember it. It had just been the vision of a void. Nothing more. "I don't know."

"Well," Neil said with a long sigh. "You put your helmet right up against the case and started pushing it."

Shawna felt as though she'd been punched. "I did what?"

"Yeah," Kate said. "That's what you did."

"Why? I mean—"

"Shawna?" Jay said. "Why don't you come back out here with me."

"Yeah," Neil said. "Probably a good idea. You might want to take a break."

"A break," she said dumbly. "Look, I just—"

"Shawna," Kate said. "Please take a break."

The tone of Kate's voice was that of a mother's, plaintive and resigned at the same time. Shawna's mother had used that tone whenever her daughter made a mess by pure accident or simply had the misfortune to be in the wrong place at the wrong time. But the meaning of the words was simple enough: you are forgiven, but I need you to leave.

"Okay," Shawna said, a flush of shame lighting her cheeks as she walked to the airlock. Stuck inside the suit, there was no way to wipe away the tears. Bleary-eyed, she went through the airlock, a soldier following too close behind her. A few minutes later, she removed her suit and prepared to leave the lab enclosure.

"Shawna," Moore's voice said over the airlock's intercom. "Please join me in the commissary when you are ready."

Shawna stared up at the all-too-visible security camera in the corner. Moore was watching her. Hell, the entire facility staff were probably watching her. She'd no doubt that when she stepped into the corridor, another soldier would be waiting to greet her. Maybe even Sarah.

Instead of giving the camera the finger, she shrugged her shoulders and nodded to it. She paused at the airlock door, her shaking hand mere centimeters away from the cycle button.

This was it. She'd fucked up. She'd lost her shit, put everyone in jeopardy, and Moore was going to fire her, as in termination of employment. Which, in this case, might mean something a little more ominous than a pink slip. She wiped away another tear, composed herself, and pressed the button.

No soldier waited for her in the corridor. The area seemed completely empty. She stepped out of the lab facility and into the wide-open area. Sarah waved to her from the security station.

Breath shuddering, Shawna fought to wave back. She waited for Sarah to beckon her, but the woman didn't. Instead, she'd already turned her attention back to the security monitors and was talking in a low voice with a security minion.

Without making eye contact, Shawna slipped through the last pair of security doors and into the elevator. While it rose, all the possible ramifications of what had happened whirled and flooded her mind with a thousand different narratives, all of them bad.

When the elevator doors opened, she paused before lifting her eyes to see who was there to greet her. There was no one. Her skin tingled with anxiety. Had the crazy bitch told everyone to get off the floor so she could kill Shawna in private?

Shawna made her way around the corridor and to the foyer. Next to the commissary door, a standing sign announced, "Closed until 1500." That feeling of unease more or less took over every other sensation. She took the last five steps slowly and deliberately, steeling herself for either a bullet or a pair of handcuffs. When she placed her hand on the door handle, her throat clicked shut on a whimper.

Before she had a chance to chicken out, she pulled. The door swung wide on the well-lit commissary dining room. The chef hadn't yet placed any food on the counters, but she noticed another carafe of hot chocolate with a sticker noting it had been brewed five minutes ago. The bad feeling melted into confusion.

"Shawna?"

She didn't jump at the sound but froze instead. Moore's voice had a strange quality to it. It didn't have its usual false, polite tone. Instead, it was more of a mother calling to a child. Shawna turned and found Moore sitting at one of the smaller tables. Apart from her, the dining room was empty.

"Hi," Shawna managed, although it came out as a hoarse whisper.

"Why don't you get a drink and come join me?"

Shawna did her best to keep her voice level, but it shook anyway. "Am I going to get a chance to drink it?"

Moore's friendly expression wrinkled into confusion fast enough to look genuine, although Shawna wasn't certain there was anything genuine about the woman. "Please. I want to talk to you about what happened. Because I don't think you explained it." Moore gestured at the floor. "I certainly don't think your team was in the mood to try and understand, either."

"That's for sure," Shawna said, sounding like Eeyore. "Not like I could have expected anything else."

Moore cleared her throat. "Shawna? I'd rather not be shouting at you. Get a drink and join me."

The strange woman dropped her eyes to the table, an index finger sliding over her tablet. Shawna stood there for a moment, not quite sure what to do. Finally, feeling awkward and paranoid, she filled a cup and dressed it the way she liked. By the time she reached Moore, the woman had already finished her own.

Moore looked up from the tablet, a sad smile on her face. "The rain's going to get worse," she said. "Canada won't shut the door."

Shawna chuckled. "I haven't been in cool weather in a long time," she said. "Not since I was in Norway."

"Not surprised," Moore said. "You were rig-hopping and lab-hopping all over Africa and East Asia. Not many of those places have a real winter."

"At least not when we were there," she said. "No."

The pause lingered between them, each second making it more awkward to break the silence. Finally, Moore said, "Tell me what happened."

Shawna stared down at the hot chocolate. She was glad it wasn't coffee. She wasn't sure she could look into a black liquid again without shivering. "I went to hold the stand for Neil and— Well—" She fought to put it into words. It sounded so ridiculous now. But it wasn't. "I looked at it. Made eye contact." She slowly shook her head. "It's like it was looking back at me, studying me, assessing me. And I just got lost in its stare. It just kept getting bigger and bigger and—" Shawna was silent for a moment. "It's like it was trying to speak."

Moore's face paled. "Trying to speak?"

Shawna laughed nervously. "I know. It sounds—"

"Ridiculous?" Moore asked. "My dear, with all the surveillance films you've seen, as well as your own experience, don't you think it's, at the very least, an intelligent creature?"

"Of course," Shawna said. "Well, Taub, much more than Poppy."

"Exactly," Moore said. "Poppy has seemed to act more on instinct rather than working puzzles. I think the records from Ben Taub make it quite clear that Taub was at least as intelligent as a dog. Perhaps much more so."

"And dogs speak to us in a different language," Shawna said.

Moore grinned. "Right."

"The difference between M2 and a dog is a bit vast, but I grant you your point," Shawna said.

"Good. Now. Is this the first time this has happened?"

"No," Shawna said, remembering the day before when she'd felt Taub 1's stare as if it were making physical contact with her. "It was watching me all day yesterday. And this morning."

"Is it the same feeling?"

"Yes and no," Shawna said. "This time in the lab? Much more powerful."

"Interesting," Moore said. "No one else has mentioned this."

"Why would they? I must be the only crazy one."

Moore sighed, wiped her face, and stared into her empty cup. To Shawna, it looked like the woman had been trying to fight back tears. "You're not," she said. "You're not crazy."

"What is with you, Moore?" Shawna said. "I read and heard the transcripts of you talking with HAL and Ben Taub. I know how you sounded. Emotionless. Robotic. Detached professionalism. I get it. But you're not doing that now. You've become Jekyll and Hyde."

Moore wiped at her face again before looking up. Shawna had been right. The bitch was at least pretending to be on the verge of a breakdown. "I know," she said. "You've seen the containments."

"Yes."

"Then you know you can see them through the glass. As if they were in a terrarium." Her voice trailed off, and her eyes had become slightly unfocused. "The first few days Poppy and Taub were here, we fought like hell to keep them from getting out. Based on our observations, we contained them the best we could with what was available. We had to evacuate the creatures immediately, you understand."

Shawna said nothing.

"The longer we waited, the more of a chance something else could happen. More lives lost. More damage. More threat." Moore picked up her cup as if to sip and rolled it between her hands instead. "I supervised the transport. I supervised the move-in to this facility. We did the best we could with what we knew. But it wasn't enough." She made eye contact with Shawna. "And now everything is inevitable."

"But you're prepared."

"Yes," Moore said. But as I've thought and heard since we discovered M2, the word 'impossible' has lost all meaning. And that means every precaution is suspect, as is every data point we've gathered and everything we think we know. And based on what I've seen this week, we need to destroy them."

Shawna blinked at the woman. Had she really just said that? "You want to destroy them." It wasn't a question.

Moore rolled the empty mug from one hand to the next, the glass scraping across the wood with a whisper. "I've always wanted to destroy them." Moore's eyes glittered with something close to madness. "Ever since I saw what they can do."

"Then why? Why all this?" Shawna raised her hands to encompass the facility. "Why didn't you just set the things on fire to begin with?"

Moore's throat clicked as she swallowed hard. Shawna thought the woman had been on the verge of saying something before thinking better of it. "I had no choice."

Shawna leaned back in her chair. "You're in charge."

Moore smiled. Shawna knew it was genuine merely because of the futility in it. "In charge doesn't mean in control. And, no, I will not elaborate. I've already said too much."

"Who is in control?"

Moore looked away to study the wall. "No one you know," she said at last. "Doesn't matter." She wiped her sleeve across her damp forehead. "M2 will be destroyed. The only question is when."

"How about now?" Shawna said.

"No. Not yet."

"Do you realize how schizo you sound right now?" Shawna dropped her mug to the table hard enough for a tendril of brown liquid to fly over the side. "Make up your mind before we're all fucking dead."

"Not. Yet." Moore's smile had disappeared, her eyes hard as

diamonds. She stood from the table and grabbed her tablet. "Soon." She took a few steps toward the door before turning. "Do you feel you can continue?"

Shawna blinked. Her brain had been turning over Moore's behavior and what she'd said, trying to find some coded meaning. "What?"

"Do you feel well enough to go back to the lab?"

The word "yes" immediately leaped into her mind, but she kept herself from saying it. Could she? "I think so. But I'm not going back inside the experiment lab."

"I'm glad to hear you say that. Now," Moore said, "I'll alert Kate that you're coming back down."

"Thank you," Shawna said.

Moore pointed at Shawna's mug. "Finish that, maybe get another. Or take one to Mis—" She blushed and rolled her eyes. "Catfish." She turned and left the room without another word.

Shawna remained looking out the door for some time. When she finally took another sip from the drink, she found it had gone cold. She swung her gaze to the industrial-sized thermos on the serving table. Another hot chocolate? Why not? And yes, she'd bring Catfish one too.

The disposable, 350ml lidded cups would keep both drinks nice and toasty. As she poured the liquid into the cups, Moore's words echoed in her mind. "Soon."

What the hell did that mean? More importantly, had the woman lost her mind? She certainly seemed close to it, at the very least.

For the first time in over a week, Shawna wondered who was really in control of this project. She'd always assumed it was Moore. Hell, they were told it was Moore, but that didn't add up either. The woman appeared to want to answer Shawna's questions but hadn't been able to bring herself to do so.

"Ears," Shawna said aloud. Ears. And eyes. Moore might be watched as closely as the rest of the facility personnel. Maybe even more so. But by whom?

Catfish called the facility a "black site," like the compounds the CIA used for storing terrorists, compromised assets, and other human beings that were never to see the light of day again. The description was close. The difference being, of course, human terrorists wouldn't eat the whole damned world.

M2 wasn't an invading army or made up of individuals who'd been indoctrinated with extremist ideologies. It was a creature. An intelligent one. While it might not be as smart as a human being, it could solve problems and was insanely dangerous to biological tissues.

This so-called "black site" was little more than a container for M2. A rigged inferno waiting for someone to pull the lever and incinerate everything.

And here we are, waiting for it to happen, she thought, *and just as vulnerable to the solution as the problem.*

Shawna finished fixing her cup of hot chocolate and started on Catfish's. As she held the cup, she realized her hand was shaking. Gritting her teeth, she willed it to steady. It didn't want to cooperate but did so anyway. Grudgingly.

When she finished affixing the lid, she walked out of the empty commissary, holding the two cups in her hand. The facility seemed completely devoid of human presence apart from her own, but she knew that was bullshit. Soldiers hid somewhere, watching, waiting, and hopefully less terrified than she was.

As she walked to the elevator, her eyes kept swinging to look at the cameras embedded in the ceiling. They were watching her. They were watching everything. The only question was, who were "they?"

CHAPTER TWENTY-FIVE

Big boom is what Givens had asked for. Catfish stared through the thick, explosion-proof glass and grinned. This was going to be it. This time, it would work. "Fire in the hole," he said softly and touched the control panel.

The gray orb in the cradle disappeared in an explosion of glittering, fiery magnesium shards. Both he and Givens watched, mouths open, as the instruments lit up with the shockwave report. The magnesium shards quickly burned themselves out as if they'd never existed, save for the scorch marks on the floor.

"Well," Givens grinned, "that worked."

Catfish slapped him on the back. "Fuck yes!"

Givens' head swung as if on a rusty hinge. "Don't touch me again."

Catfish stared at him for a moment, his happy smile disintegrating. "Okay."

"We ready to do some printing?"

Catfish already had three prototypes ready, but none had been as packed as this one. This grenade had more or less been the day's final iteration. If it hadn't worked, it would have been back to the drawing board. But now? They had something useful and workable.

"We're ready. I want to cover the science team—"

"And Sarah," Givens growled.

"Of course," Catfish said. "And Sarah. And you and me. And—"

He stopped. "Shit. How many do we need?"

Givens shrugged. "As many as we can make."

They printed the trigger mechanisms first. Of all of the components, it was the only one that required more than just slamming a shape home into another shape. While one set of printers worked on the grenade housings, Givens and Catfish carved up the charges. The magnesium had been his idea, and it was the same basic principle he'd used to turn AUV-5 into a bomb to blow up M2 in its trench. That had worked. So why not this?

Magnesium burned until there was nothing left. You couldn't put it out with air or water. An explosion would ignite and scatter it, similar to white phosphorus used during the Vietnam War, but magnesium was far more stable, predictable, and much less toxic.

Givens remained silent as his long, dexterous fingers carefully assembled the igniters. The man rarely spoke without reason and was terse when he did. Another thing about Catfish's "lab partner" that drove him crazy. Catfish didn't like silence. To him, it always felt like judgment.

"You know about the containment level?"

Givens glanced up at Catfish before returning to the igniter. "You mean the fact it's on the verge of flooding and the goddamned electricity doesn't work for shit? Yeah, I know."

The words had no malice or frustration in them. He might as well have been giving Catfish the weather forecast.

"That doesn't worry you?"

Givens shrugged. "Nothing we can do about it until something happens. Unless Moore orders us to terminate them."

"The samples, you mean."

He looked up at Catfish again, his eyes curious. "What did you think I meant?"

"Goddamned hard to tell with you."

Givens grunted. "It doesn't matter what I think or say," he said. "Matters what I do."

"And when you're an asshole?"

He shrugged again. "Just being who I am. Nothing personal." He glared at Catfish. "Yet."

The silence returned as they finished the igniters. When the first batch of grenades was finished, he and Givens loaded them, inspected them, inspected them again, and finally placed them in a storage box. Catfish pulled out a label gun and marked up seven: one for him and Givens and one for each scientist and Sarah.

Just as he finished labeling Sarah's grenade, he heard the airlock cycle. Catfish turned, half-expecting Moore to be standing there with a small cadre of soldiers. Instead, it was Shawna carrying a pair of cups.

She smiled but looked less than all there as if she had awakened from a bad dream. "Hello."

Catfish rose from the worktable and walked toward her. He knew he was grinning but didn't care. He reached her and offered his left hand. After she put the cup in it, he used his right to pull her toward him in a light hug. "Good to see you," he whispered.

She squeezed him and took a step back, his hand falling away. "Good to see you, too."

He sniffed at the cup and groaned. "More hot chocolate?"

"Well, shit, what did you want?"

"Bourbon," he growled. "And lots of it." He sipped from the cup and muttered a grudging compliment. "It's drinkable."

"Good, because it's all you're getting." She looked over his shoulder. "Howdy, Givens."

"Howdy, ma'am," he said back with a dismissive wave.

"So, what brings you here?" Catfish asked.

"Actually, it was Moore's idea. Said you might need a break."

Catfish raised an eyebrow. "Since when does she think I need anything besides a jail cell?" As he took another sip from the hot chocolate, he noticed a shadow cross her face. "Something wrong?"

"Maybe we have her wrong," Shawna said.

"Really?" He glanced over his shoulder to ensure Givens wasn't paying attention and lowered his voice. "Why?"

Her eyes lowered as if trying to find the floor. "Something happened in the lab. I—"

A wave of fear rushed over him. "Wait. What kind of accident?"

"Let me—" She paused, gathering herself. Catfish thought he saw a tear welling in her eye. "No accident. I just had a moment while I was in the lab. Exhaustion, I guess."

The way she immediately hid her face behind the cup of hot chocolate gave away the lie. He shouldn't push. Didn't want to push. He knew her last few nights had been filled with restless sleep punctured by nightmares, and she did look exhausted, but something else had happened. Something she didn't want to talk about.

"Okay," he agreed. "Go back to the trailer and take a nap now."

"Um, no," she said. "I'll help Jay with the instruments and stay out of the lab itself."

That's not what he wanted. What he wanted was for her to go up to the commissary and read a book. Or look out the window. Do anything but go back down. She was spooked, and it showed in every line on her face.

He took another sip as he tried to think of what to say, but he could say nothing that wouldn't sound condescending or demanding. The best he could manage was, "Good."

Her eyes drifted from his and studied Givens. "What's he doing?"

"Huh?" Catfish turned and saw Givens carrying a box toward them. The cardboard and foam cradled what looked like eggs. "Oh. Yeah." He grinned when she met his eyes. "We have toys. Come on."

Catfish walked her to the worktable where Givens had placed the box. The soldier leaned casually against the corner, a dim smile on his face.

Shawna reached in and pulled out a grenade with her name on it. "Whoah," she said. She rolled it around in her hands, testing the weight. "What's the blast radius?"

"Two meters. Five-second timer. It'll beep faster and faster while you cook. Just better be out of your hands before it reaches zero. Preferably long before that."

She frowned. "Just an explosion?"

"No, ma'am," Givens said. "He figured out how to make something special for M2."

"And what," Shawna said, "did you do? The magnesium worked?"

He nodded, his grin widening. "Shaved. The explosion will catch it on fire and spread it like glowing embers. Again, make sure you're well out of the way when it goes off."

"I'll remember that," she said.

"Excuse me," Givens said, "anything happen in the lab I should know about?"

She exchanged a glance with Catfish before answering. "No. Nothing. The monsters were still locked up, and there was no danger."

"No more danger than usual, you mean."

"Right," she said with an embarrassed chuckle. There was a long silence. "Well," she said, "I better get back to it."

Givens picked up the box. "I'll come down with you. Take these to Sarah. There's one for each of you."

"Oh. Great," Shawna said, placing hers back in the case, "but I can take it down."

"No trouble," he said. "I should make a face-to-face check-in anyway."

"Okay, then," she said, kissing Catfish on the cheek. "See you later."

She and Givens headed for the airlock. Just before she entered it, Catfish said, "Be careful."

Her look froze his blood. It was one of resignation. Did she know something? What the hell had happened in the lab?

"I will," she said, blowing him a kiss. The pair left engineering with a hiss of air.

Catfish stared after them for a moment, the drone of the printers providing a background layer of noise for his thoughts. More grenades were printing. They'd soon have more igniters to assemble more party favors. He glanced up at the camera in the corner of the room. Moore no doubt knew what they'd done and what they were up to.

Givens hadn't asked permission to take the grenades downstairs. He'd just done it as though it had already been planned. Or hoped for. Maybe Moore wanted those weapons available for her teams. No. Something seemed off about that, too.

There was an angle here he didn't see. He felt Moore had been playing them all along, leading them all by the nose. Her psychotic mood swings and her inconsistency in behavior all pointed to a breakdown and the obvious answer that she was batshit nuts. But Catfish was beginning to think there was something else driving Moore. Shawna had said as much.

Hating the fact he might have to trust the crazy woman after all, he headed to gather the parts for more igniters. Maybe a little manual work was what he needed to lose himself and purge the confused thoughts. Hell, maybe he could even shake off the anxiety fluttering in his stomach while images of M2 breaking out of the lab played through his mind.

CHAPTER TWENTY-SIX

Shawna stepped through the airlock and into the lab area. Jay sat on a stool at the end of the hall, his hands held before him as he stared up at the screens. He turned to her and nodded curtly. With the light reflecting off his helmet, she couldn't see his face.

She activated her headset and said, "I'm back."

Neil and Kate, still inside the enclosed laboratory, stared at her from their position behind the sample cases. She forced herself not to look at the creatures and instead walked to join Jay.

"What do you think?" Jay asked, gesturing to the screens.

Shawna took a deep breath before lifting her head to see the screens. The leftmost monitors displayed the Poppy specimens, their tendrils still pushing against the glass sides, desperate to reach one another, but the Taubs took her breath away.

A small eyestalk sat atop a surface as thick as pudding skin, the dark, dead orb leaning toward its Taub sibling. The eyestalk seemed to gaze at her, and she immediately broke her stare with the screen. After taking a long breath, she raised her eyes. The sensory organ was once again focused on the other Taub. Maybe it always had been.

"We use our eyes more than anything else," Shawna said, surprised at how calm she sounded while her heart slam danced. "Mammals in general, I mean. A lot of other species, too."

"We discussed that while you were gone," Kate said. "It's almost as if the Taubs know to use their eyes instead of blindly flailing."

"That doesn't make me happy," Neil said.

"Nor me," Kate said.

Shawna cleared her throat. "What did it do when you split it? They don't look the same size."

"We, um," Neil said, "had to just cut it where we could. It," he paused while he searched for a word, "hardened itself. Became solid."

A carapace, she thought. "What happened after you shattered it?"

"Take a look," Jay said and pointed at the screens.

One of the displays lit up with a still image, the label "Taub 1" affixed in the lower right-hand corner. The image became a video, a tight camera view of the sample case and the creature within. The shell was ill-defined and incongruous in places, and the legs were like a spider's. Or perhaps a crab's. The moment the partition began descending, the thing half-scuttled and half-flowed to move to one side, but the partition dropped like a guillotine, slicing the horror in half.

Crumbs of alien shell exploded into a mist of shrapnel, black liquid spurting from the open wound for an instant before the entire creature lost solidity. The second it had transformed, it began moving through its new prison to find the edges. Once it had, it extended the eyestalk.

"Jesus," Shawna said. "Did it just vacuum itself up? Absorb all the, the, the—"

"Debris?" Neil asked.

"Yeah. It exploded like a walnut beneath a sledgehammer. But look. No sign of any material."

"Good point," Kate said. "So what does that mean?"

"You can't let it reform," Jay said. "Once you get it into smaller pieces, you have to keep it that way. Or else."

"Or else what?" Neil said.

Jay's voice wavered with fear. "It starts chasing you through hallways."

No one spoke. Shawna changed the displays to the live feed and stared at the Taubs, watching their eyestalks twitch and jiggle every few seconds.

"Different environment," Shawna said. "Different evolutions."

"I'm coming to that conclusion myself," Neil said.

Kate took a few steps backward, shuffling closer to the airlock. "Neil? I think we should get out of the lab now. Time to go take a look at the recordings and think."

"Why?"

She pointed at the Taub cases. The creatures no longer stared at one another. They were staring at him.

"Yeah," Neil said, shuffling backward and away from the sample cases. "Good idea."

They entered the airlock and left the lab to join Jay and Shawna. Shawna barely noticed because she was too busy watching the Taubs.

The deviation in behavior had been gradual, almost synchronous, the orbs changing from their quick spin to slowly locking on Neil. He'd been the closest to the sample cases and the nearest thing they could see.

"We're going to have to destroy them," Shawna said.

"Here, fucking, here," Jay said. "We'll whack 'em and call it a day."

"Hang on," Neil said. "If we destroy them now, we're just going to have to distill more of them tomorrow. That's the riskiest part of any of these experiments."

Kate heaved a sigh. "You're right. But so is Shawna."

"You have to be kidding." Neil put his hands on his hips, looking comical in the heavy, bulky suit. "What's changed from yesterday? Same samples."

"No," Shawna said, shaking her head. "They're not. Not anymore." She pointed at the lab. The Taubs, slightly different in size, had moved forward in the sample cases and thrust their orb-like sensory organs against the glass. This time, there was no question that the creatures were watching the scientists. Studying. Observing. Maybe hatching plans.

A shiver rattled down her spine. "No," she said again. "We need to get rid of them. Now."

"Goddammit," Neil said. She thought she heard a touch of fear in his voice to match his resignation. "Okay. Fine. Fry them."

Kate didn't wait. "Security? We're going to clean the samples."

There was a slight pause before Sarah's voice responded. "If you don't mind, I'd like it if you were to vacate the lab first."

"Thank Christ," Jay said.

"Copy," Kate said. "Okay, people. Move it."

They did.

The security detail inside the hall followed them out of the airlock and into the main area. Shawna stepped a good five meters away from the thick metal walls. Four soldiers carried the large incinerators, four weapons of last resort, and, if you counted her grenade, five.

Her nerves screamed with tension. What would Moore do if the samples survived? Or if something went wrong? Flame the entire complex? She shivered again, suddenly feeling as though a cool fall wind had kissed her naked skin. Catfish was in his secured domain. Maybe he'd be protected if—

Sarah's voice boomed over the speakers. "Attention all personnel. We are sanitizing the lab. Please report to your action stations."

"Shawna?" Kate said from beside her.

She looked at Kate and noticed the exhaustion on her face for the first time. "What?"

"Come on."

The four scientists made their way to the blast doors. A single soldier remained beside the closed door, and a smaller incinerator unit was on the floor next to him. Instead of carrying the makeshift weapon, he held an automatic rifle in his hands.

The soldier cleared his throat when they reached within a meter of the door. "That's close enough."

The throng of scientists turned their backs to the door and stared at the steel-walled lab complex. From her vantage point, Shawna made out the array of monitors displaying cam views from inside the lab.

The four creatures had resumed their behaviors, desperately trying to shatter the glass and meet each other. Or eat each other. She shivered again, remembering the surveillance videos of a large M2 entity attacking a smaller one, devouring it before growing larger and becoming more dangerous.

"Attention," Sarah said over the PA. "Sterilization will begin in 5,4,3,2,1." A heartbeat later, short-wavelength UV light filled the lab. The shades still covering the sample cases lifted.

One of the Taubs slapped a tentacle at the glass, which stuck fast, almost like a sucker from an octopus. As the shades lifted and the shadows melted away, the safety zone for the M2 offspring shrank as if the sun was crawling over the horizon.

The Poppys had turned into puddles of thick black and retreated as far as they could from the killing light. One wasn't fast enough and burst into flames. The other backed up until it reached the sample case's rear edge. The liquid retracted from an amorphous puddle into a thick rope shoved against the glass as it fought to hide itself from the artificial sunlight.

Shawna switched her gaze to the Taubs, and her heart stopped. The Taub specimens had retracted into the shadows just as the Poppys, but instead of reverting to puddles, the creatures had grown thick shells, their rugose carapaces hardly reflecting the bright light.

The last of the Poppys exploded in a geyser of flame that filled its sample case. The heavy glass and steel surface shattered, sending slivers in all directions. The nearest Taub sample case rocked from the explosion, and Shawna watched in horror as zig-zagging lightning bolts of cracks shot through the glass.

The Taub smashed a tentacle into the side of the sample case, the damaged explosion-proof glass crumbling into shards. A pair of malformed limbs sprouted from its back, their ends pistoning and pushing the creature through the gap and to the floor. Against the nearly blinding white of the powerful lights, the dark form seemed like a misshapen hole in reality. Vapor rose from its stiff surface, details disappearing as a thick heat haze surrounded its shell.

A klaxon filled the room, and the steel blast door banged as its locks engaged. Shawna barely noticed—she was too focused on the remaining imprisoned Taub. Multiple pseudopods grew from its shell, sparks of fire dancing as they extended. The ends became little more than needles before the creature raised the newly formed limbs and punched down.

Kate shrieked as the overhead camera view showed the limbs smashing repeatedly, sparkling flakes of metal flying into the air. The flashing warning lights around the lab turned red and pulsed like a monstrous alien heart.

The smoking creature had somehow fractured the metal, effectively cutting a hole through the sample case's surface. It dropped through and hit the hard floor without a sound. One of the camera feeds tilted as it tried to follow the Taub's progress. Shawna had turned her attention to that feed just in time to see it zoom in on the terrifying shape lurking beneath the table and beyond the UV light's killing rays.

The vapor that had risen off its body had dissipated, but the creature's color was far from black. The Taub had grown rugose scales, their surfaces reflecting a deep brown. An eyestalk pushed its way out through the armor.

Shawna stepped backward until she hit the wall in response, her face a mask of terror. Instead of a dead orb sitting atop each eyestalk, they were more rounded, less alien, and blue with jet-black pupils. They looked nearly human.

Sarah yelled something over the PA, but Shawna suddenly knew nothing about the world beyond the feed and the thing staring back at her. It began to spin, once again returning to its impossibly black color. The creature's pseudopods formed into six limbs—four like a spider's or crab's, with the rear pair shaped like a cricket's.

Motion in another feed. Like a zombie, Shawna swung her gaze to the other screen. Through the airlock's window, she watched two soldiers armed with incinerators about to enter the lab. The creature twitched as though it had seen them. Taub 1, which she now thought of as Taub Prime, or simply Prime, seemed far more aware of where it was. She saw in her mind what it was about to do, air rushing into her lungs to scream a warning.

The airlock door opened, and a blast of fire streamed from the incinerator and torched the room's far corner. The instant the red and yellow colors began flying from the weapon, Prime leaped into the air, its spider limbs pointed like four swords, its single eye no longer spinning but twitching instead.

The soldier turned to spray the creature, but the bulky suit and weapon made it impossible. Prime's two left forelimbs punctured the soldier's shoulder, crimson peppering the white walls as if from a bloody sneeze. The camera didn't show the soldier's face, but it didn't have to. He spun in the same direction as the creature's momentum, the incinerator still pushing bright flame.

As he finished the spin, Prime leaped away from the airlock door. Fire from the spastic incinerator filled the airlock midsection, roasting the other soldier instantly. Flames licked from the ceiling and into the lab area. More klaxons, more flashing lights. Sprinkler systems engaged inside the lab in an attempt to snuff out the blaze.

Before they had more than three seconds to act, a massive explosion rocked the entire lab level. The self-contained lab, surrounded by thick walls of metal on all sides, was the safest place in the entire facility, but now there was a gaping hole where the airlock had been. A dark, thick cloud of smoke quickly gathered, completely obscuring her view.

Shawna felt a strong vibration, followed immediately by a clank of metal. The blast door had been locked.

CHAPTER TWENTY-SEVEN

The engineering test area's bright white lights suddenly dimmed, and the emergency lamps on the walls flashed a bright yellow.

As fast as he could, Catfish brought up the feeds from the lab level. The computer responded by showing him blackened windows, the words "Unauthorized" blinking in a bright red. He turned and looked up at one of the "hidden" cameras. "Moore! Show me what the fuck is going on!"

He felt the floor vibrate and heard the barely audible traces of a boom as if a firework had gone off kilometers away on a clear night. He stood from the console, his hands clenched in fists. "Moore?"

She appeared on the display, her calm, condescending smile firmly in place. "There has been an incident on the lab level. One of the creatures may have broken containment."

Catfish's skin crawled, and an icy fear rushed into his veins. Shawna was down there. He gathered up three grenades and quickly stuffed them into a tool pouch. "I'm heading down to the lab level," he said to Moore. "I'll help—"

A metallic boom filled the room. Catfish blinked and swung his eyes to the airlock. A single red LED flashed rapidly.

"Moore? What did you just do?"

The woman placidly regarded something else on her desk. Maybe another display. "You are sequestered for the moment, Mr. Standlee."

He immediately decided that anger, rather than fear, was the correct response. "Let me out of here."

"No," Moore said. "Not until I know the situation. I cannot allow you to endanger the security of the facility."

"You have any idea how you sound? Containment's already been breached."

She shook her head. "No, it hasn't. The creature is currently locked in with the rest of the staff, and it has no way out."

He shivered again. "Where's Shawna?"

Moore was quiet for a moment, her normally infuriating smile disappearing into a thin line. "She is with the others at the blast door," Moore said. "She is in no danger at this time."

"Then let them out. Let the science team out. Now."

"No," Moore said. "I'm not going to do that for the reasons I just told you."

He growled at her image, teeth grinding together. "Fine. What can I do?"

Moore leaned back in her chair. "I'm sending you schematics for the facility," she said. "I want a plan to get them out of there without causing a facility-wide breach."

"Shouldn't you already know how to do that?"

Her smile returned. "The facility was originally designed to keep things in, Mr. Standlee. Not out."

In, not out, he thought. "Got it." He'd managed to bring down his rage to at least rational levels, but he still wanted to hit something or smash a chair into a wall. That, however, wouldn't help him get Shawna out, much less help contain the creature.

He minimized Moore's con-call window and brought up his mail. Within seconds, he had the facility's schematics up on the large displays. "Okay," Catfish said, swiveling in his chair. He stopped, eyebrows furrowing. She had marked the air ventilation shafts that provided oxygen from the surface to the lower levels.

"Okay," he said aloud, trying like hell to calm himself. "Time to hack."

He'd barely begun going over the schematics when the engineering airlock hissed open. Catfish glanced over his shoulder, his face set in a disinterested glare. The look dissipated instantly into one of surprise. Givens stood just inside the room, an incinerator strapped to his back. "I'm here to requisition some boom."

Catfish grinned. "Great. Let me get some supplies, and we can go."

"We?" Givens asked.

"My friend's down there." Friend. The word sounded strange without the prefix "girl" in front of it. He wanted to smile and curse at the same time. He loved her, dammit. He pushed away from the console and stood to his full height. "Got another one of those?"

"Nope," Givens said. "But I have a smaller one out there. We'll fit you up." He pointed at the grenades. "How are you at baseball?"

"Was a pitcher in junior high."

Givens rolled his eyes. "Our savior has arrived."

"How are we getting down there?"

The soldier's face twisted in a smile that once again reminded Catfish that this guy was not all there. "I have my ways. Hope you're not claustrophobic."

* * *

McConnel looked at his partner with disgust. "Ryan. You going to stop picking your nose?"

A green and yellow glob of snot flicked off Ryan's fingers to the otherwise pristine white floor. "Bad cold, man." He pinched one nostril closed with his finger and exhaled sharply. A runner of mucus mostly escaped his nose and splatted to the floor.

"You are disgusting," McConnel said. He walked to the status panel and checked the readings. All were in the green, except for the vibration sensors. Taub was restless again, shifting and moving inside its ever-weakening metal prison. For the last several days, it had been tripping the vibration alarms off and on for hours at a time.

McConnel and the other "guards" had been given the same briefing and told what to expect should the contents of the storage tank or the oil barrel manage to break containment. They were to flip the switches on the UV array and prepare to burn the entire room with their incinerators. He and Ryan, someone he wished he hadn't been saddled with, were locked in the room with the hazards while three other guards stood sentry outside the metal containment barriers.

"Monsters," McConnel muttered.

"What?" Ryan asked, his pinky finger tucked inside his left nostril.

Sighing, McConnel crossed his arms and glared at his partner. "For Christ's sake, use a damned tissue!"

"Don't have one," Ryan said, flicking another booger to the floor.

The control panel buzzed. McConnel stiffened and turned back to examine it. "Hmm."

Ryan stepped closer so he could see the lights and the display. "What is it?"

"More vibrations," McConnel said. "It's getting frisky in there." He touched the side of his headset. "Containment to Moore."

"Go ahead."

God, that woman's voice set his teeth on edge. He'd only met her once, which was enough to convince him he didn't ever want to meet her again. But as long as her checks cleared, he'd keep babysitting the, well, whatever was inside the barrel and the metal storage tank.

"Taub is tripping the vibration alarms again. Much more strongly than before. Over."

"Copy," Moore said.

A few seconds passed, and the panel buzzed again. "Shit," he said aloud. "Damned thing's dancing in there."

"Um," Ryan said, "I don't like this."

"What?" McConnel turned from the panel. Ryan stared at the

containment barriers, his mouth half-open. McConnel followed his gaze, and his jaw dropped. Taub's metal storage tank was now riddled with dimples. As he watched, the steel's surface seemed to ripple.

"Containment," Moore's voice said over the radio, making both men jump. "McConnell? I'm reading a significant increase in activity. Over."

McConnel wanted to say "no shit" but thought better of it. "Yes, ma'am. It's, um, getting livelier. Over."

"I'm looking at the cam feed," the disembodied voice said. "I suggest you prepare your incinerators."

He found himself nodding in agreement. "Copy. UV?"

"Flood the room with it."

"Copy. Any other instructions?"

Moore paused. "I'll be sure and—"

Her voice broke off, making McConnel raise an eyebrow. "Control? Are you—"

A distant boom rattled the ceiling, making dust and ancient plaster drift around them like snowflakes. Ryan raised his incinerator as if the vibration was an enemy he could kill with fire.

"What the hell was that?" Ryan asked.

The vibration stopped as suddenly as it had begun, silence falling over the room apart from the nearly inaudible buzz of the electric lights and the low hum of the air circulation system.

"Control?" McConnel asked meekly.

The warning lights in the room flashed red. Ryan and McConnel traded glances before the two men refocused their eyes on the containment barriers, McConnel's widening in disbelief.

The storage tank marked "Taub" had a visible tear on its surface. A sliver of black, the size and shape of a knife, pushed through the tear, widening it, cutting, tearing, ripping.

"McConnel?" Ryan asked in childlike horror.

"Turn on the lights. Turn 'em up to full. Now."

The metal storage tank began flaking apart like the steel had lost all cohesion. A black talon split the tank's seam, and another immediately ripped through the top. More appeared. And more. Dozens and dozens burst through the dissolving metal tank.

McConnel stumbled backward a step, the room suddenly feeling too damned small and the tank's glass enclosure too fragile.

"Get the lights," he whispered. "Turn the UV to full."

The tank collapsed, liters and liters of thick ooze spilling out to cover the glass enclosure, bits of bright metal sparkling in the light. The black liquid shook as though churned by a mixer, waves of vibrations rippling across its surface.

"Get the lights. Just—"

The words died on McConnel's tongue as the black liquid inside the crystal clear enclosure burbled and bubbled, its color changing, lightening slightly. A crust-like chocolate pudding skin settled over the liquid, and a thin branch rose like a periscope from a submarine, its end a squashed black sphere.

McConnel's breath stopped in his lungs as he stared into an impossibly black eye that spun as though trying to see everything at once. It stopped spinning, its dead gaze settling on him. He opened his mouth in wonder as the color changed from jet black to a robin's egg blue.

"Get the lights," McConnel managed in a choked mutter.

A limb broke through the crust, its end an amorphous imitation of a human hand with an elongated middle digit ending in a sharp hook. Three more appeared, the crust rippling and bubbling. The eye switched its gaze from him to Ryan and widened, the blue as bright as a cloudless summer sky.

"Get. The. Fucking. Lights."

Ryan had stepped forward, his eyes wide and mouth open in wonder.

"Get back, you moron!" McConnel shouted.

Ryan didn't hear him, his feet plodding forward, hand outstretched. The thing inside the glass enclosure shifted its limbs, the ends pressing against the sides of the glass. McConnel could almost hear those sharpened talons scratching against the case, probing, grating, scraping to find purchase and break through.

The multi-armed lump took shape, turning itself into a nearly rectangular block of matter. The limbs continued scratching against the glass while the creature extruded more from beneath itself and rose upward, the limbs pistoning as if trying to push the glass apart.

The bright blue eye continued staring at Ryan even as the man stepped closer and closer to its enclosure. McConnel ran forward and grabbed Ryan by the shoulders, pulling him backward, the pair stumbling and falling hard to the solid steel floor.

McConnel scrambled to get up, but a strap of his incinerator had come loose, the heavy, thick fabric restraining one arm.

A sound like cracking ice, barely audible over his heavy breathing, punched through the hum of the lights and the air system. It caused him to look back at the enclosure, his eyes widening in panic. Spider webs of cracks crisscrossed the glass, partially obscuring the thing inside. Ryan was already picking himself up, his face slack and confused. The eye was no longer clear in definition, its gaze indistinct through the cracks.

He made a sound like a beaten puppy.

"McConnel? What—"

"Get the lights!" McConnel screamed as he finally shrugged the strap back on and untangled himself from the incinerator's hose and nozzle assembly.

As if in a daze, Ryan stumbled backward on unsteady feet. McConnel screamed at him again; the man's eyes finally cleared, and Ryan ran for the panel. McConnel stood, heart thrashing, and pointed the incinerator directly at the enclosure just as the glass shattered in a spray of "shatter-proof" shards.

Free from its prison, the creature's mass seemed to fold in on itself, and the limbs met in front of it, aiming for McConnel. His finger hesitated on the trigger as the limbs converged, their surfaces bubbling like peroxide on a wound. The limb grew and thickened, and a hooked talon swished ahead of it as it touched the floor and snaked toward McConnel.

Something clicked in his brain, and he finally pulled the trigger. At the same time, the powerful UV lights came to life, his eyes practically closing in response. Flame flowed from the incinerator like a river, the blast buffeting off the long limb. He might as well have pointed it at cold wrought steel.

The limb paused for half a beat, black particles dancing around it in a haze. It rose half a meter off the floor and lengthened simultaneously. McConnel tracked it with the incinerator, the heat burning his skin. The hooked end pulled back in an arc before slamming down.

The talon struck him in the shoulder and plunged into his flesh. Screaming, half-blind, and burning from the heat, McConnel stumbled in a half circle, his finger still locked on the trigger. Ryan yelled at him, but he didn't hear his partner as the continuous jet of flame hit the wall next to Ryan and gradually made its way to him.

Ryan's clothes and hair immediately burst into flame, the hose of his incinerator instantly melting from the intense heat. He had become little more than a burning matchstick, dancing like a kid who needed to go potty.

McConnel didn't notice. Red waves of pain obscured his vision, and his shoulder burned. The tentacle pulled him backward, the incinerator falling from his hands as the creature's limb tore through muscle, sinew, and shattered bone. He dropped the incinerator assembly, his hands rising to his shoulder as he fought to free himself. But it was no use.

Ryan's incinerator exploded, a whirlwind of flame consuming him and spreading to the ceiling. The delicate UV bulbs popped one by one from the heat and flame, the room darkening. McConnel lost his footing, falling backward as the tentacle dragged him toward a waiting, glistening maw.

* * *

Shawna held her breath as long as possible, not wanting to inhale the sooty black smoke still billowing from the previously enclosed lab. Sarah had killed the flashers on the warning lights, their color frozen in bright red. The displays above them were blank except for the three cameras covering the lab's exterior. The rest had been destroyed in the explosion.

"Not good," Neil said, words barely above a whisper.

Jay glared at him with contempt. "No shit."

Neil rolled his eyes in response. "No, asshole. The M2. Look around," he said, gesturing to the mostly clean metal and glass floor. "There's nothing for it to eat up here."

"Except us," Kate finished.

Neil banged a fist on the metal door. He might as well have been trying to punish a mountain. "And now we can't get out."

Shawna continued scanning the camera feeds, letting her eyes unfocus slightly to catch the barest blur of movement. At this point, she was afraid to blink, much less close her eyes against the stinging smoke. She felt as though they were forgetting something important. Something that the creature could—

"Fuck."

Kate looked at her. "What?"

"The supplies," she said. "We have the organics and rats on the other side."

"Shit," Jay said. "Not to mention the remains of two humans in the lab."

"If there are any remains," Neil said. "That was a hell of an explosion."

Sarah walked away from her console in a side shuffle, allowing her to keep her eyes on the remains of the airlock. She stopped less than a meter away but kept her head pointed toward the lab. "Listen up," she said. "We think it's still in there, but don't know for sure."

"Think?" Jay asked. "Didn't the cameras catch it?"

"We lost three seconds of video due to the smoke and the explosion. It could have escaped if it had survived the shockwave."

"I don't know how it could," Kate said. "That would have cracked its shell for sure, and we know what's inside is highly flammable."

Jay cocked an eyebrow. "What about drains? We have drains just inside the airlock."

"No," Neil said. "It would have had to change to a liquid state before the explosion. Plus, same problem. A contained fireball like that would have incinerated damned near anything."

Jay uttered a bark of laughter. "Too bad our friend Taub Prime isn't like 'damned near anything.'"

Shawna noticed they were all staring at the lab while she was the only one still focused on the displays. "We just wait for it to come out?"

"We're in lockdown," Sarah said. "The blast door is sealed, and nothing is getting out of here. Not unless Moore ends the lockdown."

"And when does that happen?" Neil asked.

Sarah said simply, "When we're sure it's dead."

In her peripheral vision, Shawna saw the security head turning to look up at the screens. "The motion sensors are mostly operating."

"Mostly?" Jay asked. "What does that mean?"

"It means," she said, "that the smoke is causing some issues. We'll have to turn down the sensitivity to get them to stop issuing false alarms."

Neil groaned. "Perfect."

The sprinklers outside the lab had only been on for a few minutes, but now she and the others were drenched. And to make matters worse, the entire level was cool enough to make you want a sweater. Now, all Shawna wanted to do was get back to her trailer, take a hot shower, and collapse beneath a heavy blanket with Catfish.

She didn't care what decontamination procedures Moore had in mind once they got out of there. She'd suffer poking and prodding of all kinds just to—

"Decontamination." The word slipped from her mouth as

though she didn't even realize she was saying it aloud. "The lift to the quarantine level. It's on the other side of the airlock."

"Yeah," Kate said. "So?"

"Where did it go once it killed the first soldier? Did it get through the airlock? Before the explosion?"

Sarah frowned and practically ran back to the security console. Shawna watched the frown deepen. Sarah looked up from the console at Shawna, her face a mask of concern.

Shawna glanced at the others before walking to stand beside Sarah. The console's displays, hanging from thick, heavy swing arms, showed four different feeds from the lab, their time stamps synced with one another. The bio-lab cameras showed the soldiers entering the airlock. Shawna glanced at another bio-lab camera and found the feed that showed the creature with its strange hybrid of limbs and body shape.

Sarah started the feed rolling at five fps, and the jerky motion made Shawna feel a little ill just looking at it. The airlock door opened, and a jet of fire flew out of the incinerator in slow motion, the flame growing by meters at a time. The creature leaped, punctured the soldier, and detached as though it had intended to spin the soldier back into the airlock.

"That's not possible," Shawna breathed.

"What?" Sarah asked.

Shawna didn't respond. Something twitched at the corner of the very bottom of the cam feed. It was difficult to see through the black smoke already beginning to cloud the airlock, but she was sure that had been the creature.

"There," Shawna said and placed her finger on the display. "Right there."

Sarah leaned forward slightly before her mouth opened in a surprised O. The look was brief but still enough to let Shawna know she'd seen it, too. "Okay, so it rounded the corner. The explosion was centered in the bio-lab airlock, so the blast was concentrated on the wall here and back into the lab itself."

Shawna stood straight. "So it could have been protected."

"Could have," Sarah said. "And you're right. It could have gotten into the chemical waste system."

"Another waste tank?" Shawna asked.

"Leads to a much smaller container on the lower level," Sarah said with a nod. "Made of the same stuff the other two have."

She felt a chill. "You mean that thing could be down there with Poppy and Taub?"

"Yeah," Sarah said and touched the radio on her belt. "Level 4, this is Sarah. What's your status, over?"

No response.

She glared at the floor and tried again. This time, there was static but nothing else. "Shit."

"What?" Shawna asked. "What is it?"

"Radio." Sarah turned and pointed to the blast door. "Pretty sure that's fucking up our send/receive. The quarantine level is no doubt locked down too." She began typing keys on the keyboard and brought up camera feeds from the quarantine level.

The feed focused on the blast door, which showed no guards. Shawna's stomach buzzed with nervous tension. Sarah switched the feed again, displaying the hallway outside the containment rooms. Three soldiers stood by the glass partition separating them from the Taub and Poppy enclosures. The soldiers were kitted up in flame retardant, silver suits, military-grade incinerators strapped to their backs, the barrels glowing with blue pilot flames.

Sarah sighed with relief. "Can't hear us, I don't think, but at least they're there." She switched to the digital comms. "Celianne to quarantine, come in quarantine."

"Harris, here," a voice said. "We're in lockdown. The level shook, and we have water dripping through the foundation, Boss. Over."

Sarah and Shawna exchanged a glance.

"How fast is the water moving in? Over."

"Fast enough," Harris said. "Given an hour or two, it might be over our feet. But that's only if we don't have another big boom. Over."

"Copy," Sarah said. "How's the kill switch?"

"Active," he said. "Just waiting for the command. Over."

"Copy. How are your charges? Over."

Harris chuckled, but it didn't sound like it had any levity. "I don't know what happened on your level, Boss, but whatever caused that explosion tripped all of our motion alarms. Guessing it was from the liquid sloshing around." Harris paused for a moment as if checking something. "We had to shut off some sensors to keep the false positives from racking up. Over."

Sarah thought for a moment before speaking again. "Copy. Harris? Are you sure they're false positives? Over."

"I—" Another pause. "No, Boss. I'm not sure."

"Then be sure," she said, the words clipped and forced. "Turn those damned alarms back on and get someone to sit by the console. I want to know if those things so much as twitch. Over."

"Copy," Harris said.

"And Harris?"

"Yes, Boss?"

"If there's a containment breach, you hit that kill switch. That's an order. Over."

"Copy," Harris said. "I'll happily hit that button myself. Over."

"Let me know if there are any, and I mean any changes."

"Copy."

Sarah sighed. "Over and out."

"The explosion," Shawna asked, "it had enough force to affect the lower level?"

"Apparently," Sarah said. "We're dozens of meters below the surface, and there's a water table right around us. Not sure the designers realized just how bad things would get down there."

"Or here," Shawna said. "So what do we do now?"

Sarah pointed to the slowly dissipating cloud of smoke surrounding the airlock. "Science team stays at that door, and my team will recon the lab."

"Recon? You're going to go looking for it?"

The soldier nodded solemnly. "Yup. So be ready to move."

Shawna patted her belt, reassuring herself that Catfish's little toy was still there. It didn't do much to stop the shivers crawling up and down her spine as she flicked her stare to the smoking remains of the lab. They'd soon have their answer about whether or not Prime had survived.

CHAPTER TWENTY-EIGHT

Luckily for Catfish, Givens was shorter, and so was his stride, but the man walked with purpose. With the boot on one leg, Catfish moved slower than he wanted, and he could feel Givens' frustration that they couldn't hurry the fuck up.

The security team on the upper floor had closed all the vents leading to the surface. If M2 wanted to ride the ductwork to find a way out of the facility, it was going to be shit out of luck. The security team would find and incinerate it before it managed to do so. They hoped.

Fortunately, the facility hadn't been designed to prevent progress to the lower floors. Three shafts sucked in air from the outside world and pumped it into the facility's secure levels. Even in a lockdown, those shafts were accessible in case of a malfunction so rescue personnel could remove anyone accidentally trapped. That shaft is where Givens was taking him.

The quiet soldier carried a large duffel in either hand. Catfish carried one duffel with a smaller incinerator strapped to his back. Givens had filled the bags with goodies, including several of the printed grenades, ammunition, and rope. Lots of rope.

The shaft's handholds were of little use to either of them. Between the supplies they carried and Catfish's boot, it made more sense to rappel. They had to lower two of the bags anyway.

Givens quickly unloaded one of the duffels and removed the

rappelling gear. He and Catfish had already donned their harnesses before heading to the maintenance wing of the engineering floor. While Givens set up the ropes for their descent, Catfish began packing the bags so they could lower them to the next level. Before long, they were ready.

The shaft held little light. Most of the maintenance lamps had gone dark due to poor maintenance, a short in the antiquated electrical system, or the simple ravages of time. The ten meters separating them from the next floor were a nest of shadows broken only by the few functional lights casting a baleful glow. Their sporadic spacing didn't help either.

When Givens was ready, they lowered the bags to the next floor as fast as they could without dropping the damned things. Catfish looked at the man as his hands alternately tightened and loosened to control the bundle's descent. "Does Moore know we're doing this?"

Givens shrugged. "Don't really give a shit one way or the other."

Catfish cocked an eyebrow. "Aren't you military?"

The lanky man half-nodded. "Was. No idea what I am now."

"Oh," Catfish said. "I always thought—"

"You can think all you want," Givens said. "But Sarah and I are just here to keep y'all safe from the bad things down there. Well, that and the facility." He looked up from the ropes. "So I'm doing my job."

"That didn't answer the question. You don't need orders from Moore?"

"Oh, she probably knows." The bundles made contact with the next level, and slack appeared between Givens' hands. He began clipping up Catfish's harness. "But she's just an employer. Sarah? She's family. She's the boss."

The shaft yawned before him, his shadow floating across the light like a dim wraith. His stomach buzzed with nervous tension, and his bowels were close to becoming liquid. Down there could be anything. M2 could already have found a way into the shaft and lay in wait for them. The very bottom of the shaft could be a gaping mouth made of infinitely caustic material that grew limbs and tentacles. He shivered.

Givens pulled three light sticks from his belt, cracked them, and dropped them into the murky gloom. The green cylinders passed through the shadows and into the darkness like streaking stars. They finally landed, creating a rough circle of illumination, making the shaft look like an open green eye.

"All right," Givens drawled. "You're gonna want to make sure you're good foot's in front. Don't bang the other, or you're gonna be in a world of shit."

"Gee, thanks for reminding me," Catfish said.

It was awkward, and, yes, he banged his boot once, eliciting an f-bomb that echoed through the shaft. The pain, once he no longer thought he'd broken every bone in his lower leg, was a welcome respite from the debilitating fear that had made every meter a shaky struggle just to hold on to the rope.

He thought he'd managed the landing pretty well, but his foot complained anyway. When this was over, he'd need a lot of whiskey. "If you ever see the surface again," he said aloud.

Doing his best to push away the pain, Catfish pulled the incinerator and pointed it downward, eyes searching for movement. There was nothing apart from the still air that seemed flavored with something acrid. With the fans powered off, only the ever-present hum from the engineering floor's lights was audible. That and the sound of Givens coming down the rope.

Givens landed, tied off the ropes, and looked at the duffel bags. "How's the leg?"

"Hurts like a motherfucker."

"Good," Givens said with a grin. "Maybe you'll be focused."

Catfish ignored him and gestured to the pressure hatch. When the lockdown had occurred, the fans had been cut off, and the ductwork leading to the air shafts had been isolated with pressure doors. It was next to impossible for someone to get out. But getting in? "Now what?"

"Think we should knock?"

Catfish smiled despite the anxiety and growing fear in his gut. "Not sure," he said. "If something knocks back, how do we even know it's a human inside there?"

"Excellent question," Givens said. "Fine. Fuck the knock." He stepped forward to the pressure door leading to the laboratory level and fiddled with a box on the wall. Catfish didn't see what he did, but the box swung open, revealing a crank.

"Manual?"

"I reckon," Givens said, "they wanted to make sure they could open her up if there was a power failure." He turned the crank, the mechanism clicking inside the wall. A red light appeared on the small gray box and flashed three times.

"What does that mean?" Catfish asked, pointing at it.

"Probably that we should close our eyes and mouths."

"Why?"

Givens put a hand over his mouth and nose and buried his face in his shoulder, eyes shut. Catfish followed suit nearly an instant too late.

Stale air whooshed by him, the scent of burned plastic and rubber much more pronounced, almost stiflingly so. He waited a moment before daring to open his eyes. The ductwork beyond, large enough for Catfish to crawl through, looked like a gaping mouth in the eerie, eldritch glow of the light sticks.

Givens had moved to the side, his incinerator nozzle pointing at the pitch-dark hole. The light attached to his shoulder harness came to life with a strong, focused beam of intense white that lanced the darkness and revealed the corpses of long-dead insects and other detritus. Givens sighed. "Guess we're lucky it's not full of water."

Catfish's heartbeat picked up. He'd just realized he'd have to crawl through the pipes with his damaged foot. "Shit."

"What?" Givens glanced at him, read his facial expression, and nodded to himself. "Tight squeeze. And we'll have to go one at a time."

Catfish was afraid to ask but had to anyway. "Front or back?"

"Hm," Givens said, his free hand scratching his chin. "That's a bit of a personal question. But I think you should go first since you won't be able to turn around easily. Not with that foot. Plus, you've got the smaller incinerator."

It was the answer he'd more or less expected. It made sense, but his skin prickled as though he'd walked naked into a cloud of ice. "Going to drag the bags?"

"Yup." Givens pulled a short length of rope from one of the duffels, laced it through the handles, and tied it off, leaving him a meter and a half long towline. "Just like that." He unzipped a small pocket on the side of the larger bag and pulled out another light like his own. "Here," he said and attached it to Catfish's harness. "Try not to shine that directly on your skin."

"It'll burn?"

"You got it." Givens grinned. "Something we did at Ben Taub, only these are much more portable."

"Right, I remember."

"Good. Then you also remember we need to hurry."

The fading, eye-watering stench of burned plastic and rubber seemed to return.

It's your imagination, he thought. *You're just smelling it because you're worried about Shawna.*

"Hurry. Right," Catfish said aloud.

Something beeped. Givens looked down at his harness and saw the red LED light on his radio. "I'll be damned," he said. "Didn't think it would work down here." He touched a switch on his headset. "Givens."

"Moore here." She sounded perturbed. "What are you doing?"

"Getting Sarah and Shawna back," Catfish said.

The radio went silent for a moment. Catfish watched as Givens' expression of concern deepened. He was pretty sure the soldier was imagining doing something terrible to Moore. He knew the feeling.

"You're at the pressure door?"

"Yeah," Givens said, his face a little more relaxed. "We are."

"Once you go through there, we'll lose radio contact. The only reason we have it now is the repeater above you. I have no cameras available on the lab level. Nothing. Both the network and the hard lines are down, so you're on your own."

"Wait," Catfish said, "you're not going to stop us?"

"Why would I do that?" Moore asked. "I can easily incinerate the lab, quarantine, and maintenance levels without damaging the facility's top two levels."

Silence fell like a hammer, and Catfish suddenly found it hard to breathe. If Moore was kidding, she sure as shit was doing a good job of playing it straight.

"Copy," Givens said. "You're closing this hatch behind us, aren't you?"

"No," she said. "I'm not."

The thin ray of light shining down from the top of the air shaft slowly melted, becoming increasingly indistinct as the shadows took hold.

"Shit," Given said, his eyes fixed above them. "What did you just do?"

"Micron filter in place," Moore said. "Will allow air in but make it impossible for anything else to get out. Unless, of course, it dissolves the filter. But I trust I'll have plenty of warning before that happens. Good luck, gentlemen."

"Too late to change your mind," Givens said to Catfish. "Let's go."

Catfish took one last look at the barely visible light above them. This shaft was one of three. Maybe they could find a way out in one of the others, but somehow, he doubted it.

* * *

Taub Prime crouched in the darkness with a single eye affixed to a dangling stalk. Most of its shell had been obliterated by the explosion before it had had a chance to burrow through the floor tiles leading to the crawl space for air, electrical wiring, fiber, and piping.

It barely had enough mass to hold solidity, but simple survival instincts told it not to transform into liquid. Not until it was sure the killing light would not return. While it waited, it absorbed its remaining limbs and regrew them beneath its surface. It probed the 10-centimeter radius with a tendril of liquid that looked more like a giant eyelash than a limb and immediately found food.

Prime's mass grew twofold in seconds as it consumed cable insulation. PVC pipe took far more time, but that material was disappearing, too. Prime shifted itself, particles rising from its liquid core to harden and buttress its battered carapace. The more mass it acquired, the thicker its shell became. Damaged and dead particles flew off its surface to cover the steel and concrete slab with nearly invisible black crumbs.

When it finished consuming the immediate area, it formed millions of cilia-like appendages beneath itself, the tiny pseudopods dancing in synchronized waves as the creature pulled itself forward to find more food.

The eyestalk, previously on the verge of breaking off, had completely reformed. Prime pushed the sensory organ upward until it reached the hole it had made. It was still too hot to consider returning to its original confines. The eyestalk lowered until it lay flat against the creature's back. Prime continued its slow march forward, new pseudopods growing to provide it with data about its environment, to get a picture of where it was, and to form a plan. A plan to eat. A plan to *become.*

* * *

Two soldiers made their way across the room to the segregated lab, the flashing red and yellow hazard lights bathing the lines of cubicles and shelves with an unnatural, blinking, garish glow. Shawna felt like she couldn't breathe, her body refusing to take in deep lungfuls. The acrid scent in the room and fine particulates of whatever hazardous materials had burned combined to make her lungs itch, not to mention her nose and eyes.

Through a trio of camera feeds, she watched the pair, armed with incinerators but not wearing nonflammable suits, approach the airlock, one covering the other.

Shawna took a deeper breath and immediately regretted it, her lungs forcing her to cough out some of the toxic air. They had to find a way to open a vent, something to suck the polluted air out of the room and replace it with breathable oxygen. She rubbed at her burning eyes while she fought to keep her focus on the screens.

The airlock, blown outward like a burst pipe, had stopped smoking, but the sheared and shattered metal edges made it difficult to get inside while wearing an incinerator. After a dozen seconds and five attempts, Sarah okayed the soldier's request to remove the weapon. He was going in armed with a UV light and a mostly useless pistol.

"He's going to die if he finds it," Shawna said.

Sarah didn't lift her eyes from the screen. "If he finds it, he'll get out of there. We just need to know where it is."

The man crouch-walked through the partially collapsed entrance and into the dark lab. The explosion had destroyed most of the lights and shorted some of the electrical systems.

"I'm in, Boss. Over."

"Status?"

"Not good," he said. "The lab is completely wrecked." He paused for a moment. "A lot of burned equipment and infrastructure. The floor took a lot of damage. Over."

"How bad?"

Shawna could almost hear the man shrug.

"Bad enough. Got gaps leading to the utility crawl spaces."

Three lights on the floor's east side winked twice before steadying, and an alert popped up on Sarah's console. "Power fluctuations," she said, her eyes sliding to peer at that side of the floor. Her hands moved across the controls and replaced the existing feeds with those of the cameras covering the east side.

One of the screens showed spare equipment, most of it on casters, and both medical and chemical supplies. To the right were the biological sample cases and cages. Shawna's mouth opened in shock.

"Can— Can you refocus on the biosamples?"

Sarah touched the controls again, and a new feed appeared. It looked down on the cages and cases, providing enough of a view to see inside the containers. If that was, there were containers.

The plastic and glass rodent pens had been turned over, their surfaces scorched and melted. The rodents were gone.

"You see it?" Shawna asked.

Sarah nodded. "Too far away from the explosion. No way the heat reached all the way back there." The lights flickered again, this time on the north side. She touched her comms. "Get out of there, now."

"Copy," the soldier said. Three seconds later, his voice rang through again. "Boss? I think we may have a problem. Looks like the chemical waste trap got blown open. Over."

Shawna felt a chill. She thought Sarah did, too.

"Copy. How bad is it? Can you close it? Over."

"No," he said. "It wasn't designed for impacts like that. It's bent out of shape. Over."

"Copy. Get out of there. Over and out."

The soldier acknowledged, and the line went silent.

"If the chemical waste hatch is open," Shawna said, "we can chase it in. Blast an incinerator down the hole and hopefully fry it in the tank."

"True," Sarah said. "Or it could just scuttle back at us and eat someone's face." She immediately shook her head. "Sorry. Shouldn't say shit like that."

The east side flickered before one of the lights went out, and a thin blanket of shadow discolored the otherwise bright, white room. The soldier emerged from the airlock, grabbed the incinerator, and carried it three meters away before re-equipping it while his partner provided cover.

"Orders, Boss?" a voice said over Sarah's comms.

"Eastside and airlock," she said.

The soldier who'd entered the lab remained in his position while his partner walked toward the shadows. He stopped seven or eight meters away from the bio-cages and spare equipment against the wall.

Shawna glanced at the blast door. The rest of the science team looked scared out of their wits. Neil especially. She was sure her face was a pale mask of tension.

She returned her gaze to the displays, her heart beating rapidly and her breath still short. If they had to run, it wouldn't be long before they were gasping. The room had grown quiet except for the air circulation system, which was doing nothing except moving the corrupted air around.

"Did the air system shut down?" Shawna asked.

Sarah nodded grimly. "Lockdown. No fresh air coming in. It's a bypass in case something escapes from the lab and tries to get out."

"So no O2."

"Nothing fresh, no," Sarah said. She looked as though she were stifling a cough.

"How much time do we have?"

"Until there's no oxygen?" Sarah shrugged. "No clue. The smoke being trapped in here isn't exactly helping."

"Then what do we do?"

Sarah looked down at her keyboard momentarily as if weighing her options. After typing a few keys, the video client appeared. She entered Moore's extension and tapped the "call" button. An alert popped up on the screen. "No network available."

She smashed her fist into the console, the metallic thud echoing in the large room. "Team. Report."

"Eastside clear, Boss."

"Northside clear."

Sarah glanced back at the screens. "Do either of you see any smoke, vapor, or anything like that? Look for floor tiles out of place, too."

A westside light flickered and went out.

Shawna's nose, already battered by the acrid smoke from the lab fire, had difficulty recognizing the new scent in the air, but she realized she'd been smelling it for a while. "Plastic. I smell burning plastic and maybe rubber."

Sarah glanced at her and nosed the air. "Holy shit. You're right." She picked up the incinerator next to the console. "Squad? It's below us in the crawl space."

Another shiver crawled down Shawna's spine. She half-turned and faced the level's west side, her eyes unfocused slightly to catch any movement. At first, all the tiles she could see looked perfectly in place, the white floor unbroken apart from the seams of the floor tiles.

Then she noticed a tile near the back wall of electrical boxes, and the emergency generator enclosure was out of place. The break in the normally white floor looked like a manic sneer. Beside it was the shadow of a long, thin branch that ended in an oblong spheroid.

She raised her hand to point. "There."

Sarah turned to follow her finger. It took her a few seconds to see it, and then her shell of serenity broke into an expressionless line, her eyes hard and glaring. "Squad. Hostile on the west side. Repeat. West side. We're between you and it. Over."

"Copy. Move up? Over."

"Move up," she said. "Ten meters apart. Give us some egress room."

"Copy."

The two soldiers carefully stepped from their sentry points. The one covering the airlock stepped closer to the blast door, providing them cover. The other soldier stood less than ten meters from the security console, his incinerator pointing at the lab. He seemed to see what they'd been looking at because Shawna saw his body stiffen.

She wondered if any of these soldiers had been shown the films and understood what M2 was capable of. Did they know it could change its form? Did they know how fast it could move if it wanted to? What about its ability to dissolve damned near anything? If they didn't know, they soon would.

Sarah swiveled one of the cameras until it focused on the area around the tile. She zoomed in on the break in the floor, the resolution pixelating before presenting a grainy image. It didn't have to be crystal clear to stop Shawna's heart.

The eyestalk was nearly bent in half but still tall enough to reach twenty centimeters off the floor. The orb spun as if searching for movement, or perhaps the creature was devising an attack strategy.

Were they that smart? She didn't want to find out, but she thought the answer was hell yes. The M2 creatures on *Leaguer* had practically laid traps for the crew as they fought to get life-saving supplies for the coming night and rescue trapped colleagues. The M2 creatures had weakened floors and walls and destroyed whole patches of ceiling so they could drop down on their prey.

The eye stopped spinning, and its space-black surface lightened until it became a deep, dark brown. The eye seemed to dissolve into itself and reform a second or two later. Shawna felt time freeze in place. The nearly human eye had returned, not spinning, not rotating, but panning across the level in slow arcs.

"Jesus," Sarah said. "Did it just—"

"It did," Shawna said. "We know Taub gestated inside a human being. Maybe it found a way to, I don't know, mimic mammalian organs?"

"Squad. I'm moving the civvies. Going to put them near the airlock," Sarah said into the radio.

"Copy."

Sarah glanced at Shawna. "Okay, time for you to do something for me. Go wrangle the rest of your team. I want you by the airlock in case things get interesting."

"They're not already?"

Sarah grinned, but it was filled more with irony than humor. "Get them over there and get them ready to move. That lab may be the only 'safe' place on this level."

"What? The airlock is broken," Shawna said. "It could easily get in there."

"It could," Sarah agreed. "But there's not exactly a lot of options here." She glared at the "no network available" message on her screen. "Goddamned thing ate its way through the network and electrical cables. Surprised it hasn't sparked a fire."

"True." Shawna looked at the lab and the broken airlock. Was there a way to secure it? Maybe something they could drag over or—

Sarah snapped her fingers, and Shawna realized Sarah had been talking. "Sorry."

"Please get them to the airlock," Sarah said. "Each of you grab a flashlight off the wall and get ready."

Shawna quickly walked to the rack of goodies behind the security desk. Eight of the rechargeable flashlights, each powerful enough to give a human being a sunburn after five minutes of exposure, hung from pegs. Shawna grabbed four of them and divvied them out. Neil took Jay's since the man couldn't hold one.

"Follow me," Shawna said, gesturing to them.

"What's going on?" Kate asked.

Shawna jerked her thumb at the lab. "She wants us near the airlock, just in case we need shelter."

"Shelter?" Jay said. "She does realize the airlock is breached?"

"Yes," Shawna said and began walking. "Come on."

She didn't wait to see if they would follow, counting on Kate to usher them along. Her fingers probed her belt and found the grenade clipped to it. It probably wouldn't save her life, but she felt better knowing it was there.

CHAPTER TWENTY-NINE

Taub Prime had grown quickly. The cabling, fiberboards, plastic ties, rubber sheathing, and other digestible material had provided it the mass it needed to escape or fight.

It continued moving beneath the floor, pausing now and then to peek through the gaps it made in the floor tiles. Prime "saw" where its tormentors stood, but more importantly, it saw the lights.

Something had caused the lights to flicker and, in some cases, go out. Confused, Prime followed the path of where the flickers and outages occurred. They lay along the same route it had traveled since first escaping. Prime deduced itself might be the cause.

The creature had lost some of its consumed material from shocks to its underside. The only reason the electrical current hadn't completely destroyed it was the solid shell it had secreted. The fragile feeding pseudopods had disappeared in flashes of light, but Prime regrew them quickly and repeated the process. Maybe whatever had destroyed its feeding pseudopods was also responsible for the behavior of the lights. It had never seen that happen in the lab, leaving it to conclude in simple, logical steps that it was the cause.

The creature stopped moving and extruded four short, muscular pseudopods from its belly, flanks, and dorsal surface. In a few seconds, the pseudopods' off-black color turned to that of heavily creamed coffee, except for a sharp hook that remained nearly black. Prime tentatively moved the limbs in unison and swept the area in an effort to encounter the phenomenon again. The belly appendage received a jolt of electricity, and the hook disappeared in a flash. It continued searching the area with the three remaining sensory organs. Nothing.

Prime pulled the mass back into itself, regrew a belly pseudopod, and searched further ahead. The feeding end was once again destroyed.

A sudden vibration caught its attention, and it cut a hole in the tile floor large enough for its eyestalk to surface. Its tormentors were returning to where Prime had been born, the place of fire and light.

With no light, it could shed its armor, take any shape it wanted, and feed without fear. Prime dissolved more of the fiberboard material to replenish its lost mass. It would have to feed as it moved, replacing its pseudopods when they were destroyed. It could do that. There was more than enough raw material, and it could even grow while it set about its task, watching the lights for cause and effect. Anything to get to its tormentors. Consume them. *Become.*

* * *

As they reached the entrance to the metal laboratory enclosure, Shawna saw another bank of lights go out. The overheads, which had once been ridiculously bright, dimmed. Portions of the room now had shadows and, in some places, gloom.

"Sarah?" Shawna yelled.

"Get in the lab. Now," Sarah responded, taking a position to cover the scientists' flank. "Get in and see about the quarantine lift. It might be your only way out."

"Is she fucking crazy?" Jay asked.

Kate pushed him inside the lab. "Shut up and move."

Neil followed Kate inside the enclosure, Shawna bringing up the rear. The air still smelled of fire and burned flesh. She held a hand to her mouth, desperately attempting to stave off the coughing, but it didn't help. They couldn't stay here long without suffocating.

With the light aimed before her, Shawna stepped past the other scientists and swept the area. The destruction was surreal. The bio-lab's floor had been completely swept clean of nearly anything non-metal. The displays were fried, and the screens cracked and broken from the intense heat. Somewhere in there were the corpses of two men, doubtlessly burned beyond all recognition or destroyed by the shockwave. *Maybe*, a voice said in her mind, *they got off lucky.*

"Maybe they did," Shawna said aloud in a breathy whisper.

"What?" Jay asked.

"Nothing," Shawna said. She pointed her light back to the floor while making sure not to shine it on anyone's skin.

"Do we really want to do this?" Jay asked. "I mean, that's the quarantine level."

"Yes," Kate said, "and it's also where Poppy and Taub are still contained. Taub Prime, however, is not."

"I know that," Jay snapped.

"Look, if Sarah and her crew kill Taub Prime, we can end the lockdown," Neil said. "Then it won't matter what level we're on."

Jay took a step back from them, his weary face barely visible in the dim ambient light. "Know what that lift is rated for?"

"Not a clue," Shawna said. "You, Neil, and Kate go down first. Just send the lift back up when you're down."

"What are you going to do?" Kate asked.

"Wait for you to send it back up," Shawna said.

Her heart should have been hammering, panic and fear threatening to overwhelm her. Instead, she felt calm. Having something to do, something other than being chased, gave her purpose. "Good luck," Shawna said to the scientists and pulled the steel lever.

An alarm sounded from the partially melted consoles, but it wasn't loud enough to be anything more than annoying. A red light blinked over the platform, and the lift descended into the shaft. Kate waved to her as the tops of their heads disappeared from view.

Sarah yelled something at her men, but Shawna couldn't make it out. As soon as she left the platform and strode to the broken airlock, hoping to listen in, the serenity that had covered her like a blanket began to rip apart. Sarah had returned to the desk, her incinerator pointing away from the lab.

"Shawna? You're supposed to be gone," Sarah said.

She nodded. "I know. I sent them down first. No idea what that platform is rated for."

"Bullshit," Sarah muttered.

Several more banks of lights either flickered or had gone out. Shawna switched off her flashlight and looked around the large room but saw nothing out of place. Heart beating fast, she walked to the side of the airlock to sweep that wall. Something was out of place, and it wasn't from the fire.

She walked as fast as she dared into the gloaming, the flashlight shaking in her hands, the beam cutting through the gloom in a spasmodic dance. She stopped in place, eyes widening. One of the tiles a few meters away had a ragged tear down its middle. The rip had formed like something had eaten through it from below or above. "Shit."

"Everything okay?"

Shawna was afraid to turn around. She swung her light and traced a path across the floor. Several other tiles had been damaged in the same way. She slowly turned and continued following the path with her light.

"What is it?" Sarah called out, her voice echoing off the ceiling and the far wall.

Shawna found another tile across from the security desk. "It's under the floor."

"Say again?" Sarah called.

"It's under the floor. It moved over there," Shawna said, pointing to the generator enclosure. As if on cue, the lights above the generator shed flickered and went out. That's when she heard the sizzle.

Sarah turned from the security desk, her incinerator aiming at the gloom beyond. "Get in the lab. Now," she said.

As Shawna turned, something moved near the generator shed. Time seemed to stop as a thick, black limb broke through the tile floor, fiberboard, and insulation with a cloud of dust. Another followed, dug into the floor, and the creature pulled itself upward.

Sarah yelled orders, her incinerator sparking a short flame that split the shadows for an instant. In the flash, Shawna saw more than just legs. Prime was over four times its original size, eyestalks protruding from its thorax, and discolored, malformed fangs filled what looked like a mouth.

Two more gouts of flame lit the room, and the nearby sound of the incinerator finally pulled her brain out of neutral.

"Shawna, goddammit, get in the lab!" Sarah yelled and walked toward the creature.

Shawna ran to the airlock and bumped her head as she moved inside, eliciting both a shock of pain and a ripping sensation on her scalp. A scream from outside the lab punctured the air but sounded strangely distant through the lab's walls. Shawna snapped her head around just as flares of fire lanced the darkness beyond the broken airlock. A storm of sizzling static replied to the incinerator blasts, and Shawna heard someone yelling.

The lift light flashed yellow. With all the instructions and warning stickers burned off and its controls half melted, she had no idea what it meant. She hit the button for the lift return, but it only flashed yellow again.

Near panic, she shined her light into the shaft and saw the stainless steel platform rising through the darkness. While it ascended, every second an agonizing eternity punctuated by the yells of Sarah's team and the hurricane whoosh of the incinerators, Shawna swung her head to look behind her, terrified the thing would get in here before she could escape.

The sound of the flame-throwers ceased. She heard Sarah yell something about vents but had no idea what she was talking about. It didn't matter. A few seconds later, the lift quietly appeared before Shawna, and she stepped onto the platform. The lift paused for a long second before descending. A moment later, she was in the shaft and looking upward, waiting for Taub Prime to pour down on top of her.

CHAPTER THIRTY

It didn't take long for Catfish to realize he'd made a huge mistake. His foot screamed at him with every movement. A tear of pain threatened to roll down his cheek, but he fought it off by gritting his teeth. He wondered if he'd have any enamel left on them by the time the day was done. "Assuming that's not all that's left of me," he said to himself.

The airshaft led into the ductwork that criss crossed above the laboratory level. The metal dimpled beneath his knees as he crawled, but he barely noticed. His powerful flashlight easily eliminated the darkness before finally petering out some five meters ahead. The corners and bends in the duct design didn't exactly help him in figuring out where he was.

He knew they should be nearing the lab, maybe entering above its generator or the other infrastructure equipment. Somewhere up ahead, they'd find a vent they could drop through. He hoped.

"Nothing yet?" Givens asked.

"No," Catfish said over his shoulder. "Nothing but more metal."

"You going to make a joke about a TV dinner?"

Catfish grinned. "Fuck no."

Givens loosed a grunt that might have been his version of a laugh. "Somebody should."

Although they spoke quietly, their voices echoed through the vent, along with the scrape of the incinerators occasionally rubbing against the duct's ceiling. He couldn't imagine how they would have fit inside normal-sized ductwork even without the tanks on their backs. Then again, when you were twenty or thirty meters below ground, you wanted to ensure you had enough air.

A sound hit his ears, and he stopped, head cocked to listen. Voices. "Givens?"

"I hear it," he said. "How many?"

"Two, I think? Maybe—"

Before he could say "three," the whoosh of incinerators blasting fire drowned him out. He felt a rush of heat pass by his face as if from a desert wind. An instant later, a sizzling sound, loud and as if it were next to him, filled the duct, followed by a bang that briefly interrupted the wave of static.

Catfish froze, his body instantly seizing up. That sound. He'd heard that sound when M2 dissolved sheetrock. Wood. Human beings. Somewhere up ahead, an incarnation of M2 had broken out of its cell, and it was right next to a vent leading to their duct. Even now, a tentacle might be snaking its way around the—

A bolt of pain rattled through Catfish's foot, breaking his brain's downward spiral into panic. Howling and terrified, he glanced over his shoulder, certain he would see an impossibly black talon slashing at his face.

Instead, it was Givens. The man's face had turned scarlet, and Catfish suddenly realized Givens had been yelling at him.

"Asshole. Get that incinerator ready! We have to push!"

Push. The word rattled around his brain, looking desperately for something to cling to. Push.

This psycho, a calm voice said in his mind, *would like you to go toward the sound of certain death. Ready?*

"Are you out of your mind?" Catfish yelled at him, the pain still making him see stars.

Givens reared his fist back to punch Catfish's boot again. "Sarah and Shawna are down in that," he said. "We have to get down there.

Blast it if you see it."

Another wave of heat accompanied a chorus of incinerators. The sound of sizzling receded in volume, but it was closer, just the same. Much closer.

Catfish moved forward, his handheld incinerator clutched tightly in one fist. The duct dimpled beneath him, but he hardly noticed. A junction up ahead offered them two ways to continue: right and left. The sounds echoing through the vents now seemed to come from everywhere.

"Could have split itself," Catfish whispered.

"What?"

He didn't answer. Would it do that? Wouldn't that leave it more vulnerable? From what he'd seen aboard *Leaguer,* not to mention the film from the other two incidents, it was all or nothing with M2. It was cannibalistic. He couldn't imagine why it would split up in that case.

The skittering sound of a giant spider running across a thin tin roof echoed through the duct.

"Go left," Givens said. "Stay a meter or two from the junction and cover that side. I'll do the same on the right."

Catfish obeyed without a word, flashlight shaking from his movement and the shivers crawling down his spine. The darkness at the end of his duct flickered as though firelight were reflected through an open vent. He squinted as he tried to see if a vent was up ahead.

The skittering sound paused, and Catfish felt another tingle down his spine. He'd been so busy looking for a vent he hadn't focused on what was down the other end of the duct. He thought he knew now.

The flickering light from a vent further down the duct illuminated something in the shadows. Or rather a solid shadow. His eyes widened, and he pulled the trigger.

A jet of fire flared across six meters of metal, the flash illuminating the thing. The creature filled the duct except for two crab-like legs that jutted from its front. It had a maw ringed with fangs, each pointing toward a small opening that glistened like a strong light on heavy oil.

The thing ducked its head, its mouth shutting and turning a more tannish color as the fire roared across its surface. The metal beneath him began to warm as the thing danced in the duct, the rattling sound practically deafening him. It made no noise, which somehow made the burning thing all that much worse.

The fire quickly died except for a few flames still smoking on the thing's back. The creature stopped moving. Catfish held his breath, waiting for it to come toward him while his heart thrashed, but it didn't move.

"What are you? Why didn't you burn?"

His flashlight raked across the creature, eliciting vapor but nothing more. The creature's color had changed from jet-black to a lightly creamed coffee and had grown a shell. In the halo of bright light, he watched dimples appear around its mouth and on its short, thin limbs. It was changing in front of him, the mouth opening again, the teeth silently vibrating like saw blades.

Its legs scrabbled at the sides of the duct, sharp talons grinding into the metal for purchase. It moved toward him.

Screaming, Catfish triggered the incinerator while shuffling backward. Another blast of fire erupted and scorched the duct's metal surface before he finally aimed directly at the creature.

The flames washed over the creature's shell but hardly slowed it. A rage of panic sizzled across his brain, and all he could do was hold the trigger down and keep moving backward.

His knees burned, both from effort and the quickly heating duct surface. The boot clomped into the metal again and again, and sharp waves of pain rolled across his already shorted-out nervous system, but he kept moving.

The creature's skin became lighter and lighter, crumbs of black rising from its body like a pulverized lump of coal. It was shrinking.

The legs grew darker again, but the creature had retracted its head into itself like a turtle hiding in its shell. It continued moving forward slower and slower.

The constant gout of flame crisped and singed his unkempt beard and eyebrows. His knees shrieked with pain as the metal beneath him soaked up the heat. Catfish was faintly aware he was yelling hard enough to rip his throat, but he didn't stop.

The creature ceased moving, its limbs and sensory organs disappearing into its shell. The shell now looked more like stone rather than something biological. Catfish finally dropped his finger from the trigger and breathed in painful gasps while waiting for it to move. It didn't.

Givens yelled something, but Catfish couldn't understand it. Christ, his knees hurt. Felt like he'd pressed a red-hot iron against them. And was that plastic melting? Maybe his boot had—

His vision blanked momentarily before reappearing, a field of stars racing across the world. An instant later, the pain rocked him, and he turned sideways in the duct. Givens crouched less than a meter away, his fingers snapping.

"Hey!" Givens yelled. "Move. Forward!"

Woozy from the encounter with the creature, not to mention Givens' cuff of his head, Catfish seemed stuck in neutral. He caught movement over Givens' shoulder, and his eyes widened.

The vent beyond had become mouths, talons, and mandibles, all vibrating in the light. In the center of it all, a single blue eye blazed with malevolent intelligence.

With a yell of his own, he turned in the tight space and crawled forward as fast as he could. The creature he'd torched might still be alive, but he didn't care. He pulled back a fist and struck the burned shell as hard as he could. He barely registered any surprise when the carapace shattered, and a much smaller thing sprouted tiny legs from its thick shell before skittering toward the duct exit.

He reached the torn vent where the creature had first entered and tumbled through the gap without even bothering to see where he'd land. He dropped nearly a meter before striking metal and plastic and struggled to raise himself to point his incinerator back at the ceiling. Two seconds later, Givens dropped through with a yell, his incinerator pointing upward.

Flares of pain spread through Catfish's nervous system. His boot had hit the metal first, but he still had enough sense to look for the other creature. The smaller M2 entity sat at the edge of the metal box they'd landed on, its tiny legs trying to carry it off the housing. Catfish blasted it with the incinerator just as its surface rippled with black bubbles. The creature exploded into a fireball of flame before disappearing into a cloud of hardened crumbs.

A blast of fire rocketed past his face and toward the vents above them.

"Hey!" Catfish yelled. "Cease fire!"

"Fuck that!" Givens said and pushed Catfish hard.

Catfish rolled off the top of the generator housing and fell into a row of cardboard boxes. Lightning bolts of pain flashed across his back and elbow, making tears run from his eyes. His daze broke when he heard Givens screaming.

He looked up just in time to see a set of limbs push through the rip in the ductwork. Catfish, vision blurred with pain and panic, pointed his incinerator at the open vent. A spray of mist settled over his face. He watched with horror as the limbs retreated, Givens' upper torso impaled by one of the alien-looking appendages. The soldier's face rolled to one side, his eyes staring down at Catfish as if in lamentation. The limbs lifted back into the duct, the metal shearing Givens' remains at the neck, his head dropping to the floor with a wet crunch.

Catfish didn't hear his own yell of rage as he pulled the trigger, and a jet of fire lit the dark room. The flame belched into the duct, eliciting the smell of burning flesh and something altogether unrecognizable. He continued holding the trigger until his incinerator ran dry.

"Hey!" someone yelled.

Instead of turning, he continued staring at the ductwork. Something dripped down from the generator housing and splashed his cheek. He managed to keep from vomiting, knowing full well Givens' body had been torn to shreds and likely consumed.

"Catfish!"

The voice finally broke through the fog in his brain, and he turned. Sarah stood in the ambient glow cast by two other flashlights, aiming her incinerator at the ductwork from which he and Givens had appeared.

"It—" He swallowed hard. "It got—"

"Come to me," she said, her voice both commanding and sympathetic.

He walked backward, his eyes still focused on the vent above the generator. Catfish only stumbled twice before reaching her. "I'm sorry," he said.

"Where did it go?"

"Back into the vent," Catfish said. "It got Givens."

He heard the sound of her teeth clicking together. "I know. You've got blood on your face."

"Where's Shawna?"

"In the lab." Sarah's voice had grown choked, weaker somehow.

He looked down at the useless incinerator in his hands. "I'm empty."

"Yes," Sarah said. "You are. We have one more incinerator left. It's by the security desk."

The darkness of the room made it difficult to orient himself. Without the baleful ambient glow cast by the powerful flashlights, the room would be completely pitch. He stumbled toward the security desk. His hands, bruised, scraped, and bleeding from his time in the duct, fumbled with the straps of the incinerator. Givens' shrieking scream, the most terrible sound he'd ever heard, rattled around his mind, coupled with the image of the alien limbs dragging the man's remains into the ductwork.

Dazed and exhausted, his foot sizzling with pain and his legs burning, Catfish bumped into the security desk. The tanks clanked as he dropped the weapon.

"Catfish?"

He heard Sarah's voice, but her words barely made an impact. He was too busy searching the rack for the spare incinerator and not finding it. "What?"

"Get to the lab. Now."

The tone of her voice made him turn around. Then he heard the sound of talons rattling through the vent as if on a plate of thin aluminum.

"Where?" he asked in a small voice, although he already knew. It was near the generator. It ceased for an instant and started up again. Now, it sounded as though it were all around him, all around the room.

Catfish turned back to the rack, his eyes finally focusing on the collection of tools. There was the other incinerator. He pulled it from the rack and shuffled into the straps as quickly as his trembling hands allowed.

"Get into the goddamned lab," Sarah said again, her voice nearly a growl.

He looked at where her light pointed, and the breath in his lungs emptied in a rush. A long limb, thick at its base with a hooked talon jutting from its end, had snaked out of the vent. A terrible squealing, rending sound echoed in the room as the creature ripped at the duct, trying to tear through the metal and escape.

Sarah's incinerator came to life, as did the other soldiers'. The jets of fire roared from the weapons almost loud enough to obscure the sound of the creature ripping its way through the ductwork.

Catfish's brain finally kicked into gear, and he ran as fast as he dared through the near darkness and to the lab. "Shawna!" he shouted.

Not waiting for a response, he crouched through the broken airlock and into the darkness beyond. He yelled her name as he frantically scanned the area with his flashlight, but he saw no one. "Where are—" He stopped mid-sentence, his eyes finally recognizing the open lift shaft.

He aimed the flashlight into the shaft, the light reflecting off old steel. The lift, still at the bottom, was empty. Shallow metal rungs ran up the sides. Catfish cursed, knowing damned well his booted foot couldn't fit into the rungs.

A scream erupted from outside the airlock, followed by a storm of static and the whoosh of the incinerators. Sarah yelled something, but he couldn't hear what it was. The lab shook as something massive slammed into it. Catfish turned to peer out the fractured airlock, but he couldn't see much of anything apart from the brief flash of an incinerator.

He maneuvered until he had a sightline and poked his head out. In the glow of his flashlight, he saw what looked like a deformed spider tearing through the remains of the large room. The sound of frying bacon rose as a long proboscis lanced through the raised floor, consuming anything the creature could digest. Flames licked off the creature's surface, but the thing wasn't burning. It was growing.

The creature suddenly paused, one of its eyestalks swiveling in his direction. A cold blue eye stared at him with curiosity. He held his breath, his mind frozen at the sight of the creature. The bright light cast by the flashlight raked across M2's surface, eliciting tendrils of smoke but nothing more. The creature's eyestalk bent in his direction as if growing, lengthening to get nearer to him. A pair of mandibles hungrily clicked together as though in anticipation. Then it rushed him.

The creature covered the ten meters, separating it from the lab in less than two seconds. Catfish had time to stumble backward further into the lab before the creature smashed into the steel wall. The lab trembled and burned detritus shook loose from the ceiling like dust.

Panicked, Catfish ignored the bright flares of pain from his foot and walked away from the airlock as fast as he could. A tentacle swept through where he had been, its hooked talon scratching at the floor as it tried to find him. Instead of trying to run away, something he couldn't do, he lifted himself onto the console and rolled over the shattered glass pane and into the specimen lab.

The remnants of the protective glass dug into his back and side as he landed on the floor. He screamed in pain before covering his mouth to dampen the sound. God, it hurt. The glass had ripped through his clothes, and warm trickles of blood streamed down his perforated skin.

Something slapped the wall beyond him. Catfish's breath stopped when he looked up. His flashlight, flickering in a near strobe, showed a hooked tentacle licking the air above him. Taub Prime was searching for him.

He hit the flashlight hard with his bleeding palm, and the light stabilized for a moment. Rather than pointing it at the tentacle, he used it to illuminate the area around him. Shattered glass, shattered instruments, shards of metal, and blackened streaks from fire surrounded him. The tentacle bent toward him, its end flicking back and forth, trying to find something to shred, tear, or grab.

Heart hammering, Catfish used his bleeding hands to push himself backward along the floor and away from the probing tentacle. He kept the light shining to the side of the creature, not wanting to give it a hint of where he was. Could it sense light? He didn't know, which was reason enough to try to stay in the dark as long as possible.

The tentacle continued sweeping, lengthening to reach the floor. A brief wave of static filled the lab. The tentacle's end was no longer solid but glistened like liquid as it vacuumed any consumable material. Catfish continued shuffling backward, his body shuddering in fear.

Several seconds passed before the tentacle once more became solid, retracted from the opening, and disappeared. Catfish held his breath, the light still focused on the floor, the ambient glow barely illuminating the observation room beyond the lab's shattered glass windows. It was gone.

He stayed where he was a few seconds longer, afraid that any movement might alert the creature to his position. Then he heard a shuffling, sliding sound as though something was being dragged across the floor. Static, much louder than before, drifted through the shattered windows. The creature was still inside the lab enclosure, but now it sounded as though it were near the quarantine shaft.

The shaft, Catfish thought. *Jesus. I have to*— He raised himself from the floor with a silent howl of pain, the wetness of warm blood on his skin making him wince. His lacerated back and arms burned, but he ground his teeth to bite back the pain and not give it a voice.

He cautiously shined the flashlight over the floor beyond the broken windows. No tentacle. Barely daring to breathe, he swung the light in a slow arc toward the airlock. His breath hitched, and his mouth opened in horror. What he saw at the lab airlock entrance broke his brain.

Something like a jet-black millipede moved its long, thin body through the damaged steel. Hundreds and hundreds of tiny legs clicked on the hard floor while it moved further and further toward the quarantine shaft. As he watched, the thing's head sprouted two sets of eyestalks, each bending to peer into the shaft and the level below.

Catfish aimed his flashlight at the wall nearest the shaft to provide ambient illumination. He wished he hadn't. The creature seemed to be sniffing the air or perhaps sensing the light. The rest of its body entered the airlock, its rear flipping up like a scorpion's tail, three sharp talons jutting from its flipper-like end.

The thing paused, the black orbs of its eyestalks spinning crazily. One of them swiveled toward him. Catfish killed the light and froze in place, his breath coming in ragged gasps. More clicking, more radio static, more fear. He closed his eyes, fearing what might be approaching him in the dark. If it was going to move through the lab interior, he'd have no chance. There was nowhere to run to. He was finished.

The seconds passed like an eternity. Then he heard the sound of liquid as if dropped on a tile floor, but thicker, so much thicker. Oil.

Catfish opened his eyes and stared into the darkness, head cocked to one side as if to hear better. Taub Prime dragged itself with the sickening liquid sound of sewage sliding over concrete. Its legs no longer clicked on the floor, and suddenly, he realized what it was doing—it was going down the shaft.

He carefully hoisted himself back over the window sill and into the lab's observation area. Clicking the light back on, he panned its beam over the immediate area.

Polished steel glared back, the reflection nearly blinding him. He slowly walked forward, his shoe and boot crunching on shattered glass and metal remnants. When he turned the corner, he saw the creature's tail jutting up from the shaft before disappearing. He stumbled to the shaft and carefully looked down into it without a thought.

The bright light from the quarantine room below wavered as the creature descended, its thick body groping at the sides of the shaft. It had shed its legs for strong limbs, the ends so much like rudimentary hands and fingers that his skin crawled at the sight.

He shined the flashlight into the shaft, the UV's brightness set to full. The light skittered across its carapace, eliciting tendrils of vapor but nothing else. An eyestalk grew from its rear, a cold blue eye staring at him with disinterest from its end. The creature didn't pause but continued down the shaft. Catfish watched until it hit the floor and dragged itself out of view. It was on the quarantine level now, and there was nothing he could do.

CHAPTER THIRTY-ONE

When the lift finally reached the bottom, Shawna turned to see the three scientists standing a few meters away. Jay's face had gone pale, but she supposed all of them looked terrified.

"You made it," Kate said with a smile.

Shawna nodded. "Yeah. Okay, we need to—"

A shout echoed down the shaft, although it was completely unintelligible, and the four turned their heads toward the sound. Another volley of noise drifted down into the quiet quarantine level.

"Jesus," Jay said, his voice tight and timid, "it's killing them."

"We have to move," Shawna said.

"Where?"

Shawna turned to look at Kate and finally realized where they were. The lift connecting the lab to the quarantine area had deposited them in a safe room. Well, not safe, exactly. It was little more than another lab. Sealed. Metal. Glass. Locked from the outside. They were trapped.

"Shit." Shawna stepped to the pressure door separating them from the rest of the level. The word "Unauthorized" glowed like an epithet from the control panel. Shawna put her bracelet against the sensor. The door buzzed angrily, and the word blinked before steadying. Fighting panic, she let her eyes take in the entire door. Then she saw an intercom.

She punched the button and yelled, "Hey! Anyone there?"

No response. Beyond the quarantine enclosure's glass windows, the brightly lit observation area was completely deserted. Before its lights had been blown out, the science lab had been filled with light and devoid of shadow. This part of the quarantine level was barely illuminated past the confines of the relatively small isolation cubicle. As it was, the four of them stood less than a half meter apart, the walls uncomfortably close.

"Where the hell are they?" Jay asked.

Shawna stabbed the button again. "Hello? We're in the isolation room. We're not infected, but we need help!"

No response.

Neil shivered and crossed his arms. "What if— What if there's no one on this level because of the lockdown?"

Shaking her head, Kate pointed at the glass separating them from the rest of the level. "They're supposed to have guards on this level at all times. But in here? Probably not a big concern unless the alarms were tripped."

"Um, the alarms were tripped," Jay said. "So where the hell are they?"

Shawna thought for a moment and pressed the button. When the light turned green, she cleared her throat and spoke very slowly. "Moore? If you can hear me, we're trapped in the isolation room. Can you disengage the locks?" She released the button and stepped away as though it might bite her.

The silence lingered, the whoosh of an unseen air circulation system the only stimuli apart from their labored breathing and the dim sounds from the shaft. Sighing, Shawna stepped back to the intercom and moved to press the button.

"Moore here." The voice made the four of them jump. A staticky crackle floated beneath her words. "My apologies for the delay." The light above the airlock turned green, and the pressure seals disengaged. "I had to make sure none of you were infected."

"Of course, we're not infected," Jay said. "The fucking thing is still up there."

"Yes, it is," Moore said. "For now."

Shawna's spine tingled. "For now?"

"Please exit the room," Moore said.

Jay opened his mouth to ask another question or maybe yell a stream of curses, but Kate pushed him to the open hatch. The four of them stepped through the isolation airlock and into the observation hallway. The hatch shut behind them, red lights glowing above the steel.

"We have lost the science level," Moore's disembodied voice said over the PA. "I have no way to know what has happened there, much less the situation."

Shawna found the comms panel and activated it, eliminating the need for an intercom button. "What about engineering?"

"Engineering is secure," Moore said. "Apart from an air shaft, Mr. Standlee and Mr. Givens used to make their way to the science level."

That tingling feeling turned to ice. "What? What do you mean?"

"Mr. Standlee and Mr. Givens descended to the science level some time ago. They have not reported in."

"Great," Jay said. "Our rescuers."

"What do we do now?" Kate asked. "We can't go back up."

"No," Moore agreed. "That would be unwise. May I suggest you activate the UV lights in the isolation room in case M2 decides to escape using the lift shaft?"

"Shit." Shawna turned and looked at the control panel. She quickly found a label marked "UV" and pressed it. The isolation room's interior became intolerably bright through the observation windows. "Okay. Now, how the hell do we get out of here?"

"You don't," Moore said.

Kate and Shawna exchanged a glance. Lip quivering, Kate cleared her throat. "What do you mean we don't?"

"You don't leave the level until the escaped M2 creature is destroyed."

Neil pounded a fist on the control panel. "And how do we do that?"

"I suggest," Moore said, "that you make your way to the blast door. I'll alert the remaining guards on the level that you are on your way there."

"Fanfuckingtastic," Jay said. "Can't believe you didn't send them to let us out."

When Moore spoke again, Shawna suddenly realized how much trouble they were really in. "They have been busy. We have a possible containment breach. Which is another reason you should make your way to the blast door immediately."

"Oh, shit," Shawna said. "You said remaining guards?"

Jay's eyes widened, his face growing more pale. "What does—"

Neil grabbed him by the shoulder and pushed him toward the observation room's exit while Jay stuttered.

Shawna stared at the speaker in the ceiling. "How bad is it?"

"Please leave the observation area now," Moore said.

Kate tugged at her shoulder, and Shawna finally turned. Without a word, they headed through the open hatch and into the corridor beyond. Red warning blinkers flashed on the walls, and the overheads filled the world with incredibly bright white light.

* * *

Moore's eyes flicked from one feed to another as she desperately searched for egress points to protect. Ways M2 could get out. Her monitor displayed the old blueprints of the facility's quarantine level. It was the last level before the maintenance floor and the foundation upon which the facility had been built.

The air shafts were the logical weak points, so those had been the first areas mined with thermite and Semtex. According to her other engineering consultants, none of whom could examine the facility nor know its exact nature, an explosion in the air shaft shouldn't cause a breach in the steel and concrete walls protecting the facility from the water table. That, however, was little comfort. The moment she'd visited the facility's quarantine and maintenance levels, she'd known all bets were off. Cracks. Water leakage. Any significant explosion might create spiderwebs of fissures in the thick walls. The water would begin seeping through cracks, further damaging the concrete until leaks became streams. Then rivers.

The Taub descendant was loose on the science level, but she could do little about that. The trick would be finding a way to extract the survivors without breaking containment.

"Containment's already broken," she said aloud, eyes still dancing from one feed to another. The Taub creature broke through to the remaining glass shield. If it managed to fracture it, she'd have no choice but to detonate the sets of explosives ringing the lowest level, followed by quarantine, followed by science, and, at last, destroying the engineering level. All of it. Collapse the entire fucking facility into the earth itself. If M2 managed to survive that, it might crawl back to where it came from.

"Fat chance."

The facility was decades old, and its security measures were not meant for something like M2. It had not been designed to contain a creature that grows and grows with everything consumable it touches. A creature that can change its form to fit purpose and adapt faster than its human captors. M2 was smarter than they'd suspected and intelligent enough to form strategies and avoid obstacles, all while feeding and feeding and feeding.

"I should have destroyed you before they had a chance to bring you here."

Moore wiped the moisture from her eyes and forced herself to focus. There had to be a way. Just had to be.

* * *

Catfish repeatedly hit the lift controls, but they didn't respond. "Fuck!"

His voice echoed in the mostly enclosed space, hurting his ears. Another bolt of pain rose from his damaged foot, clouding his vision with stars.

Something metal clanged outside the airlock, and Catfish froze, his flashlight shivering in his hands. He waited in the dark and the ensuing silence for the sound to come again. He didn't have to wait long. It sounded like metal sliding across metal. No clicks. No static. Nothing that sounded like M2.

He turned and faced the airlock, sweat dripping from his forehead despite the coolness of the room. The clang and slide didn't come again, but he heard footfalls—combat boots on the raised floor. He stuck his head out of the airlock, half expecting a tentacle to cleave it, and shined the light toward the sound.

Sarah approached from the equipment racks. Her clothes were covered in grime, torn in places, and her face lacerated by God knew what. Her incinerator dangled from her hands, its blue pilot light no longer lit. She smiled at him.

"Holy shit," he said. "You made it."

"Yeah," she said, voice barely above a whisper.

He moved out of the airlock, wincing with each step. With the adrenaline no longer spiking through his bloodstream, the pain and fatigue were descending on him like a shroud.

"You okay?" he asked between clenched teeth.

Sarah limped, and one of her arms hung straight down as if she couldn't move it. "Dandy," she said, shrugging the incinerator off her shoulders. It clanged to the ground with an echoing metallic bang. "It went into the lab."

He nodded, although he wasn't sure she could see him. "It went down the shaft."

The head of security froze in her tracks. Her head slowly tipped back before she howled in rage. When she looked back at him, her eyes looked dazed instead of sharp with anger. He made his way to her and put his arm around her waist.

"Sit down," he said, "before you fall down."

He guided her to the blast door separating them from the elevator corridor. The thick steel was still in place, blocking their egress, but at least it was something to rest their backs against. When he had her situated, he sat less than a meter away.

The room's silence was creepy, especially without the normally pervasive hum of equipment. It was like sitting in an abyss with a penlight to illuminate it.

"Did Shawna and the science team make it out okay?" Sarah asked, her eyes closed.

"Yeah," he said. He turned off his flashlight. Damned thing was doing little more than flickering now. *Cheap piece of shit.* "That's the problem. M2 went down there too."

"I heard you," Sarah sighed. "At least they have power. If the UV lights are still working, they should be able to keep it enclosed."

Catfish chuckled, but it sounded more like a sob. "It doesn't give a damn about UV anymore. It's beyond that. Did you even manage to hurt it with fire?"

She was silent for a moment. "Only when it was stupid enough to show us something we could hit. We blasted it, all three of us, and torched the shit out of it. It destroyed the generator and leaped into the vents. Didn't see it after that until you and—" Her voice broke off, and he could hear her trying not to cry. "Until you came out."

He nodded in the dark. "Must have split itself. Or something."

"Split?"

"Yeah." Catfish scratched at the prickling, itching cuts and burns on his arm. "I burned the one that was coming for me. But another one was behind it on the other side of the vent. That's the one that followed us out." He winced, realizing he'd said "us."

"We might be fucked," Sarah said. "If it comes back, we have nothing left to fight it with. All the incinerators apart from yours are drained. We're nearly down to harsh language."

"Did that work at Ben Taub?"

She laughed, but it had no mirth in it. "No. It didn't."

They were silent for a moment.

"So we just die here."

"Yup," Sarah said. "This is where we die. If they don't stop it."

Catfish's lip trembled. Meters below him, surrounded by steel and concrete and blocked off from any possible exit, Shawna and the science team were at the mercy of the M2 entity. He was betting it was hungry after its attack and the damage that had been done to it. If it had been damaged at all.

His boot was becoming painfully tight from swelling. To make matters worse, the trickle of liquid he felt on his toes had to be blood. He'd probably split his remaining stitches and reopened the wound. He tried to move, but the pain hit him like a truck.

"Well," he said through a groan, "if it comes back, serve me up for dinner. I'm not going anywhere."

"Same," she said. "Dislocated my arm."

He laughed. "Maybe I'll get some sleep."

"No sleep," she said with a yawn. "Shock. No sleep. Not yet."

Catfish closed his eyes anyway and moved his hand. He found her palm and put his fingers in hers. She cringed at first and then clenched his hand.

Not love. Not want. Just two human beings trying to take comfort while they waited to die.

"—grenades," Sarah muttered a moment later.

He yawned and stared at her. "What?"

She stirred, and her eyes blinked owlishly. "Forgot we still have grenades."

The blast door boomed as the locking mechanism clicked open.

* * *

Prime knew the light was dangerous. It protected itself by growing a thicker carapace before dropping into the room and curling its long body beneath itself. Within its hard shell, the creature reformed, hardened new limbs, and finally extruded them from its thorax. The creature extruded a solid hood over itself and grew a short eyestalk beneath it. The overhang kept the UV light from directly smashing into its vulnerable liquid form. Tendrils of vapor still rose from the eyestalk, the ambient light almost setting it ablaze, but it only needed the appendage for a second or two before it reabsorbed the sensory organ and the hood.

The incongruous lump of alien shell rippled as two thick limbs formed, each of their ends becoming disturbingly like human hands with long talons for fingertips. It pulled itself to the wall where it had seen the glass, the same kind of glass that had imprisoned it in the place of its birth. It had seen that barrier shatter and knew it could do the same.

Static filled the room as its liquid belly absorbed flakes of dead skin, construction debris, traces of old cleaning chemicals, and plastic. Not the meal it wanted, but it would have to do for now.

The creature reached the wall, and a single limb with a wide, flipper-like end emerged from its belly. Prime hardened the shell around the new appendage and its vulnerable underside. The creature deflated as it shifted more and more of its mass to its ventral side. Then it pushed.

The wide flipper acted like a foot, giving Prime enough leverage to raise itself. When it was at the right height, it swung its makeshift arms before springing them into the glass. The sharp talons crashed into the transparent barrier, spider webs of cracks suddenly covering the observation windows. Prime swung its limbs repeatedly, the flipper broadening to provide more leverage and allowing the creature to rock back and forth for more power.

Prime smashed at the glass five more times, its limbs wheeling backward before swinging over its head and crunching into the window. Vapor rose from its body, the harsh UV lights burning off its outer shell. It couldn't stay in here forever. It had to escape before it expended too much of its mass. It also knew what was beyond the room. It sensed *another.* Another to help it *become.*

Prime felt the glass give way in an explosion of material, a brief rain of shards pattering over its shell. The creature's arms stopped swinging and moved forward through the glass. The finger-like appendages experimentally gripped the edge of the sill, the digits digging their talons into the soft plastic and aluminum of the console.

It reabsorbed the foot back into its belly and pulled itself into the observation room. The vapor stopped pouring from its back when it struck the steel floor. It was safe now. The quarantine room filled with static as it consumed everything it could. The *other* was closer now. All Prime had to do was find it.

CHAPTER THIRTY-TWO

A klaxon screamed from the embedded speakers, making conversation nearly impossible. Warning lights flashed red in an ominous strobe, giving the bright white overheads a pink tinge. They moved past stacks of storage crates, Kate shepherding them toward the blast door and the elevator corridor.

Shawna looked past the surplus incinerator tanks, thick sheets of aluminum, and instant concrete, her eyes focusing on the containment room beyond. Three figures stood near the thick steel enclosure's door, their incinerator blue pilot teardrops visible even under the assault of the UV lights. She wasn't sure, but she thought one of the men was shaking either from adrenaline or fear.

She nearly bumped into one of the crates when a large dimple appeared on the steel wall. The three soldiers jumped back, and Shawna stopped in her tracks. Another dimple appeared with a low boom that caught the barest edge of her hearing.

"What the—" Jay said, his head turning in that direction.

One of the soldiers yelled, and the sound of shattering glass echoed through the room. A dark shape flipped through the broken entry door, and the three incinerators came to life.

The blasts of fire washed over a shadowy limb. The soldiers' yells rose above the crackle and whoosh of the jets of flame. A large, dark, amorphous form scuttled out of the room and lunged at the closest man.

The tentacle they'd been firing upon whipped and took out the legs of one of the soldiers. He fell backward to the floor, his feet no longer attached to his body. His incinerator went out as he crumpled to the deck just before the tentacle whipped again and removed his head.

The remaining guards shuffled backward, trying to escape the creature, but it was moving too fast. Instead of focusing on the tentacle, they'd concentrated their fire on the creature's hardened shell, the flames licking impotently off the surface. The tentacle's hook slashed and cut one of the men in two at the waist. The remaining guard turned to run. The tentacle flashed again and buried its hook in the man's back.

Shawna screamed. The incinerators were out. The three guards were down. The crackle and spit of static filled the room as the creature, still smoking and surrounded by a veil of heat haze, plopped down on the first body. She watched in horrified fascination as the body disappeared and the creature grew larger. In less than five seconds, it had completely consumed the corpse and was moving to the next.

"Run!" Kate yelled.

Shawna finally tore her eyes away from the sight and followed the scientists through the maze of crates to the blast door. When they were less than five meters from the thick metal door separating them from the elevator corridor, a loud boom echoed out of the quarantine observation room, accompanied by the tinkle of broken glass on metal.

The four scientists, panting and puffing, turned as one to peer over the clutter of crates and supplies. Something was coming out of the quarantine lab. Shawna watched in horror as a brown form advanced through the entrance, its centipede-like body adorned with eyestalks and all too human arms jutting from its back.

For a moment, she was certain it was staring at her. Even across the fifteen-meter distance, its dark blue eyes seemed to pierce her consciousness, ripping and tearing at her mind. Another sound caught her attention, but she didn't dare break her stare with the thing. She needn't have bothered anyway.

The creature's eyestalks flipped toward the containment room, its segmented arms flicking at the air in an uncanny pantomime of human movement. The thing she'd named Prime had changed direction and curled its body around the lab to face the containment area.

The ever-present wave of static suddenly ceased, leaving Shawna and the scientists gaping at the sight of Taub. It had consumed the bodies and everything else in the area and now appeared as a quivering lump of glistening dark matter. Freed from the danger of the UV lamps, Taub had returned to liquid form. Its surface puckered and bubbled. A crab-like eyestalk rose from its center, a dead black orb rotating at high speed at its end.

The clicking of dozens of tiny, spindly legs on the metal made her shift her eyes to Prime. The creature had rounded the edge of the lab, its eyestalks pointing at Taub like spears. The two creatures stared at one another in a deathly silence. Shawna held her breath as she waited for something to happen, the sound of Neil quietly sobbing in terror barely registering in her consciousness. Crunching and crackling finally broke the tableau.

Prime's centipede body morphed before her eyes, the legs retracting into its middle, the creature slowly lowering itself to the metal deck. Prime's elongated body widened, its surface hardening into a shell. Four new legs, each crackling and spitting as it grew a new carapace, extruded from the squat shape. Instead of looking like arachnid limbs, these were more mammalian, the hind legs composed of joints and ending in wide analogs of human feet.

Prime's body had reformed into something that looked like a human being had been stretched and pulled, the nose replaced by a misshapen snout sporting black, glistening teeth. Now the size of a massive Grizzly bear and just as thick, the creature raised its head in a silent howl, its shell wriggling and writhing as short spikes appeared on its back and sides.

Taub quickly reformed itself, crab-like legs sprouting from the lump of dark ooze, chelicerae and mandibles taking shape as it widened and lengthened its body. Three legs sprouted from its bottom and lifted a malformed torso into the air. The wide head sat atop the short, squat, thick body, a pair of human-like limbs crunching and crackling as they pushed through the outer shell. The nightmarish thing stared at its offspring with alien hunger.

As if on a silent count, Prime pushed with its hind legs and leaped nearly three meters through the air, crashing down into the metal floor like a sledgehammer. Taub pulled itself forward on two legs, a third limb dragging behind. Taub's taloned, thick arms reached forward as if hoping for a deadly embrace. It didn't have long to wait.

Prime sprang forward again, its front legs kicking upward as it moved through the air and hit Taub like a linebacker. The noise of brittle eggshells smashing into one another filled the air, along with a cloud of dark crumbs and particles.

Taub fell backward to the steel deck with a crash. Prime, the four-legged monstrosity, sat on Taub's torso, Prime's multiple arms rising and falling like hammers as it pounded at the creature's carapace. A new short, broad limb extruded from Taub's torso, pushed upward like a piston, and sent Prime flying off its chest.

Prime landed on all fours, its arms shortening and its quizzical blue eye staring at its progenitor. Taub shook, its three "legs" retracting into its torso, and its shape was already beginning to change.

Readying itself for another attack, Prime lurched forward and to the side, doing its best to flank Taub and avoid a counterattack. But Taub had plans of its own. Taub's foot-like appendage tapered to a spear point and swung to the side, tracking its assailant. Its surface crackled as it reformed, the squarish torso becoming a squat, oblong body. Six legs sprouted from its flanks, their ends wide and flat. A pair of dark fangs, their color lightening as they hardened, jutted upward from a wet maw. A new appendage grew to match its spear, but this one looked more like a three-fingered gripping hand, each digit ending in a hooked talon.

Now looking more like a misshapen roach or beetle, Taub scuttled backward as Prime approached. Prime's arms raised upward like scorpion tails, the appendages flicking and slashing at the air in random arcs. Taub retreated, its spear and gripping hand continuing to track those of its quadruped enemy.

Without warning, Prime leaped forward, snout down, arms held at a nearly 90° angle. Taub prepared for the attack and used its gripping appendage to shove the creature aside and jab with its spear. The sharp limb met Prime with the sound of a desiccated locust shell crushed beneath a heavy boot. Prime fell to the side, its shell quickly regrowing bits of shattered carapace. Taub reached for it, but Prime danced away with a grace Shawna hadn't expected possible.

Taub moved sideways, its legs clicking loudly on the metal floor. The point of its spear looked dull and sheared. The limb retracted a few centimeters, and the point reappeared and renewed. Taub's body seemed to shorten, the crackle and spit from a grease fire filling the air. Prime had shrunk in the same manner.

A hand grabbed her shoulder. "Shawna! Get down!" Kate yelled. She barely noticed.

Prime circled Taub, the roach-like thing scuttling to keep its fanged mouth aimed squarely at its attacker. Prime lunged, but Taub moved backward in a flash, its gripping hand slapping the side of Prime's snout with the crunch of spring ice.

Hard, dark matter puffed in a cloud as part of Prime's head disappeared, revealing a bubbling cauldron of black. Prime shuffled backward as if stunned, a shell forming around the glistening hole. Taub immediately shot forward and rammed the quadruped in the flank, knocking it sprawling. The spear reared back before piercing Prime's hindquarters.

A cloud of crumbs so small they looked like black mist exploded off Prime's back. One of its legs cracked at the base and folded beneath it. Taub grasped Prime by its short neck, and the digits pressed into Prime's outer shell.

Prime's flank shivered as a mouth with serrated teeth extended from its torso and bit like a snapping turtle. Black sawdust spat off Taub's third segment, the leg disappearing, leaving a large, ragged hole in the beetle creature's armor. Taub reared back or tried to, but Prime held fast, its mammalian features melting into arms and tentacles. It plunged them inside the opening and widened it with rips and tears. Taub's remaining legs pulled back, but Prime extruded a new appendage resembling a mosquito proboscis. The beetle shrunk in size, its shell fading into a glassy liquid while Prime drank it.

Shawna watched Prime grow, its surface rippling and bubbling as it consumed its parent. A moment later, Taub transformed into a puddle of liquid before Prime rushed forward to absorb Taub's remains.

Prime's body crackled with static as it widened and lengthened. It rose from the floor on two legs, its abdomen, and chest festooned with appendages. It turned toward her.

Then everything went blue. She suddenly found herself looking at nothing. No creature. It had been there and then—

Someone grabbed her shoulder and pulled her backward. She stumbled and fell to her ass, her hands scrambling to find purchase. A yell of anger and fear erupted behind her, and something flew over her head.

An incendiary grenade exploded with a fiery bang. A set of hands grabbed her shoulder and dragged her, screaming through the open blast door. Another grenade flew over her head, her view of the ceiling becoming unfocused. She dropped her head just in time to see something rounding the corner of the burning crates, its silhouette undeniable. Prime walked on two legs, four arms growing out of its torso, the top two flexing their taloned digits, the lower two looking like octopus tentacles.

The other grenade detonated out of sight, and a secondary explosion followed close behind. The enormous, thick steel door closed with a bang. Something crashed into it from the other side, the boom echoing in the elevator corridor.

Hands lifted her to her feet. She turned and saw Catfish, his head slightly bowed and panting like a dog. He was covered in lacerations, clothes streaked with grease and filth, and clutched a grenade in one hand. His boot was melted and half-broken.

A wave of dizziness spread over her, and she wobbled as Neil and Kate took her weight. Catfish jerked a thumb to the elevator.

"Move," he said through gritted teeth.

After two steps, Shawna finally got her feet under her. Kate moved away, Neil's arm remaining around Shawna's waist. A moment later, Kate had Catfish by the hip, one of his arms over her shoulder. They stepped as though she were a crutch.

"The elevator is unlocked," Moore said from the speakers, her voice even and calm. "I suggest you hurry."

A new set of klaxons erupted from the ceiling.

"Warning. Facility destruction in three minutes," a robotic voice bellowed. "Evacuate the facility immediately."

Unable to hear anything over the sirens, the four scientists and Catfish made their way to the elevator. With its doors open and interior lights flashing an angry red, the steel box suddenly looked safe and inviting instead of like a claustrophobic coffin.

Once inside, the door descended and closed. The elevator's floor rumbled beneath her, and the group jerked as one as it rose much faster than normal. A moment later, the door opened to a new set of sirens.

"—in two minutes," an electronic voice calmly shouted through the speakers. "Evacuate the facility immediately."

Two men dressed in military uniforms stood on either side of the elevator. When the door fully opened, they reached into the car and plucked Catfish out as though he were a pile of laundry. One soldier lifted him onto the other's back.

"Hurry," someone yelled, and the soldier with Catfish walked quickly through the pulse of red lights that seemed much brighter than the overheads. The robotic voice droned as the group moved past the conference room and into the lobby. The heavy glass doors hung wide open, and another group of soldiers waited outside. Several of them carried large incinerators, and a turret had been placed several meters away from the doors, a weapon's long barrel covering the exit.

The man carrying Catfish continued ahead as though being chased by something unseen. Shawna felt like she was walking through a dream beneath the cold, rainy fall sky. The group made their way to a large, thick green tarp. Neil led Shawna to a canvas lawn chair and carefully guided her into it. A hand reached for hers. She turned dumbly in that direction and looked into Catfish's pale, grizzled, bloody face.

He smiled at her, a tear dripping from one eye. "Found you," he whispered.

She squeezed his fingers and held them tightly. A man appeared at Catfish's side, a medical caduceus on his sleeve. He rolled back Catfish's shirt and plunged a needle into him. Catfish turned to look at the man for a moment before his face slackened.

Her daze evaporated as he closed his eyes. "What? Wait!"

A hand touched her shoulder. She whipped around and looked up into Moore's deadpan expression. "Just a sedative," she said. "We need him immobilized until we check him out."

Shawna brushed the woman's hand from her shoulder. "Check him for what? He can't be infected!"

Moore nodded. "No. He can't. But he's damaged his leg again, and we need to check his burns. We don't want him getting sepsis."

A swirl of unreality swept over her.

"Doctor Moore?" a soldier said. "All personnel evacuated."

Moore didn't shift her gaze from Shawna's. "Thank you, Lieutenant. You may proceed."

Klaxon sirens went off around them, the air splitting with their low to high-pitched swell.

A grin spread slowly over Moore's face, and she squeezed Shawna's shoulder like a mother reassuring her daughter. "It's done," she said.

The ground trembled beneath them, the tarp shaking off a storm of droplets. A muted roar underlay the sound of the rain and the whisper of a breeze. The trembling ebbed and disappeared along with the last of the sound. The din of crumbling concrete, an entire foundation crackling as it fell apart, filled the air. Shawna turned to look at the building they'd spent so much time in.

The facility's walls had collapsed into a pile of rubble, fractured wood, chunks of sheetrock, and metal. Black smoke billowed from the building's corpse like the dying gasps of a giant animal. Soldiers slowly moved forward and took positions around the collapsed husk, their incinerator pilot lights glowing blue in the twilight.

"Ah," Moore said quietly. "You think that looks bad? Imagine what the quarantine level looks like."

Shawna met her gaze again. "What did you do?"

"Detonated the thermite charges. Turned the entire floor into an inferno before setting off multiple Symtex charges. After it blew, the lab level got the same treatment. Then engineering." She shrugged. "Was the plan all along."

"How do you know it's destroyed?"

Moore bit her lip. "I don't. We never will. Not unless it reappears. Until then," she rubbed her arms as though to warm them, "we'll search for it once the facility is pronounced safe to examine."

"That could take weeks," Shawna said dumbly.

Moore turned her head and looked back at the smoking wreck. "It will take weeks. But that'll be my problem." She turned to Shawna. "Rest. We're taking all of you to the infirmary. And we need to get your concussion looked at."

Shawna blinked. "I don't have a concussion. My head is fine."

"Okay," Moore said. "But we're going to check you anyway." Her voice had become strange in its cadence, as though it were more of a question than a statement.

The soldier with the caduceus appeared in front of her and held out two small cups. "Take this," he said. One paper cup held two pills, the other water. "I don't want you going into shock."

Moore's hand squeezed her shoulder. "Take them, Shawna. This will all be over soon."

Shawna took the pills, that dreamlike shroud returning and drowning her thoughts. After swallowing and polishing off the paper cup of water, the medic smiled at her and took the cups.

"You let me know if your head starts hurting, okay?"

"Feel woozy."

"That's the shock I'm worried about," he said. He grabbed her wrist, his fingers pressing down on her vein. He peered at his watch, following the second hand with his eyes. Finally, he released her arm and nodded. "You're okay. We'll get you warm."

His words had become fuzzy, distant, as though he were speaking through gauze. Her vision wavered slightly, and the pressure on her shoulder increased.

"Almost over," Moore was saying. Her voice faded into silence, and soon, the rest of the world did, too.

CHAPTER THIRTY-THREE

She awakened upon a comfortable mattress in a private room. Phantoms had removed her clothes, bathed her skin, and placed her body in the bed. At least, that was her theory. Had to love whatever cocktail they'd hit her with.

When she finally got her bearings, she realized her door glowed with a red light. She stood, headed to the door with bleary eyes, and read the word. "LOCKED." It didn't stay that way for long.

Just as she heard the footsteps in the hall, the light went green, and the lock clicked. A knock at the door.

"Shawna? It's Dr. Moore."

She stared down at the thin carpet, wondering where this room was. Where had Moore taken them this time? The fucking moon? Shawna stepped back with a sigh. "Come in."

The door swung open, revealing a hallway that looked too sanitary to be anything but a medical facility—private, by the look of it. She had no idea if that was a good or a bad thing. Moore wore a lab coat over a white blouse, dark slacks covering a pair of what might have been combat boots. Her hair looked like it had grown several more strands of white in the past few hours. Or was it days?

Moore stepped into the room and closed the door behind her. Shawna noted that it didn't automatically lock.

"How are you feeling?"

Shawna forced a smile. "Great, of course. Little fuzzy, but getting doped tends to do that to you." Moore's stoic expression didn't change. "Then there's that other thing that always happens. You being a bitch. And me wondering if I'm going to get shot."

The woman's lips twitched once before turning up in a thin smile. "Your criticisms are noted," she said with an icy tone. "Anything else?"

"Oh. How could I forget? The part where I ask you where Catfish is."

Moore nodded. "I wondered when we would get to that part." She looked expectantly at Shawna as if demanding her to say the words.

Shawna said nothing.

After a moment, Moore's smile disappeared, and she gestured to the bed. Shawna sighed and sat on its edge, her shirt and gym pants making her look like the prisoner she was.

Moore stood still as a statue while her face held all the warmth of a reptile. She finally held up a finger. "You were drugged for both your safety and ours and so that certain medical tests would be possible." Another finger. "You're in a private facility a few kilometers outside Houston." A third finger. "You will see Mr. Standlee shortly."

Shawna blinked.

"Oh, and, of course," Moore said, crossing her arms, "you are not going to be shot."

The woman's posture seemed less hostile than her disposition. Shawna wondered if Moore's psychological warfare tactics were ever going to stop.

"So now what?"

Moore's smile reappeared with a little less ice in it. "I'm going to explain a few things, and then we'll get with the group."

"Group?"

"Yes," Moore said. "Debrief. Something to do while we endure quarantine together."

She raised an eyebrow. "Quarantine?"

Moving her hands to her lab coat pockets, Moore glanced behind

Shawna toward the window, Shawna following her gaze. Sunlight filtered through a canopy of trees, casting shadows over the forest floor.

"It's a nice place for quarantine," Moore said. "Better views than last time."

Shawna rolled her eyes. "How long of a quarantine?"

"Two days. It's more observation than quarantine. We've already been given a clean bill of health. So to speak."

"Observation," Shawna said, rolling her eyes. "And what are we being observed for?"

"Psychotic and schizophrenic behaviors," Moore said casually. "It's just a precaution."

"Why would you—" She blinked. "You don't think—"

Moore returned her stare. "I don't think what?" she prompted.

And that was the question. Why had Shawna suddenly felt defensive, like Moore had accused her of something?

"What's going on?"

Moore's face relaxed, and Shawna felt as though something had happened here. Just now. Like a decision had been made. "Do you remember what happened in the lab?"

"When?"

"When you approached Taub 1 in the lab. When you came to talk to me."

A chill ran down Shawna's spine. The eye. That eye had bored into her like a laser and seemed to read her thoughts. Then she'd found herself near its containment box, hand reaching for it.

Shawna swallowed hard. "Yes."

Moore's expression lightened. A little. "Good. What about at the end?"

"The end?"

Moore moved to the wall and leaned against it with one hand. She sighed. "The end. At the blast door."

Prime reformed into a humanoid form, its features both androgynous and amorphous. "Yes."

"And what do you remember?"

Shawna told her. While she listened, Moore's head twitched every few seconds in a curt nod. When Shawna finished, Moore looked disquieted.

"And?"

It took Shawna a moment to understand what she meant. "And then I got pulled into the hallway."

Moore's light expression disappeared. "Did anything happen after it reformed?"

"No," she said too quickly. Had something else happened? There was something. Maybe. But. "No. Nothing I remember."

Nodding, Moore straightened herself and stood rigidly, her arms held tightly at her sides. "I want to show you something," she said, heading to a small control panel by the bed. She touched a few buttons, and the screen came to life. "NO INPUT" flashed several times before going dark. Moore pulled out a phone and swiped a few times. The darkness on the screen disappeared, replaced by four squares of images.

After a moment, Shawna realized she was looking at views from the surveillance cameras on the quarantine level. The split screens were frozen in time in a way she didn't understand at first. The upper left showed the stacks of crates, Shawna's torso and head clearly visible. Her reverent expression, too.

The upper right showed her what stood just out of frame on the previous view. Shawna's heart stopped in her chest. A jet-black body. A human body. No, she realized it wasn't. But it was close.

The creature's skin was too smooth, and its limbs had too many joints. Its feet were too wide, and the thing had no genitals. The proportions were wrong in most places, making the shadowy thing appear uncanny. Disturbing.

The image in the lower right, however, is what made her catch her breath. Moore had already zoomed in on it, framing the creature's head so it was fully defined. The reflection of light shining off glistening liquid created a white spot in the image, but it was clear enough. Shawna was looking at her own face. It lacked lines of stress or laughter and was too damned smooth. Instead of two eyes, one large blue orb stared out from its face. But the nose? The ears? The forehead and the jaw? It was her. It was Shawna.

"Do you understand why I am concerned?" Moore asked.

Shawna blinked at her, still trying to process what she'd just seen. A humanoid form wearing her face reached out to touch her with one of its arms.

"I don't remember that," Shawna said. "Not like that. It was coming for us. It was like it teleported."

Moore nodded slowly. "But it didn't."

No. Prime hadn't teleported at all. It had walked around the crates and stopped two meters from Shawna, its hand extended toward her. Before Shawna could close the distance to it to grasp it, Kate had pulled her backward and dragged her toward the open blast door. Catfish had already thrown one of the grenades, the object flying over her head before landing and detonating.

Prime had stumbled away, but Catfish had thrown another, which landed close enough to catch the creature on fire. After the blast door closed, Prime smashed into it repeatedly.

"This timestamp matches the one of you getting into the elevator," Moore said.

The split screen showed the two feeds side by side. Moore fast-forwarded a few seconds, and something started to happen. Prime left the door and ran to the other side of the lab, the side closest to the elevator shaft. Its humanoid form transformed into arms and legs holding up a stretched torso. The arms reached to the ceiling, its dark legs pushing against the floor. Adorned with talons, the misshapen hands shredded the ceiling panels and exposed the ductwork. Prime then leaped, its thin shell crumbling away as the liquid pool disappeared.

"It made it to the engineering level," Moore said, "just before the detonation." She turned off the TV and stared at Shawna. "Any questions?"

The room fell silent, which only added to Shawna's anxiety. "What—" Shawna's voice had turned to a croak. She cleared her throat and tried again. "What do you think happened?"

The thin smile returned, but Shawna thought Moore's bottom lip quivered before regaining its rigidity. "I don't know," Moore said. "There are dozens of theories, and all of them are about as insane as the next."

Shawna shook her head. "Name your top three."

"Top three," Moore said. "That's difficult, but I will try." She held up a finger. "There is something different in your physical, mental, or, um, spiritual makeup that attracted it to you rather than anyone else." A second finger rose. "Next, we have the theory that the creature hypnotized you and tried to take your form at the end to save itself. To replace you. Or become you." She held up the last finger. "And third, that you've been able to control the creature all along. Which sounds better?"

Shawna didn't know what to say because the rest of Moore's words had been lost. Shawna had checked out of the conversation when Moore said, "Attracted." Attracted. Attracted to or by a monster. Bride of Frankenstein bullshit. But it had fractured her ability to absorb the rest of it.

"Now," Moore said. "Which of those bothers you the most?"

Shawna shook her head. "The first."

"The first? You mean it's more likely you've been controlling it?"

"What?" Shawna stood from the bed. "What do you mean I've been controlling it?"

Moore wrinkled her eyebrows. "The theory. That's one of the three."

"It was?" Shawna slowly sat.

"Did you not hear what I said?" Moore asked in confusion.

"Heard. Didn't listen."

Moore relaxed slightly but didn't lean down, didn't offer any comfort. "Why not?"

The second one. "Oh. It was trying to take my form. That was the other one."

"Right," Moore said. "Which of those three is your favorite?"

She looked up at Moore. "Number two is definitely the most reassuring."

"That's what I thought," Moore said. "We're reviewing the videos where the team interacted directly with the creature. Jay had the least contact since he was always ensconced in the observation hall."

"Lucky him," Shawna said.

Moore ignored her. "You, Kate, and Neil, on the other hand, dealt with dispensation and the physical experiments. If it was attempting to become anyone, I would think it would be someone it spent time with. Of course, that means it could have chosen any one of you."

"Makes sense," Shawna said. "Maybe." She glared at Moore. "One and three are ridiculous."

"Which is why we're all going through quarantine. Which is also why you'll be staying here for a while longer. Observation, of course."

"Observation? For what? For me to grow tentacles?"

The smile disappeared. "If that had been a concern, I would have already incinerated you."

Shawna's heartbeat, the flush of anger she'd felt, froze. The matter-of-fact look on Moore's face was enough to know she meant it. She wondered just how close to not waking up she'd been. If, instead of a sedative, they had just given her something to put her in a coma and die. That would have been safer for them.

"Observation," Shawna said with reluctant acceptance. "For how long?"

"Until we are satisfied."

She looked up at Moore with a quizzical expression. "You said 'we.'"

"Indeed I did."

After that, Shawna was allowed to rejoin the rest of the team. The scientists had been somewhat subdued around her, Neil and Jay looking terrified to be in her presence. Kate, although cautious, had chatted with her. Kate had asked Shawna what she remembered. Shawna told her, and Kate went quiet, her skin paling slightly. Then she'd reached out and squeezed Shawna's hand. "We're alive," she'd said.

* * *

Shawna waved goodbye to the black sedan as it sped away from the parking lot. She'd assumed that watching Jay, Neil, and Kate leave would close some kind of psychic wound. If they left, if she left, the past would disappear into the ether, and the nightmares would go away.

Shawna made her way from the front of the building to the path running through the trees. It was time for a walk, and she needed to get some space anyway. She'd been trapped on the ocean, she'd been trapped inside the earth, and the last thing she wanted to be was trapped in a new prison. But even these little excursions made her unable to deny where she was. It was a nicer cell with better conditions, a good rec room, movies, and trips to the city for clothes. But it was still a prison.

Her feet padded along the thick blacktop path, large pines and oaks sprouting to the sky, unhindered by human manicuring. A forest split in two and allowed to exist, for the most part, as it always had. So long as humans could travel through it for pleasure, there was little need to do more. Too much had been done already.

Sunbeams cascaded through the browning leaves and the growing number of bare branches. Another front was due tomorrow, bringing more rain and dropping temperatures. She'd need another sweater if she wanted to continue her walks. And she did. They were one of the few things keeping her sane at this point.

Somewhere in the canopy above, a squirrel chittered, and something fell to the forest floor. Pinecone. Damned things were everywhere, along with brown pine needles and yellowing oak leaves. Not to mention the offal of downed branches and rotting wood.

Shawna scanned the trees, looking for birds, but heard only their song. A breeze rattled the dying leaves in a corpse rustle of sound. For no reason she could think of, she shivered.

Jay. He and Kate were on their way to the airport, and both of them were heading to Denver. She planned to stay there permanently. The same with Jay. Shawna wondered if they would start their own research lab or maybe go to work for one of the bio-chem firms up there. Maybe. Perhaps they'd be able to. Shawna wasn't so sure she could say the same for herself.

Still saddled with a teenager at home, Neil was staying in Houston for now. The scientist had seemed diminished, something in his fundamental worldview completely cracked and shattered. Moore had said the government would provide psychiatric counseling for any team members at a moment's notice. Shawna hoped Neil took her up on that.

The only real question was where Sarah had gone. She'd disappeared without a word once they released her from quarantine. Shawna had been surprised by that, although Sarah had seemed distant and lost in her own world during the debrief. Maybe the strain of seeing her partner die had been too much on top of everything else. Or maybe she'd already accepted another assignment, hopefully something less dangerous than Miskatonic University.

Shawna doubted she'd see any of them again, not even if M2 reappeared. What was the point? After what had happened, there was little reason to try and study the creature again, not unless a major scientific breakthrough allowed them to examine its "cellular" material. Shawna wasn't sure humanity would ever figure that one out. Besides, there were no more samples and no more matter to study.

Just petabytes and petabytes of data. That alone would keep Moore's team of scientists busy for decades.

She damned well knew Moore had her own science crew. Kate and her team hadn't been the ones to debrief Shawna and Catfish to begin with. Who were those people if they weren't Moore's?

"In charge doesn't mean in control," Moore had said in the commissary after Shawna had nearly let one of the Taubs loose.

Yes, Shawna thought. *So who is in control?*

"But we're still alive," Shawna said aloud, her feet nearly silent on the path. A bluejay flew through the lower limbs and chirped in irritation. Maybe she'd gotten near its nest. Or perhaps it was warning her of an impending dive-bomb sortie. She didn't know shit about birds, but it was enough to make her stop for a moment.

Distant birdsong, the sound of cars on a highway a few kilometers away, and the tree branches rustling in the breeze. Sound. Sight. Free.

Shawna began walking again, suddenly feeling watched, which was stupid. She knew she was being watched. All the time. While she slept. While she showered. While she ate. While she and Catfish fucked. They were watching. Taking notes. Waiting for her to— Her to what?

That was the part Moore still hadn't divulged, which somehow made it worse. To know she was some kind of goddamned experiment while they insisted her house arrest and supervision were just precautionary. Precautionary, her ass.

If it was just for observation, Moore would have moved on. But she hadn't. Instead, she was there every day, never taking a day off, and presumably "working," parsing data, putting together suppositions and theories. Now and then, Shawna would sit in with Moore, and they would discuss the various experiments and what Shawna thought of them. Not much had changed in her mind.

"Prime evolved," Shawna had said after they'd watched it form a blue eye on the recording. "Taub, when it infected Krieger, had to be a single particle. Or something akin to that. Maybe it didn't really display any specific traits of Poppy because of that. And it had evolved to win a fight."

"The fight to live?" Moore had asked.

Shawna had thought for a moment. "Not live. Adapt."

"Overcome?" Moore said.

She knew Moore had meant to riff on the old saying, but the word had chilled her. Overcome. Annihilate? No. "Consume," Shawna had finally said.

Since quarantine, Shawna had spent an hour a day with a woman named Val. Val asked her questions about her feelings, emotions, and dreams. Val was supposedly there to listen to the things Shawna couldn't, or wouldn't, talk to Catfish about. Shawna had talked, but that didn't mean she could trust Val. How could you trust someone when everything you said was being recorded? Observed. Analyzed. Categorized.

When she told Val about the dreams, the woman seemed to get a twinkle in her eye, which, of course, meant that's what they wanted out of her—to see what secrets hid within her mind and discover if her encounter with Prime had triggered a kind of fugue or delusionary state. Maybe something else.

Shawna took a left rather than continuing down the path. She wanted a nap. The dark circles under her eyes spoke to sleepless nights with nightmarish moments. Every night, every damned night, she saw Prime standing before her, its hand outstretched as if to caress. Or grab. Or simply make contact. And every time she saw it, she woke up screaming, and it took meds to calm her back down.

She sighed and walked to the Guesthouse's side door, waving to Pete, the guard, on her way through the lobby and into the interior. Today, she'd meet with Val and get asked how she felt about the others saying goodbye. And what would she say? Relief? Loss? Or just an emptiness? She didn't know.

The third floor held the room she and Catfish shared, and that's where she was headed. He'd had a medical appointment, and the doctors were doing their best to repair the damage he'd done to his foot, so she'd have it to herself. It's what she wanted anyway.

She wasn't supposed to sleep during the day. It would ruin her cycle and make it more difficult to sleep during the night. Fuck that.

She flung the curtains open, allowing the bright day's light to fill the room. Yawning, she undressed and cracked the window.

She wanted to hear the breeze through the trees. She wanted to smell the end of Fall. But most of all, she wanted to sleep in the light.

ABOUT THE AUTHOR

A writer and Parsec Award winning podcaster from Houston, Texas, Paul E Cooley produces free psychological thriller and horror podcasts, essays, and reviews available from Shadowpublications.com and iTunes. For more than a decade, Shadowpublications.com has brought unabridged, original content to the ears of podcast fans.

While best known for his Parsec Award winning sci-fi/horror series The Black and The Derelict Saga, Paul also writes traditional horror as well as alternate historical fantasy.

He has collaborated with New York Times Bestselling author Scott Sigler on the series "The Crypt" and co-wrote the novel The Rider. In addition to his writing, Paul has contributed his voice talents to a number of podiofiction productions.

He is a co-host on the renowned Dead Robots' Society writing podcast and enjoys interacting with readers and other writers.

To contact Paul:

Mastodon: @paul_e_cooley@vyrse.social

YouTube: https://youtube.com/paulecooley

Email: paul@shadowpublications.com

Want to know when a new book or podcast presentation is released? Join the Shadowpublications.com mailing list:

http://mailinglist.shadowpublications.com

Made in the USA
Monee, IL
08 January 2025

76159832R00184